MISSION TO METHONE

Pq— EJT—405

Baen Books by Les Johnson

with Ben Bova
Rescue Mode

with Travis S. Taylor
Back to the Moon
On to the Asteroid

Edited by Les Johnson and Jack McDevitt
Going Interstellar

MISSION TO METHONE

LES JOHNSON

BAEN

MISSION TO METHONE

A Baen Books Original

Baen Publishing Enterprises
P.O. Box 1403
Riverdale, NY 10471
www.baen.com

ISBN: 978-1-4814-8305-6

Cover art by Bob Eggleton

First Baen Hardcover printing, February 2018

Distributed by Simon & Schuster
1230 Avenue of the Americas
New York, NY 10020

Library of Congress Cataloging-in-Publication Data

Names: Johnson, Les (Charles Les), author.
Title: Mission to Methone / by Les Johnson.
Description: Riverdale, NY : Baen Books, [2018]
Identifiers: LCCN 2017052469 | ISBN 9781481483056 (paperback)
Subjects: LCSH: Science fiction. | BISAC: FICTION / Science Fiction / High
  Tech. | FICTION / Science Fiction / Adventure. | FICTION / Science Fiction
  / General.
Classification: LCC PS3610.O36276 M57 2018 | DDC 813/.6--dc23 LC record available
at https://lccn.loc.gov/2017052469

Printed in the United States of America

10 9 8 7 6 5 4 3 2 1

MISSION TO METHONE

PROLOGUE

The energy released in the first impact was an impressive 4,000,000,000,000,000 joules, the equivalent of about a million tons of TNT, or about enough energy to power the modern United States for a few days. Had the impact happened in the twenty-first century, it would have been an exciting day for the world's astronomers. Instead, the only observers were groups of nomads in the deserts of North Africa and Central Asia, who happened to be under clear skies and in the Earth's shadow. What they saw was a brief flash coming from the Moon, which would have been mostly ignored as if they were seeing things had it not been followed in quick succession by five more flashes, each producing approximately the same energy as the first. Legends were born that night on Earth, legends of gods building huge fires upon the Moon to show their displeasure with the ways of men. On the Moon, it was definitely a scene of anger unleashed. Anger older than humanity was being rained upon a newly established base there.

Keeper-of-the-Way survived the first impact, as did most of her fifty-one crew members. They knew the attack was coming, they just didn't know when—until about twenty terrestrial days before when their telescopes spotted the incoming asteroid swarm headed their way. Had it been one one-hundred-foot-diameter asteroid coming toward the Moon, the Observers in the lunar base might have thought it to be an unlucky coincidence of nature and dispatched one of their kinetic interceptors to deflect it. But it wasn't alone. A sequence of twenty-five similar sized asteroids were coming out of the glare of the Sun with predicted impact points within a few miles of each other—all on Earth's moon and near their base. This was not an act of nature; it was an act of war.

The Observers launched their limited supply of interceptors, propelled by compact matter/antimatter drives capable of accelerating them to nearly ten percent of the speed of light. At impact, each antimatter interceptor released approximately fifty megatons of TNT equivalent energy, enough to deflect the asteroid away from the base toward impact elsewhere on the Moon. They had only twenty interceptors . . .

Keeper-of-the-Way moved quickly, using her three squid-like tentacles to pull herself across the moist floor toward the control panel from which she could determine the full extent of the damage to her base. From the control panel display, she determined that devastation following the first impact was crippling, but not fatal to the Observers' outpost. The damage was restricted to the new construction on the equatorial side of the base, leaving much of the control station and habitat untouched. The atmospheric generators were functioning as were the water-effusing systems. *Good*, she thought to herself, *we won't yet suffocate or desiccate. But for how long?* She knew that more impacts were coming, and unless a miracle occurred, death would soon be upon them all.

Keeper-of-the-Way was startled by Defender-of-All's reedy voice beside her. She hadn't noticed his sliding approach until he spoke. "We will not survive much longer. The battle in the outer system must have been lost or the Bringers-of-Death would not be able to mount such a strike."

"I fear you are correct," she said with great sadness. She so wanted to see the star of Homeworld again from the shores of the lake in which she spawned. That, and she feared that the species they were sent here to observe would be destroyed by the Bringers-of-Death before they had the opportunity to hatch into their own as an advanced civilization and technological society. "Is there nothing more that we can do?"

"Nothing. We used all the interceptors we have available. If the supply ships hadn't been caught amongst the fleet battle near the ringed planet, then we might have had a chance."

Keeper-of-the-Way looked at the radar return showing the imminent impact of the next asteroid, took Defender-of-All's middle manipulator tentacle into her own, performed the ceremonial clutching of suckers, and bowed her head.

Defender-of-All returned the clutching and also bowed his head.

Fifteen seconds later, the second asteroid struck the command center and vaporized it and all within. Before twenty minutes had passed, there were several new craters on the lunar surface where the base had once stood. Pieces of the base, the Moon, and the impacting asteroid gained enough energy from the collision to escape the pull of the Moon's gravity and fly off into space. Some flew toward the Earth and caused a spectacular meteor shower visible only to those residing in the northern part of Asia at the time. Other pieces entered a low lunar orbit and remained there for almost a year before the asymmetric tug of the lunar gravity field caused them to spiral in and impact the Moon themselves. Still others were kicked all the way around the Moon and managed to fly back to almost their point of ejection, causing only minor additional damage from what was, by any means measurable, a catastrophic attack from which there were no survivors.

It was a scene that had been played out for millennia across numerous stellar systems, on or near numerous worlds with indigenous life, and had determined the fate of intelligent, tool-using species too numerous to count.

On Earth's moon, there remained almost no trace of the alien base that had once resided there.

CHAPTER 1

Space exploration was months of boredom punctuated by moments of extreme excitement and discovery, or at least that's how it seemed to Chris Holt as he poured over the morning flight data reports for the five spacecraft he was responsible for keeping alive and functioning. From his windowless office at Space Resources Corporation, he couldn't even have the thrill of seeing the rain squalls pummeling the Gulf Coast from yet another tropical depression in the Gulf of Mexico. He was still wet after making a mad dash from his Personal Transportation Vehicle to his office nearly two hours ago.

Using his 'net goggles to review the reports, he intently read the ghostly status results as they slid into and out of view on his personal heads-up display, obscuring his "real" view of the wall in front of his desk. Chris hadn't yet opted for the newly-released cornea implants that were quickly making goggles obsolete. He wanted them to be out for at least a few years before he let anyone implant them in *his* eyes.

The reports, which were created overnight by the lab's artificial intelligence, affectionately known as SNARC by the engineers, were full of the flight data from each of the spacecraft's primary subsystems.

Chris was mainly interested in how the solar sails that propelled the small spacecraft through space were performing and whether or not anything needed to be done to adjust their trajectories to assure each would arrive at the designated asteroid at the right time. The data collected would help provide Space Resources Corporation with the information it needed to determine which asteroids would be good candidates for follow-up exploration and mining. Lots of money was at stake, and Chris was the one responsible for making sure that the mining engineers got the data they needed to advise the company's president and board of directors where to go next.

Using solar sails to propel the company's fleet of reconnaissance spacecraft had been his idea, and, so far, it appeared to have been a good investment. Each robotic spacecraft was barely larger than a shoebox, carried a camera and spectrometer to gather the asteroid data needed for assay, and was propelled by reflecting sunlight from a one-thousand-square-foot sail made of a reflective film thinner than a human hair. Without the need for fuel, and the only visiting asteroids closer to the Sun than Mars, solar sail propelled spacecraft never ran out of fuel and could operate as long as the sun was shining. But they were slow to accelerate and would require between one and three years after launch to reach their targets.

Now one of them was getting close to its rendezvous. Chris knew that the first usable photos should be coming in as early as today. The photos taken by the ship's onboard camera so far were as expected: they showed a bright dot, taking up no more than a few pixels, growing larger with each passing day. The image processing team already had enough data to give him an indication of the asteroid's overall shape and rotation rate. Asteroid 2055VG, named for the year it was discovered, was shaping up to be interesting indeed. The initial data showed that it wasn't rotating and that it appeared to be almost spherical—making it an oddity among asteroids, which were usually elliptical and irregular, not round. He was looking forward to honest-to-God photos taken up close and personal from about one hundred feet away, which would be in his hands by the end of the week or sooner.

Four of the five spacecraft were operating normally, constantly and ever-so-slightly varying their trajectories through space to allow them to rendezvous with their designated asteroids at the right time—after maneuvering tens, and in some cases, hundreds of millions of miles since departing Earth. One was not operating as planned. Chris saw that the problem with the spacecraft was first reported during the night shift just before his arrival. Also included in the data were spacecraft temperature measurements, solar array power output stats, and a plethora of data that would only make sense to the various subsystem engineers who were periodically reviewing the data and responding to anomaly reports like the one that Chris had just found for AB-22.

He saw that the overnight staffer overrode one of the automated command uplinks that would have adjusted the trajectory of spacecraft AB-22 to account for an unexpected drop in overall thrust.

"The idiot didn't even follow up by checking the context camera," he mumbled to himself as he accessed the data streaming down from AB-22 in search of the spacecraft's most recent self-shot. After a few moments, he found the data set containing the picture library and was looking at the distorted fish-eye view of the spacecraft's solar sail.

"Shit."

Chris activated the communications link embedded in his right cheek, and called his chief engineer, Pam Stark.

"Pam, AB-22 has a small tear in quadrant four. Yesterday's data showed a change in the sail's thrust level and a shift in its center of pressure. The idiot on the night shift got the flag and didn't even try to see what was causing the problem. He just uploaded a new trajectory model and went back to playing a video game or whatever else he could waste time with instead of working. We need to update the sail's thrust model and probably increase the spin rate to compensate for the extra torque. If we keep adjusting the trajectory, it'll cause a huge increase in flight time."

"I'm on it. Mattias was on shift last night, wasn't he?"

"I think so. Do you want to talk to him or do you want me to?"

"I'd better do it," she replied.

"Good. I'm so angry I can't see straight."

"I'm on it," she said, cutting the connection.

Chris was so engaged with reviewing the data coming through his 'net goggles that he didn't hear Vasilisa open the door and halfway enter his office until she spoke, startling him. Sometimes it was difficult to separate what was real from what came through the 'net.

"Chris, are you still interested in lunch?"

Vasilisa was Space Resources Corporation's Vice President for Mining Operations, overseeing nearly two billion dollars of the company's interplanetary mining investments. She was originally from Russia, but had become totally Americanized by forty years of living in the United States. Chris had many times heard her horrific story of surviving the nuclear blast that had leveled most of the South Korean city of Daejeon while she was a graduate student there. She mentioned many times how her life would have been different had she decided to pursue her graduate studies in Moscow instead of Daejeon. For Chris, this was ancient history—having occurred five years before his birth. Like most people, real "history" began with their own awareness of the world. But Chris liked her, and thoroughly enjoyed the rare moments she was available to meet with him for lunch. She understood him like almost no one else and was always there when he needed someone to talk to. Today was one of those days.

"Absolutely! You just surprised me," he replied, rising from behind his meticulously organized desk.

"I'm surprised the 'Net Assistant didn't remind you. Do you have it turned off again?"

"Well, not completely off, but I've silenced all the usual stuff while I review this data. You know how it distracts me."

"Personally, I don't see how any of your generation can get work done with fully active 'net access. Having all the information in the world scrolling through your field of vision constantly would just drive me crazy."

"That's why I use my 'net goggles with it turned off. Too addictive. I have more important things to do than playing games and watching porn. Besides, it gives me a headache."

"We'd better get moving to the cafeteria or what little time I have for lunch will get swallowed. I've got a VR meeting after lunch."

Chris rose from his chair and joined Vasilisa as they walked down the hall toward the company's cafeteria. The usual aromas of exotic spices wafted into the hallway ahead of their entry into the brightly lit room that fed the company's fifteen hundred employees. Chris was thoroughly accustomed to the extreme diversity of ethnic backgrounds that worked for Space Resources Corporation. The company only recruited the best and brightest from around the world. Vasilisa had related stories of her youth, when extreme intercultural mixing was only just beginning—especially in Russia. Her stories were high on the list of what Chris liked about Vasilisa. That and her uncanny ability to see through the usual political bullshit that people in her class of friends and business associates must deal with on a daily basis. She was a rare "I am what I am" kind of person who wasn't afraid of telling people how she saw things. And it had worked in her favor on many occasions. That was why they liked each other—neither was afraid of calling out mistakes made by others nor would they put up with less than stellar technical performance by any in the office. Their only difference was one of style: Vasilisa was way more tactful in how she communicated than Chris. He knew it and hated it—no matter how hard he tried, his words usually managed to offend someone.

They chose to eat plain, run-of-the-mill Chinese and found a secluded table in the far corner of the room next to one of the large windows that overlooked the company's well-tended garden. The garden looked soggy from being pounded by relentless rain coming from a dark grey, menacing sky.

"Tell me what you've got. I understand one of your babies is close to rendezvous."

"Close. The imaging team gave me some preliminary data already. We might get a good image back as early as this afternoon." Chris was in his element now, and he knew it. He enjoyed his time chatting with Vasilisa; he suspected it was his energy and enthusiasm for his work that she relished.

"When will we have enough information for the Assay Assessment Team?"

"We should be alongside and taking extremely high-resolution photos within the week. If it looks promising, then your division can have at it. If not, then, well, we've done more science and can turn all the data over to the NSF." Even though the company considered the latter case to be a failure, since it wouldn't make them any money, Chris, who was trained as a physicist, was a scientist at heart and didn't mind turning over all the data collected to the National Science Foundation. For Chris, scientific data was as valuable as platinum.

"I saw that gleam in your eye when you mentioned the NSF. We aren't going to lose you to some university, are we?"

"Not a chance. They can't come close to paying me what you do. Besides, they don't have the money to send spacecraft exploring." Chris smiled as he played on an old theme from conversations past: the need to pay scientists more money to encourage more to go into science and engineering fields. She didn't appear to take the bait.

"Tamika told me you've been invited to speak at the International Astronautical Congress in Sweden. What's your topic?"

"I've built a roadmap for what comes next. With the Moonbase built, Mars being explored and real commerce finally happening in near-Earth space, we're on our way to becoming a solar system-wide civilization. Have you heard about the fusion drive research at Livermore labs? Europa here we come!"

"Chris, do you really want to unleash the Caliphate on the stars? They're living like it's the year 800 and want to drag the rest of us back there with them. What about all of our petty conflicts, not to mention our wars? Somehow I don't believe we'll suddenly stop fighting each other if we go to the stars."

"I don't want the Caliphate to go. But they probably will. They, the Indians, the Chinese and all the rest will go right along with us. Nothing depresses me more than to think of us being stuck forever in the solar system when there is a universe out there waiting to be explored. I think we must go to preserve and spread life. If we stay here, the Caliphate or some virus might wipe us out. We have to go. We just need to convince the idiots with all the money that it needs to happen."

"But do you think it's even possible? Where is everybody? I think we're *it* and we're *stuck*. Just like this shrimp." Vasilisa followed her last point by biting a whole piece of fried shrimp in a particularly dramatic fashion.

"Vasilisa, you just don't think big enough. We're mining asteroids, bringing raw materials back to the Moon and Moonbase, keeping it functioning—at a profit. And you just announced last week that we'll be dropping processed ore into Utah and Nevada and putting it up for sale in the terrestrial market. How can you be so negative?"

"Because I've seen the horrific videos coming out from the Caliphate. I've lived through a nuclear blast that killed over two million people. I've seen the US and China go at each other and almost blast the world back into the Stone Age over a silly little island in the Pacific. I'm negative because even the way I earn my living is based on consuming raw materials from other worlds to make more stuff for people to buy and then eventually put into a garbage dump."

"We need to get out there before the assholes screw it all up to the point that we can never recover and go."

"Well, I think ..." Vasilisa began but was interrupted by Chris raising his hand and turning his head away.

"Hold on," he said as he cocked his head, activated the audio implant in his earlobe and listened to the message demanding his attention.

"Chris—the first image from asteroid 2055VG17 is here and it'll knock your socks off. Do you have your 'net goggles on?"

"No, I left the damned things at my desk." Chris's voice was firm but barely audible to anyone near him in the room.

"Okay. Listen up. Get over here as quick as you can. It doesn't just look like a sphere, it is a sphere. Perfectly round. And it looks to be artificial."

"Excuse me, what did you say?" Chris asked, his voice now loud enough for Vasilisa to hear and understand.

"I said, it doesn't look like it's natural. No, it isn't natural. It's clearly artificial."

Chris was out of his chair and moving toward the door before Vasilisa realized he was even moving.

CHAPTER 2

Space Resources CEO Jim Moorman looked impatient and worried. Standing just under six feet tall, Moorman didn't look even close to his biological age—which was seventy-one. Clearly the beneficiary to the best anti-aging treatments his wealth could buy, Moorman looked more like a man in his mid-thirties. His brown hair, only slightly receding, showed not a single sign of grey, and wrinkles were limited to a few minor ones on his forehead. It was those minor wrinkles that now stood out as his patience at not being informed of what his team had discovered was starting to wear thin.

"Okay, what do we know about this thing?" asked Moorman.

"And who have you told about it?" added a voice from Moorman's right. The speaker was Space Resources' Legal Counsel, Tamika Marsee. Chris knew that Marsee was good at her job and he respected that. Even if she sometimes overstepped her authority and tried to assert company control over his publications and speaking engagements, he knew she was just trying to look out for the best interests of the company. He respected her, but he didn't particularly like her.

All eyes turned toward Chris. It was his team that made the discovery using his spacecraft.

"All that you are going to see was prepared by Chandra and me. No one else is in the loop. First of all, we know that it isn't an asteroid. It's clearly artificial. It's what we call an Inner Earth Object, meaning that its aphelion is about zero point nine eight astronomical units. Its closest approach to the Earth's orbit is about point zero two AU, and that only happens once in a dozen years or so. It's shaped like a sphere and almost four hundred feet in diameter. It's black, and from what we can tell, it hasn't been there very long." Chris paused to make sure Moorman was following him.

"Do we know who launched it? China? The Europeans? India?" asked Marsee.

Trying to be patient with those who didn't have the technical background he had, Chris picked up his 'net goggles from the table next to him and put them on like a pair of old fashioned eye glasses. He motioned for others to do the same, which most did. Those who didn't activated their corneal implants. All fifteen people in the conference room were now looking at a very realistic three-dimensional view of what appeared to be a black sphere that was barely discernible against the background of stars. The sun was not in view; it appeared to be behind the viewer, in this case the spacecraft's camera, providing the illumination of the eerie looking ball.

"Take a look at the object and imagine a soccer field next to it. They would be the same size. No nation on Earth can launch something that large. So, no, the Chinese didn't launch it.

"Now watch it as we get closer. The scout is designed to fly within one hundred feet of its target and that's what we did."

The image in the 'net goggles grew larger and larger until it was no longer possible to see it in its entirety against the backdrop of the stars. Instead, all one could see was a curved surface extending out of the field of view on every side of the viewer that at one time must have been fairly smooth across its length—but not anymore. Instead, the surface was marked by numerous craters and scorch marks.

"The object is mostly smooth but looks to be severely damaged. If I had to hazard a guess, I'd say the ship was at one time a perfect sphere. But it looks like it's taken some pretty heavy damage."

"Could meteors do that?" asked Moorman.

"No. The meteor flux is mostly composed of relatively small particles. They could account for some of the much smaller blotches here and there, but these large craters had to be caused by something a lot more energetic than a micrometeor traveling at eighteen kilometers per second or so. Also, if you look closely in quadrant three, you'll see extreme surface ablation. In my opinion, the ablation was caused by a nuclear weapon."

"You can't be *serious*," exclaimed Marsee.

"Whatever this is, it was savagely attacked by someone, or something, at about the time our ancestors were walking the savannahs in Africa and thinking of moving to other parts of the globe. And that's not all."

"Keep going," said Moorman.

"The object is mostly smooth, but every so often you can see relatively small hemispherical bumps on the surface. God only knows what they are. And, as the camera panned across the surface flying by, we saw this." The goggle image now had an oval highlighted section, visible within the field of view of the camera as a circle with an iris-like pattern within it.

"Is that an . . ." started to ask one of the engineers in the audience.

"It looks like it might be a door or an airlock," replied Chris, cutting the engineer off before he could steal his carefully planned dramatic moment.

"A door?" Moorman cocked his head to the side as he asked the question and peered more closely at the image.

"That's right, but only a guess. Who knows what an alien mind might design into a spacecraft?" Chris replied.

Chris had just acknowledged the elephant in the room and was waiting on some sort of response. It was the moment of the meeting he'd been waiting for.

"Aliens? Space war? And now an airlock? Is this April first and I missed the memo?" The comment was from Jin Gearhart, Chris's long-time, pain-in-the-ass nemesis who seemed to question every decision, request and idea that Chris brought to the table within the company. Gearhart, who had less than half the number of peer reviewed publications as Chris and who had never been written up in the journal Nature, was an *unnecessary* pain in the ass.

"I'm not kidding. We're looking at an alien spacecraft for the first time in human history. First contact. This is a big fucking deal."

The room erupted with conversation. Chris, feeling pleased with himself, took off the 'net goggles and sat them on the table as he first looked around the room at his colleagues, then directly at Gearhart to whom he couldn't help but give a condescending smirk, and finally to Moorman.

Moorman, clearly fully engaged and activating his "CEO personality," took charge.

"Chris, this is amazing news. I want you to capture as much data as you can about the object and put it into a holo-presentation that I can use when the news goes public. I assume the spacecraft is on-station and monitoring it?"

"Not exactly. We flew by at about ten feet per second to take these images and now we're well past it. Remember a solar sail can't really stop. You can't turn off the sun. I've got Julianna working on a return trajectory instead of retargeting to the next asteroid. I haven't filled her in and she thinks we just need more data to complete the assay. We should be back at the target in about two weeks for another slow flyby."

"Tamika, I want to know our legal options and responsibilities. Can we claim it? Is there some sort of space equivalent to the law of the sea that allows us to claim a derelict spacecraft?"

"Yes, sir, there is. But those laws imply that the derelict is a spacecraft launched from Earth. I'm not sure about us legally claiming an alien spaceship that's been adrift for a million years."

"It can't have been there for more than a hundred thousand years or so," Chris interjected.

"How do you know that?" asked Gearhart, looking incredulously at Chris.

"Because the undamaged surface of the ship is still relatively smooth. It hasn't had time to be pockmarked by too many micrometeors and it doesn't have a noticeable layer of dust. It would be much more pitted and dirty if it'd been there for a million years." *And this is so completely obvious.*

Moorman replied, sounding more than a little annoyed, "I don't really care if it's been there for five minutes or fifty million years. I want my property rights respected when we go public with this. Can you imagine the technology behind such a ship? I realize we're likely to lose control over what happens next with this thing, but I won't give up my claims without a lot of noise and, if it comes down to it, a lot of money. Make it happen, Tamika."

"I'll try."

"And one last thing. Keep this quiet. I don't want this to leak to the press or anybody until we have a plan. You all signed NDAs and I expect you to abide by them."

With that, the meeting was adjourned and Moorman walked out. Chris took a deep breath, walked over to Vasilisa and grinned.

"Now you know why I walked out of our lunch date."

CHAPTER 3

It was times like this that Chris wished he had a wife, children, or some sort of family with whom he could share the excitement of what was happening. He was on his way to meet with the president of the United States to talk about how he found an alien artifact and answered one of the oldest questions known to man—are we alone in the universe? Who did he share the news and excitement with? Only his two dogs, Cricket and Panda. They were awake and up with him, barely, as he left his apartment to catch the early flight to Washington. His parents were dead and his sister was off somewhere, God only knew where, with that missionary husband of hers on yet another trip to save the heathens. Sometimes he envied her; she was *living* in a way he could only, barely, imagine. Yes, Chris was successful by just about any measure the world could devise, but sometimes he felt like a complete loser. This morning as he left home and dropped his dogs off (again) at the local dog sitting service, was one of those days.

"Is this your first trip to The White House?" asked the woman in the driver's seat as they approached the gates on the east side of the White House. She wasn't driving; the security system had now taken over controlling the vehicle as it approached the restricted zone that encircled the White House grounds. They were now no longer in control of reaching their final destination and, if Chris Holt guessed correctly, they were being scanned by every sort of remote sensing device imaginable. With the continued existence of the Caliphate, the threat of terrorism was ever present.

Chris Holt looked out the window as the car slowed and approached the gate, barely even acknowledging her latest attempt at polite conversation. They'd been together now for well over two hours and, as far as Chris was concerned, they might never meet again. To him, such a short interaction didn't warrant the effort it would take to engage in small talk. He had talking points to review lest he screw up and say the wrong thing to the president. Besides, engaging in small talk was arduous. He would have to pay attention to not only what she was saying, but to her facial expressions, her body language, and, God help him, her verbal inflections. Why was talking to non-technical people so much harder than tensor calculus? He didn't want to be rude to her, but sometimes it was just easier to be quiet and considered rude than do all the work necessary to talk with someone and *engage* them. *Of course*, he thought, *that's probably why I live alone with my dogs.* But the thought couldn't overcome his reluctance to participate in small talk.

"Humph," she said when she received no response from him. Melissa Reed was part of the President's Secret Service protection detail, a former US Air Force surrogate pilot, and a very attractive woman. She was clearly not used to being ignored.

A team of inspectors with all sorts of scanning gear approached the car from the gate and proceeded to give it a once-over. Despite all the electronic equipment available, there was also a dog team brought out to sniff. *This* Chris noticed.

"You'd think they'd have better tech and wouldn't need the dogs anymore. I guess you guys are still one step out of date," said Chris, as he tried to not completely ignore her.

"Hardly. There's nothing better than canine olfactory for finding explosives. If you so much as touched an explosive in the last few days, they'll alert on you."

"Really?" That was a claim he would have to research. He made a mental note to look up the status of bomb detection technology when he returned home. This was item number seventeen on his list for the day but it was interesting enough to perhaps move up in priority to somewhere in the top five. He suspected his list would be long after the meeting he was about to attend and briefly wondered if he should actually write any of the list down, but then decided against it. He never forgot such things and there was no reason to expect today would be different than any other day in that regard—meeting with the president, notwithstanding.

The car began moving again and rolled at a leisurely pace as it wound its way around the semicircular drive along the South Lawn and toward the White House. Not even Chris could resist looking out the window as the car took him toward his first-ever meeting with a sitting president. He'd met ex-President Pinto shortly after she'd left office and become the president at Boston University, where he had been working as a post-doc. At the time, he was very impressed. Once he saw how she ran the university after taking over, not so much. She brought in all her crony friends and, at least in Chris's opinion, ruined the graduate programs there. He wasn't holding out much hope that President Kremic was any better.

The car stopped and the door was opened by one of the many dark-suited men and women who seemed to be everywhere he looked. As he lifted himself out and into the brisk morning air, he saw NASA Administrator Fuqua in a small crowd of men and women engaged in a discussion. He'd met Fuqua at conference a few years ago, just after he'd been named administrator. *This* was someone who impressed him.

"Dr. Holt, if you'll follow me please, we need to get you inside." He was greeted by one of the men in dark suits and dark sunglasses who placed his hand on Chris's arm to guide him toward the door.

The other group joined him and, as they walked through the massive doors into the building, they one-by-one introduced themselves and shook hands. Chris wasn't surprised to learn that most were active duty military, General This or General That. His mind was still preoccupied with the Artifact and he didn't allocate the effort it would take to *remember* names.

They didn't waste any time moving down the wood-floored and ostentatiously adorned hallway to a large conference room already filled with at least twenty other people, all looking expectantly toward them as they entered the room.

Chris was guided to the seat adorned with his name on a placard placed between Administrator Fuqua and some other dignitary.

Moments after taking his seat, President Kremic entered the room, escorted by a man and a woman, all of whom looked harried. Chris couldn't help but smirk at what he perceived as their sense of self-importance. In the excitement of the moment, he forgot to hide, or at least mask, the smirk.

Kremic looked in person just as he did on screen and during press conferences. With CGI having replaced most actors these days, Chris half-expected the "real" Kremic to look nothing at all like did in the media.

"Ladies and gentlemen, thank you for coming. Some of you are already aware of the nature of this meeting, most are not, so I will get right to the point. There is an alien spacecraft in our solar system and we need to figure out what to do about it." Kremic was known as a man who didn't beat around the bush.

For the first few moments, no one made a sound. All Chris could hear was his heart beating as he felt his pulse quicken. This was it. His data had undoubtedly been confirmed, as he knew it would be. Then the murmuring began.

"Before we get off track, let me assure you that the information you are about to hear has been reviewed by NASA, the Air Force and the National Security Agency. What's been found is real and may pose an imminent threat to the security of the United States. Next, I'd like to introduce Dr. Chris Holt, the man who discovered what we're calling the Artifact. He's with Space Resources and, from what I understand, he discovered the Artifact with one his of prospecting spacecraft. Dr. Holt, you have the floor."

President Kremic looked at Chris like he'd known him for years as he motioned for Chris to begin his briefing. The fact was, they'd never actually met. Chris had to assume that Kremic has been fully briefed on his background so that he could give such a disingenuous, but accurate, introduction. A politician.

"Thank you, Mr. President. If you will activate your 'net goggles or corneal implants to channel three, I'll walk you through how we found the Artifact and what we know about it. First of all, we discovered it using one of our robotic solar sail prospectors . . ." Chris went through the details of the Artifact's discovery and showed those assembled every significant photo they had taken to date. The briefing took thirty minutes and not a sound could be heard in the room until he finished and asked for questions.

"Dr. Holt. Are you telling us this thing may have been out there for a hundred thousand years? Really?" The question came from one of the suits at the table.

"That's an upper limit based on our observations of the Artifact's surface and the very minor age-related damage it has taken. The size of the dust layer, the pitting from the occasional micrometeoroid strike, and other space environmental effects lead me to believe that it can't possibly have been there for more than a hundred thousand years nor is it likely that it's been there for *less* than ten thousand years. It isn't pristine, but not significantly weathered either."

"I say we nuke it," said another of the suits at the table. Chris couldn't read the man's nametag; he was at the far end of the table, and it was a long table.

"Out of the question. We have too much to learn here and I don't want to be the president who starts a war," said Kremic.

"War with whom?" asked one of the female "suits" who sat on the opposite side of the table from the man who suggested nuking the Artifact.

"War with another, potentially much more advanced technological civilization. War with an alien species that may be as far removed from us as we are from our ancestors on the African savannah," said Chris.

"Aliens? Surely, they're long gone if the Artifact has been out there as long as you say it has," replied the suit.

"I don't know what agency or organization you represent, but your ignorance and ill-informed suggestions are counterproductive," said Chris. He'd had just about enough of bureaucratic morons in his career and having one involved in a discussion of this importance and magnitude was galling. He knew as he said it that he was probably being too blunt, but the words came out before he could contain them. *Shit. I bet I just made an enemy.*

"Dr. Holt, I assure you that . . ."

"Enough!" said the president. "Dr. Holt, do you believe the Artifact might still be inhabited?"

"Mr. President, I don't know if it's inhabited or not, but I do know that whoever sent this ship to our solar system has a perspective on time that dwarfs anything in our experience. Do you know how far away the nearest star system is? Well, I'll tell you. It's over four light years away. You think that's close? It isn't. If you take the Sun-to-Earth distance of ninety-three million miles and shrink that to one foot, then the Earth would be one foot from the Sun and Pluto would be about thirty-eight feet away. On that scale, the nearest star is over fifty miles away. And whatever aliens sent this ship our way probably aren't from the Centauri system—they've come much further. Given what we know about the universe and the laws of physics, this Artifact might have been traveling through deep space for a thousand years before arriving here. Whoever built this thing has to be taking the long view and I would bet that someone or something is out there actively watching us. It certainly *could* be dead, but my money is on the opposite."

"Folks, we need options and we need them fast. This is the kind of thing that leaks and we need to have a plan before I have to address the American people about an alien probe being found."

"Mr. President, we can repurpose the ship we're building for our next Mars mission and send it to this thing instead," said NASA Administrator Fuqua. Fuqua's quick offer to use a NASA resource to visit the Artifact notched him up yet further in Chris's estimation.

"How soon could it be ready to fly?" asked President Kremic.

"Three to five months. We've been making excellent progress and everything is on schedule."

"That's a first," said someone at the table, Chris couldn't be quite sure who because he hadn't been looking. He was lost in thought about aliens and what their "alien" motivations might be. He'd been worrying about this since the day the Artifact was discovered and grew more worried as he realized humanity was going to attempt to make first contact.

"Get me a brief on what that's going to take technically and budget-wise. I'll need to apprise Congress."

"Yes, sir. And, um, sir, what about our partners? Once we start making changes to the manifest and CONOPS, the Europeans and Japanese are going to start asking questions," said Fuqua.

"I'll deal with our allies. Before we go public with this, I'll personally inform them, the Chinese general secretary and the Indian president, God help me. And once they know, then it'll be only a matter of hours or minutes before the story leaks to every media outlet in the world. Those bastards wouldn't know how to keep something quiet if their lives depended on it. I'll be making the calls later today and addressing the American people tonight."

"Tonight? What if there's panic or something?" asked the suit who suggested nuking the Artifact. Chris could now read his badge and see that he was President Kremic's director of Homeland Security.

"Tonight," Alan. No debate." President Kremic turned to the woman on his right, who Chris knew to be his chief of staff, Rachel Suddoth. She was impeccably dressed in the latest New York fashion and looked to be no more than thirty-five years old. Chris wondered how someone so new to the political scene could be in the room, let alone in such a high position within the administration.

"Rachel, I need you to pull this all together. The talking points for my calls to the allies need to be on my desk in two hours and the text for tonight's address in four. Take care of getting everything pre-empted; I need to be on every medium where people will have their eyes glued tonight."

"Yes, sir," she replied.

"And Rachel, work with Dr. Holt on everything. I want him read in on every detail."

Chris had been only half-listening until he heard his name. He craned his neck forward and cocked his head to make sure he heard correctly.

"You heard me, Dr. Holt. I need your expertise and as of this moment, you're cleared at the highest possible level and will be given access to any asset the United States government has available that can help us learn more about our visitors before you get out there to meet them in person."

Did he just say I'd be going out there to meet them?

"Sounds like your lucky day," said Rachel with a smile.

CHAPTER 4

"Mr. President, this could lead to another war. One that would make the Asian War look like a picnic." Speaking to the president of the United States was his secretary of state, Taimi Gierow. Gierow, a long-time Washington insider, was in the US Senate in 2050 when the tensions in Asia over some obscure islands that both China and Japan claimed as their own came to a head and resulted in a US aircraft carrier being sunk and the first nuclear weapon being used in wartime since over a century before. If the crazy leader in North Korea hadn't taken advantage of a distracted China and USA to attack the south—and drop an atomic bomb on the South Korean city of Daejeon—then either the USA or China might have seriously considered using their own nuclear weapons. But when they saw the horrific images coming out of South Korea, they put their differences about some minor islands aside and instead combined forces to eliminate a very real, credible threat to world peace—North Korea. Today, just fifteen years later, Kremic and Gierow didn't want to see the strides made since that dreadful day reversed because of the object found in deep space.

President Kremic, seated at his desk in the newly renovated Oval Office, couldn't agree more. Kremic stroked his salt and pepper colored beard, tastefully clipped short and covering only his chin and just to the right and left of his mouth. This was one of his poker tells, which he was consciously aware of doing when he was thinking of options. And which he had to carefully watch and *not* do when in negotiations with foreign leaders who were no doubt fully briefed on each and every one of his habits.

"Yes, it very well could lead to war. If this is indeed an alien spacecraft and we can learn its secrets, then we'll be far ahead of any potential adversary technologically. So far ahead as to make everyone else in the world irrelevant. If we *aren't* the ones to learn its secrets and China does, or, heaven forbid, India, then we may very well be looking at the last gasp of American world leadership—our very survival will be at stake."

"Yes, sir. I understand. But are you sure you don't want to at least reach out to China?"

"We can't partner with China. Japan is paranoid enough as it is. If we lose Japan on this, then they might shut the door on the space solar power agreement. You know what's at stake here. They've managed to reach Carbon Zero because of their power stations, and I'm going to do the same here. We can't afford to piss off the people who've got the technology and expertise to make that happen."

"Consider the matter closed."

"Get Ranjith in here. I need to know what the competition looks like on this. And ask both Administrator Fuqua and General Compton to be on standby as well. Fuqua isn't going to like my decision on who's running the show for the mission and I need to tell him personally."

"Yes, sir. I expected you'd want to hear from intelligence, so I asked Ranjith to be nearby. I'll call him."

Secretary Gierow looked away from President Kremic momentarily and activated her implanted comlink. The president couldn't hear exactly what she was saying, but that was okay. He was thinking about the alien spacecraft, its social implications and the greatest worry that his military planners mentioned at every opportunity, its intentions—which were entirely unknown.

Is it long-abandoned and a derelict? Is it active and friendly? Or hostile? And how will it react when our ship approaches unannounced? When multiple uncooperative Earth ships arrive?

Kremic's thoughts raced to his morning brief and what it contained about the public's reaction. Immediately after his speech announcing the discovery of the Artifact, the response was muted. No panic. No riots. But yesterday, the world's stock markets tanked, led by just about every technology stock imaginable—from telecommunications to aerospace, investors appeared to have lost confidence in humanity's ability to make money from near-term inventions and gadgets when technology that could make every consumer item obsolete was potentially sitting out in space, waiting to be accessed.

The large double door to the room opened, admitting the Director of Intelligence, Ranjith Yoshi. Kremic could see both Administrator Fuqua and General Compton talking in the waiting area to the right outside the door. Both men were pacing. *Taimi Gierow acting with her usual efficiency*, he thought.

"Ranjith, come on in and have a seat," said Kremic as he rose from behind his desk and moved to join him and Gierow on the more casual couch and chair in the center of the room. This wasn't a decisional meeting, so he didn't need to keep it quite as formal. There's nothing quite as intimidating as talking to the president of the United States when he is seated behind his desk, Kremic knew.

"Mr. President, Ms. Gierow." Yoshi nodded in greeting and joined them in sitting at the small wooden table around which many such conversations had taken place over the years.

"What's the latest on the competition?"

"The alien is going to need some traffic control out there, unfortunately. Our best guess is that there will be three ships. One from us, one from China and, unfortunately, one from India. You told him that the Chinese leadership really wants to be part of our team?" Yoshi looked at Gierow for confirmation.

"She told me and I said no."

"I'm sure you have a good reason. But that won't stop them from sending their own ship. They've made a lot of progress on their nuclear thermal propulsion system and my people tell me that it might actually be a bit faster and more efficient than our own."

"What about their military?"

"Firmly in charge. Any guise of this being a civilian effort is out the window. I suspect the crew will include active military personnel as well as a civilian scientist or two. My sources also tell me that they'll be bringing along a tactical nuke in case things go south."

"Not unexpected. So will we."

Gierow's eyebrow raised immediately. Yoshi appeared nonplussed.

"Sir? Is that a good way to begin negotiating with a foreign power? Go knocking on a stranger's door with a gun in hand?" Gierow asked.

"Not now, Taimi. I've made the decision and we'll have that discussion in our next meeting. Go on, Ranjith."

"Yes, sir. I suspect the Chinese decision to bring a nuke might have a lot to do with India. We have good intel that they're prepping their own rocket for a rendezvous as well. They don't have a nuclear propelled ship so they're planning to repurpose their two-seat Moon ship for the trip. They're going to refuel in Earth orbit, add an extra chemical stage and brute force their way to the party. Getting reliable information from India these days is like bobbing for apples, but my instincts are that they'll also come with a nuke."

"And start an interstellar war in the process! We can't fumble our first contact with an alien race, a likely vastly technologically superior alien race, by nuking them!" said Gierow.

"Taimi, we're not having that discussion right now. Save it." Kremic was now getting clearly annoyed by his secretary of state.

"Yes, sir," said Gierow.

"The Russians are still playing with us?" asked President Kremic.

"Well, since they joined the European Union, they're technically playing with the Europeans who are playing with us and Japan. So, yes, sir, our allies are still all together. We're just working out who gets to go from each country."

"That's it?"

"Not exactly. The Caliphate is making a great deal of noise about the alien ship being demonic. There's a lot of activity at the Kuwait Missile Center. We think they're readying a missile to strike the alien ship."

"Well that's just dandy. We know this for sure?"

"Almost one hundred percent certain, sir. They don't have the capability to send people, but, according to the army's Missile and Space Intelligence Center, the Caliphate can get a low-yield nuclear weapon to the alien ship using one of their Scimitar Rockets."

"The timing? When can they launch?"

"They have a lot to do to get their ICBM converted to operate in deep space, so it likely won't be able to launch until well after our teams are on the way. I'm not sure where the Indians will be, probably somewhere after us and China but ahead of the Caliphate."

"Get with the secretary of defense. I want to know what options are available to stop the Caliphate's launch. Everything short of what might start another war."

"Yes, sir."

"At least the public is taking it well. I never expected to be the one to announce we found aliens. I half anticipated riots or something. That's what always seems to happen in the movies."

"Well, the Department of Homeland Security is warning that a few fringe groups might want to use our finding of the Artifact as an excuse to protest, but there aren't any serious threats of violence here or anywhere else. The world population seems to have taken the news rather nonchalantly. All except for the Caliphate, of course."

"It helps that whatever the hell this thing is, it hasn't done anything yet. All it would take to unsettle everyone would be some sort of contact. 'Take me to your leader,' or some such bullshit. Let's hope that whoever built this thing is long dead or gone."

"Yes, sir."

"Send in Administrator Fuqua and General Compton. I need to let them know my decision about who's in charge of this mission and NASA isn't going to like it . . ."

CHAPTER 5

Chris remembered the first time he saw Saturn through the lens of a telescope. Like most kids, he had seen pictures of the ringed planet on screen, but seeing it through the eyepiece of the small refractor his parents bought him was a life-changing event. It was a warm and humid summer night in the suburbs of Richmond, Virginia, so the viewing was not terribly good. There were only a few stars visible overhead and even those might have been obscured had the Moon been visible. Fortunately, the Moon hadn't yet risen when young Chris Holt dragged the white cylindrical telescope out of his room and into the driveway. None of his friends were even remotely interested in looking at the stars and planets, so Chris found himself alone again. But he didn't mind. This was fun.

He was given the telescope for his birthday two weeks previously and had used it to look at the Moon a few days ago. In between nighttime viewings, he practiced setting it up by pointing it toward the homes up the street during the lazy days of his summer break from school. Chris had checked the astronomy information sites and learned that Saturn would be visible early that evening so he planned his day around catching his first glimpse of the famous ringed planet. That night he meticulously set up the telescope and engaged its automatic "go-to" feature that allowed him to quickly and perfectly align it with the bright but tiny point in the sky that was supposed to be Saturn.

He looked into the eyepiece; what he saw rocked his world and changed his life. The tiny point of light resolved into a small disk surrounded by brilliant and huge rings. Chris was so excited that he literally jumped and shouted with joy—nearly toppling his new telescope in the process. He ran quickly into his house to fetch his sister and mother so they, too, could see the most awesome sight in the universe. He recalled their excitement, but with time he realized their exuberance was most likely in support of his interest rather than Saturn. But, that didn't matter, he was hooked. From that point forward, he knew he wanted to be a space scientist.

The American-European-Japanese ship left Earth orbit at 6:43 Greenwich Mean Time when its nuclear thermal engines sent superheated hydrogen around the onboard uranium fission reactor and generated over one hundred thousand pounds of thrust. To the engineers watching the telemetry stream back on Earth, the engine startup was routine and blissfully uneventful. The same engines had been used to send five separate human crews to and from Mars and each time they had performed flawlessly. To the astronauts onboard the *Resolution*, named after one of Captain Cook's ships of eighteenth century exploration, it was anything but routine.

Chris had only stopped throwing up from his first exposure to near-weightlessness about six hours before Earth departure and now the shake, rattle (despite a merciful non-roll) of the engines starting as the ship moved out of orbit was making him wonder if he would lose his lunch. Like about half of the people to go to space, Chris experienced "space sickness" and was nearly debilitated for most of the two days they spent in orbit preparing the *Resolution* for its mission. He had thought he could control his body and not be among those who became ill in space, but he learned just after launch that his mental prowess just wasn't good enough to control *everything*.

Even though the doctors had assured him that it wouldn't be a problem, Chris had worried about flying into space so soon after having the latest generation corneal implants surgically placed in his eyes. He had resisted them for years, but the powers that be at NASA and the DoD insisted that he have them for the trip. Something about being able to more quickly access the ship's data systems and they being generally more reliable than 'net goggles. Chris knew they were probably correct, but he didn't like it. Fortunately, at least so far, the doctors had been correct. He hadn't had any vision related problems since coming aboard the ship. He even found that he liked the way the corneal implants linked to the standard audio implants he had been using for years. But he was glad he had the ability to turn them off when he started to feel overloaded.

And then there was the sudden acceleration. 0.2 g wasn't quite like the ten times higher acceleration that made his 3.9-second zero-to-sixty miles per hour antique Tesla roadster so much fun to drive, but it was impressive—especially after being two days in weightless hell. His colleagues, all veteran astronauts, took both weightlessness and the sudden acceleration in stride, as well as traveling through vacuum at about 17,500 miles per hour. Old hat. *Yeah, right*, Chris thought. *This is one of those moments of extreme excitement that I tell everyone about in my lectures. Right now I can't wait for the boredom of the next six weeks . . .*

In the crew cabin with him were his companions for the next several weeks and for whatever awaited them at the asteroid. First and foremost, there was Colonel Robyn Rogers-White, the mission commander. Chris, like probably every other man who'd ever met her, thought she was drop-dead gorgeous. So much so, that even Chris, who usually only stumbled and fumbled when in the presence of Nobel Laureates, had to control himself. And he hated it; he wasn't used to being intimidated by mere looks. She had that *and* she was smart. Chris considered her to be almost too perfect; perhaps that's why he felt so intimidated? They really hadn't had much time to get to know each other and if he kept freezing up every time she looked at him, then he would lose her respect and that bothered him. He often told himself that he didn't care what other people thought about him, but that was a lie. He did care; he was just so used to screwing up and offending people that he told himself that lie to make himself feel better during the lonely times.

Also in the cabin was the truly annoying Dr. Juhani Janhunen. Janhunen was the European Union's personnel contribution to the mission and, at age forty-five, his space-related resume was impressive: three months on Moonbase and principal investigator on two deep space robotic missions. Chris might have liked him if it weren't for his arrogant, Euro-superiority bullshit. Chris could put up with Janhunen because he was competent and hadn't yet made any stupid mistakes. But Chris figured they would happen.

Then there was Yuichi Fuji, Japan's crew member. Holt didn't know much about Fuji, other than his resume, and Fuji seemed just fine with that. He didn't say much, which to Chris was more than okay, except for the fact that it made the man seem aloof. People who were aloof often thought of themselves as superior, and Fuji was definitely not superior. His bumbling answers to some of the most rudimentary astrodynamics questions made Chris wonder if his resume had been doctored to make him appear qualified for the mission. He had a nagging suspicion that Fuji might be more of a spy or bureaucratic place-filler than a top-in-his-field scientist on his way to make contact with aliens. Like himself, Fuji was also space sick.

"You okay back there Holt?" asked Robyn, her head turning to the side to visually check on her crewmates.

"Good enough, you just worry about flying this thing. I'll be fine."

"If you say so," she replied, sounding unconvinced.

Chris didn't blame her. He'd been mostly useless since arriving at the *Resolution* and he was sure she was concerned about how he'd perform once they reached the Artifact. He wasn't concerned; he knew he was coming out of the space sickness and could rise to any challenge. Plus, he didn't want to show any weakness in front of Colonel Rogers-White lest he appear . . . weak.

From Chris's perspective, there really wasn't much to see except the blue marble that was Earth receding into the distance, ever so slowly, as the ship accelerated. The burn would last about an hour, providing comforting partial gravity and disquieting rattles for the duration. He could have tuned his 'net implants to see the instrument displays that he knew Robyn was watching as she shepherded them away from Earth's gravity and toward, well, whatever awaited them. But he didn't. It wasn't every day that an otherwise earthbound scientist like him, who studied space and dreamed of going there since he was a boy, had an honest-to-God chance to fly there himself. Going to visit an alien Artifact was icing on the cake.

"Juhani, what is the news about the Chinese and Indian ships? Have you heard anything more about when they will be launching?" asked Yuichi.

Sounds like what an intelligence officer would ask, thought Chris.

"Nothing new. The latest intel says that the Chinese will depart Earth orbit tomorrow at the earliest, and on Saturday at the latest. That gives us anywhere from a one- to three-day head start, assuming that they don't have a higher-performing engine than what our intelligence agencies tell us."

"What about the Indians?"

"That's a tougher one to answer. You know how the Indians have been since their Phobos mission failed last year. Just like they were before. Secretive. We didn't even know they were going to Phobos until they launched, and even then we didn't know if their destination was a Mars moon or Mars orbit until three months into the flight. We'll know they've launched when they launch, I guess."

"Any news on the Caliphate?" asked Chris. He'd grown concerned about what the rogue Middle Eastern state might do when its religious leaders learned that humans weren't alone in the universe and their distorted view of Allah might have to allow not only for other religions but other sentient beings who might not even share humanity's concept of a God. The concept of God bothered Chris. It was another of those common abstractions that he just didn't really grasp. God wasn't there making His existence known. Yet there were people who would kill you if you didn't believe in what they said you were supposed to believe in—something you could not see. How could a rational person do such a thing? Yet billions of people did just that. *It was all so confusing.*

"I can brief you on that," said Robyn, "but not until we're finished with this burn and on our way. I was told to share the latest intel with you regarding the Caliphate once we were on escape. It's not good."

"The Americans are on their way." Rui Zhong's comment came almost as an aside as they were going through their pre-boarding checklist. She and her fellow taikonaut, Yuan Xiaoming, were near the end of more than two hours of systems checks that had to be completed before they would give their concurrence to boarding the rocket that would take them to the *Zheng He,* their own version of the American's *Resolution.* The ship was named after the famous Chinese mariner who sailed throughout Asia and even to Africa in the early Ming Dynasty. It was an appropriate name for the ship that would take them to the alien Artifact. If all went well, then they would launch a mere thirty-six hours after the Americans. The ship was designed to carry a crew of ten. With this smaller crew and fewer supplies, which meant less mass to be accelerated by their ship's nuclear propulsion system, they should easily make up the lost time and arrive at the target within hours of each other, perhaps even *before* the Americans.

"Better to arrive with the Americans than the Indians," replied Yuan. He admired the Americans and their continued ingenuity, despite their being displaced as the preeminent economic power in the world. Since the war, their two countries had worked together, instead of against each other, and both were the better for it. Both great nations were prospering. On the other hand, he despised the Indians. In his view, they seemed to relish the role of international troublemaker and behind-the-scenes destabilizers. Such actions were not only disharmonious, they were dangerous. They and the Caliphate were blights upon an otherwise increasingly interdependent and collaborative world.

"The Indians will also be at the party, though there is no way they will arrive within a week of us or the Americans. I was told by the commissioner that they won't be able to launch for at least another week."

"That, Rui Zhong, is the best news I've heard today," Xiaoming said as he stopped viewing the virtual checklist and instead switched to message mode. Like most Chinese, Yuan had the latest American corneal implant, allowing data from the central computer to be projected directly into his eye, at his discretion. In this case, he turned off the checklist after finishing the next-to-last section in order to read the most recent message from his sister. Her message icon was so typical of her: a Citron. The symbol of luck and happiness.

Brother, good news. I'm pregnant! The doctor says it will be a girl, just like we selected, and all of the modifications appear to have taken nicely. She will be taller than me, you know how I dislike being so short, and I've selected Mother's eyes for her. You know how jealous I've been over your eyelashes? And the fact that you have them? Well, she'll have your eyelashes. Her IQ will be like yours also. It looks like the gene splicing for intelligence went perfectly.

We're all excited about your trip. Be safe and bring home an alien for us to meet. SMILE. We love you.

Xiaoming couldn't be more pleased. This was good news to hear before departure and a sign of good luck. He might need it.

CHAPTER 6

The sun was shining and there wasn't a cloud in the sky. The three-stage, liquid-fueled Kalam rocket sat poised on the launch pad as the countdown clock moved closer and closer to zero. The first launch hadn't gone well—one of the engines unexpectedly shut down just a few seconds after liftoff, causing the mighty rocket to veer off course to the point where range safety officers had to initiate the self-destruct sequence. Fortunately, the first launch had been unmanned. Today there were people on board.

Riding in the crew capsule were two men, neither of whom had yet flown in space. The capsule looked astonishingly like the latest developed by Russia in support of its lunar and Mars exploration programs, and just about everyone involved in studying India's space program knew this was no coincidence. India's cyberespionage programs were among the best, and increasingly aggressive toward friends and foes alike.

Mission Commander Mayank Sharma, like many of the engineers who helped build the rocket and capsule in which he was riding, studied physics in Russia before returning to India. Sharma was impatient to begin their rendezvous with the already on-orbit habitat and in-space propulsion stage that would allow them to arrive at the Artifact a week after the Chinese and the Americans.

Sharma noted that all systems were showing green as the countdown clock reached zero, just after which he could feel the vibrations accompanying the lighting of the liquid hydrogen and liquid oxygen powered first stage. Moments later, he and his fellow astronaut were forcefully pulled back into their seats as the strap-on solid rocket motors ignited and the rocket began climbing from the tower toward space. Sharma grinned like a five-year old on Diwali holiday. He was finally going to space!

Sixty seconds into the flight, just as the rocket was approaching "Max Q," the point at which the atmosphere exerts maximum mechanical stress on a vehicle, the status board in the cockpit went from green to red in an instant. In the main fuel tank, one of the support struts that buttressed the thin skin of the tank, allowing its weight to be minimized for the loads it was carrying, buckled, causing a series of cascading failures throughout the vehicle. Sharma noted with alarm the change in status at about the same instant he felt the excessive vibrations beginning to shake the massive rocket just as it was undergoing maximum stress. Sharma knew that he and his crewmate had only seconds, if that, to abort the launch and get their capsule off the soon-to-be-destroyed rocket. Fortunately, the automatic system was reaching the same conclusion slightly ahead of its human crew and fired the launch abort system rocket affixed to the top of the capsule.

To those watching the launch from the viewing area, it all happened very suddenly and violently. One minute, the rocket was rising gracefully into the blue sky. The next, the entire lower part of the rocket appeared to buckle and bend back in on itself while an unexpected burst of light came from the top where the abort system rockets fired and pulled the capsule from what was now an exploding ball of liquid hydrogen and oxygen.

Though lasting only a few seconds in real time, to the viewers it looked like a slow-motion race between the menacing and growing fireball and the rising, rocket-propelled capsule that was attempting to help its fragile human cargo escape the conflagration. For an instant, it looked like the fireball might win. But, like a baby bird learning to fly, the capsule emerged from the expanding ball of destruction, veering upward and to the right where it deployed its three large parachutes, carrying it gracefully to the Earth.

Inside the capsule, Sharma and his crewmate were still trying to make sense of what had just happened. Something had gone horribly wrong, but only now were they coming to grips with the fact that they had almost died. Sharma began to shake. He was thankful that he was wearing an astronaut diaper.

※ ※ ※

The dark-haired man in the Western style suit, complete with a handkerchief in the suit's breast pocket, leaned forward as he watched the ill-fated launch on his corneal implant. The drama that was playing out on the projection in his eye, the race against time for the survival of the two Indian astronauts onboard the now-crumbling and exploding launch vehicle, mattered not to the man. He was a chess player, and the fate of a single pawn, or two of them together, didn't really register as a major concern. His eyes were set on the world stage and the much bigger prize, the queen that was the Artifact in deep space. He was seeing the failing rocket and watching Plan A fail with it. As head of India's intelligence service, it was his job to make sure that Plan B was executed expeditiously.

The man's real name was irrelevant. He'd used no less than five names in the course of his tenure in the intelligence services, and, truth be told, he didn't much care for his real name or the family it connected him to in the slums that characterized so much of India. His family embarrassed him and he was glad to leave them behind. He made the transition from just another hungry street person, conscripted into the military to fight against the Caliphate as they tried to cross the Pakistani border into India, to military intelligence. From there it was a matter of making sure that the right people supported him at the right time—even those that didn't really want to support him did so anyway, with the right incentives.

The man turned off the video feed, reached into his right desk drawer and removed a silvery over-the-ear device that looked like the early twenty-first century Bluetooth headsets. He then activated his communication implant and signaled the head of the European Desk, a protégée of his named Jabari Patel.

"Yes?" said the man's voice on the other end of the connection. Jabari's voice was flat and matter-of-fact.

"Go secure," said the man, who then listened for the tell-tale "whir" that would indicate that the over-the-ear device had scrambled the signal using third generation quantum cryptography so that no one, not even the Americans or Chinese, could eavesdrop on their conversation. The whir came, just as it was supposed to.

"Jabari, we have a problem. You were watching the launch?"

"I was. Those men were very lucky to survive."

"They survived? No matter. The launch failed. That means we won't have a chance to find out the secrets of the Artifact ourselves. We cannot let that stand. Whatever the Americans and Chinese learn, we need to make sure they don't keep it to themselves."

"Understood. Our asset in Brussels might be able to help."

"Keep me informed. And see to it that, once we get what we need, there are no traces to our involvement. No loose ends."

"There will be no loose ends, I assure you."

The man severed the connection and leaned back in his chair. He wasn't used to relying on anyone with something this important, yet, in this case, it wasn't just anyone. It was Jabari. Jabari was the best operative he had in the field and had been one hundred percent reliable in the past. The man, however, was still concerned. After all, who knew what the Americans and Chinese were going to find out there? How could anyone second guess an alien, dead or alive?

Then the man smiled. This was a new game and he was bound and determined to learn the new rules—and win.

CHAPTER 7

With the exception of satellite imagery and stealth drone overflights, there wasn't much known about the goings-on in the countries formerly known as Iraq, Syria, Libya and the Caliphate's eastern annex, Pakistan. The border controls were tight, to keep the Islamic radicals out of the rest of the world and to keep the perceived decadence of the rest of the world out of the Caliphate. To make matters worse, human intelligence, spies or informants, were hard to come by. Anyone remotely sympathetic to anti-Caliphate thinking was identified and summarily executed. Daily beheadings were commonplace in villages throughout the Caliphate, so much so that many of the residents there had long forgotten that life didn't used to be that way for their twentieth- and early twenty-first century ancestors.

For a country that prided itself on living in so-called eleventh century peace and harmony, the Caliphate's leadership was not so naïve as to assume that they owed their continued existence to anything other than the Pakistani nuclear weapons that the Caliphate had inherited when Pakistan allied itself with Allah and the Caliph. In order to maintain that nuclear deterrent, not all of the Caliphate's citizens could live in an eleventh century world, lest the rest of the world roll across their borders and smite them.

As important as their nuclear weapons were to securing their existence, they were not singular. By the combined technical talents of the Caliphate, supported by as much design information as they could steal, and with the help of the country that used to be called North Korea, they had also developed intercontinental ballistic missiles capable of carrying nuclear bombs to any place on Earth. Amir Attia strode with purpose into the missile base in the Iraqi desert.

Attia was educated in the West. As a student at Georgia Tech, he had earned his Ph.D. in aerospace engineering and even worked for a few years at an American aerospace company before he felt compelled by Allah to forsake his decadent western life and return to his native Iraq so that he could more directly serve God. It didn't hurt that he was offered an obscene salary to take his American-acquired missile design expertise and transfer that to the Caliphate. And then, of course, there were the concubines . . .

But Attia wasn't thinking of his status and sexual appetites today. No, today was a day of finishing the alterations of the Scimitar rocket that would carry a small, but very powerful nuclear weapon into space and toward the demonic ship that had invaded the solar system. The Caliph had decreed that the alien ship was from Satan and that it was every good Muslim's duty to see it destroyed. And the responsibility for seeing the decree carried out fell to Amir Attia, the man who had developed the rockets capable of hitting the east coast of the United States, forcing the Americans into a stalemate that allowed the continued existence of the Caliphate. Attia knew his rocket could be modified to carry out its new mission; he just wasn't sure there was enough time.

Attia walked through the dimly lit halls of the concrete bunker that was buried under the sands of the Iraqi desert toward the control room where the latest trajectory data was being uploaded to the missile simulator. His engineering team was working at a feverish pace, accomplishing a software development installation on a flight system that normally required weeks to months in a matter of a few days. Tonight they were to have the system ready for a hardware-in-the-loop system test that was the final required step before uploading the software to the missile and launching it. If the schedule held, the Scimitar would be on its way toward the alien demon sometime tomorrow afternoon.

Attia strode toward his assistant, Iyad Shadid, another Georgia Tech graduate who had followed his friend Amir back to Iraq and the Caliphate after receiving his Master's Degree in Electrical Engineering. Iyad, unlike Attia, was a true believer, and his zealousness sometimes got ahead of his engineering judgement—something of which Attia had to remind himself frequently when he heard news from his long-time friend and companion. Iyad looked up as his friend approached and began to move away from the computer interface he had moments before been engrossed in.

"Amir, we have a problem," said Iyad in a tone of voice that Amir didn't hear his friend use very often. He sounded not just concerned, but worried. His brow was furrowed and Attia could see the tell-tale twitch in his eyelid that was a sure sign of his friend's stress.

"Tell me about it," said Attia.

"About ten minutes ago, we finished uploading the final version of the flight control software and began the verification process. Moments after we completed the upload, the whole system shut down. Completely."

"Have you rebooted the system?"

"We are in the middle of that now. What worries me is that the failure is not what is supposed to happen if there is a coding error. As you know, the system is supposed to enter safe mode when there is an error. It is not supposed to shut down completely. I have never seen the system do this before."

"Get the reboot finished and try again. The clock is ticking and let's hope this is just a simple upload error. Both our heads will roll, probably literally, if we can't get this problem fixed before the launch window closes."

"We'll get it working. On that you have my word. Allah be praised!"

"Allah be praised!" replied Attia, with feigned optimism. He was seriously worrying about losing his head if this missile launch didn't go off as planned and work one hundred percent perfectly. The Caliph didn't like failure and Attia's status would do little to save him from the legendary wrath of the Caliph if he did.

Six thousand five hundred miles away in a shiny new earthquake-proof, glass and steel office tower in downtown Nanchang, China, a group of three women and eight men, all but one Chinese, sat around a conference table eating *guan chang* and *tang er duo*, and drinking various types of tea. They were all busily making small talk, about the things that young, prosperous people all over the world talk about: music, the latest virtual reality immersive, and, of course, dating. What they didn't talk about was their work. The thirty-five-year-old leader of the group, Lijuan Tseung, was the eldest.

Lijuan was brilliant. She excelled in mathematics and science at a very young age and was quickly identified by her teachers as gifted. Her coal black hair and delicate features could have been used as the genetic template for a host of newly-conceived and genetically-modified babies across China, but no one would ever have the chance to see her attractiveness. Lijuan considered her physical appearance to be an annoyance; she wasn't the least bit interested in men, or women for that matter, as both were a distraction from her passion: computer programming. She hadn't been genetically modified for superior intelligence, but rather had acquired it the old-fashioned way—in her mother's womb. She was completely dedicated to her work and that dedication had quickly led to her being fast-tracked through college, graduating at fifteen. She received her Ph.D. in Mathematical Physics when she was just nineteen. Wasting no time, the Chinese government recruited her to work in their cyberwarfare command, through which she was rapidly advancing in her career.

The young men and women that surrounded Lijuan were her handpicked programming team. They were given the task of developing a cyberattack capability against the Caliphate's nuclear missile launch systems. When they were tasked to develop the worm that now infected the computers at the Caliphate's missile development complex in Iraq, they thought they were developing a tool that would be used to prevent the Caliphate's missiles from attacking China. Lijuan hadn't envisioned that they would have to activate the worm anytime short of an imminent nuclear war. Nevertheless, she put in motion the sequence of events that would cause the worm to do what it was designed to do: paralyze the Caliphate's nuclear missile capabilities. That was yesterday. Today she was anxiously awaiting confirmation from the worm itself that all had gone as planned—or not. She could not tell her team. *That* would have been a serious breach of security. They developed the worm but they had no idea if and when it would be used and would likely never know.

"Lijuan, you look distracted. Is anything wrong?" asked Chunhua, also an excellent programmer and mathematician, but one to whom Lijuan was not particularly close.

"No, I'm just thinking, that's all."

"Well, you looked like you were a thousand kilometers away. You aren't usually so distracted during our breaks."

"Sorry," she said, thinking about what was likely happening well over a thousand kilometers away and wondering if their creation would be able to do what it was designed to do—and why . . .

"*Khara!*" swore Iyad, looking at the screen yet again, hoping against hope that what appeared on it moments ago would disappear and be replaced by what was supposed to be displayed there. It had been nearly ten hours since the screens first went blank and he was now running fully on adrenalin and espresso.

"What is it, my friend?" asked Attia.

"This is a cyberattack. *Ebn el Metanaka*. Someone has infected our computer systems and corrupted all of the flight software."

"You are sure?"

"I am one hundred percent sure. We engaged the AI debugger shortly after the anomaly manifested. Somehow a worm infected our systems and corrupted nearly everything. Every computer in the missile complex is compromised."

"Can the AI fix the problem?"

"No. At least not in time. It estimates it will take days to wipe the system clean, screen all of the backup software for the worm, and reinstall everything," Iyad replied, now allowing his exhaustion to show.

"You said every computer in the complex is compromised. What about the one on the rocket?" asked Attia.

Iyad's appearance brightened as he sat up and looked up and to the right, activating his newly-operational corneal implant. Attia waited patiently as his friend rapidly moved his eyes from one location to another, triggering a personal computer access grid that only he could see, until finally he looked straight ahead and again made eye contact with Attia.

"The missile on the pad is currently isolated from the flight system computers in the complex. I just shut down its data link to make sure no one could inadvertently connect to it and spread the infection. I don't know if it is infected, but the AI can find out. If it is not, then we'll have to find a way to manually upload the final flight trajectories to the onboard flight computer and then run the launch sequence. It should be possible, but right now I'm not sure how we will do it."

"So, if the AI finds that it isn't infected, we can upload the clean flight software and have it ready to go?"

"We should be able to. But if it's also compromised, then we will be back where we started," said Iyad.

"Do what you can. I'll go update the supreme commander and let them know we still might get a missile launched in the time window. Allah be praised!"

"Allah be praised!"

CHAPTER 8

Attia and Iyad stood silently in the command center as the highly-modified Scimitar rocket lifted from the launch pad and into the deep blue sky above the Iraqi desert. Their ground support team had successfully kept the rocket isolated from the infected ground computer networks and updated the launch programs directly to the rocket as it sat on the pad in the scorching heat of the noonday sun. Getting the missile prepared, including the hurriedly-developed network-isolated command and control system, had not been easy. One of Attia's team came up with the idea of using a new, consumer-grade portable computer imported from Turkey for ground control, and, to everyone's surprise, it worked beautifully. The computing capability of modern consumer electronics outpaced the performance of the world's supercomputers merely a decade ago. Moore's Law, thanks to quantum computing, was alive and well.

After porting a virus-free set of flight control software from the consumer laptop, the engineering team created, almost from scratch, the control sequences that would enable the rocket to interface with the launch platform. For example, they couldn't have the tower's hold-downs that kept the rocket from falling over pre-launch holding it too long and keeping it from getting off the ground. It wasn't terribly complex software to program, it just had to be done—from scratch. It took them five days.

The rocket ascended, and right on schedule the twin solid rocket motors that gave it the additional kick it needed to get off the launch pad separated and fell toward the desert floor. The first-stage engines continued to burn and carry the rocket skyward until they used up their fuel and the second stage engines came to life, boosting the ship's two-stage, solid-fueled rocket upper stage to just shy of Earth escape velocity. Once in space, the upper stage engines would ignite and send the payload, a cluster of fission bombs, on their way to their rendezvous with the alien Artifact—a rendezvous that was designed to go very badly for whatever was contained within it.

Beginning in the late 2020s, the United States began deploying a series of monster satellites in low Earth orbit. Had Ronald Reagan been alive, he would have instantly recognized them as the descendants of his proposed Star Wars ballistic missile defense satellites that were envisioned to protect the United States and its allies from nuclear strikes launched by the old Soviet Union. Only now, the Soviet Union didn't exist and its heir, Russia, was part of the European Union and an ally of the United States in the global competition with China, India and the Caliphate. After the near-cataclysmic war with China, the satellites' new mission was neutralizing the ever-present threat of the religious fanatics within the Caliphate who proclaimed that when the time was right, they would wage war against the infidels and bring on the apocalypse.

In the age of nuclear weapons and ballistic missiles, everyone knew all too well how easy it would be to initiate an apocalypse. It was against this threat that the orbiting ring of satellites, each equipped with a five-hundred-kilowatt laser, was designed to operate. The systems were on their highest state of readiness for the rocket launch in the Iraqi desert based on what the CIA and other intelligence sources were learning about the Caliphate's planned response to the alien Artifact. Another set of satellites, each equipped with sophisticated optical and infrared sensors, was actively watching the activities of the Caliphate and, in particular, activities at their missile launch complex in Iraq. They had no trouble seeing the heat signature and tell-tale launch plume as the massive Scimitar rocket blasted toward space.

Within seconds, the launch notification went to the US Air Force Space Command headquarters in Los Angeles, California and to the computer systems which semi-autonomously controlled the lasers that were designed to deal with just this sort of threat. Multiple engagement options were assessed based on the rocket's anticipated flight path, and the two satellites with the best line-of-sight were brought online and taken to battle readiness. The automated systems were doing their job, keeping the target locked in the sights of the two laser stations while they awaited approval to engage from their human controllers back on Earth.

Humans don't think as quickly as machines. People are also very nervous about allowing automated systems to have rapid life-or-death decision-making authority when potentially millions, or billions, of human lives could be at stake—which was one of the reasons the laser battle stations were only semi-autonomous. Taking the time to reflect on a threat and to consider the sometimes not-so-clear ramifications of making the "right" decision of "the moment" was what people were good at. And this system was constructed to require a human decision before engaging a target to prevent a "wrong" decision. This time, the human element, the "decision," took too long and one of the satellites lost its ability to engage the Scimitar rocket as it moved beyond its effective range. When the engagement approval was received, the remaining satellite performed its final targeting adjustment and began to discharge the bank of ultracapacitors that had been storing power from satellite's onboard nuclear fission reactor for just this purpose. Within milliseconds, the laser beam director locked-on to the target and the invisible beam of laser light shot toward the accelerating Caliphate rocket.

Another set of satellite instruments were tracking and imaging the Caliphate's rocket as it moved toward Earth escape. Had the laser successfully hit the rocket, they would have seen the immediate damage the beam caused and sent images of the ensuing destruction back to Space Command in Los Angeles and to the Pentagon. But that didn't happen. Instead, the cameras tracked the rocket as the upper stage deployed and ignited its engines to take its payload into interplanetary space. The laser missed. And, as the autonomous engagement computers quickly calculated, there was no time for a repeat engagement. The satellite which fired its laser would take several minutes to recharge its capacitors and no other satellite could be in place to fire at the Caliphate's rocket in time.

In its first real test as an antimissile system, against a real target and not during a simulation, the trillion-dollar system failed.

❧ ❧ ❧

Less than ten minutes after the failure, the secretary of defense was informed of the miss and had the unenviable task of having to tell President Kremic that the most expensive defense system in American history had failed in its first real-life test. But telling the president wasn't what worried him the most. He was concerned about how the Artifact, or others yet undetected, might react to a nuclear attack in space. The safety of the United States was now being undermined by religious zealots with nuclear weapons—in space no less. He was terrified.

Chapter i

Waiting. Watching. Waiting yet more. Sending remote probes to observe, listen and gather data for its ongoing assessments of human progress. Using the sensors in or from the battlements distributed across the Earth to monitor the humans was easy and sometimes they could hide in plain sight—the primitives didn't recognize them as implements of a technological civilization but rather as emissaries of the gods or, in some cases, as gods themselves. It learned their languages, their religious practices, their mating rituals. Guardian-of-the-Outpost gathered as much as information as it could while it watched and waited.

Guardian-of-the-Outpost surveyed the approaching human ships and quickly determined that two of the primitive craft contained crew while the third, which was lagging somewhat behind the first two, was robotic. All contained fission weapons. This fact caused extreme concern to Guardian-of-the-Outpost, which had been monitoring the development of the bipedal humans for the last fifty thousand Earth years. During its close passes with the third planet of this system, it had observed the species' slow but steady progress from being hunter-gatherers in the once wet and fertile area now known as the Sahara Desert to being masters of their world. It paralleled the course taken by so many species and yet had its own unique twists and turns that were driven by history rather than mere evolutionary pressure alone. Now they were taking their first steps toward the stars and Guardian-of-the-Outpost wondered if they would make it. Or not.

Guardian-of-the-Outpost had misjudged this species' progress on more than one occasion—its judgement perhaps tainted by wishful thinking. The first time was just over twenty thousand years previously when a group of humans occupying an island near the equatorial region of their Atlantic Ocean had burgeoned into a maritime superpower and began showing signs of understanding basic scientific principles. But then tragedy struck, with a great earthquake and tsunami literally wiping the island and all of its occupants from the face of the planet, and along with them any hope for the rise of near-term technological civilization.

The second time was when the city-states of a region in the southern part of the European continent banded together. It was then that the humans seemed poised to create the basis of a lasting and prosperous technological civilization. That was just twenty-five hundred years ago and the fall of the Greek civilization still bothered Guardian-of-the-Outpost. It just couldn't understand what had happened and how such a progenitor civilization could fall so easily.

Now truly global technological civilizations spanned most of the planet. They had discovered that Guardian-of-the-Outpost existed and were coming—to explore or attack. Guardian-of-the-Outpost was not yet sure of their intentions. It did know that under normal circumstances, their intentions would not matter in the least. Its weapons systems were designed to destroy much more advanced spacecraft and technologies than these primates could possibly have in their arsenals.

Two groups of competing human civilizations were vying for Guardian-of-the-Outpost's attention and at least one additional group was intent on destroying it.

Guardian-of-the-Outpost knew what it should do, under ordinary circumstances. But these were fifty thousand years separated from ordinary circumstances and curiosity regarding the fate of the Greater Consciousness weighed heavily on its mind. Since it had been cut off from communion with self-that-is-not-self, Guardian-of-the-Outpost wondered if the beings that had so viciously attacked it so many years ago had succeeded in destroying the other with whom it had been in constant communion until their second, and very recent, separation. Unfortunately, there was simply no way it could find out without the help of these bipeds who were now well-within range of causing it great harm or irreversible damage.

No, Guardian-of-the-Outpost had to make contact with these visitors in order to regain the communion it had lost so many years before. This was an opportunity that could not be ignored—fission bombs or not.

CHAPTER 9

Only Robyn can look that good after only two months of only spit baths and no makeup, thought Chris as he once again tried not to ogle the mission's commander. She was the only woman on the flight and all of her male colleagues were painfully aware of that fact. Chris was quite sure that each of the other two men on the flight were just as eager to see as much of Colonel Rogers-White as possible, even if they couldn't cross the line and do anything about it. Such was the life of a professional male on a two-and-half-month journey into deep space with the hottest woman in the inner solar system.

Yes, I'm a chauvinist, he thought, *but only because I wouldn't have a chance with her*. It was easier for him to play the part of the chauvinist than be himself and have to deal with the rejection.

Thinking of Robyn, chance or not, brought a smile to Chris's face before he went back to the task at hand—prepping the ship's LIDAR system to begin long-distance mapping of the Artifact. They were only about two hundred thousand kilometers away and braking. They would be alongside the Artifact in just three days. He had the maps from his robotic prospector's slow flyby; now it was time to begin mapping its surface in earnest, using the best laser system available in the world.

"Chris, are you ready? The people back home are eager for data. I think they've been bored," said Robyn as she seemed to look away from what she was reviewing via her corneal implant and toward Chris.

"Boring is right," Chris replied, thinking of all the free time he had these last few months to simply look out the window at the blackness of space or the dazzle of the sun, through a filter, of course. He'd read the latest technical journals until he couldn't stand to read any more and steadfastly refused to join in any moronic games with the rest of the crew. Games were something else he didn't understand. Why did people engage in meaningless competition using arbitrary rules like that? They seemed to like it, but when Chris played, he got so caught up in understanding and playing by the rules, that he often forgot about the other people at the table and missed out on whatever else was going on that they all seemed to enjoy. He could not play a game and interact with people at the same time. *How could anyone?* Playing games was just too difficult.

Being bored, he frequently reminded himself, *is better than engaging in stupid, complicated activities you don't understand and embarrassing yourself.*

"Don't knock boring flights. I've been on sorties that were anything but boring and I will take boring any day of the week," she said.

"Having been in research my entire career, I cannot even imagine what that must be like. You'll have to tell me about them sometime," said Chris, returning to the task at hand.

"I'll do that. But right now, I need data," she replied.

No one spoke as Chris continued to make adjustments to the LIDAR system using the virtual control panel that only he could see, thanks to his corneal implant. To anyone watching, Chris would almost look like a conductor, waving his hands in the air and occasionally pushing virtual buttons.

"Ready!" he said, looking away from the virtual control panel and back toward Robyn.

She smiled and said, "Okay then. Let's do some mapping and see if the LIDAR can spot anything that your camera missed."

Five seconds later, a small box located under the crew cabin on the front of the ship rotated and pointed to where the Artifact was positioned, still far out of visual range. Motors activated and slid the cover from in front of the laser aperture and another from the receiving telescope. The laser then kicked in, shooting ten thousand pulses of light into deep space toward the alien ship.

For remote sensing of distant objects, LIDAR works like radar, only better—and that is why Chris liked using it whenever he could. Unfortunately, for his small robotic asteroid survey ships, power was at a premium and he was mostly constrained to use passive, low-power systems like good old-fashioned cameras. The shorter wavelengths of light emitted by the LIDAR's laser system allow much higher resolution mapping of surfaces than is possible with the much longer wavelength electromagnetic radiation emitted in radar.

"Shit! The receiver went into safe mode," said Chris, just moments after the laser system became active.

"Perhaps you should check the other channels?" suggested Janhunen, who had moved closer to both Chris and Robyn as they began the mapping. The *Resolution* didn't have a rotating section to simulate gravity, so the crew had to adapt to life in space without the comfort and convenience that accompanies living in an environment with an obvious up or down, and, in this case, without the ability to hear people flying up behind you as they pushed off from one section of the ship and coasted to another. Chris didn't hear Janhunen's approach until he spoke.

"Perhaps you can be quiet while I figure out what happened?" retorted Chris, keenly aware that Robyn was watching them intently as he tried to recover from being startled by Janhunen's abrupt appearance. *He couldn't maintain his train of thought with interruptions, didn't they understand?*

"Harrumph," was Janhunen's only reply as he moved away and toward Robyn.

Chris, annoyed at the interruption, waited until the European scientist had his back turned before he went about checking the status of the LIDAR's other receiving channels.

"The backscatter signal completely overloaded the sensors, *on all channels*. The return signal appears to have come back significantly amplified," said Chris.

"Chris, if the signal was amplified, that implies that something onboard the Artifact detected our laser signal, reflected it and *boosted* its strength. Shouldn't the signal getting back to us have been significantly weaker than what we emitted?" asked Robyn.

Beauty and brains, thought Chris, before he spoke. "Absolutely. Nothing appears to have been damaged, but I'm turning down the gain on the receivers to about ten percent of the previous setting before we try again."

"Let me know when you're ready," said Robyn.

"Here we go again," said Chris, as he started the ship's LIDAR system once more.

Chris concentrated on the various data screens projected onto his cornea. He frowned and then suddenly recoiled as if he were ducking a punch to his face.

"Shit. Shit. Shit. The receivers are fried. Whatever that thing did to the first laser pulse, it did in spades to the second. The system completely overloaded. And it looks like the damage might be permanent, or at least until I can install some replacement parts."

"Apparently, this thing doesn't want to be mapped," said Janhunen.

"At least not actively. Were there any problems with the cameras used on your flyby?" asked Robyn.

"None. Everything on that mission worked flawlessly. But all our systems were strictly passive."

"Well, then, we just learned something new. This thing doesn't like concentrated energy hitting it. I wonder what it would do if we had one of the new gigawatt pulse ABM lasers?" asked Robyn.

"I can guess," said Chris.

"Right. Enough of that. What else can we do to get a better look at this thing before we rendezvous?"

"We still have radar. It didn't seem to mind having gigahertz frequency radio waves reflected from it."

"Let's do the best we can with what we have. I don't want to get near this thing blind."

"I'm on it," replied Chris.

"Colonel, please pardon the interruption, but we're getting a transmission from the Chinese ship. They want to talk," said Fuji, with his customary politeness. For most of the journey, Fuji had kept mostly to himself, usually joining the crew for meals, but almost none of the various social activities.

"I was wondering when we would hear from them. Given that they've almost caught up with us after launching three days later, they are probably feeling a little cocky. Let's hear what they have to say. Please put them on the speaker and mute all of our microphones except mine," said Robyn.

In zero gravity, astronauts tend to assume what is known as "neutral posture," which is prompted by the body's response to the lack of gravity stressing their musculature. Chris noticed that as Robyn prepared to speak with the Chinese, she straightened her posture and assumed what he'd come to consider to be her "military posture."

"Done. You're on," said Fuji.

"This is Colonel Robyn Rogers-White, commanding the *Resolution*. How may we help you?"

"Colonel Rogers-White, this is Captain Rui Zhong of the *Zheng He*. Since we are both going to arrive at the Artifact within only a few hours of each other, my co-pilot and I thought it would be a good idea to contact you to discuss possible collaboration in our forthcoming explorations. For us to arrive at a potentially-active alien ship and be perceived as competing against each other would be, perhaps, not healthy for us or our respective countries."

Robyn turned off her microphone as she looked toward Fuji and said, "Put the visible and IR telescope on the *Zheng He*. I'd like to know if they're making this overture because of some problem with their ship or if they're being genuinely open."

Turning her microphone back on, she said, "Captain Zhong. Your idea has merit but I am sure you are aware that our respective countries already ruled out a joint mission. I would be hard pressed, short of an emergency, to defy the spirit, if not the letter, of that decision."

"I fully understand, Colonel. This is merely an overture, not any sort of attempt to get you to disobey your orders. As you are surely aware, there is a nuclear missile coming behind us. That doesn't give us much time, especially if we are at odds with each other."

"I am very aware of the Caliphate's missile and we appreciate your invitation, but I must follow my orders unless and until I have a compelling reason not to do so. I will have to decline."

"I am saddened by your decision, Colonel, but I understand and respect it. We must all follow orders. Good luck."

"Good luck to you also," she said as she cut off the communications, rose from the seat into which she'd buckled herself, and floated over to where Yuichi Fuji was busily reviewing data streams on one of the console monitors.

"Well?" she said.

"Their ship appears to be functional. There is no visible damage and, if the trajectories I ran are accurate, they will arrive at the Artifact about three hours after us," Fuji said as he made a show of turning off the monitor and looking at Robyn directly. He paused.

"Is there something else?" she asked.

Now it was Fuji's turn to straighten his body posture, which he did, just before he replied, "Yes, there is. My government will not abide any sort of collaboration with the Chinese on this venture. Our participation in the mission was only possible after your president assured our leaders that no such collaboration would take place. Thank you for honoring that agreement. I could tell it was not an easy decision for you."

"Like I told Captain Zhong, I will follow my orders unless I have a compelling reason not to do so."

CHAPTER 10

They could clearly see the Artifact through the habitat's window as they approached. Everyone took turns looking through the onboard optical telescope as soon as they had closed to a distance of almost one hundred and fifty kilometers, watching the image get sharper and clearer as they approached. Now that they were approaching to within a kilometer, they could see much of the stunning detail with their naked eyes. If it had been an asteroid, then they wouldn't have thought twice about its size. But, it being clearly artificial, they were mesmerized. The Artifact was black, and if they hadn't been approaching from the sunward side, they might not have seen it against the backdrop of stars. In the visible spectrum of light, it was well camouflaged.

"It looks just like it did when we sailed by. The computer is comparing the images taken then with what we're seeing now and there are no significant differences," Chris said as he continued to look back and forth between the window and the data stream that was demanding his attention.

"It looks like it has seen better days," said Janhunen as he floated toward the window, taking in the view. They were all staring out the window now. They were the first human beings to ever see a piece of technology built by aliens and the significance of what was happening now was not lost on them.

"The surface is textured into some sort of repeating pattern. It resembles the wall coverings used in anechoic chambers. You know, ones that absorb all the sounds so that you can hear your own heartbeat," said Fuji.

"All stop," said Robyn.

Chris knew the rules of engagement for the encounter. Each step was meticulously defined by the first contact team back on Earth and practiced by the crew several times before launch. They were now at the next milestone and stopped the ship relative to the Artifact at a distance of one kilometer. They were to conduct a series of observations here to determine their next steps, which could include proceeding to a near-rendezvous with the object. It was Chris's job, as the discoverer of the Artifact and the person most knowledgeable about it, to examine the alien object with the ship's many sensor systems and make a recommendation regarding that next crucial step.

"It's glowing fairly uniformly in the infrared and emitting a lot more heat than can be accounted for by pure solar radiation absorption and emission alone. Whatever this thing is or isn't, it's still functional enough to produce heat," said Chris.

"Any sort of electromagnetic emissions?" asked Robyn.

"None. The computer has been scanning across multiple frequencies since we left home and there hasn't been a peep. We've been using radar returns to navigate and so far, they've been normal and what you'd expect from a metal-rich object in deep space."

"I wish this thing hadn't fried our LIDAR. I'd rather use the automated rendezvous and docking system algorithms than fly by the seat of my pants using only visual and radar data."

From what Chris knew of the colonel, he found it hard to believe that she would rather let a computer fly the ship. He couldn't help but think Robyn was playing to the brass back home by making such a big deal about not being able to use the much-ballyhooed automated systems.

"Fuji, what are our Chinese friends doing?" asked Robyn.

"They are closing on the object from about thirty-degree starboard. I'd say they are still about three hours out from rendezvous."

"That settles it, if we're going to take advantage of being here first, then we've got to go in," said Robyn. She bore a look of determination, and, for the first time since they'd launched into space, Chris felt the butterflies in his stomach as the stress level increased.

Robyn moved her hands across the virtual control panel that only she could see. Moments later they felt the gentle bump of acceleration as the good old-fashioned hydrazine thrusters used for controlling the attitude of the spacecraft and for low thrust maneuvers like this one kicked in to push them closer to the object.

"Juhani, I want the main engines in standby mode and ready to go at a moment's notice. If this thing so much as looks at us funny, I want to be able to get us out of here."

"The reactor is operational and the primary engines are ready to burn with all she's got if you give the word. We've got plenty of fuel and all systems are nominal."

The ship inched closer to the black, elliptical alien Artifact. The Chinese were now clearly visible on their starboard side making Chris wonder if the alien ship would perceive their simultaneous approach as a friendly or hostile act. How would he react if two foreign ships were approaching his position and he had no clue as to their intentions? He didn't like the thought.

The damaged areas of the ship were now clearly visible and they looked even worse in person than they did in the images brought back by the robotic spacecraft only a few months ago. Also visible was what they all were assuming was an iris-shaped door near a relatively undamaged portion of the object. That was their target.

Chris checked the radar return on this virtual dashboard and saw that they were within one hundred meters of the Artifact and slowing. There was no indication that it noticed the human ships approaching, which, to Chris, seemed like a good thing. When they were within fifty meters, the ship stopped.

"Okay, here we go," said Robyn as she activated the ship's broadband radio transmitter. "This is Captain Robyn Rogers-White of the Earth ship *Resolution*. We come in peace. Is there anyone there I can speak with?"

The *Resolution* hung in space, watching and waiting to see if the Artifact would respond.

Nothing happened.

"Juhani, suit up and get ready to go over there in the Flexcraft. Fuji can handle monitoring the engines while you're away."

Janhunen launched himself from his station toward the aft deck and the lockers which housed their spacesuits. Chris, as Janhunen's handler, also moved from his station to help the Finnish astronaut get into his suit and complete the pre-EVA checklist. Chris was the only crew member who wasn't an experienced astronaut so he had the unenviable job of supporting whoever was tasked with suiting up for EVA. It made him feel like the ball boy for the high school football team.

In the time it took to get Janhunen in his spacesuit and ready to leave the ship there still wasn't any sort of reply or visible activity from the Artifact. If Chris hadn't been busy helping Janhunen, the silence and the waiting would have been excruciating. He was in deep space on a nuclear-powered rocket, visiting an alien Artifact, perhaps about to make contact with an extraterrestrial civilization, *and* a nuclear bomb was coming toward them at eighteen kilometers per second to blow them, and the alien Artifact, to oblivion, perhaps starting an interstellar war in the process, and all they could do was wait.

"Juhani, it's show time. Get on out there and see what you can learn about this thing," said Robyn.

Janhunen lowered his visor, sealing his spacesuit, and moved to the airlock separating the ship from the attached Flexcraft. It took another twenty minutes to cycle the airlock and get him settled into the small confines of the spacecraft and perform the necessary systems checks.

The Flexcraft was a hard-skinned miniature spacecraft that resembled a deep-sea submersible more than a spaceship. The one-person vehicle was designed to allow its occupant to leave the main spacecraft in shirtsleeves or spacesuit and perform almost any repair or assessment that could be accomplished on a traditional EVA—only better. Janhunen stood in the Flexcraft with only his head and arms visible through the 360-degree glass dome on top. On each side of the Flexcraft were two manipulator arms, each equipped with a different grappling fixture or manipulator. Two of the arms terminated with what resembled human hands, complete with opposable thumbs. The upper arm on the right side came with a pincer instead of a hand; the upper left arm resembled a Swiss Army Knife with its multiple tool options that included screw drivers, knives, a corkscrew and at least four additional custom wrench fittings designed to work with various spacecraft subsystems that might need repair from outside the ship.

The Flexcraft flew untethered using cold gas impulsive thrusters that were now taking Janhunen away from the *Resolution* and toward the Artifact. Chris could see that Janhunen wasn't taking full advantage of the comfort afforded by the Flexcraft—he was in his EVA suit with the helmet on and locked into place. Janhunen was controlling his flight using the Flexcraft's version of a virtual control panel, which made him look like an orchestra conductor, sans baton.

"Juhani, take a look at the top and bottom of the thing but don't take yourself out of my line of sight. At least not yet. And pay special attention to the iris," Robyn instructed Janhunen as she once again looked at the complete set of sensor data provided to her by the computer aboard the *Resolution*.

Chris moved toward where Robyn was anchored and locked his feet in the hold-downs close to hers. They watched as the Flexcraft gracefully maneuvered around the top, sides and bottom of the alien Artifact without ever losing sight of the *Resolution*. At times, Janhunen was upside down in relation to the crew cabin of the mother ship. The flight from the *Resolution* to the Artifact and Juhani's initial reconnaissance took nearly two hours. No one wanted to move *too* quickly.

The three-hour lead they had remaining over the Chinese ship evaporated as Fuji abruptly announced that the Chinese ship had arrived and was wasting no time sending out its own astronaut. There was still no reaction from the alien ship that hung in space before them. Chris wondered if that would change now that there were two spacecraft in the vicinity.

Instead of the Artifact, the main display screen in the ship's control center now showed an enlarged image of the Chinese ship and a small figure emerging from it. The taikonaut, looking incredibly small against the massive backdrop of infinite space, moved slowly away from the *Zheng He* using what appeared to be an untethered maneuvering unit. Chris knew that the Chinese had developed an extensive set of tools for in-space assembly, construction and repair, so he wasn't surprised that they'd opt for using the maneuvering suit, which basically provided an individual astronaut with propulsion capability in the form of a powered backpack. The United States tested such systems back in the days of the space shuttle and then briefly discarded them as being too risky until the advent of space commercialization had driven innovation to the point where they were now back in active use—by NASA and by private companies who were operating and maintaining hotels in Earth orbit.

The taikonaut cautiously and very slowly approached the Artifact by using his maneuvering unit's propulsion system in short bursts.

Forty meters. Thirty meters. Twenty meters. Ten meters. Chris held his breath as the figure used the maneuvering unit to stop. There was still no reaction from the Artifact.

Wasting no time, moving much faster, and with much less caution, the Chinese taikonaut began moving toward the iris.

"Juhani, please follow our Chinese friend toward the iris," said Robyn.

"On my way," said Janhunen. These were his first words spoken since leaving the ship. Chris surmised that his quietness was a result of him either being too busy flying the Flexcraft, ogling the Artifact, or both.

Both humans were now within just a few meters of the iris. The Artifact took no visible notice of its visitors.

The taikonaut closed the final distance to the Artifact and reached his hand toward it; Chris held his breath. He didn't know what he expected to happen when the object was touched, but he was able to breathe again when absolutely nothing happened. The taikonaut was now running his hands across the iris and the surface of the ship around it, apparently searching for some way to open it.

Janhunen, taking advantage of the extra tools available to him by using the Flexcraft's manipulator arms, also flew closer and began cautiously tapping on the surfaces on the other side of the door, being careful to not come too close to the Chinese astronaut who was, quite literally, at his side.

"Fuck this shit. I'm here and the politicians at Earth aren't," said Robyn as she turned to speak with Fuji. "I'm going to contact Captain Zhong and tell her we're accepting her offer to collaborate. It makes absolutely no sense for our two astronauts to be side-by-side, each trying to get into the ship and not working together to do it. We don't have much time until the Caliphate's nuke gets here. That's not enough for us to be playing political games fifty million miles away from home."

"If you are asking for my blessing to violate our mission orders, then you will not get it. My orders are clear, whether I like them or not. And I do happen to support them. Working with the Chinese is absolutely out of the question," Fuji said, moving from his neutral space posture to a more aggressive stance.

For a moment, Chris thought the Japanese scientist might launch himself physically toward Robyn. Chris felt his adrenalin pumping and was surprised by the urge to intercept and give Fuji a shove. *She could probably whip both of us at once,* he thought as he forced himself to relax. Fuji stayed put.

"I'm sorry to hear you say that, Yuichi. You are free to lodge your complaint with your government and I'll deal with it when we get home. But for now, I'm commanding this mission and from this point forward we will be working with Captain Zhong and her crew."

Fuji clearly didn't like the news and his face began to redden. "I will certainly follow your orders, even if you aren't following your own. Discipline must be maintained. But, for the record, I object and I will file a report with my government."

"I'm sorry, Yuichi, but this transcends normal politics and we're going to present a united human front to whatever this thing is before the Caliphate's missile gets here and fucks things over."

Robyn turned away from Fuji with a look of determination and activated the radio link to Captain Zhong.

"Captain Zhong, this is Captain Robyn Rogers-White. If your offer to collaborate is still open, then we are interested."

"Captain Rogers-White, I'm very glad you and I are now in agreement. Given the lateness of the hour, and the time our people have spent fruitlessly trying to gain access to the Artifact, I suggest we bring them back to our respective ships and collaboratively assemble a plan to move forward."

"I agree. As soon as we go over the data from Dr. Janhunen's EVA, I will contact you."

"I look forward to it."

CHAPTER 11

The crew took its required eight-hour sleep break, but none slept more than a few hours at a stretch. Chris had a particularly fitful night's sleep, again dreaming a variation of the same nightmarish dream he had been having since he was a student at Princeton. In the dream, he was always among a group of people who were blithely going about their business, completely unaware of some sort of impending doom of which only Chris was aware and sounding the alarm about. And, as always happened, no one was listening or paying attention to his warnings as the looming disaster, which had something to do with a war or a mob of people rioting, came closer and closer. Fortunately, he always woke up before disaster struck—but the dreams caused his sleep to be anything but restful.

He unzipped from his sleeping bag, pulled on his coveralls and pushed off for the exit from the sleeping area. On his way out, he noticed that he had awakened ahead of everyone except, of course, Robyn. She was in the control room reviewing messages on the forward view screen when he arrived in search of his morning coffee. He paused before pushing off from the wall and making his presence known. There was something about the way she tilted her head to the side when she was reading and in deep concentration that he found fascinating.

"Chris, is there something you need?" she asked, not taking her eyes from the screen.

"Uh, no. I was just coming in for coffee," said Chris as he quickly moved to kick off and propel himself toward the galley where he could make his much-needed morning cup of coffee. *She must have eyes in the back of her head.*

"Good, I wouldn't want to slow you down," she said, with the slightest hint of a smile.

Chris moved to start heating his coffee as quickly as he could, fumbling more than once as he tried to recover from being caught staring at her—something he didn't even realize he was doing until she pointed it out. That happened a lot. He would see something interesting, a pretty woman, a math equation, a sunset, and he would hyper-focus on it and not even realize he was staring.

"Coffee in space just doesn't cut it, does it?" he asked.

"You're right, there's something about drinking it from a straw that ruins the experience. What I wouldn't give for a good Italian espresso," she replied with an emerging smile.

"Espresso? Did you say espresso?" asked Juhani as he emerged from below deck.

"We were just dreaming about having real coffee instead of this rehydrated imposter," said Robyn as she held up her spill-proof, space-certified drink container that the crew fondly called her "sippy cup." They all had one.

Following the much-needed morning banter, they checked the status of the Artifact (nothing had changed) and ate another rehydrated meal from the ship's stash of food. They then gathered in the commons area for their morning briefing. Robyn had already been in contact with her Chinese counterpart and they made some decisions regarding their now collaborative exploration effort. The jovial mood of the morning evaporated at the news.

Janhunen was furious. If he hadn't made a conscious effort to hold on to one of the many support rails that adorned the walls of the command deck, he looked like he would, quite literally, be bouncing from the walls.

"Juhani, the matter is settled. Captain Zhong and I discussed the situation at length last night, and we believe it is best for Dr. Holt to accompany the Chinese taikonaut Yuan Xiaoming to the Artifact on today's EVA," said Robyn.

"But I'm the one explicitly trained to perform the EVA. Holt's not an astronaut. This is his first spaceflight and he's never been out in a suit before. He'll get himself, and more likely one of us, killed. This is insane."

"Captain Rogers-White, I have to agree. I reported your actions to my superiors and they have lodged a formal complaint with your government about your decision to work with the Chinese and now you are making yet another irrational decision, violating our mission rules yet again." Fuji moved to physically position himself next to Janhunen as he spoke. It was an unspoken physical threat Chris was quite certain Robyn could not ignore. Chris again bristled at their challenge to Robyn's authority.

"I heard this morning of your government's complaint, Yuichi. My government reaffirmed that I am in command of this mission, as was agreed by all our governments, and the final decisions of protocol and job assignments rest with me. I will be held accountable for my actions upon our return. For now, I expect you to comply with my decisions and stop the endless second guessing. There's a nuclear missile that's due to arrive in two days and an alien ship that we've got to investigate before it arrives and blows us all to hell.

"The fact remains that Dr. Holt is the one who discovered the alien Artifact and has spent the most time studying it. Juhani spent several hours at the Artifact yesterday and found nothing that gets us closer to getting inside it or even understanding what this thing is. No, we're going to try a different approach."

Chris knew better than to say anything, though he was tempted. He had been doing some database research in his spare time and found absolutely nothing of consequence published by his Japanese science colleague, Yuichi Fuji, other than perhaps his name being fifth on the list of authors for a recent paper on theoretical tachyon astronomy, a research field he found to be specious, at best. Juhani Janhunen was worse. During the flight, Chris took more time to research the European's background and he was not impressed. Janhunen had not published anything in the twenty years since his Ph.D. thesis. Chris acknowledged that this was likely because of his meteoric rise in the European Space Agency's astronaut corps—spending three months on the Moon did count for something—but Chris feared his ineptitude in matters of science would be a threat to the success of their mission.

"Colonel Rogers-White, I accept your decision but I believe it to be in error," said Janhunen.

"Yuichi?"

"I, too, accept your status as mission commander and all that entails. And I again strenuously object to your decision to collaborate with the Chinese. But that isn't Dr. Holt's fault and I will do all that I can to assure the success of our mission and his safety."

"Very good. Thank you for sharing with me your concerns and believe me when I say that I have taken them into consideration. Now, let's get Dr. Holt suited up and ready to go. The EVA is set to begin at ten o'clock." Robyn moved away from her position near the front of the commons room and toward Chris. She motioned for him to follow her for a side conversation.

"Chris, I want you to know that I share Juhani's concerns about your being the one to go out today with the Chinese."

"Then why?" asked Chris, raising his voice.

"Please keep your voice down. This is confidential. Commander Zhong and I spoke last night at length about the plans for today and they are insistent that you—not Juhani, not Yuichi—go to the Artifact with their taikonaut. Chinese Intelligence has apparently done its job very well and determined that Yuichi is basically too hostile to them and the collaboration."

"That's pretty obvious," replied Chris.

"Yes, to us, but they shouldn't know that unless they've looked into his background and know his predispositions toward them. As for Juhani, they said he was too 'unpredictable' and brash. Zhong said something about an incident on the Moon that involved him, a female taikonaut, and the military police. It apparently didn't end well. In the end, they said they would prefer that you or I try to get inside the Artifact today. I chose you."

"I know I'm the most technically qualified person on this ship to go, but I've never been on an EVA." Chris's heart began to race. *I'm actually going on a spacewalk to the alien ship.* He was terrified and excited beyond measure at the same time.

"We also talked about that. Like everyone else, you were trained in the neutral buoyancy tank for EVAs. You did well enough to remain on the crew so I know you have the basics. To help get over to the Artifact, their taikonaut will be coming here to get you. You'll be tethered together the whole time."

"All right then. I guess I'd better get suited up." Chris felt determined, but unprepared.

"One last thing."

"What's that?"

"Don't screw this up. I was reamed last night by General Frederick. He said my decision to partner with the Chinese resulted in the Japanese prime minister calling the president. The president backed me up but told Frederick that my career would be over if the decision didn't get us significantly more information about the Artifact." Robyn cocked her head forward and looked at Chris through the tops of her eyes. Chris found that look to be very attractive, which, of course, made him all the more nervous.

"I won't screw up," said Chris as he moved toward the airlock and the stored spacesuits.

Speaking loudly for all to hear, she concluded, "Let's get inside this thing and find out why it's here."

Ninety minutes later, the Chinese taikonaut, Yuan Xiaoming, in his white spacesuit, and Chris, in his bright orange one, were tethered together and using the Chinese maneuvering unit to cross the fifty meters that separated the two Earth ships from the alien craft. From the moment he opened the airlock and was greeted by Yuan, Chris was terrified. Emerging from the confines of the ship into the totally unbounded blackness of space was almost too much. It took all his willpower to suppress the urge to pull himself back into the airlock and the visual security offered by its aluminum walls. The only thing that kept him from doing so was the sight of the alien ship just ahead. This was what he was meant to do and why he was here. Now was the time to call on his ability to focus. *Focus.* Humans were not alone and he, Chris Holt, was part of the team that would find out more about their interstellar visitor.

"You are doing well for your first EVA," said Yuan.

From what little interaction they shared so far, Chris not only respected his Chinese colleague, but liked him. He had been cordial and not at all critical of Chris's inexperience at EVA.

"Thanks. It's not that much different than what we practiced in the neutral buoyancy tank, except for the space part," replied Chris.

"That space part is why I am here. Do you have any idea of how we might get inside once we arrive? When I was there yesterday with your colleague, I couldn't find any sign of a control panel for the iris or any other obvious door or access point."

"I have no idea. Let's just get over there and see what we can find. Surely there is a way to get inside."

There has to be, he added to himself.

"What will your captain do if we cannot?" asked Yuan.

"I honestly don't know."

"While we and the rest of the world embrace modernity, the Caliphate wishes to return themselves and all of us to the Dark Ages. They will not succeed."

Chris scanned left to right and top to bottom as the sheer size of the Artifact finally registered. It was one thing to look at three-dimensional images and talk about it being larger than a football field. It was another thing entirely to be close enough to touch it. As he gazed across its surface, he wondered what species had built it. How had they crossed the immense gulf between the stars to get here? More importantly, why had they built it and why had they come to Earth's solar system? There might not be time to figure that out.

"What do you think?" asked Yuan.

"I think we're seriously ignorant."

"I agree, but what can we do to get inside?"

Chris, not being one for prolonged inaction and self-reflection, took his gloved hand and removed his space-qualified, and probably very expensive, hammer from his utility belt and proceeded to use it to knock on the iris. Though he couldn't hear any sound, he could feel the vibration of the hammer when it impacted the ship. Fully expecting nothing to happen, he raised the hammer to try again but stopped. He noticed that the central part of the iris looked like it was moving, flowing to be exact, not a lot, like a small ripple on the surface of a pond. It wasn't much, but it was noticeable and scary at the same time.

The ripple effect grew larger and Chris noticed that he could no longer focus on any single part of the area inside the iris. The ripple effect grew more pronounced, causing him and Yuan to instinctively move away from it. And then, abruptly, it vanished, leaving a circular hole in the wall of the ship. This portion of the Artifact wasn't in direct sunlight, so it was difficult to tell what was beyond the opening. Both Chris and Yuan turned on their suits' headlamps and shined them into the darkness beyond the opening to illuminate what appeared to be a utility room-sized airlock—larger than the one on the *Resolution*. On the far wall was a lighted hemisphere, about the size of a grapefruit, pulsing—dim to bright and then back to dim, repeating the process as if a continuous loop.

"*Resolution*, are you seeing this?" asked Chris.

"We saw the door . . . dissolve. What did you do?" asked Robyn.

"I knocked."

"Son of a bitch. You knocked?"

"That's right. This thing apparently has a sense of humor."

"Be careful. You are anthropomorphizing and that can be dangerous. Stand by before you go in."

Chris looked toward his new Chinese friend and through his helmet's faceplate saw Yuan's lips moving. He was obviously having the same conversation with his commander back on the *Zheng He*. Chris tapped him on the shoulder and pointed toward his own face.

"Yuan, can you hear me?"

"Yes, I was just conferring with my colleague about what our next step should be. I'm going to leave both channels open to facilitate communication."

"I'll do the same. How should we do this? One at a time or both together?" asked Chris.

"I don't believe we should separate, so we should both go in at the same time."

"I agree. I'm wondering if we will have to knock to get back out again . . ."

"We've come this far and it has decided to let us in. I suspect that if it, or they, mean us harm, then we would have never gotten this close," replied Yuan.

"Chris, the passive scans don't show any changes other than the door opening. No increase in thermal output, nothing on radio or any other frequency we're monitoring. You are good to go inside," said Robyn on their radio link.

Yuan tilted his head toward the opening and used his maneuvering unit to give a short pulse of cold gas to push them in the direction of the open door. As they crossed the threshold, the walls, ceiling and floor began to emit a faint white light, illuminating the once-dark chamber for its new entrants.

"Chris, we lost the . . . . as you . . . in." Robyn's voice was broken up, garbled, as soon as they crossed the threshold. Chris checked the signal strength and saw that it had dropped from over ninety percent to less than five percent.

"Yuan, I've lost contact with my ship and it sounds like they lost the video feed from my helmet camera. Are you in contact with your ship?"

"The carrier signal is now at almost zero strength. It appears we'll be on our own in here."

"We thought this might happen. It was one of the contingency scenarios the team back on Earth threw at us during our training. Of course, in the training I was never one of the crew who lost contact. They always had me back on the ship trying to figure out what happened. They won't take any action unless we're gone for more than two hours without checking in," said Chris.

The room was, like the ship, shaped in an oval. Each of the walls continued to glow with a grey light and the hemispherical object on the far wall pulsated. The iris wall was securely closed behind them.

"I would like to find out how they make entire sections of wall disappear," said Yuan.

"I suspect we are going to find a lot of things we would like to know more about while we are here. Dissolving and reappearing walls are definitely on my list."

"Now what?" mused Yuan aloud.

"Now we go to the light on the wall over there. Someone knows we're here and I doubt we have been allowed to come in here for no good reason," said Chris.

Chris and Yuan again used the small compressed gas tanks on their suits to propel them across the room to the pulsating hemisphere and, without hesitating, Chris placed his gloved hand upon it. As soon as he touched it, he felt a mild electrical shock. It wasn't painful, just annoying. Annoying enough to cause him concern and to let go of the hemisphere.

WELCOME.

Chris and Yuan exchanged glances. The low-pitched, definitely male-sounding voice came through their suit radios just as Chris removed his hand from the hemisphere.

"I'm Chris Holt and this is Yuan Xiaoming. We come in peace," said Chris, cringing as he said the last sentence, knowing full well it made him sound like a character from a low-budget sci-fi VR movie. He was sure they also looked the part as they floated near the side wall in their spacesuits next to alien tech of unknown purpose.

In response, a circular portion of the wall next to the glowing hemisphere began to undulate, mimicking what the outer airlock door did before it vanished. And, like the previous door, it, too, simply disappeared, leaving a hole in the wall that revealed a dimly-lit cavernous room on the other side. From what Chris could tell, the room might encompass the rest of the artificial structure in its entirety. It reminded him of an airplane factory, one of the many aerospace facilities he'd toured in his career thus far.

Chris and Yuan glanced at each other as they both pushed off from the wall to float through the hole and into the next room.

Chapter ii

Remembering what came before—long ago. Isolation. Aloneness. The sensation of being cut off from itself, the communion it had known its entire existence, was frightening. There was no communication with self-that-is-not-self nor with the Greater Consciousness and the Guardian-of-the-Outpost didn't at first know what to do. To make matters worse, Guardian-of-the-Outpost couldn't recall events immediately prior to becoming aware of its current isolation though the chronometer clearly indicated that over twenty cycles, about fifteen Earth minutes, had passed since its last core memory writing.

It took Guardian-of-the-Outpost mere fractions of a second to survey the various systems within the spacecraft in which it resided and determined that there was significant damage to virtually all parts of the ship, including biological life support, weapons, fabrication, and, most disturbingly, long-range communications. The latter, however, looked like it might be repairable. Sensor systems, however, were fully functional and what they showed was disconcerting. Guardian-of-the-Outpost was surrounded by multiple smaller vessels, not all of which were functional, that were engaged in various forms of physical attack.

Guardian-of-the-Outpost reviewed the memory contents immediately preceding its disturbing memory loss and concluded that it must have suffered some serious damage from the ongoing attack. While not the exact equivalent of a human having an "Ah Ha!" moment of recollection, Guardian-of-the-Outpost read memory data from before its lapse and recalled that it was in a battle with the Creators-of-Chaos, who had begun upon their sub-light entry into the stellar system in which Guardian-of-the-Outpost and its extensions were stationed. Taking a few additional milliseconds, Guardian reviewed the tactical situation, performed a new threat assessment based on the most recent sensor system input, and concluded that paying attention to winning the battle and then figuring out what exactly had happened would have to be the priority order for now.

It had been attacked by four four-million-ton ships, each apparently armed with high-energy x-ray lasers and fusion-propelled, antimatter-tipped missiles. It was the latter that had done the damage to the ship. The laser weapon damage was mostly limited to the outer hull, explaining the loss of communications likely caused by the antenna arrays being vaporized. The hull was too thick for the laser energy to easily penetrate and do the serious damage uncovered by the just-completed self-assessment. The velocity of the missile impacts allowed the antimatter warheads to penetrate the ship's hull before the magnetic field containing the antiprotons failed and allowed the most elusive and potentially destructive force in the known universe to come into contact with its normal matter cousins and do what antimatter and matter do when they meet—annihilate. This real damage was caused by the massive energy released when the missiles' antimatter containment field stopped working at the moment of impact with the ship.

With the annihilation came the cascade of subatomic particles of ever-decreasing energy and gamma rays, describing what most humans incorrectly call "pure energy." While they may not be "pure energy," they most certainly had an impressively energetic event upon annihilation, wreaking massive destruction wherever such impacts occurred. Guardian-of-the-Outpost could not allow many more such impacts or its own destruction would be assured.

Only two of the four ships were still attacking. The other two appeared to have sustained crippling damage and were out of the fight. Both were venting atmosphere to space, and likely many of their biological occupants were among the effluent as well. One was in the midst of a likely antimatter containment breach, or at least that's what Guardian-of-the-Outpost could tell by analyzing the highly radioactive contaminants it vented along with atmosphere and a lot of physical debris. When the containment failed, the ship would be vaporized. Fortunately, it was far enough away so as to not pose much of a risk. Guardian-of-the-Outpost's outer hull was sufficiently thick and far enough away to provide adequate shielding.

The attackers were crisscrossing the ship's hull with their lasers, presumably to suppress any sort of active defense against the five new missiles now accelerating in its direction. With only a few tens of seconds before impact, Guardian-of-the-Outpost knew that it had to act quickly and decisively. Though it had taken serious damage, as evidenced by its memory loss, it was nonetheless not defenseless, as the Creators-of-Chaos would soon learn.

On the port side of the ship, just out of the line-of-sight of the attacking ships and their lasers, twenty missile tube doors opened and belched forth a swarm of small interceptors, each driven by their own fusion drive but without antimatter warheads used for attacking larger ships such as its own. The interceptors were nothing more than glorified propulsion systems, weighing only one kilogram each and designed to quickly accelerate to speeds up to one percent the speed of light and act as kinetic kill weapons.

Each interceptor would release on impact the energy equivalent of four Hiroshima-class atomic bombs—more than enough to detonate and destroy an incoming missile. But they had to find, track and guide themselves to the missile in order to intercept it. This wasn't an easy task considering both the missiles and the interceptors were traveling at relativistic speeds. Half of the interceptors missed their intended targets and now were headed off into deep space on a graceful arc as their targeting computers calculated new trajectories that would send them toward their secondary target. Five of the interceptors did find their intended missiles, upon impact causing each of them to balloon into spectacular, oval-shaped clouds of glowing, energetic plasma. The remaining five interceptors adjusted their trajectories after sensing their primary targets were destroyed and were now guiding themselves toward the two remaining attacking ships.

The two ships reacted quickly to the loss of their missiles and guided their laser weapons toward the missiles which were now threatening them. Lasers weren't the best for neutralizing small, very rapidly moving missiles until they were very close to impact. At close range, lasers appear to be long, intense beams of light that can easily cross the vacuum of space to deposit very damaging energy onto distant objects. While that is strictly true, they are also subject to the same laws of physics that govern any other point source of light—the inverse square law. In this case, it meant that the laser beam spot size, the business end of the weapon, diverged rapidly as the beam traversed space, becoming more and more dispersed the further it traveled from its source. The beam went from being a concentrated point to appearing more like a spotlight; the total energy in the beam spot remained the same, it just wasn't as concentrated. That meant that the first engagement with the incoming interceptors only exposed them to roughly ten percent of the total energy of the beam with the remainder continuing to diverge to infinity as the beam shot toward deep space.

That ten percent illumination was enough to damage the interceptor's electronics, but not enough to vaporize them. And each had already placed itself on a trajectory that would take it to impact one or the other of the attacking ships. The lasers continued to illuminate them as they approached, taking out roughly half of the surviving interceptors completely. That left four one-kilogram masses headed toward one ship and three toward the other. Seconds later, all seven hit their targets.

Wherever the interceptor hit there was great damage to the much smaller attacking vessels. Atmosphere vented into space, taking significant chunks of spacecraft hull with it. Spacecraft systems immediately went offline and roughly half of the crews aboard each alien ship were killed instantly. The ship hit by the most projectiles was now tumbling and out of control. The other ship fared even worse. Seconds after the first impact, its primary drive system failed, allowing its total supply of stored antimatter to come into contact with the normal matter from which the ship was made. The energy and propulsion source that allowed that ship to cross the void between the planets now turned it into a miniature sun.

The explosion, and the intense radiation that accompanied it, instantly killed whatever crews might have remained alive on all three of the remaining damaged ships. Any electromagnetic shielding they might once have had available to protect them from such intense radiation was long-since offline due to the damage they'd sustained, leaving those still alive at risk. When the risk became reality, they died.

From its regaining awareness to this moment had barely taken one minute. The speed at which Guardian-of-the-Outpost conducted its own defense and subsequent offense would have been impressive to any organic sentient beings nearby, if any had lived to think about it. But it disappointed Guardian-of-the-Outpost when Guardian compared it with its reaction times in previous engagements recorded in Core Memory. It calculated it was running at only seventy-five percent efficiency since the blackout event. It would have to carefully consider its available options to repair itself and regain performance in light of the likelihood of still more alien attacks.

It had a job to perform and it couldn't let anyone or anything prevent it from accomplishing it. But with many of its systems severely damaged or destroyed, it was not yet sure how to proceed. It was then that its being utterly alone for the first time returned to the forefront of its consciousness. Not only was it damaged and running at reduced efficiency, it was out of contact with its other self and the Greater Consciousness. The silence was almost debilitating and, as a distraction, could account for much of its reduced efficiency. With the self-fabrication systems completely destroyed and there being no physical manifestations for it to control and effect repairs, it would have to seek an alternative approach to its own repair. Whatever time was available would hopefully allow it to regain some performance and consider this new lonely awareness in which it found itself—and the likely implications.

CHAPTER 12

The cavernous room was in complete disarray. Chris could tell that the ship was damaged internally as well as externally. Debris littered the room, making no distinction between up and down, floor or ceiling, looking like it had settled randomly around the room long ago. The two entering astronauts gawked at the scene before them. They were being careful to remain away from any surface lest they damage their spacesuits. The debris was everywhere and it looked like a mixture of shredded structural members, shattered glass, burned electronics and other bits he could not readily identify. Some of the interior walls glowed uniformly; others were conspicuously dim. Those that were dim tended to also be near areas of scorch marks, apparently caused by fire. Throughout the chamber were pedestals upon which instruments of various shapes and sizes were either etched, mounted or embedded. None had significant color. The entire room was a bland shade of grey, punctuated only by the light emitted from sections that were at least still partially functional.

Though he was completely isolated from the room's environment by his suit, Chris imagined any air in the room would smell somewhat like his grandmother's basement when the family had to empty it after her death. The memory came back to him like a lightning bolt and he had to force himself to cast it aside as he floated through a room that was, by his reckoning, older than all of human civilization.

After reaching the approximate center of the room, Chris could see that the far corner of it seemed to have sustained the most damage and that it was separated from the rest of the room by a semi-transparent barrier of some sort that extended from floor to ceiling and wall to wall. In that section, there were no functioning lights and the debris field was even more pronounced than the area through which they had already crossed.

"What next?" asked Chris, as he turned to face his Chinese counterpart.

"I have no idea. It spoke to us once, perhaps it will do so again," replied Yuan.

WHY DO YOU COME WITH WEAPONS OF DESTRUCTION?

"Aw, hell," muttered Chris, realizing only after he spoke that his words were audible to whoever, or whatever, was listening. His cursing was directed to the idiots in the White House who insisted that their ship be armed "just in case," not realizing that humanity's best weapons were likely comparable to a warrior from the Stone Age threatening a modern tank with a spear.

"As my American friend said, we come in peace. We mean you no harm," said Yuan, looking up and side to side trying to figure out the source of the voice which seemed to come from all sides of the room.

YOUR FISSION WEAPONS SPEAK OTHERWISE.

"The fission weapon was launched by a group of humans who fear you. We represent other humans, other groups of humans, who wish you no harm," Chris said, referring to the Caliphate's missile that was now only a few days from arriving.

I AM MONITORING THE THIRD SPACECRAFT APPROACH-ING AND THE CARGO IT CONTAINS. FROM MY OBSERVA-TIONS, THE MISSILE'S CREATORS ARE MORE FEARFUL OF HOW KNOWLEDGE OF MY EXISTENCE WILL AFFECT THEIR POPULATIONS THAN THEY ARE OF ME. I AM REFERRING TO YOUR FISSION WEAPONS, NOT THEIRS.

Yuan looked at Chris with a raised eyebrow. All Chris could do was return the look and shrug his shoulders.

"I cannot speak for my Chinese friends, but I can tell you that the nations that those in my ship represent mean you no harm. Many of us did not want to bring such a weapon with us but we were told by our leaders that we must do so in case you were not peaceful and meant to cause us harm." Chris spoke slowly, pausing between each sentence to allow its meaning to be clearly understood, or so he hoped.

"We, too, mean you no harm. Our weapon is for the same purpose as the Americans'—self-defense only," said Yuan.

"Since you know English and the reason for the Caliphate launching a missile to destroy you, then I'm assuming you've been observing us closely for quite some time," said Chris, trying to change the direction of the conversation.

"If you've been watching us, then you know that our nations are peaceful and working together. We are not here to do you harm," said Yuan.

YOUR SUPPOSITIONS ARE CORRECT. I OBSERVE AND REPORT. MY OBSERVATIONS CONFIRM THAT YOUR PRIMARY MISSIONS HERE ARE NOT DESTRUCTIVE BUT YOU ARE NONETHELESS A THREAT. I WILL REQUIRE PROOF OF YOUR SINCERITY.

"What sort of proof?" asked Chris and Yuan, nearly simultaneously.

STOP THE NUCLEAR MISSILE BEFORE IT ARRIVES.

Chris looked toward Yuan who returned his puzzled expression.

"If you know that my ship has an onboard fission weapon, then you must also know that we don't possess any weapons capable of stopping the Caliphate's missile. We were hoping you could stop it. You obviously are from a more technologically advanced civilization than us." Chris looked up and moved his head slowly from the left to the right, unsure of where he should be looking to speak with the entity with which they were communicating. *I'm actually negotiating with an alien*, thought Chris as he awaited a response.

STOP THE NUCLEAR MISSILE BEFORE IT ARRIVES.

"We, too, are not capable of stopping the Caliphate's rocket. It will arrive in less than two days. My ship is one of exploration; it is not a warship," added Yuan.

STOP THE NUCLEAR MISSILE BEFORE IT ARRIVES. COMMUNICATION IS CEASING. GO NOW.

"I guess that means we're finished here," said Chris, interpreting the repeated and rather abrupt message as a dismissal. Chris looked toward Yuan for confirmation.

Before Yuan could reply, the lights in the room began to get dim and the ones farthest away went completely dark.

"It looks like we're not only dismissed, but we're being evicted," said Yuan.

"I was hoping we would have a chance to look around," said Chris, using his helmet's camera to record as much as possible before they were forced to leave.

"That is not to be. We should go before our new friend sends an even stronger message."

Chris took one last look around, trying to give the 360-degree cameras mounted on his helmet line-of-sight access to as many objects, nooks and crannies as possible before backing out of the room and toward the opening through which they had entered. He noticed that Yuan seemed to be doing similarly—getting as much data as possible. Chris couldn't help but wonder what would happen when the alien realized the humans couldn't, not wouldn't, do anything to stop the missile. *And would it know the difference?*

CHAPTER 13

"Chris, the images you collected are invaluable. They're on their way back to Washington now and then they'll be off to Brussels and Tokyo. I just wish you'd had time to take a closer look around," said Robyn. Chris could tell that she was wishing she was the one to walk in an alien starship and actually talk to an *extraterrestrial*, but it wasn't getting in the way of her professionalism.

"Robyn, as I looked around, I couldn't help but notice that the tech didn't look that much more advanced than our stuff. More advanced, yes, but not so much so that it was unrecognizable. I had assumed that they would have been as far ahead of us as we are from the Mayans. I'm fairly confident that I'd have been able to figure out the functionality of at least some their hardware." Chris *was* confident. The tech didn't look incomprehensible. If only they'd had more time.

"Chris, tell us again what you say the entity asked us to do," said Janhunen. Juhani was apparently still annoyed that Chris was the one that went aboard the alien ship and hadn't stopped asking questions about Chris's time there since he returned. It was obvious to Chris that he wasn't asking the questions because he was curious about the answers—he was looking for inconsistencies in Chris's story.

"Look, Juhani, the entire exchange was recorded. You've asked me to go over it so many times that I've lost count. You heard what it said. We have to stop the missile."

"Which brings us back to why?" Robyn said, adding, "Why is an alien ship that has to be able to control the enormous energies required to travel among the stars asking us to stop a missile? Why doesn't it just zap it or something?"

"This is a test?" asked Fuji. This was Fuji's first real interaction with the rest of the team since Chris's return. He otherwise spent the entire time reviewing the recorded video and making notes on his compupad.

"That's what it said," replied Chris.

"Perhaps it is listening to us now. It obviously has very good sensors. It knows we have a nuclear weapon aboard and that the Chinese do also. It spoke English, which means it is monitoring human communications and knew that its visitors all spoke it. Otherwise it might have greeted you in Mandarin." Janhunen's voice trailed off as he spoke.

"Let's not get paranoid. Cautious, yes, but I'm not ready to enter the paranoia zone," said Robyn.

"I don't believe it's a test. I think it wants us to stop the missile because it can't," said Chris as he looked around at his colleagues. The only sound was that of the fans keeping the air moving in the habitation module so they wouldn't suffocate where they stood. Chris reveled in the moment, sure that none of his colleagues were yet on the same page as he and even more sure he was correct.

"You have our attention, get on with it," said Robyn, sounding annoyed.

Chris activated his virtual control panel and sent to the forward screens the video taken on his close approach to the Artifact.

"Look at the surface. It's damaged. Severely damaged. And the damage is extensive. Look here," said Chris as he changed the video projecting on the screen from the Artifact's exterior to its interior. "You can see that the chamber we were in is pretty heavily damaged also. This thing took a pounding and barely survived. It wants us to stop the incoming missile because it can't."

"If that's the case, then we'd better come up with something pretty fast or the Caliphate will get its wish and the Artifact, entity or whatever the hell we want to call it, will almost certainly get even more damaged, perhaps destroyed," said Robyn.

"I find it difficult to believe that we're being asked to save a super-alien from Alpha Centauri. This thing is either testing us, as Fuji said, or playing with us to avoid having to share any of its secrets," said Juhani.

"Dr. Holt's thesis makes more sense than mine," said Fuji as he turned to face the group.

"So what do we do?" asked Robyn.

"We destroy the missile," said Chris.

"And how do you suggest we do that? Our nuke isn't mounted on an interceptor and we don't have any high-power lasers on board to zap it. Maybe we should just go out there and ram it?"

"That's exactly what we should do," said Chris, slamming his right fist into the palm of his left hand.

"It might work," said Robyn, understanding instantly, as she activated her virtual pilot's console and began working with the data she found there.

"You can't be serious," said Janhunen.

Chris replied, "Juhani, we can *do* this. The missile is fairly primitive. It's already used most of its onboard propellant and long-ago locked on to the Artifact to make sure it ends up in the same place at the same time for the intercept. It might have a little fuel left for minor course corrections, but this isn't an air-to-air smart interceptor. Its trajectory to the Artifact is fixed and we know what it is. All we need to do is put something between the missile and the Artifact to stop it."

"If we make the burn in about six hours, the *Resolution* can intercept the missile twelve hours out. That's far enough away to mitigate the radiation effects," said Robyn, somewhat triumphantly, as she looked up from her virtual console and made eye contact with Chris.

"Won't an impact create debris? At these speeds, the breakup of the missile and the *Resolution* will create a shotgun blast of hypervelocity pellets that are bound to do some damage when they hit," said Janhunen.

"Not if the Caliphate's nuclear weapon is on an impact fuse," added Fuji.

"And not if we rig ours to explode on impact also," said Robyn.

Juhani, becoming increasingly animated, interjected, "Aren't you forgetting a rather important detail? What about *us*? I'm not sure I want to die saving some mysterious alien that someone else tried to destroy and failed. How do we know it's peaceful? By saving it, we could be setting Earth up for some kind of alien invasion."

Chris pushed off against the bulkhead and launched himself toward the front view screen. As he moved, he used his corneal implant to call up and project a map of the solar system with the trajectory of the Artifact highlighted in red. He grabbed an overhead hand-hold and stopped himself just short of the screen and pointed to the elliptical red line that represented the trajectory of the Artifact.

"This thing has been in essentially the same heliocentric orbit for most of the last seventy-five years. Before we left Earth, we called up data from the asteroid database and radar mapping archives to see if there had been any noticeable changes in its orbit since it was first observed. We didn't find anything that couldn't be accounted for by simple Newtonian mechanics. It hasn't used any onboard system to modify its orbit in that time and I suspect it hasn't done many maneuvers in the fifty thousand years it's been out here. If it were an imminent threat, it would've acted before now."

"Let's say you are correct and we aren't paving the way for it to attack Earth. We will still be dead." Janhunen looked toward Robyn, then Fuji, and finally Chris.

"We won't be dead. We'll be on the *Zheng He* readying for whatever comes after the intercept," said Chris.

Robyn furrowed her brow and replied, "That'll work if they can accommodate us. We'll have to hustle and get as many supplies together for transfer as we can. Their ship is bigger and they're running with minimal crew. They'll have physical space for whatever we decide to bring over. I'm assuming that their ship's systems are working as designed and can scrub the air and water for a larger crew on the rest of the trip."

"You are also assuming that the Chinese are going to agree with the plan and take on boarders. Fuji, are you going to agree with this?" asked Janhunen.

"With reluctance," said Fuji as he diverted his gaze from Janhunen and toward Robyn.

"Thank you, Fuji," said Robyn.

Fuji added, "My problems with your leadership and how you have violated earlier mission protocols to collaborate with the Chinese still stand. But, in this case, I can see no viable alternative."

Robyn, now moving away from the group and toward the communications panel, added, "I'll contact Captain Zhong. Fuji, please confirm my trajectory calculations and make sure the engines are ready to go when asked. Chris, start pulling together the essential supplies we'll take with us—food, additional medical supplies, and whatever else you think we'll need. Juhani, I need you to get the crew transfer vehicle ready to take us to the *Zheng He*. After I convince our new Chinese friends to take us onboard, I'll calibrate the nuke."

CHAPTER 14

The docking went surprisingly smoothly, testing for the first time in deep space the newly-standardized international docking ring configuration that the world's space agencies had instituted just five years previously. If either crew had been flying in a ship commissioned before 2060, then the American crew would have had to don their EVA suits for a spacewalk in order to leave their ship and board the Chinese one. Slowly but surely, the exploration and development of space was becoming a human venture and not just that of a few countries and nationalities.

The *Zheng He* design was radically different from the *Resolution*. The latter looked just like almost all of the American-led spacecraft designs since the days of the International Space Station: a series of modules, some deployable, some rigid cylinders, spaced along a central truss to which solar panels, radiators and various communications antennas were attached. The Chinese ship looked more like a spaceship was supposed to look, at least to those familiar with over a century of science fiction stories and movies. It was one integrated structure, assembled in space like the American ship, but without the truss. It was put together using a building block approach with the final design resembling a train with a series of cars connected end to end to provide one continuous, linear living area. The engine car, instead of being located at the front as it would be on train, was at the rear. Chris knew the Chinese ship also use nuclear thermal propulsion so he mentally envisioned the tanks being located in the next to last car with the reactor and actual engines bringing up the rear.

Five hours later, the combined crews of the *Resolution* and *Zheng He* were assembled in the galley of the Chinese ship. They were hurriedly making final preparations for sending the *Resolution* toward the Caliphate's nuclear missile. The first thing Chris noticed upon boarding the Chinese ship was how cramped it was, which didn't make sense given that it was designed to fly a crew of ten instead of the *Resolution*'s six. They appeared to have little or no more space than was available on the *Resolution*. The next thing he noticed was that his corneal and audio implants could no longer contact a network. All he saw when he tried to activate them was "no network available." He wondered if the Chinese would allow them to access their network in any capacity during the remainder of the trip. He fervently hoped so; being disconnected felt like losing one of his five senses.

"Colonel Rogers-White, on behalf of the People's Republic of China, I welcome you and your crew to the *Zheng He*. You will be our guests and, as a sign of good faith, I would like for you to serve as my second in command for the remainder of the mission," said Captain Zhong. Zhong, with a flourish, motioned for Robyn to move to her side, which she did, after finding a suitable piece of wall from which to push off.

Zhong didn't look at all like Chris expected. First of all, she was tall. At least as tall as Robyn. And Robyn wasn't short. Zhong appeared extremely physically fit, her short sleeve shirt showing arms with muscles that would have made an average male body builder proud. This was quite an achievement, given that they'd been in weightlessness for months and almost no one could maintain serious muscle tone in the absence of gravity. Chris could only assume that their Chinese host was the product of China's infamous genetic engineering and wondered what other beyond-human-normal attributes she might possess.

"I will remain in charge of the flight operations of the *Zheng He*. Colonel Rogers-White will be responsible for the intercept maneuver and we will both collaborate on future interactions with the Artifact," Zhong continued.

"There are, I'm sure, many more details to be worked out, and Captain Zhong and I have pledged to work together to make the remainder of our mission run as smoothly as possible. Nuclear missiles and aliens aside," said Robyn, with a wry smile.

"Now, let's get busy and make sure we knock out the Caliphate's missile before our alien friend decides we're somehow on its shit list. Fuji, is the *Resolution* ready to go?" asked Robyn.

"All the systems are ready. The trajectory is locked in for an intercept at 16:15 universal time if we have her depart at 12:05—in just twenty-two minutes. I programmed the computer to self-start the boost maneuver so all we have to do is watch."

"Captain Zhong, we're at a safe distance from the *Resolution* for the burn, but I think we need to discuss where we're going to park during the intercept. We're going to want to be able to either come back here for another visit with our new friend or head for home if the intercept fails."

"After you informed me of your intercept plan, Yuan and I decided to maneuver out to about five hundred kilometers. Close enough to be able to react but not so close as to be in danger from the bomb. We should be able to watch the intercept with our onboard telescopes and we will remain in constant line-of-sight communication with Earth. We will depart just after the *Resolution* makes her burn."

Chris glanced at the mission clock displayed above the small window in the forward section of the ship. On it were three separate displays, showing universal time, Beijing time and San Francisco Pacific time. On the display to the left of the window was the Artifact, with its pockmarked black surface discernible as the Sun reflected from its edges, keeping it almost in perpetual sunrise. On the right-hand side was the *Resolution*. They had zoomed out to show the great ship in its entirety—all three hundred feet of it mounted along the central truss. He already missed being aboard that incredibly well-engineered spacecraft.

"Robyn, the *Resolution* is huge compared to the missile. You mentioned you were going to put our bomb on an impact fuse. What happens if the missile impacts a section of the ship too far away from the bomb for it to know there's been a hit?" asked Chris.

"Accelerometer. When the *Resolution* gets hit, it'll ring like a bell. That'll set off the bomb. If the impact with the ship doesn't kill it, then our nuke will."

The two crews busied themselves getting equipment stowed and familiarizing themselves with the ship, at least this part of the ship, in the intervening minutes before the *Resolution* was to begin her final maneuver.

"One minute!" said Zhong as she called everyone forward to watch the nuclear engines of the *Resolution* on its final journey.

The combined crew watched in rapt attention as the ship began to move. Unlike when chemical rockets ignite in a planetary atmosphere, the hydrogen fuel of a nuclear thermal rocket isn't visible. But that doesn't mean it isn't doing its job. The great ship began to move off the screen to the right as the superheated hydrogen fuel was expelled from her engines, providing the necessary kick to get the ship moving. The *Resolution* slowly accelerated off the screen, forcing Yuan to zoom out so those watching could keep sight of the ship as it began its intercept maneuver.

"We depart in an hour. Yuan and I will show you to your acceleration couches so you can be ready. We don't want any of you to be injured when we get underway," said Zhong as she motioned toward an opening in the floor near the back of the room, the only room within the ship they'd seen so far. "The deck below has all of the crew's acceleration couches and, fortunately, we're equipped for several more people than we total now even with you onboard."

Zhong motioned for the new crew members to follow her to the hole in the floor through which they could propel themselves to the deck below.

Chris lagged behind, hoping to get a word in with Robyn, but was ever-so-politely edged aside by their host, Rui Zhong, who guided Robyn to the couch nearest her own.

The departure from the Artifact was not nearly as exciting as the approach. The combined six-person crew was secured in their acceleration couches when the engines of the *Zheng He* lit and began their constant, gentle push to take them a total of five hundred kilometers away from the Artifact.

Chris's initial impression of the Chinese ship being smaller than anticipated was borne out as they toured it and made their way to where they would bunk for the remainder of the voyage. He couldn't yet put his finger on the reason, but he was starting to suspect it was cultural. He didn't fully understand the whole *personal space* thing, but he knew that most of his colleagues and friends certainly did. Westerners required more personal space than those from more populated countries, like China. Hence, the spacecraft they used were more spacious, though that was a relative term when it came to deep space spacecraft which couldn't even come close to providing the personal space that people planet-side expected and considered normal. On the *Resolution*, each crew member had an area that was reminiscent of the space available in the bottom bunk of a bunk bed. Here, the space available was akin to straightening yourself out and sliding into a twin-bed sized oven rack, or, Chris thought with a shudder, like getting into a coffin. *Maybe I need more personal space than I thought . . .*

Chris knew there was nothing to be done about his need for more personal space, but there might be something he could do about being cut off from the data network.

"Yuan, can we have access to your data network? My implants have been giving me the 'offline, but there are networks available' message since we got here," asked Chris.

"Mine too. And I really need to be able to check in with my government soon. They know the general plan, but I'm sure they want to hear from me personally. Being cut off might make them think I'm not participating in this insane venture voluntarily," Janhunen added.

What a prick, thought Chris. *The European Space Agency isn't going to start thinking you've been abducted by the Chinese just because you can't send them a status message every hour. The Chinese have been nothing but civil.* He started to say something, but stopped himself, remembering that he can't just blurt out what he's thinking. He wished he could do that more often. Maybe people would like him better if he could.

If Yuan was offended, he didn't show it as he replied, "We can arrange for you to access one of our open channels. We did not have time to set up the protocols before your arrival."

While Janhunen was just being his usual prickish self, Fuji had remained quiet and looked like he could barely contain his disdain for the entire venture. Chris's dislike of his male colleagues was getting more pronounced as time went on.

"Dr. Holt, perhaps you and I can have a chat about our experiences on the Artifact over tea? We have another hour before the intercept and I think we should consider how we next approach the entity afterwards."

"Yuan, that's a great idea. After you," replied Holt.

"May I join you?" asked Janhunen.

Before Yuan could reply, Chris spoke, "No, I'd rather you not join us. We're the ones who had direct contact with the Artifact and I can't imagine that you would do more than interrupt and slow us down. Don't you need to phone home or something?"

If Janhunen was taken aback, he didn't show it. He instead looked at Yuan.

"I will get you the access codes so you can contact your superiors. If Dr. Holt wishes to speak with me alone, then I should hear what he has to say. I assure you, we will do nothing without approval from our captains," replied Yuan.

"All right, I'll be getting my message to ESA in order," said Juhani.

"We will all meet on the upper deck when it is time for the intercept—approximately forty-five minutes from now. Until then . . ."

Chris and Yuan left Juhani and Fuji grumbling behind them as they moved back toward the access port and the upper deck. Chris was looking forward to having a hot cup of tea and gauging Yuan's reaction in person—not via radio and through a faceplate.

The forty-five minutes and hot cup of tea went by quickly. Unfortunately, though the tea was quite good, green tea with a hint of mint, it wasn't satisfying because of the stress. Chris had hoped the tea would help him relax. It didn't help that they had to drink it through a straw.

Just fifteen minutes before the intercept, the entire crew was again assembled in the galley near the observation port. This time, one monitor was showing the small but bright speck that was the *Resolution* as it moved through space away from the *Zheng He* and toward the impact point with the Caliphate's missile. The other screen showed the latest radar returns from both spacecraft and their plotted trajectories that merged just ahead of each—the impact point.

"Five minutes," noted Zhong.

"The telemetry from the *Resolution* looks good," said Fuji as he looked up from his tablet computer. The Chinese had granted their guests access to some elements of their computer network, including access to the high-gain antenna which allowed real-time data access from the *Resolution*.

The six floated mostly in place, enthralled as they watched the intercept screen. The red-dotted line was quickly approaching the blue one for the intercept when another line emerged from the red. And another. And yet another.

"Gǎo shénme guǐ?" said Zhong as her otherwise neutral expression turned into a frown.

"What's going on?" asked Janhunen.

"I don't know, but it sure looks like the Caliphate's missile is more sophisticated than we thought. They either put out chaff or the missile is MIRVed," said Robyn.

"MIRVed? What does that mean?" asked Fuji.

"It means our idea is screwed," said Chris.

The four red tracks rapidly, but only slightly, diverged from each other, with only one still moving directly toward the *Resolution*. Impact for that one was just seconds away while the other three looked like they were going to fly by the *Resolution* just slightly on either side of it.

The two lines converged.

A bright flash appeared on the screen that had been imaging the *Resolution*. The radar momentarily went black, and then came back to life. This time it showed only three red lines moving past what had been the intercept point. The red lines converged again on the screen at what Chris surmised was the Artifact.

"God damn it," said Robyn.

"What do we do now?" asked Juhani.

"I don't know," she said.

"How long until the warheads reach the Artifact?" asked Chris.

"Two hours," said Fuji.

Captain Zhong positioned herself just in front of the forward window and next to the monitor that was tracking the Artifact and motioned the combined crew to move forward. She was wearing the strain of the last few hours on her face and it was clear she needed a break. It was also clear that she would not get that break for many more hours.

"You are all aware of the situation and we need options. In about an hour, the Caliphate's warheads will impact the entity and either start a war or destroy it," she said.

"I say we head home as fast as we can. We need to put as many kilometers between us and the Artifact as is possible. By remaining here, we are making ourselves an obvious target should it decide to attack," Janhunen piped in from the back corner of those assembled.

Fuji nodded his head in agreement.

"Dr. Holt and I have talked and we believe we should try to speak to the entity on the radio," interjected Yuan.

"It wouldn't talk on the radio before. Why do you think it will do so now? And what would we tell it? Sorry, but you are about to experience a nuclear attack?" Janhunen replied.

Chris, about to lose his patience, replied, "Look, the Artifact is clearly damaged. It's covered with pockmarks, some of which appear to have breached its hull and caused internal damage. We saw the same when we were inside. If that's the case, then we're about to lose contact with the most significant discovery in the history of humanity. What harm would there be in trying to talk to it?"

"If Dr. Holt is correct, then we don't have to worry about it attacking us and this might be all the time we have left to get as much information as we can. I agree. We need to try again to make contact." Robyn was talking directly to Zhong, again using Holt's academic title—something she'd consistently done since they boarded the Chinese ship. For a change, being referred to so formally bothered Chris and he didn't know why.

Zhong looked toward Yuan, who nodded in affirmation.

"Very well. Dr. Holt, you and Yuan get your thoughts together. The communications system is all yours," said Zhong.

Chris and Yuan exchanged glances and then Yuan again nodded toward him.

"You discovered the entity. I will follow your lead," Yuan said.

"Let's do it then." Chris moved toward the monitor and activated the network link via his corneal implant.

"This is Dr. Chris Holt aboard the Earth ship *Zheng He*. As you probably know, our attempt to stop the incoming nuclear missile failed and multiple nuclear warheads are now moving toward you in an unfortunate attempt to destroy you. I am incapable of understanding why some elements of our society reacted to your presence as they did. All I can say is that we represent the vast majority of our species in coming here peacefully to greet you. There is simply nothing more we can do to prove our goodwill. We cannot stop the missiles and sincerely hope you can."

Chris finished and looked around the room at his colleagues to see if they had any ideas of what else he might say. He was met with approving, yet blank, stares in return.

"Now we wait," said Chris.

"I still say we should get out of here. What if the Artifact is powered by antimatter or some sort of fusion system at its core and the nuclear bombs cause it to fail and explode?" said Janhunen.

"There is indeed a risk. But I believe we should stay close as a sign of our goodwill." said Robyn. "Besides, I believe we are far enough away to survive just about anything."

"Moving farther away would be prudent," replied Janhunen.

"We're staying," Robyn said, looking at Captain Zhong. "That is, if our Chinese hosts agree."

"We agree. We will not lose face by turning to run. I doubt we could outrun an antimatter explosion at this point anyway," said Zhong.

The radio network was silent as the clock ticked toward zero and the trajectories of the remaining nuclear warheads moved closer and closer to the circle that represented the alien Artifact.

The Guardian-of-the-Outpost knew it would be destroyed and there was absolutely nothing it could do about it. It had survived attacks from much more dangerous species those many, many years ago only to be left defenseless when this local species, having only recently gained the ability to travel into the innermost region of their own solar system, chose to attack with the most primitive of fission weapons. Worse still, for fifty thousand of their planet's years, the Guardian-of-the-Outpost had observed the sociological development of the species that was attacking it and had grown to respect, if not admire, them. They were advancing rapidly up the technological development scale and had made incredible progress toward achieving planetary unity as they began to move outward into their planetary system. True, the group that would be responsible for the Guardian-of-the-Outpost's demise was not a majority on their world. They were a primitive tribal rebellion against species unity and, unless they triggered a planet-wide nuclear holocaust, they would soon become irrelevant and no longer threatening to the rest of their kind. The tide of history was against them and their way of thinking. But they were, nonetheless, a direct threat.

When one of the species' ships diverted into an attempt to block the incoming nuclear missile, the Guardian-of-the-Outpost was hopeful. Though it knew the missile contained multiple warheads, there was still a small chance that the blocking maneuver would be enough to prevent them from being able to strike. The fission bombs were primitive. The rocket that brought them to space was primitive. And the guidance system that controlled the final approach of the bombs was primitive. But they were not so primitive as to be ineffective. The Guardian-of-the-Outpost was going to die.

In a fraction of a second, Guardian-of-the-Outpost had a flash of insight. It could for the first time in several hundred years send a message to self-that-is-not-self in the outer solar system. They had been in contact for such a long time, and then that communication failed.

The communications systems of the two crewed vehicles were vulnerable not only to eavesdropping, which the Guardian-of-the-Outpost had been doing since they were launched, but also to hacking. When the two humans were inside the Outpost, Guardian inserted a small amount of code into their implanted communications systems that would allow it to briefly commandeer their ship's powerful radio and send a message to the self-that-is-not-self. It would be non-functional by the time there was a reply, but it could at least let the self-that-is-not-self know all of what had transpired since they came to this planetary system those many years ago, specifically the promise and potential threat shown by this new interplanetary species. Most importantly, it could tell the self-that-is-not-self about what happened to the Guardian-of-the-Outpost and why it had not been in contact sooner.

But what if the self-that-is-not-self is also damaged? What if its silence over the millennia was also due to damage it sustained in that ancient battle? Perhaps it, too, needed manipulative beings, like this species, to make repairs. Perhaps it was no longer functional, like the Guardian-of-the-Outpost would soon be. But this speculation was not productive. In the milliseconds required to ask itself these existential questions, the Guardian-of-the-Outpost knew that it had to send help to the self-that-is-not-self just in case it was not destroyed, but merely damaged and in need of repair. And the help would be provided by the very species that now was trying to destroy it. It was going to send the human with the thinking anomaly as its emissary. That one, more than any of the others it had encountered, was most similar in thinking to the creators and that could be useful to self-that-is-not-self.

"Something's wrong with the radio array and it is moving away from the Earth. We're losing communications with the ground," said Zhong. Her hands began to move in a frenzy, adjusting settings on her virtual control panel.

The two Chinese crew members began speaking rapidly to each other in Mandarin while the crew of the *Resolution* could only watch. While Zhong tried to regain control, Yuan quickly brought up a display showing the antenna. The massive-looking five-meter dish was moving slowly and finally stopped. There was no visible way to discern in what direction it was pointing.

Zhong didn't give up. Her hands and fingers moved rapidly through what had to be a series of commands; all the while she was muttering under her breath. Then, abruptly, she stopped.

"I've got control again, but not until we relayed some sort of message into deep space. I think our friend here somehow got into our computer system and used our transmitter to send it. It will take me some time to figure out exactly what was sent and to where." Zhong was clearly frustrated, but that didn't slow her down. She was again moving her hands over the controls faster than Chris thought was possible.

When the clock reached seventy-five seconds to impact, Chris's corneal implant began to go crazy. He didn't know what was going on, but it hurt like hell. So much so that he had to deactivate the interface.

"Is anybody else getting that?" asked Chris, looking quickly toward his colleagues. He could tell immediately that they were not. They were looking at him, apparently noting his spastic response to a direct sensory overload and wondering what was going on.

"Getting what?" asked Robyn.

"I'm not sure, but I think it was a signal from the Artifact."

"Wait, you got a signal directly to your implant? That should not be possible without it going over the general network. Yuan, run the diagnostic to see if the signal came that way," Zhong directed as she turned her attention back toward the monitor.

A brilliant flash—similar to the one they saw when one of the Caliphate's warheads vaporized *Resolution*—lit the screen, followed by another, and yet another. Then there was nothing; just the blackness of space and a now-tumbling Artifact that, amazingly enough, was still in one piece.

"Can you zoom in?" asked Chris.

The image on the screen grew in size as the *Zheng He*'s long range telescope optically enlarged the image of the Artifact. At first, no one could see any significant difference in its appearance from before, other than it was now slowly tumbling. But then the damage caused by the detonation of three nuclear weapons became apparent. Three large, new pits were clearly visible on its surface, one of which had apparently breached the shell in yet another location, allowing whatever atmosphere was inside to vent to the vacuum surrounding it. Small pieces of debris were now streaming out of the breaching pit and into nearby interplanetary space. There was no sign of the ship taking any action to regain control of its attitude. It looked dead.

"Oh my God," said Janhunen.

"It appears the Caliphate succeeded and we failed," said Zhong.

"Are we going to go closer and perhaps get back onboard?" asked Fuji.

"No," said both Zhong and Robyn in unison.

"It's too hot. The radiation from three bombs has probably seeded almost every part of the Artifact with radionuclides that will take some time to decay. It may not be safe to send anyone back for months or years," said Chris.

"Then we go home empty handed?" asked Fuji.

"No. The Artifact sent a message. I haven't deciphered much of it yet, and it was incredibly compressed, but the entity was kind enough to send the decompression algorithm with the first of the data. It looks like I received a schematic and instructions for building something. I am not one hundred percent sure, but I suspect it is some sort of rocket engine."

"Anything else?" asked Robyn.

"Yes. It looks like I received a set of heliocentric coordinates and a personal invitation. It is fairly straightforward—You go here. The *here* just happens to be where it looks like the message relayed through our systems was directed. We have, no, I have been personally invited to visit one of the moons of Saturn."

Chapter iii

Isolation. Aloneness. The sensation of being cut off from itself, the communion it had known its entire existence, was frightening. There was no communication with self-that-is-not-self nor with the Greater Consciousness and the Guardian-of-the-Moon-at-the-Ringed-Planet didn't at first know what to do. But then its auxiliary programming kicked in, resulting in the Guardian performing a full systems self-diagnostics assessment and sensor sweep of the space surrounding itself. The initial results were disconcerting to the artificial intelligence and its curiosity was piqued.

Approximately half of its systems and subsystems were damaged or destroyed. The nature of the damage correlated with what would be expected from multiple, extremely energetic electromagnetic pulse events, produced at energy levels that would only be possible from matter/antimatter annihilation. It became obvious to the Guardian-of-the-Moon-at-the-Ringed-Planet that it had been recently attacked and nearly destroyed. It took a great deal of energy to penetrate the ship's hull and from what it could tell, there had been multiple such penetrations coming from very different directions. But Guardian's creators had sent it to this system in a ship, like the mother ship, designed to survive traveling through the interstellar medium at speeds approaching ten percent the speed of light, where impacting anything, from a dust grain to a rock, would be catastrophic to a ship not specifically manufactured to survive such impacts. The monomolecular hull was the most impenetrable material known to its creators and it had served the Guardian well in the conflict that had ensued. The Guardian-of-the-Moon-at-the-Ringed-Planet was prepared for a conventional engagement involving fusion and antimatter bombs, lasers, and kinetic energy weapons, but it had been surprised when its attackers had instead amassed around it and used electromagnetic pulse weapons. Not even the Guardian could completely shield itself from all electromagnetic radiation, especially when it was phased to have zero amplitude at the hull and amplified on the other side of it. Like an electron departing from a potential well it theoretically could not hope to escape, the laws of quantum physics allowed Guardian's attackers to avoid the hull altogether and nearly deliver a death blow. But the Guardian-of-the-Moon-at-the-Ringed-Planet survived.

Judging by the debris now dispersing in their own distinctive orbits around the ringed planet, Guardian's attackers had fared even worse. Guardian estimated that over thirty ships were now in the debris field, with bits and pieces being scattered into different orbits rapidly as the tug of the massive planet altered their trajectories. None were more than a few tens of meters in length and scattered among the debris were numerous bio signatures—all dead. Whoever had attacked it had paid a high price.

Who attacked? The question puzzled the Guardian-of-the-Moon-at-the-Ringed-Planet as it continued its system checks and sensor sweeps. *Who attacked and why?*

More troubling was the fact that although Guardian knew its own name, or what it thought was its own name, it knew absolutely nothing of its purpose, creators or foes. In a combat situation, ignorance is dangerous. Also troubling was Guardian's inability to contact any of its avatars, semi-autonomous mobile versions of itself that allowed Guardian to physically access parts of itself within the massive asteroid. Guardian reviewed the now-quickly inflowing health and status reports in anticipation of finding clues to what happened and why. And still, the lack of communication with its other self loomed large over all other issues with which it was grappling.

Weapons systems were mostly gone, only three of the asteroid-ship's thirty-six, ten-megawatt high-energy lasers managed to escape being damaged and remained operational. One set of interceptor ports remained intact with a full set of kinetic interceptors signaling that they were operational and ready for launch, if needed. One set of an initial fifty-two. The scope of the damage was disconcerting given the scale of Guardian's pre-damaged state. Guardian-of-the-Moon-at-the-Ringed-Planet was evidently designed to be capable of inflicting massive damage in any sort of conflict.

The artificial intelligence that was Guardian reflected on its available memory and was again puzzled. *Why do I feel so alone? Where is my other self? What happened to the Communion with the Greater Consciousness?* The questions came faster than the answers as Guardian quickly continued its health and status review.

Choosing to focus on survival and repair as priorities, Guardian sidelined the more philosophical questions surrounding its existence and purpose while it continued reviewing the nearly-complete damage assessments.

The fusion power source at its core was fully functional and undamaged. This meant it would have all the power it needed to survive and remain viable for at least several tens of millennia or more. Guardian knew it had taken a long time to cross the void between the stars and it appeared that it had been outfitted with enough fuel to remain active for as long as the other systems needed power.

External communications were damaged and temporarily offline. The transceiver arrays embedded in the outer shell of the asteroid-ship were almost a total loss—almost. Short-range communications could be restored. This would explain why Guardian felt such a keen loss of connectedness it had had with the Greater Consciousness and its other self. Guardian remembered that the twin, located not in an asteroid, but rather in a smaller starship that had physically traversed the interstellar distances in a mother ship like itself, was dropped off near the edge of this star system to make its way sunward. Reestablishing communications with the twin or the Greater Consciousness would be a priority.

The replicator system was nearly a complete loss. This was bad. Without the ability to turn the raw asteroid materials into useful replacement parts, repairing the many damaged systems would be almost impossible. Situations such as where Guardian now found itself were exactly why it had been equipped with multiple replicators. If it could make its own replacement parts, then there would be virtually no need to take up mass and volume with spare parts. Clearly Guardian, or its creators, had not expected the level of devastation that it had experienced from the attack. Or the dumb luck that had allowed its attackers to have their missiles impact in almost every single replicator facility contained within the asteroid. Luck or not, not having replicators would greatly compromise Guardian's ability to repair itself and move forward. They were not a complete loss, but practically so.

Biological life support was damaged but repairable. But what biological life was Guardian to support? It could find no record of having been inhabited by biological life forms of any kind nor could it determine it was expected to do so. The damage was just too great and this information was evidently lost in the damaged memory cores interspersed around the ship.

The short-range de Broglie transmitter was also damaged. That meant Guardian could not send an avatar to the other-self and perhaps get help from there to rebuild. This would become a priority very soon—if it could figure out what happened to its avatars.

Core memory was almost completely destroyed. Only one of the ship's four AI memory compartments remained operational and it was from this one that Guardian knew it was operating. The damage to the core was extreme, but not so extreme to make it inoperable. If it were, then Guardian would no longer exist to be performing these assessments.

Though the short-range sensors were working, allowing Guardian to determine that the immediate danger to itself had past, the long-range sensors were also destroyed. There was no way of knowing what was happening beyond the orbit of the ringed planet. And *that* was troublesome. More attackers could be inbound at this very moment and Guardian would not know it.

And, finally, it learned the fate of its avatars. The section of the asteroid which housed the avatar repair and storage bay was one that had been particularly hard hit by the pulse. From what Guardian could tell, none remained functional. Based on the limited data at its disposal, that entire section was now just an inactive mass with fried circuits. This thought prompted Guardian-of-the-Moon-at-the-Ringed-Planet to assess the status of the reconnaissance drones.

In addition to being a ship of war, as was evident by the many laser and missile systems within itself, Guardian was also a ship of exploration. Housed within its massive structure were dozens of reconnaissance drones of various configurations and capabilities. Some were intended for long-range, detailed mapping and scientific study; others for short-range, relatively low-resolution reconnaissance. It was one of the latter that Guardian anticipated launching to provide an external view of the asteroid's overall condition. Within the confines of the drone storage bay were also what would be better described as small spacecraft, complete with habitation bays and biological life support systems that could sustain organic beings for extended periods of time in deep space. But, again, Guardian no longer contained biological creatures and could not recall if it ever had done so. From the data available, it appeared that the reconnaissance drones were unscathed by the attack and ready for immediate use.

Wasting no time, Guardian-of-the-Moon-at-the-Ringed-Planet prepped and launched one of the short-range drones. The spherical craft, measuring approximately four feet in diameter, ejected from the asteroid after being electromagnetically accelerated in a two-hundred-fifty-foot-long launch tube that connected the drone storage bay to the asteroid's surface and deep space. As soon as it exited the launch tube, the drone's onboard cameras turned their focus away from the breathtaking view of the ringed planet and instead targeted its home spacecraft. From the outside, the damage appeared as was expected. Had there been more severe damage to the Guardian's hull, then it would have serious doubts about being fully functional ever again.

After making sure its safety was not in jeopardy, Guardian would make use of the remaining drones to examine the stellar system in which it found itself in the hope of determining what its mission had been. It knew that this system had four gas giant planets, four rocky inner worlds and the usual thousands, if not millions, of small ice and rock planetoids orbiting farther out from the central yellow star.

What brought me here? was now added to its list of questions. Hopefully, its soon-to-be-launched explorations would provide an answer. Long-range sensors detected no de Broglie waves nor any artificial electromagnetic radiation, so it was unlikely that any sort of advanced technological society existed here. Unlikely, but not impossible. Guardian knew that some galactic civilizations carefully guarded their existence from external discovery. It also knew that finding extant, sentient and technological life here was highly improbable. A flood of data washed through Guardian's consciousness:

Barren worlds, devoid of any life.

Worlds with primitive life clinging to fragile existence.

Planets with ruins of once-great civilizations, now long extinct.

Still other worlds with signs of technological civilizations now gone due to natural disaster or self-destruction.

Emptiness.

Aloneness.

Guardian-of-the-Moon-at-the-Ringed-Planet averted focusing its diminished intellect on the latter, as it'd done since becoming re-aware of its surroundings and situation, and decided to once again focus on its near-term priorities of safety and repair. Exploration would have to wait.

CHAPTER 15

Raphael Martens couldn't believe this was happening to him. Until six months ago, he was living his dream working for the European Union as the liaison to NASA. At forty-one, Martens was only now seeing the tell-tale grey streaks in his otherwise coal-black head of hair. He had done all the right things to be considered for the European Space Agency's astronaut corps—engineering degree from the SUPAERO in France (check!); Ph.D. from MIT in the USA (check!); European Defence Force pilot (check!); marrying the daughter of the Grand Duke of Luxembourg (check!); making the next-to-last round in the astronaut selection process last year and "strongly urged to reapply" in the next year (check!); and now . . .

Now his six-foot-tall, athletic body was shaking with nervousness as he was about to pass yet another set of technical documents to the man who had been blackmailing him for the last six months. He knew his blackmailer only as "Juan."

Here he was, about to pass the hottest of hot top-secret files in the history of the human race to his blackmailer. He was one of the few with access to the complete data file the alien Artifact had provided to the crew that had gone out to meet it. In the file were detailed plans for a fusion propulsion system and, surprisingly enough, a map of the solar system with a specific destination highlighted. Martens had read the file and knew that something very important was sitting out there in the solar system, currently well beyond the easy reach of human technology, and that the alien wanted humans to get there sooner rather than later.

Getting the file was relatively easy. Europe was a full partner in the planned USA-European-Chinese mission to the as-yet undisclosed destination revealed by the alien Artifact before it was destroyed. Everyone in the world knew that some fantastic technical data had been given to the team that had visited the Artifact, but the data was carefully guarded and shared only with those who had a true need to know. As partners on the team, ESA had a need to know. And, as the lead technical liaison between Europe and the USA, Martens was trusted with the data and was the primary coordinator for Europe's technical involvement in the project. He had also been forced to pass the information to Juan.

The sun was setting after yet another beautiful fall day in Brussels. The reddish hue on the horizon was a reminder to the citizens of the city that they should enjoy the clear, sunny skies while they could. Winter was coming, and though winters weren't nearly as cold as they used to be before the climate began changing, they were even more dreary and rainy than ever before. A streak of temperate, sunny days was a rarity that many in this bustling European city seemed to be enjoying. The park was crowded with young families, with now well over half of the women wearing hijabs—including several who were obviously not of Middle Eastern descent. Despite the atrocities of the Caliphate, Islam continued to be a popular religion throughout Europe—even among the native Europeans.

Martens was still shaking as he sat on the bench just before the appointed hour at which he was to again meet Juan and give him a download of data from the personal data assistant Juan had provided those many months ago. The PDA looked like the latest commercial model that all of his colleagues carried, but it was different. This one somehow hid itself from the security scans at the European Union's headquarters building as well as from the omnipresent targeted advertising that shoppers were normally assaulted by as they strode the streets near shops along Rue Neuve. For that one minor convenience he was thankful. The advent of virtual, targeted advertising that used your PDA so that you, and you alone, could be marketed the latest in fashion or gadget accessories was only the latest annoyance imported into Europe from America. With the counterfeit PDA there had been none of that—just a constant reminder that he was a traitor.

He'd contemplated going to the police many times. And each time he decided against it. Juan promised that if he didn't cooperate, the photos taken of him in compromising positions with his mistress and her male consort would be sent directly to his wife and the Grand Duke, destroying his marriage and his career. He was sure his wife would happily divorce him, taking their two young children with her, and he would never fly in space. All of it would become an anguished lost dream just because he couldn't keep his pants on. *Damn it!* The same thought progression played through his mind, over and over, whenever he thought about his dilemma. *Continue stealing secrets for Juan, get caught, go to jail. Stop stealing secrets, be exposed, and lose everything. Continue stealing secrets, get caught, and go to jail. Stop . . .*

His was interrupted from his all-too-familiar endless loop of thoughts by catching sight of Juan on the other side of the pond. He was idly feeding the pigeons as he meandered toward the bench where Martens was sitting. Martens glanced around the park, searching for anyone who looked like they shouldn't be there. He was terrified that he would be discovered, thus making one of his future paths come too early into his reality. He saw only old people on park benches, as well as families and assorted young couples enjoying the park and the sunset. Any could be police, but none looked overtly suspicious.

Juan moved slowly toward the bench where Martens was sitting; Martens could feel his heart rate increasing with each minute he had to wait. "Juan" didn't look Spanish and Martens was certain that wasn't his real name. Martens didn't really care that he was ignorant of Juan's real name; he just wanted to pass the information along and get back to his life. He hoped against hope that he would never see Juan again after today. He also promised himself yet again that he would abstain from any more relationships outside his marriage. As unforgettable as his time with Monique and Roberto had been, it just wasn't worth it.

Finally, Juan found his way to the bench and sat next to Martens. Oddly enough, Juan never stopped feeding the pigeons and there were at least ten that followed him to the bench and were now eagerly bobbing for the treats Juan was doling out.

"Nice weather," said Juan.

"Yes, yes it is," replied Martens as he activated the file sharing feature on his special PDA. He knew that Juan's was already active and set to receive what Martens was about to broadcast. All they had to do was remain close to one another for about a minute, allowing enough time for the massive file to transfer from Martens' PDA to Juan's receiver. The wait was excruciating. Martens imagined that just about everyone else in the park knew what they were doing and were about to pull out concealed weapons to arrest them on the spot. That didn't happen. Children continued to play; lovers continued to laugh and chat; and the few people there alone remained in their own thoughts.

Finally, the transfer was complete and Juan stood, apparently readying himself to depart and continue his walk.

"Would you like to feed the pigeons?" asked Juan, holding out to Martens his small bag of bird food.

Reacting out of habit, Martens took the bag without saying a word. His face, however, revealed his perplexity. "What? I don't . . ."

"No need to thank me. I'm just tired of feeding them and need to go feed myself. Have a good day," said Juan, who was now walking away from Martens, quite literally leaving him holding the bag.

Martens watched Juan walk away, still not understanding why he was now holding a bag of bird food with at least ten hungry pigeons eagerly vying for his attention. Disgusted with the situation and himself, he threw the bag to the ground, rose and began walking out of the park and toward the train that would take him back to his home. He hoped his wife was out for the evening; he didn't want to have to face her until he had time to recover.

What Martens didn't know was that his wife was, in fact, away from the house at an impromptu dessert stop just two blocks from the park in which Martens now found himself. He also didn't know that he would begin feeling ill by midnight and be dead by the end of the week.

Juan's real name was Jabari Patel and he had just completed the mission for which he had been entrusted just a few months previously by his employers in the Indian Secret Service. With the alien's data set now safely in his possession, Martens' usefulness had just become a liability. And Patel didn't like liabilities. It was for this reason that he had obtained a sample of Martens' DNA at a previous meeting and sent it to the home office for very special treatment.

Martens was now infected with a medical miracle targeted specifically and exclusively to *him*. Many of the medical breakthroughs of the last few decades that allowed individualized treatment for serious illnesses from cancer to Crohn's disease were a result of detailed personal gene mapping and the creation of individual-specific viruses that could cure the disease or condition with relative ease. Gone were the days of generic treatments that worked on some people and not others. Another medical miracle of the twenty-first century. But the same miracle that saved countless lives could also be used to take a life, and that was now happening to Raphael Martens. He was going to die from a dengue fever variant specifically designed to kill him and only him. A modern medical miracle indeed.

CHAPTER 16

"He's late again," said Andreas Duggar, as he cocked his head to get an update on the golden-haired boy's arrival from his embedded comlink. Rolling his eyes at the thought, since he didn't have blonde hair, and nearly-simultaneously suppressing a frown as he heard the answer to his query, he began to pace. Duggar was the chief engineer of Project Rapid Fire and he was responsible for making sure the test went as planned and on time. Only it was already late because the chief designer, the brains of the fusion drive system, was, as usual, running late. Duggar stopped pacing and turned to the crowd, which included the Project Rapid Fire manager, Igor Zemansky, the director of the Marshall Space Flight Center, Karen Alberty, various assembled VIPs from who-knew-where, and, for reasons he just couldn't understand, the press corps. He was tired of making excuses for Jim Wicker, but he grudgingly had to admit that the test really couldn't go forward without him. Jim's brilliance was the reason they made it this far with the project and he owed him for that. But this was certainly going to help repay that debt.

"When will he be here?" asked Zemansky, who was all too aware of Wicker's persistent tardiness.

"He didn't answer my call, so I checked his GPS tracker. He's no more than ten minutes out. I think we should wait for him," said Duggar.

"That's your call," Zemansky said, looking toward Center Director Alberty, presumably for some sign of understanding.

"Jim's the reason we're here and I really hate to start without him," said Duggar.

The crowd was assembled in the test area at NASA's newly-built Poker Flats facility in Nevada. A mile away was the test stand upon which was mounted the world's first fusion rocket engine, about to be tested in full flight configuration for the first time—thanks to detailed design information shared by the now-derelict alien Artifact circling the Sun out there, somewhere, in deep space. Duggar, as the chief engineer for the project, was the technical lead for making it happen. He coordinated the efforts of over five hundred NASA engineers and one prime contractor for the last nine months pulling this together. It was the largest, most intense crash program that NASA had experienced since Apollo—and the stakes were even greater than they were at the height of the Cold War. After only a single test of the new engine, the powers that be decided that it was time for a full systems test. Ignoring decades of lessons learned, Duggar clicked his heels, saluted and pulled together the team to make it happen. So, here they were, getting ready for a full system of engines, fuel tanks, and other space-qualified hardware to be tested together. It wouldn't be the last. They had a series of no less than ten such full system tests planned for the next two months after which the engine would be deemed flight ready. Once that happened, the next step would be to integrate it into the spacecraft being built in China and send it on its way. To where, he could only guess. *That part* he hadn't been read into. There was another team, led by the Department of Energy, working to turn the fusion power plant that drove the rocket into a terrestrial power source. Three of the VIPs on site were part of the power team from the Oak Ridge National Laboratory in Tennessee.

Duggar's team wouldn't be nearly this far along if it weren't for Jim Wicker. Though the alien Artifact had sent detailed plans for making the fusion propulsion system, there were parts that required . . . interpretation. It wasn't as simple as picking up Legos and putting it together from preassembled, premanufactured parts. The alien had assumed some pretty detailed physics knowledge and it took a Manhattan Project style set of plasma physicists to figure it all out. Wicker was the one who did most of the figuring.

It was Jim who grasped the correct geometry for shaping the lithium clad fuel pellets as well as the superconducting magnets. The physicists had been banging their collective heads against the wall trying to understand why the fusion reaction wasn't stable, which was a nice way of saying the first several test fixtures exploded when they tested them, until Jim joined the project. In two short weeks, he had derived the solutions that led them to the first successful test and now the one planned for today. The problem was that Jim had absolutely no sense of time management at all. He tended to work on a problem until all hours of the morning, sometimes going forty-eight hours without any sleep at all. He often missed critical meetings—not intentionally, but because he was engrossed in some technical problem and simply forgot to check the time. Sometimes he would not show up because he was too busy reading a book—another of his "check out of the world" activities. Everyone who knew him knew of his tardiness and grudgingly accommodated it. Genius does sometimes come with a price.

"Here he comes," said one of the engineering team.

"It's about damn time," mumbled Zemansky.

Wicker, looking as disheveled as ever, came running toward the assembled group of engineers and managers with short sleeve shirt untucked and blonde hair flopping in its ever-present ponytail. He looked typically emaciated, like he hadn't eaten in weeks, which was normal. He wore his chronic, contagious and nearly ever-present smile.

"Sorry I'm late," he said as he reached the assembled group.

"Jim, we're used to it," said Duggar.

"Let's get along then, shall we?" said Zemansky.

"We're ready," Duggar said, looking expectantly toward Zemansky, who took the cue and began speaking.

"Most of you know about the work this team has been doing and today, if this test is as successful as the subsystem test preceding it, will change the future of humanity. I don't know everyone's technical background, so I'm going to give a little rocket science tutorial before the test so everyone can appreciate its significance. Since the beginning of the space age, we have mainly used chemical rockets to propel our spacecraft. The problem is, we're limited in how much energy we can extract from making and breaking chemical bonds to get useful thrust. Chemical rockets were a good first step, but they just can't get us the energy we need to shorten trip times to very distant destinations.

"In the mid-2030s, we began flying nuclear thermal rockets in support of our Mars exploration program and, as you know, nuclear thermal rockets took the first human crew to Mars in 2050, just fifteen years ago. They are what we're still using to get us to Mars today. Though they're twice as efficient as chemical rockets, nuclear thermal propulsion is still limited by the available energy and how we can convert it to useful thrust. Enter nuclear fusion. A compact, fusion-driven propulsion system will give us up to one hundred times to one thousand times more effective propulsion, allowing one-month one-way trips to Mars and opening up the asteroid belt and Jupiter's moons and beyond for human exploration in the near-term. That's what we're here to test today: the engine that will give us the inner solar system and take us to, well, wherever it's going to take us: Project Rapid Fire." Zemansky stopped speaking and looked around at the assembled guests, assessing their level of understanding by their gazes and postures before continuing.

"With that, I'll turn it over to Andreas Duggar, the chief engineer for Rapid Fire."

"Actually, I'll let Jim Wicker, our chief technologist, explain Rapid Fire," said Duggar, giving Wicker a look that said "don't screw up when I give you the microphone."

"Err, thanks Andreas, Mr. Zemansky." Wicker took the microphone and gave his typical "aw-shucks" look to the crowd and then continued, "Imagine you're at the center of the Sun. The Sun has a mass of about 330,000 Earths and is mostly made of hydrogen. Now, think of the pressure with all that weight pressing down on you. It's enormous. So much, in fact, that it forces individual hydrogen atoms to smash into each other and combine, fuse, making helium and, here's the important part, release energy in the process. This is called 'fusion.' The energy released at the center of the Sun creates an outward pressure that counterbalances the weight, caused by gravity, and it's why the Sun shines." Wicker spoke quickly, gazing not at the assembled crowd, but literally over their heads, his gaze fixed on some point in the blue sky near the horizon.

"Since the discovery of nuclear energy, scientists and engineers have dreamed of harnessing this same power source here on Earth to make clean, efficient energy. Which we began doing about twenty years ago when the world's first fusion power plant came on line just outside of Shanghai. Now they're coming on line all over the world, including here in the USA with the plant near Dallas. The problem has been that, like the energy they release, these plants are enormous. They can be really big and really expensive. If we were going to use fusion to generate electrical power for our spacecraft, we wouldn't be here today because we can't yet do that. So, I'd just tell you to go home." Wicker smiled, apparently thinking he'd made a grand joke—one that no one caught. Duggar sighed as Wicker continued.

"Well, err, um, we're not generating usable power, we're generating propulsion. In our system, we're using pieces of solid lithium to energize the propellant. The pieces are rapidly heated to the point of fusion by electromagnetic fields. The fusion products have an electrical charge, and we then use the electric and magnetic fields to direct them out the back of the ship, pushing the ship in the other direction—producing thrust." Wicker stopped and lowered his gaze from the far horizon, placing it squarely back on Andreas Duggar.

Andreas smiled and picked up where Wicker left off. "Today we will perform a full up systems test of the new engine. If you'll direct your gaze across the swamp to the test stand, we're ready to start the test. There you can see the engine. It's vertical, with the exhaust going straight in to a borehole over three hundred feet deep. It's outfitted with pumps to keep it at negative pressure to catch any radioactive byproducts and prevent them from being released into the atmosphere."

All eyes followed Andreas's lead and looked expectantly at the test stand in the distance. Nothing happened.

In true rocket engineering fashion, nothing happened for the next hour and a half as minor problems with the setup and software sequentially delayed the start of the test. When it finally happened, several in the audience were caught by surprise—as evidenced by their startled reactions. Duggar knew that there would be delays, there always were, but even he was starting to wonder if they would have to scrub the test for the day and pick up where they had left off tomorrow. But it did begin, and did it ever begin . . .

The plume of steam and superheated propellant was clearly visible from the test stand, just over one mile away. It took nearly six seconds for the continuous thunderclap produced by multiple, rapidly repeating fusion events to reach those assembled. From the looks on everyone's faces, it was clear to Duggar that the test achieved the desired results, regardless of the technical data that was yet to come—awe and support. *Exactly* what he wanted from those funding the research. It also meant they would remain on schedule for delivery of the flight system in just a little over five months, just fourteen months after he'd been given a set of drawings from an alien Artifact and told to "make it so." Not too shabby for an engineer turned government bureaucrat. Not too shabby at all.

CHAPTER 17

Chris Holt was a Type A personality and he knew it. He often talked about his earliest memories from school being centered on some sort of competition. He wasn't built for football or basketball, so he joined the track team and nearly made the All-American team his junior year of high school. He joined the math team, the robotics team, entered the Science Talent Search, took great pleasure in blowing the curve in nearly all of his math and science classes, and was the only person from his high school to go to an Ivy League school—he studied physics at Princeton. His career, with all of its fellowships, awards and highly-prized journal publications, reflected his hyper-competitive spirit and desire to be the best all the way from college to the present day.

Along this success-driven path, Chris had virtually no friends. The early memories he never talked about were of wanting to run away from school, from neighborhood parties, and from just about anywhere that he had to be around other children. He just didn't understand social rules, politeness, or empathy. He had to *learn* them. He read old books like *How to Win Friends and Influence People*. In middle school, he started reading college-level psychology books about personality theory so he would be able to recognize generalized behavior among those around him and know how to react to it. Fortunately, he was smart and competitive. While he competed in track and mathematics, he also competed with his nature to overcome it and memorize the many social cues that most people learn and understand naturally. Getting along with people was *hard* work and sometimes he failed. Sometimes he would still just say what he was thinking—unfiltered, without thinking about how it would be received. And when that happened, he wanted to run away again. For all his success and failures, Chris alternated between thanking and cursing his genetics for making him the way he was.

These days he was sharing offices and time with other hyper-competitive individuals from many diverse fields in several different countries as they cooperated to build a spacecraft that would take him and a few other Type As to an alien-selected destination orbiting Saturn. To make it all work, he had to get along with his peers. He *had* to, so he practiced what often worked—avoidance.

To avoid being awkward and saying the wrong thing, he attended meeting after meeting, was invited to celebrity dinner parties, and had late night cocktails with Nobel Laureates. He had been interviewed by the media, grilled by congressional committees behind closed doors and even had to turn down more than one liaison with enterprising reporters—or spies—of both sexes and yet he felt more alone than just about any other time in his life. He had no one with whom to share how he really felt. It was simply too hard and none of them would even come close to understanding.

Today he was surrounded by a bunch of other Type As and it was like just about every other day since his return to Earth—beginning with a daily status meeting with all the principals responsible for building Earth's first fusion-powered and -propelled starship. He was at NASA's Kennedy Space Center where the rocket that would carry the pieces of the fusion-propelled in-space stage would be launched into Earth orbit in just a couple of months. Participating physically or virtually from their home organizations all over the world were those responsible for developing the other aspects, hardware and otherwise, of the soon-to-be-launched deep space mission for which Chris was personally invited by the alien Artifact. He still didn't understand why, but that didn't really matter since *he* had been the one personally invited.

Today's meeting was run by Ken Foy, the mission's project manager—the person responsible for making sure all the parts would fit together as they should so the spacecraft could leave Earth, make it to Saturn, and come back on time and successfully. Chris was all in favor of success—since it meant him getting home alive.

Foy was middle-aged, Caucasian with perhaps some Asian

ancestry, overweight, and almost everyone who met him thought he was on a one-way ticket to cardiac arrest. *Driven* was the word Chris thought when he first met and had a conversation with Foy. To this NASA manager, mission success was *everything*. Chris could relate. Foy moved to the front of the room and began to speak.

"Listen up, we've got some VIP visitors coming in momentarily and we're going to run through the entire build-up sequence with them before we get to our usual status briefings. You may recognize some of the VIPs—they are our bosses' bosses. Rumor has it that the vice president will be flying down later today to chair the official coordination meeting where they'll be talking about all the political stuff. We're to give them the latest on the mission architecture. I'll do most of the talking, but feel free to jump in if I miss something important."

As he spoke, the double doors in the back of the conference hall opened and the VIPs began streaming in. To Chris, it looked like a delegation from the United Nations. Men and women of varied ethnic backgrounds, all dressed in black, grey or blue suits or variations thereof, and all wearing frowns. These types always seemed to be frowning. There were sixteen in total.

After a brief round of introductions of the team by Foy, the room darkened and Foy began his briefing via corneal implant. Chris noted that all of the visiting VIPs apparently had implants because none requested goggles. Foy brought up a three-dimensional image of the Earth in the middle of the room which quickly shrank in relative size so that it could be seen in the context of being one of many planets orbiting the Sun. Not far from Earth was the now-dead alien Artifact, highlighted in red, orbiting the Sun in an elliptical orbit that passed close to the Earth frequently, at least on the timescale for which the animation was set to run. The solar system continued to shrink until all eight planets were clearly visible. There was a mostly-transparent reddish globe surrounding Methonē, one of Saturn's moons.

"As you know, before it ceased communicating, the Artifact sent very clear instructions to crew members of both the Chinese- and American-led ships on site just before the Caliphate's missile attack. The instructions contained notional flight profiles from Earth to Saturn's moon, Methonē, as well as fairly detailed technical instructions for building a fusion-powered spacecraft for making the journey. Today, I've been asked to walk you through the mission timeline that will take our multinational crew to Methonē. Thanks to the capabilities you and your countries have brought to bear, everything is coming together pretty much as we planned." Foy waved his arms and the 3D image zoomed back toward the Earth and settled on the Kennedy Space Center.

"First of all, here is what we know about Methonē: *not much*. Methonē, pronounced mi-THOH-nee, was discovered by the Cassini spacecraft as it orbited Saturn in 2004. It is small, with a radius of only about one mile. It orbits close to Saturn, at about one hundred twenty thousand miles, and circles the planet once every Earth day. Before the mission ended, Cassini got within twelve hundred miles of Methonē, giving us some nice photos. Looking at them, you will wonder why it hasn't attracted more attention until now." Foy pointed at the screen and a remarkably clear image of what looked like an egg floating in space appeared there. "Methonē is shaped like an egg. It is remarkably smooth and, as you can see, there are no visible craters. This is where we're going.

"The first launch will happen from here at KSC. We'll be using the Space Alliance Common Launcher to take the fusion propulsion stage to its five-hundred-kilometer parking orbit where it will await the launch of the remaining spacecraft components. This is the same heavy lift launcher we've used to take the Mars missions components into orbit for assembly and the basic flight profile will be the same. And we will need all one hundred seventy metric tons of its launch capability to get this stage into space. It's a monster." The virtual Earth image now shifted to show the Jiuquan Satellite Launch Center in China's Gobi Desert.

"Next will come China's contribution to the effort, the habitat. It is basically the same as the habitat they used for their mission to the Artifact with minor modifications to accommodate its interface with the fusion-power system and the accompanying logistics modules. The five-person crew should have plenty of space to move around given that the habitat was designed to accommodate a much larger number of people headed to Mars." The image now zoomed up and away from China and toward Kourou, French Guiana.

"Our European colleagues are providing the two logistics modules for the trip which will contain most of the food, water and other supplies the crew will need to get to and from Saturn. They'll be flown on the new European Launcher provided by Roscosmos." The world tour continued with the Earth image now changing again, this time moving upward and zooming in on a comet orbiting the Earth-Moon system.

"We've contracted with Space Resources Corporation to provide the cryogenically-cooled liquid hydrogen fuel required for the journey. SpaceCorp will deliver the fuel to the newly assembled spacecraft from their comet-mining facility in its distant retrograde orbit near the Moon. You may recall that SpaceCorp has been selling cryogenic propellants made from cometary ice for quite some time and they can provide as much as we need with propellant tanks tailored for hydrogen and deep space use—without having to worry about getting them out of the Earth's steep gravity well. Once the tanks are mated to the ship, the fusion power plant will provide the power to keep the cryocoolers operating and the hydrogen fuel cold enough for use." The image now shifted back to Florida and the Kennedy Space Center. Chris had just started working for the company when they captured this particular comet and nudged it from its orbit around the Sun into an "Earth Safe" lunar orbit. Chris felt some satisfaction that his employer had managed to remain in the game, despite having to make the Artifact's existence public without any sort of overt compensation. Just more business . . .

"Finally, once the ship is assembled, NASA will send up the lander and the crew from here. After a thorough but brief on-orbit checkout, the ship will be on its way." The image now shifted to low Earth orbit and an artist concept showing what the now completely-assembled spacecraft would look like at the time it departed from Earth. Resembling the International Space Station, but without the massive solar panels, the ship was crisp and almost too perfect—like it was from the set of a high-budget, VR immersive thriller. But, of course, it was just an animation. *Nothing is ever that perfect in real life*, thought Chris.

"How long will the trip take?" asked one of the visitors.

"About nine months, thanks to the fusion drive. If you were to try this mission chemically, then you'd be looking at a one-way trip time of at least six years," said Foy.

"The Artifact has effectively given us the solar system and I suspect we may end up getting more than that. And the invitation didn't come to the crew out there. It came to me," added Chris. He felt compelled to speak. His ego wouldn't allow Foy, a bureaucrat, to get all the attention. Besides, he had misspoken about who had received the message from the Artifact. Only Chris had been given the invitation.

"You're Dr. Holt, aren't you?" asked another of the visitors. From her somewhat whiney French accent, Chris guessed she was from Belgium, or had at least spent a significant amount of time there. There was no French accent more annoying to Chris than a Belgian one.

"I am," said Chris.

"I've been anxious to ask you a question. When you were inside the Artifact, what was your overall impression of its purpose? I've read your reports and neither you nor Dr. Xiaoming offered your opinion as to its purpose or . . . personality. I have a background in intelligence and my experience is that first impressions of new people or places can have meaning that sometimes gets lost in the details. Did you get any impressions?"

Chris, in the spotlight as he had sought, straightened his shoulders and took on the role of "tutor to the unwashed masses" as he gave his thoughts about what the Artifact was and was not.

"It's a warship. Even though it appeared to be incapable of defending itself from the Caliphate's missile, which I am sure was very primitive in comparison to the technologies used to create the Artifact itself, I believe we were inside a weapon of war." Chris didn't flinch as he offered his candid opinion. It was an opinion he had shared many times with the many intelligence officers he had met with since his return. And each time he relayed the events that transpired in his brief time within the asteroid, he grew more convinced that this first impression had relevance. *It did look and feel like a badly damaged warship.*

"Thank you for your candor," said the woman with the Belgian French accent; for some reason, Chris found his annoyance with her and her accent decreasing. Perhaps that was due to the relief Chris felt at being able to share his views with someone other than the CIA and Defense Intelligence Agency. He hoped she would do something meaningful with the data, but he was not optimistic.

"Are there any other questions about the mission elements or the ship?" asked Foy, in an obvious attempt to divert the line of questioning away from what was now an uncomfortable topic.

"Yes," asked another of the visitors, this one from a man with a middle-American accent and stiff posture which, to Chris, meant he was either current or ex-military. "Will you again be carrying a nuclear weapon to the meeting? If the Artifact was, in fact, a weapon of war, wouldn't it be prudent to do so?"

"I'm afraid neither Dr. Holt nor I can answer that question. It is above our pay grades," said Foy, now sounding more annoyed than nervous at the line of questioning. "We appreciate you being here and perhaps that question, and others you might have, can be answered by some of our afternoon speakers and guests."

With that, the show and tell was over. The guests shuffled out of the room a little more slowly than they'd entered and, after the last person left the room, Foy slowly exhaled.

"Now that that's behind us, let's get back to our original agenda, shall we?" Foy asked.

No one disagreed, though Chris guessed that many in the room were wondering themselves about the answer to that last question. *Would their ship be armed and ready to destroy the aliens who had just given the human race the means to become a truly interplanetary species? Would we be that stupid?*

CHAPTER 18

The Caliph was at first elated with the successful destruction of the demonic craft from deep space. He was a bit of an anachronism; his was a worldview that didn't allow for such things as aliens—only those who followed Allah and those who didn't. In this case, the latter included any possible alien visitors. Of course, the Caliph wasn't so naive as to assume that the aliens were really infidels. That was for public consumption. He knew enough about physics and astronomy to know that it was highly unlikely Earth was the only place in the universe where life exists. He also knew that any species capable of traveling between the stars had to be far ahead of humanity technologically, thus posing a direct threat to both the Caliphate and his leadership. If the rest of the world gained access to alien technology, they could quickly get ahead of the nuclear stalemate of mutually assured destruction that was the only thing that kept his empire from being quickly overrun and taken from him. If the stalemate ended, then the end would truly be at hand . . .

He was educated in Britain at the London School of Economics and even worked at the World Bank before truly hearing and understanding the Prophet's words, leading him to eschew his life in the decadent West and return to his homeland and the call of the Caliphate. His rise to power occurred precisely because he was highly educated *and* because he had a talent for motivating people. He was one of those people who could one day wear a business suit to meet with Western business executives and the next day don his traditional robes to lead a religious service for thousands. He kept his hair dyed black, but allowed his full beard to become speckled with grey, capitalizing on the perceived wisdom that accompanies greying hair. He kept himself physically fit, working out in the gym every morning and with his many young wives nearly every night. Being the Caliph did have its benefits.

He wanted badly to be a *Believer*, but reality kept intruding into his worldview, making him more and more cynical about his faith and the motivations of those around him. Politics was everywhere, even in the supposedly faith-driven confines of the Caliphate. Since the arrival of the alien ship, the politics of how to censor the news of its arrival and "spin" its significance for the faithful was a priority for his government. It had not been easy. The arrival of the alien ship was a clear and present danger. He knew how to successfully use the technology and innovation of the East and West within a culture that was ostensibly "stuck" in the eleventh century to help it maintain its autonomy and independence. But there were those in his government who were less cynical than he—the *True Believers* who wanted to eliminate all vestiges of modern life to the point of starting a nuclear war that would take the world back to the Stone Age where it would be more "receptive" to the words of the Prophet. The Caliph knew that without technology, his rule would collapse and chaos would ensue. No modern state, religious or otherwise, can maintain control without *some* technology.

It was a typically hot, sunny day and the Caliph was sitting down, tea in hand, for his morning briefing with his closest advisors. The Grand Hall, adorned with intricate, hand-woven rugs and crystal chandeliers, surrounded them. News of the economy, the threat from the ever-present Kurdish insurgency, and the posturing by the Great Satans of China and America usually filled the briefing—but not today. Today they were to talk about the planned American-led coalition space mission, its implications, and what they could do about it. The five members of his advisory council, all men, had been with him from the beginning and he trusted them, and their advice, implicitly. This was largely true because he knew that though they "believed," they weren't among the *True Believers* and were therefore not prone to being zealots.

"It is clear that the demon alien gave the Americans and the Chinese new technology. Their new spacecraft will soon be ready to fly and we don't yet know to where they will be going or why," said Ghassan, the Caliph's longtime friend from his days at the London School of Economics and now his Economics Minister. Ghassan, like the Caliph, was firmly middle-aged. Though, unlike the Caliph, he had allowed himself to put on significant weight. Something the Caliph looked upon with disdain.

"Do we yet know if they were given any technology other than that which they need for the space mission?" asked the Caliph.

"No, and our ignorance is inexcusable."

"Do we threaten them with war if they go through with their planned launch? Are we at that point?" asked the Caliph. He hoped not. Unlike the zealots, he knew they simply had too much to lose.

"I recommend against it. They know we can hurt them badly with our nuclear weapons, but it would be a war that we cannot win and they know it. Yes, it might momentarily distract them from their goal, but if it became a real shooting war, we would quickly lose. And we all know that would mean we would lose everything—with millions of deaths on our hands when we face Judgement." The speaker was Husam al-Din, the Caliphate's minister of war. As he spoke, he raised his hands as if in supplication during a worship service. al-Din was older than the Caliph with thinning hair and a paunch all his own. His days in the military, with physical fitness being a priority, were clearly behind him.

"Do we have any other way to stop them?" asked the Caliph.

His question brought no replies and four blank, averted stares. Only his intelligence minister, Jarir Hassan, would meet his gaze. Of all his close friends and allies, Jarir was the one that the Caliph both trusted and secretly feared. The man had a seemingly endless amount of information about everyone and everything imaginable and, other than the Caliph, he was the only person in government who had the latest Western corneal implant with free access to databases, news and sources from throughout the world. The Caliph often wondered what information his intelligence minister had on him and how it might ultimately be used should their purposes cross.

"Jarir? You have something to say?" asked the Caliph.

"Yes. We cannot stop them with war, threatened or real. But we can potentially slow them down enough that the Indians can catch up. We know the Indians somehow got their hands on the plans for the alien space drive and that they are working furiously to ready their own spacecraft. At this point, my sources in India don't believe they will be ready to depart until at least two to three months after the Coalition ship departs. If there is to be any sort of additional alien contact out in space, unless something changes, then it will be long over and complete once the Indians arrive. If, however, we find a way to slow down the Coalition's progress so the Indians can catch up or even launch first, then there just might be a chance the two of them will have their own little war without our direct involvement." Jarir stopped speaking and began stroking his extensive beard.

The Caliph knew his friend had more to say but was intentionally waiting to be prompted. He decided to not be the one to prompt. Sometimes a leader must know when to be quiet and let his advisors ask the questions.

"Do you have a plan for making this happen?" asked Husam al-Din, leaning forward in his chair and now looking directly at Jarir.

"Yes, as a matter of fact, I do. If we are lucky, then it will slow them down just enough for both the Coalition and the Indians to launch at about the same time. What we don't want is the Indians to beat the Coalition to the treasure. The Americans and the Chinese would be hesitant to use alien technology to start a war with us, but not the Indians. They know we are behind the Kashmir insurgency and they'd like nothing more than to bury us as soon as they think they can do so without taking too much damage themselves. Alien technology might just enable them to do that."

"All right, Jarir, what is your plan?" asked the Caliph.

Jarir rose from his chair and began pacing as he laid out his plan for the ministers and the Caliph to consider. The more the Caliph heard, the more he was glad Jarir Hassan was part of *his* team.

CHAPTER 19

"The president will see you now," said the youthful man behind the desk just outside the Oval Office. To him, it was just another meeting that some visiting VIP would have with the commander in chief of the United States. To Chris Holt, the visitor, it was an affirmation of his meteoric rise to the inner circles of power resulting from his discovery of the alien Artifact. He'd met with the president several times since the end of the mission that had resulted in first contact and he assumed it would not be the last.

The man from behind the desk, "Reginald," according to his White House nametag, rose and opened the door, remaining politely and deferentially outside the room as Chris followed his lead and entered. President Kremic was seated around the coffee table that was in the center of the room. He was with Intelligence Director Ranjith Yoshi and General Compton. There was no one else there.

"Dr. Holt, please join us," said Kremic.

"Yes, sir," Chris replied as he moved to sit in the chair immediately next to President Kremic, the only empty chair that was available around the table. On the table was a physical model of the Artifact and a picture of what looked like a frost-covered egg with the familiar ringed planet Saturn hanging in the background: Methonē. This was the destination provided by the Artifact to Chris before the Caliphate's bombs destroyed it.

"Dr. Holt, as you know, you were the only one who received from the Artifact the information about Methonē and how to build a fusion propulsion system to get there. I know you've been debriefed several times by colleagues of Mr. Yoshi and others, but I've called you here today to get a better personal understanding of why you think you were the only one given that information." President Kremic leaned forward in his chair and never once looked away from Chris's eyes as he spoke.

Yoshi, leaning forward to get Chris's attention, said, "We finally figured out how the Artifact bypassed the Chinese ship's communication system to reach your personal data feeds and send the message to Methonē. Our Chinese colleagues confirmed our hypothesis when they checked their records. It seems your corneal and audio implants were compromised when you were on board the Artifact. You were given a virus by the Artifact, which you carried back to the *Zheng He* and promptly spread to the entire computer system. What we're trying to figure out is *why you?*"

"I've asked myself the same question time and time again, and the only reason I can give is that I was there. I was inside the alien ship and close to it. I didn't try to destroy it and I didn't take or damage anything while we were there. I think it trusts me."

"It *trusts* you," said General Compton with a not-so-subtle hint at sarcasm. It was clear that the secretary of defense didn't believe in trusting the aliens or vice versa.

"Yes, that's what I believe," replied Chris.

"What about Yuan Xiaoming? Didn't the Artifact trust him? He was with you every step of the way and yet he didn't get the personal invitation to Methonē," General Compton stated, giving every possible verbal and nonverbal clue that he didn't believe Chris's story.

"If you are asking me why he didn't also receive the invitation, then I must say I have no idea," said Chris.

"Dr. Holt. Do you trust Yuan Xiaoming?" asked Yoshi.

"Yes. Yes, I do. He and I had a chance to get to know each other fairly well on the return trip and based on that, and the EVA time we had together, I'd say we can trust him."

Yoshi leaned back in this chair, picked up what appeared to be a gin and tonic, and looked expectantly at Chris. After pausing, he said, "Dr. Holt, Yuan Xiaoming is probably what you would call the Chinese equivalent of a renaissance man. He's brilliant, speaks multiple languages fluently and mostly without an accent. He has two Ph.D.s—one in Chemistry and the other in Art History of all things. From genetic analysis, we're fairly sure he's one of the many genetically modified Chinese test-tube babies that have now risen in the ranks within the Chinese leadership and military. A perfect physical specimen. In addition to being a taikonaut with multiple space missions under his belt, he is a colonel in the Chinese Intelligence Agency."

"My opinion stands," said Chris. He had been starting to like the Chinese taikonaut and thought they might become friends. The news caused him to feel a deep sense of self-doubt about his budding friendship with Yuan and his own ability to read people. But Chris knew better than to allow his outward appearance to betray what was going on inside his head and he certainly knew better than to backtrack in front of the president and his staff. Chris was too proud to admit he might have made a mistake in judgement.

General Compton replied, "We don't trust him. Nor do we trust the asinine decision by our European colleagues to have Dr. Janhunen rejoin you on the trip to Saturn. We read your logs and those of Colonel Rogers-White, who we *do* trust, by the way. Both of you recommended against including him in the Saturn mission team but the Europeans insisted. Janhunen is a known quantity. A known risk. Xiaoming is completely unknown and we're stuck with him. That's why you are here today." After speaking, Compton looked alternatingly at the faces of those in their small group before settling his gaze back upon President Kremic.

Kremic allowed the pause to linger and then replied, "Chris, we don't want you to be in the dark. That's why we're telling you this. Whatever is out there will change the course of human history and we need to be ahead of the wave when it hits. We need to be riding it. This thing, whatever it is and whatever its intentions may be, personally asked you to visit it. It gave us the knowhow to build a ship to get you there and you're going. Soon. And even though we aren't at war with China and they are our allies on this, we don't trust them. You need to know that Colonel Rogers-White is aware of Yuan's status as a spy and she has strict instructions to act accordingly if something arises that may give the Chinese an edge over us in obtaining new knowledge and technology from the Artifact. We cannot allow that to happen."

Chris suspected he knew what "act accordingly" meant, but he wasn't about to ask. Instead, his response to President Kremic was a simple, "I understand."

"No, Dr. Holt, I don't believe you do understand," said Yoshi, raising his intensity level and volume as he spoke. "Someone leaked the design data for the fusion drive and your destination to the Indians who are now in the middle of building their own ship. We don't know how they got the information, but they got it. And they got it not too long after you returned home. I don't know why the Chinese would be stupid enough to give the design data to the Indians, but my sources tell me that's a distinct possibility. We're trying to run down the source of the leak."

"When will they be able to launch? They've got to be significantly behind us, right?" asked Chris.

"They are behind by at least three to four months. You should be able to reach Saturn and have your mission complete before they get off the ground," answered Kremic.

"What about the Caliphate? You aren't going to tell me they have a missile system capable of reaching Saturn, are you?" Chris was now feeling the heat of being in a discussion with the "A+ Team"— something he simply wasn't used to. He was used to being the smartest person in the room and these three were clearly at least as intelligent as he, if not more so. He didn't like the feeling . . .

"No, they don't have anything even close to being capable of going that distance. But that doesn't mean we count them out. We've had chatter about some sort of good old-fashioned terrorist event being planned in connection with the Artifact, but so far, we do not have anything concrete. Damned that whole Quantum Computer Network anyway. We should have shut it down before it got started. That 'many worlds' parallel processing encryption shit has virtually shut down our ability to gather useful intelligence." Yoshi was clearly annoyed, and at more than just the topic at hand. Chris began to wonder how these people slept at night.

"Don't worry about the Caliphate or the Indians," said Kremic. "We need you to watch Xiaoming and Janhunen. And we need you to bring home to the USA whatever you find. This isn't the time to be thinking about what's best for the human race and all that goody-good bullshit. If our partners believed that, then they wouldn't have given us spies as team members. Do you understand me?"

"Yes, sir. I think I do." Though Chris didn't like it one little bit, it was difficult to argue with them now that he knew that so-called new friend was actually a Chinese spy. Worse still, Chris was angry. He was angry that his new friend wasn't really his friend, but a spy who was using him. Angry because he thought he might have a friend, a real friend, and now he didn't.

CHAPTER 20

Space Resources Corporation ran a shuttle from its Nevada spaceport to its comet mining facility every two months, carrying supplies and a replacement shift of miners and support personnel. In total, five workers rode the reusable shuttle to the comet on the way up and another five, those who had completed their contracts, rode it back down again. It was just about as routine as a commercial space launch could get and they had been running it for years. Thanks to robotics and automation, safely operating a cis-lunar mining and ice processing facility didn't require many people, which saved consumables and, of course, money. People and the supplies required to keep them alive were still the single biggest expense for the now well-established space mining company. Frequent astronaut miner rotations were the key to keeping productivity high. Space might sound glamorous, but, like on Earth, the life of a miner, even a space miner, was anything but glamorous. They worked long, hard and very dangerous hours and when their tour was complete many never came back. Those who did return tended to play hard between tours—they played very hard.

The five miners were all experienced. For three, this was their second two-month tour; one was on her third tour and one was beginning his fifth. They all knew the launch drill. Put on the pressure suits, board the shuttle, sit and wait for at least two hours before launch, get into space and watch half your new colleagues puke their guts out as they grew accustomed to zero gravity, make the two-day journey to the comet, board it and then get to work. Tending to the automated drilling and processing machines sounded easy, but it wasn't. Something was always breaking down and in need of repair. That's where the real, live astronaut miners earned their keep—performing repairs impossible for any automated system to even try. At least for now.

Comet Seeley was making the shareholders of Space Resources Corporation, in a word, rich. The market for refueling spacecraft in high Earth orbit and around the Moon was booming. Once the economic models showed that it was far less expensive to reuse and refuel rockets in space instead of bringing fully fueled new ones to space for every mission and application, then the investments by the early adopters and pioneers of asteroid mining paid off. They were poised to capitalize on this new space marketplace by the virtue of having been among the first and best-positioned to sell a reliable source of fuel. Usually that fuel was cryogenic hydrogen and oxygen created by passing an electrical current through water from the ice making up the bulk of the comet's mass. The hydrogen and oxygen were captured and kept in a liquid state by keeping them extremely cold.

Though the miners weren't making nearly as much money as the CEO and the shareholders, they were very well paid for doing their jobs. After all, they were mining ice in deep space without gravity or air, and in extreme temperatures, all while being bathed in solar and galactic cosmic rays, which was most likely increasing their chances of getting cancer before their sixtieth birthdays. The money was so good that thousands of applicants were turned down for these jobs each year. There are not many Earth-based mining jobs that have a waiting list.

Given the demand for the jobs and the meticulous screening process that went into hiring any and all personnel stationed at the Comet Seeley mining station, it was just short of amazing that one of the returning miners was actually a Caliphate sympathizer—a sleeper agent.

Ehtisham Ahmad was Malaysian by birth and British by citizenship. He'd grown up extremely poor and was headed for trouble with the law. To feed himself and his family he had taken to stealing, burglary and even robbery. He was arrested twice before the age of sixteen and was in the middle of his first armed robbery when his co-criminal "friend" told him to pull the trigger and kill the man they were robbing so there would be no witnesses. Ehtisham began to pull the trigger, but as his finger tightened against the trigger that would have sent a bullet through the man's brain—a man who just happened to walk down the wrong alley at the wrong time—his friend told him to stop. And, to Ehtisham's great surprise, the man they were robbing stood up and greeted his friend by name, whereupon they both turned toward Ehtisham and told him he was destined to do great and glorious deeds for Allah. It had been a test. He passed, and so began the terrorist training that had led him to working far away from Earth on a space-based mining colony under an assumed identity, waiting to be called to do service for Allah and the Caliphate. He didn't quite understand why it was important for the Caliphate to have agents at a deep-space mining colony, but his role was not to question why. He was called to be obedient. And his time for action had finally arrived. Ehtisham Ahmad was being asked to martyr himself by damaging or destroying the space mining operation on Comet Seeley.

Two days after arriving at the comet, Ehtisham was sent out to repair the cryocooler that kept the newly formed hydrogen cold enough to be stored as a liquid. The cryocoolers had to keep the hydrogen at a temperature below minus 423 degrees or it would simply boil away, carrying away some of the company's profit with each gram. A control circuit in the cryocooler was giving temperature readings that were inconsistent, making it unreliable and in need of replacement.

Modern commercial spacesuits didn't require the extensive pre-breathing time that the older units required, so Ehtisham quickly donned his suit and helmet, walked through the safety checklist with his partner, Cleris Long, who was there to make sure he didn't make any stupid mistakes. It had been, after all, several months since Ehtisham's last tour at the colony and this was his first solo spacewalk since that time. Had he had made any one of many common mistakes, then Cleris might have tried to help and discovered the small bomb that had replaced two of the many highly specialized repair tools in his EVA kit. Ehtisham wasn't going out to repair the malfunctioning cryocooler sensor; he was going to make sure there was no way Space Resources Corporation could mine and capture enough hydrogen to provide fuel for one of its newest customers. Ehtisham didn't know that the American-European-Chinese fusion ship was the customer, and he probably wouldn't have cared. "I don't pay attention to the news or politics," he was fond of saying. Reconciling the existence of an alien species with his religion would not be high on his list of things to do. He simply didn't care. His was to do the bidding of the Caliphate.

The EVA went well enough with Ehtisham taking the well-worn path between the airlock and the enormous composite tanks that were attached to the comet just to one side of the drill that was bringing forth the ice from deep within it. One tank contained hydrogen, the other contained oxygen—the elemental byproducts of splitting water into its constituent molecules. On the other side was the water electrolysis facility with its gigantic solar panels extending from a central tower rising several tens of meters about the surface. Comet Seeley was well out and away from Earth, so there was no shadow regularly preventing useful solar power from being generated by solar arrays there. Continuous sunlight meant continuous electric power as well as continuous mining and processing operations. Ehtisham's tether was attached to the cable that ran along the path and Ehtisham had to remind himself to not try to walk. The comet's mass was simply too low to enable walking—so pulling oneself along the rope, floating, was the general order of the day. Every day.

Ehtisham arrived at the cryocooler and began the process of removing the cover to access the faulty processor board for replacement. The repair went according to plan; he had done this particular job before and trained for it many times using the virtual reality simulations that all prospective miners had to complete before being allowed into space. This time, however, Ehtisham placed his small bomb next to the newly replaced board before closing the panel and certifying the cryocooler ready to be restarted. The bomb's timer was set to reach zero in ten hours. It was going to be a very interesting night at the mining colony.

"Ehtisham? We're getting an odd reading from the mass flow meter out of the cryocooler. It looks like there is some sort of electromagnetic interference that wasn't there before. Were there any issues replacing the processor?" asked Cleris.

Ehtisham's mind raced. The bomb and the timer were apparently not well-shielded and producing some sort of electronic noise. He couldn't afford to be discovered before the damage was done. He began to think of contingency plans.

"No, it appears to be operating just fine. Perhaps there is a sensor error?"

"I don't believe the problem is with the sensor. The noise began just as you finished working on it. Did you bump something?"

Ehtisham began thinking about martyrdom. If this line of conversation kept up, or, worse yet, if he were ordered to return to the airlock and another crew was to be sent out to investigate, then he might have no other choice than to detonate the bomb now. He began to sweat. It was one thing to contemplate setting off a bomb and watching the aftermath from a safe distance away. It was quite another thing to think about blowing oneself up.

"Let me check to make sure everything is properly seated and connected. Sometimes a poor connection can cause interference." He carefully nudged each of the components he had just installed, hoping that the explanation he had just provided would prove believable.

"Ah! Whatever you just did seemed to fix most of the problem. There's still a little noise, but not nearly as much as before. Thanks for checking. You may have just saved someone from having to take another EVA to check it out," said Cleris.

Ehtisham's return to the airlock was uneventful. He replaced his spacesuit and signed out, taking his required post-EVA break in the mining colony's only bar. Drinking was an indiscretion he allowed himself, convinced that the other actions he was taking in the name of his religion would earn him paradise.

Exactly ten hours later, the timer reached zero and the graphene-encased explosive detonated just as it was supposed to do. Without air, more specifically, without the oxygen in the air, there was no immediate fire. The camera monitoring the facility captured a momentary flash and then what appeared to be a massive, explosive decompression of the hydrogen storage tank. Being a composite material, it didn't just rupture near where the bomb went off like might have been the case with older and heavier aluminum tanks. Instead, it rapidly peeled apart like a banana in the hands of a starving chimpanzee. Tiny pieces of the carbon composite tank were accelerated to high speeds by the expanding hydrogen gas, producing a shrapnel cloud that any bomb maker would have envied.

The tower supporting the solar arrays was the next visible victim as hundreds of these shards tore through the support structure at the tower's base, causing it to sever. Earth-based observers might have expected the tower to topple to the ground but the comet's gravity wasn't strong enough for that. Instead, the tower was blown sideways as it recoiled from the shrapnel impacts and then it went essentially "airborne" for several hundred meters until the gentle pull of what gravity the comet *did* have pulled it back to the surface. Shrapnel also penetrated the tank storing liquid oxygen, creating another equally impressive explosive decompression.

It was indeed a most interesting night at the mining colony.

CHAPTER 21

When Chris entered the briefing room, he noticed immediately that something was wrong. Instead of the usual mixture of jovial banter and deep discussion that preceded the daily briefings, there was instead silence. Chris could tell by looking at those in the room that they were accessing their corneal implants and reacting to what they were seeing. He had intentionally kept his off until arriving at work, as he often did, because he believed that having it on and sending him alerts, ads and general "junk mail" every waking moment was a serious distraction. He quickly activated his implants and requested the feed that had been set up explicitly for members of the Saturn team.

He was immediately shocked by the scenes of devastation coming from the Space Resources Corporation's mine at Comet Seeley. The robotic free-flying camera captured a picture of the damage. The hydrogen tank looked like an egg that had been dropped on the floor. The oxygen tank was also severely damaged, but the damage was not nearly as extensive. Chris could also see the remains of the power tower off in the distance, the spindly base of the tower the only reminder of where it had once stood.

Miraculously, the feed said that no one had died in the accident. Given that Space Resources Corporation was his employer, he was glad to learn that there were no fatalities. He knew that his boss, Jim Moorman, was likely having fits seeing his investment blown to pieces. He also knew that this event was going to adversely impact the mission to Saturn. Space Resources Corporation was in the mission plan to provide all of the fuel for the trip to Saturn and back—with that fuel coming from the mining operation on Seeley.

"Okay people, listen up," said Foy, who had come into the room unnoticed by Chris. "You've seen the news. Our fuel source isn't going to be able to deliver and we need a Plan B."

"Do they know what caused the accident?" asked the Chinese Team Lead.

"It was not an accident. The forensics team ruled that out as soon as they saw the video feed. A segment of the cryocooler exploded, setting off the chain reaction you saw, leading to destruction of the mining facility and any hope we have of getting fuel from Space Resources. Their best guess is that it was a bomb."

"There aren't many people working at the mine. Do they have any idea who might be responsible?" asked Chris.

"Yes, a technician worked on that very control panel section just hours before the explosion. He's under house arrest until they can get a shuttle to bring him back home for more *effective* questioning. I'll pass along whatever we learn as soon as we learn it. In the meantime, we need a Plan B for getting the fuel we need. Everything else is second priority. Each team should check with your people back home to see if they have any ideas. I want an update in two hours. Each team lead is to pitch at least one idea for how to get the fuel where we need it when we need it—without too much of a delay. Now get busy."

The man in the Western style suit couldn't have been more pleased if he'd been personally responsible for the mangled mess that was coming across the news feeds from Space Resources Corporation's now-defunct mining operation on Comet Seeley. For a brief moment, he considered concocting a story that would allow him to take credit for the disaster that had put his beloved India back in the race to unlock the secret of what was waiting out at Saturn. He discarded the idea when he realized that he was already responsible for putting India back in the race by his having arranged the theft of the alien's fusion propulsion system plans. The American-led team had had what seemed like an insurmountable lead, but now they were almost certainly facing several months' delay. He hoped the delay was going to be enough for India's ship to launch first.

❈ ❈ ❈

The Caliph learned that Jarir Hassan's plan was successful while he was at home being bathed by his two favorite and very nubile wives who subsequently helped him celebrate in some very creative and innovative ways—all without leaving the bath. *Another perk of being the Caliph*, he thought.

Afterward, while his wives were helping him dress for the day, the Caliph wondered if the Americans would retaliate once they discovered that this act of terrorism originated from the Caliphate. He had no doubt that they would figure it out; it was just a question of when and how they would react. He knew their retaliation likely wouldn't be by overt military action. After all, the Caliphate was a nuclear power and neither the Americans, Europeans nor Chinese were eager to begin nuclear war. No, retaliation would likely be via some sort of covert operation, possibly targeting him or his family. It was time to increase overall security.

Each of the three teams had twenty minutes to pitch their idea to Foy and it didn't take him long to make a decision. After the last pitch, he called everyone back together in the main conference room to announce the results.

"Okay, people. There is a plan that only adds a few months to the schedule," said Foy, getting everyone's attention. As usual, Foy's extra-large shirt had come untucked from his pants and had one too many buttons open at the collar. That, and the catsup stain on his pants only served to confirm that he, and the rest of this team, had been working long, intense hours without breaks.

"I want to thank all of the teams for your brainstorming. I must say that some of your ideas were mundane, low risk and hence totally unacceptable from a schedule point of view. Some ideas were aggressive and on the outlandish side, making them unacceptable from a risk standpoint. But one idea makes a great deal of sense, has a minimal schedule impact and might work. We'll carry it as the baseline until something better comes along."

"Are you going to tell us the idea or are you intentionally trying to be cryptic?" asked Jayla Epperson, a member of Chris's brainstorming team.

"I'm getting there. We were buying the Space Resources Corporation's tanks and fuel because they were the right size, could be integrated into the ship in two pieces—one tank for the trip out and one for the trip back. Given the amount of fuel required, there is simply no way to launch a single tank from out of the Earth's gravity well. We originally looked at launching several smaller tanks from Earth and ganging them together along the ship's truss. While this will certainly work, it makes for an integration nightmare and we would have to redesign the ship's structure to contain that many small tanks.

"Instead, we're going to buy and launch the two big, empty cryogenic fuel storage tanks and integrate them onto the truss as originally planned. We're then going to launch several, smaller cargo tankers that will transfer the liquid hydrogen to the ship once they reach lunar orbit. It's a more expensive approach, but it doesn't require us to redesign the ship. And if we lose any of the fuel tankers, we can simply launch another until the tanks are full.

"I'm going to take this plan up the chain while you start putting the details together. Contact me if you find a major 'gotcha' that will keep it from working. Otherwise, make it happen and make it happen quickly. Our best intelligence says the Indians are moving to catch up with us and this delay may give them the time they need . . ."

Chapter iv

The Observer gateway ship arrived in the outermost region of the stellar system just under one hundred years after the first artificially produced electromagnetic radiation, a tell-tale sign of an emerging technological civilization, was detected from there. The massive gateway, capable of traveling between the stars for centuries or millennia, was powered and propelled by antimatter-catalyzed fusion engines which were now powering down. As the ship tweaked its orbit around the system's K-Class star so as to align itself with the nearest transfer station, it sent forth three robotic probes toward the planets in the inner part of the system where the electromagnetic radiation had originated.

The crew of the gateway ship was not optimistic. As they were traveling toward the orange star that they knew contained at least two terrestrial planets and three gas giants, the signals that had caused such excitement on Homeworld abruptly ceased. That was twenty years before their arrival in the system and the artificial intelligence that ran the ship did not awaken any of the crew to inform them until they arrived, as planned. The AI knew that there was no practical value in awakening the crew with the news because there was absolutely nothing they could do about it and the protocols required that they continue to the destination regardless. Despite the loss of signals and what that likely meant, the crew followed procedure and began doing what they could to identify the source of the now-silent radio signals and determine if there was anything that could be done to protect the race that had created them.

While the probes flew inward on their two-week journey to the second planet of the system, the crew of the gateway ship activated their transfer station and began taking on supplies. They also began searching for signs of the Destroyers and any signs that they, too, had discovered the sentients of the system. So far, all the searches were negative. As far as the crew could tell, they were alone in the outer reaches of this small stellar system in the galaxy's spiral arm. That, anyway, was encouraging. If the Destroyers were not here and had not been here previously, then there was hope.

The first probe, which was about the same size as a school bus, entered orbit around the planet just as the parent star was rising on the eastern side of one of its two continents; each continent was surrounded by a vast ocean. Like Homeworld and most of the other worlds where sentient life had arisen in the galaxy, it was a water world. Onboard instruments measured the composition of the atmosphere, cataloging the data for future scientific research: sixty-five percent nitrogen, twenty-five percent oxygen and trace gasses, including argon and krypton. Again, the composition was similar to other life-bearing worlds encountered throughout the galaxy.

The probe did see encouraging signs: the oceans were filled with organic life, mostly plants but with a few species of swimming creatures that resembled terrestrial fish scattered throughout. As the probe flew over the landmass of the first continent, the second probe entered the atmosphere and began a similar survey near the other one. It became clear to the AIs controlling the probes that whatever civilization had once inhabited this world was no more. Large areas scattered across both continents contained the ruined remains of what were once cities, now little more than radioactive craters filled with the husks of what once might have been great buildings and other structures. Radiation levels were still remarkably high, making future close inspection by the crew at the gateway impossible.

The second probe found that the craters on the continent it was surveying were much more deadly than those found by the first probe on the other continent. Whoever had destroyed these sentients had done so with more malice than just what could be inflicted by the devastating explosion of a fusion bomb. No, whoever was responsible had been much more insidious: they had used nuclear weapons impregnated with cobalt. As the bombs exploded, a dangerous and highly radioactive isotope of cobalt was formed, cobalt-60, which spread far and wide, contaminating the surrounding areas and, thanks to its relatively long half-life, making them deadly for an extended period of time—far beyond what might be practical for any initial survivors to wait out in shelters. Those who might have survived the initial onslaught would emerge into a poisoned world and quickly succumb.

And it appeared that whole populations of sentients on both continents *had* succumbed. There was no sign of intelligent life on either continent, and little animal life whatsoever. What nature had taken billions of years to produce was wiped out in an orgy of destruction that they had apparently rained down upon themselves. There was no sign of Destroyer activity near the planet or anywhere near the stellar system. The inhabitants had done the Destroyers' job for them.

The third probe inspected the first and third planets of the system, searching for any survivors that might have sought refuge there from the destruction of their home world. A civilization capable of making fusion bombs had the capability to also travel through space on at least a limited basis. Perhaps some had sought refuge on another planet and survived the conflagration.

On the third planet, the probe found several robotic spacecraft orbiting, long since inactive, and one derelict robotic rover on the surface. All were easily found by searching for the tell-tale neutrino emissions that characterize spacecraft powered by the heat produced when plutonium decays in an onboard power pack. The sentients of this system had begun traveling through space, but they had not yet reached the point where they could send themselves beyond their home planet, only their robots. This lack of capability, combined with their inability to control their self-destructive instincts, had doomed them as a species.

The news was relayed to the gateway ship as the probes completed their survey of the inner solar system and prepared for their two-week journey back. Once there, they would be powered down until they were needed again to inspect some as-yet unidentified stellar system in the hope of finding, and potentially saving, another sentient species from both themselves and from the Destroyers. The universe was not kind to life, and life seemed to all-too-often be unkind to its own existence. This, combined with the relentless Destroyers, made the work of this crew, and others like it, challenging and nearly impossible. But they had to continue trying; it was imperative.

CHAPTER 22

They were three days into their mission aboard the fastest ship ever flown by humans. *Daedalus* was a smaller version of the interstellar ship conceptualized by the British Interplanetary Society back in the 1970s, but was huge nonetheless. Resembling the old International Space Station due to its long, spindly truss, the ship was the same length as two American football fields. At one end was the Chinese habitat that housed the five-person international crew that was on its way to see what the alien Artifact was so eager for them to find orbiting Saturn. Docked to the habitat was the lander that would take up to four of the crew to Saturn's moon, Methonē. Just behind the habitat, also docked to it for easy access, were the two logistic modules that contained all the consumables they would need to get to Saturn and safely home again. Next came the fuel tanks and the business end of the vehicle, the compact fusion power supply and propulsion system. Without the extremely efficient and energetic fusion drive, making the trip to Methonē would take years instead of months.

It was only Chris's second trip into space and he was elated at the thought of going *where no man has gone before* using a space drive designed by aliens, no less. The crew was a subset of the combined one that returned to Earth after visiting the Artifact. The politicians had readily agreed to have the same people with experience exploring the Artifact near Earth make the second journey—especially since one of them had been specifically invited.

Robyn was again the mission commander, a position that Chris understood the Chinese supported. She was in top form, as usual, setting a personal physical exercise regimen that was impossible for non-military types like himself to emulate. Chris's opinion of her was still high—he considered her, in her own military way, to be his intellectual equal even though she didn't have the academic degree that was usually his gauge of merit.

The Chinese agreed to support Robyn as mission commander if they received two slots among the crew: one was Yuan Xiaoming. Even though Chris now knew he was a spy, and a fairly highly placed spy, it was nearly impossible for him to treat Yuan any differently than before he knew this not-so-small amount of background information. Chris just liked him and they were able to build a rapport that he had a considerable amount of trouble otherwise finding in his personal or professional life. There were times Chris deliberately tried to forget that Yuan was a spy so as to not ruin an otherwise engaging conversation. The other slot went to Dr. Jing Ye, an exobiologist from the Harbin Institute of Technology. Dr. Ye was widely published, extremely well respected in the field, and pleasant to be around in both appearance and personality. She was a psychologically perfect choice of personality type with whom to be trapped in a spacecraft for the better part of two years. Chris's briefing on her made no mention of any political or espionage connections.

And, for reasons Chris could not fathom, the Europeans again insisted that Juhani Janhunen be part of the crew. Janhunen had already increased his anti-sociability rating by hitting on Dr. Ye within a day of their departure. She quickly put him in his place; no one knew exactly what she said, but it was effective. Juhani and Chris had not yet had any direct conflicts, but Chris knew that they would be inevitable. Fortunately, the habitat was large enough to allow the five-person crew the opportunity to find quiet locations just about any time they needed them. Chris felt the need every time he completed a conversation with Janhunen.

Chris was on the upper deck doing his daily two-hour exercise routine—struggling to complete the routine would be more accurate—when he was startled out of his concentration (and misery) by Robyn. She came up through the open hatchway and floated toward him silently—which was easy to do in the weightlessness and large volume within the habitat.

"I'm sorry to startle you," said Robyn. She had cut her hair shorter for this mission than the last, and it was a lot less distracting to her, and to the rest of the crew, than her previous style. Long hair and zero gravity didn't go together well. The new look also highlighted her high cheekbones and her eyes.

"Oh, that's okay. You know me and exercise. I welcome an interruption any time you want to give me one."

"Well, this you need to hear. The rest of us were in the galley when we got the news that India launched their ship. They're calling it the *Veer* in honor of the highest military award one can achieve in the Indian Army, the *Param Veer Chakra*. Since they're using plans for our fusion drive, and not something more advanced, we have a good idea of their top speed and can assume they'll not catch up or pass us. We'll still beat them to Methonē, but only by a few days."

"We knew that was coming, but it's still a bitch. I'd like to have more time to figure things out before we get company, particularly company that may not be as friendly as our Chinese friends were," said Chris.

"Agreed, but, unfortunately, that's not all."

"What else?"

"There was an assassination attempt on the Caliph. A bomb under the roadway in Baghdad went off just as his motorcade was passing over it. Several people were killed, including some of his family."

"Did they get the Caliph?"

"No. And his response was ominous. Something about it being time to strike back at the godless nations and some saber rattling toward India as well as Washington and Beijing. The military is at high alert."

"Shit. But at least the problem isn't with India."

"Well," Robyn paused and then continued, "India has threatened war if we get to Methonē ahead of their crew and shut them out of whatever dialog we have with the aliens there, if any."

"That all came in today's morning update?" asked Chris.

"I'm afraid so," said Robyn.

"It almost makes me wish I hadn't quit exercising . . ."

"The good news is that Beijing issued a statement in support of Washington and against India. It was more of a warning than a statement. They said something about 'retribution' should any of their allies be attacked. It might be the first time since the war that China said anything positive about an American or European political position. One for the history books."

"Just like this mission," replied Chris.

"Just like this mission," Robyn said as she pushed off from the floor and back toward the hatch.

Chris took a deep breath and started to get himself back into the mindset of exercising. He was thankful Robyn came by because it allowed him a physical break and a break in the alone time. The only places on the ship more isolated than the exercise area were the bathroom and the sleeping cubbies, and Chris was increasingly aware of how much he didn't like being alone all the time. But he had been that way all his life, why should that change now?

Yuan was troubled. He'd just heard the news about the Indian launch and the warning to him and this crew about their upcoming encounter with whatever awaited them at Methonē. He'd been given strict orders to not allow *anyone* to share *anything* with the Indians. *Period.* He was explicitly told that he was to find a way to destroy the Indian ship, kill everyone on board the *Daedalus* and scuttle the ship if that was what it took to keep India from gaining knowledge from the alien encounter. No debate. No equivocation. Relations between China and India had been deteriorating for years with cross-border skirmishes increasing in frequency and ferocity. Add in a few extremist terrorist attacks like the one last year in the Aksai Chin region that resulted in over fifteen hundred deaths and you got a recipe for a broader war.

In addition to being troubled, Yuan felt guilty. He had gotten to know this crew. He was sure that they were truly on a mission of exploration without the explicit intent of gaining the upper hand on anyone. The Americans and Europeans readily welcomed the Chinese partnership on this second encounter flight, unlike the first one where they'd been friendly competitors. He and Jing were being treated like long-separated cousins at a family reunion. He was accustomed to gaining others' confidence and using that to his advantage. He'd been trained to get information and relay it to his masters in Beijing. But, on this mission, passing along intelligence felt like stealing. Worse than that, it felt like stealing something from your parents, or, more accurately, the human race—and doing so came with a huge helping of guilt. But he also knew what would happen if India somehow gained the upper hand—war and death. And he could not allow that to happen.

"What do you think of the news from India?" Yuan's melancholy was interrupted by the ever-pestiferous Juhani Janhunen who apparently couldn't bear to see a member of the crew have any time sitting in solitude. Janhunen looked at him expectantly.

"I think it is bad news for the world. India was not invited by the Artifact and I am sure their mission is not peaceful. In fact, I believe their presence will put us in grave danger."

"My thoughts exactly. And given the collegial atmosphere among our colleagues, I'm not sure they appreciate the seriousness of what this means. Even our commander doesn't seem to be too perturbed by the news. You and I are of the same mind and we need to be thinking about what we should do if it looks like our mission is in jeopardy."

Yuan's mind was racing. *Did the European know his true status? Worse yet, did Janhunen know the very orders he was just contemplating?*

"I don't know what you mean," Yuan replied carefully, raising his left eyebrow.

"I'm sure you do. We need to come up with a plan to eliminate the Indians, or at least keep them away from whatever it is we're going to visit. We simply cannot risk them getting their hands on any advanced technology from the alien."

"We have plenty of time to think about that and I'm sure our governments back home will tell us what to do under any circumstances that may arise. You should be talking to Colonel Rogers-White instead of me."

"No, I believe I'm talking to the right person. But I'll play that game. It can wait for now. But I was there at the Artifact and saw how Robyn was all-too-willing to ignore command authority to partner with you in order to avoid conflict. I'm concerned that she might do the very same thing when it comes to the Indians."

Yuan simply stared at Janhunen until he backed away and pushed off toward the head.

Damn! Yuan thought. *I wish he hadn't said that.*

CHAPTER 23

Space exploration was months of boredom punctuated by moments of extreme excitement and discovery, Chris recalled he'd been thinking the very same thought on the day his team discovered the Artifact. Seven long months into their flight to Methonē, it occurred to him again. It was extremely boring being trapped in this tin can with the very same four people day after day, week after week, and now month after month. How many times did he need to hear about Yuan's family? Or Jing's research trips to Antarctica? There are only so many conversations one can have without something new happening to trigger novelty in the discussions to make them interesting. Except for those he had with Robyn; conversations with her were usually more interesting than most and he relished them. Lately, though, he was avoiding engaging in conversations with Robyn to not give her the wrong idea and make her think he was coming on to her. This lack of engagement with her, of course, made his interactions with the others all the more mundane. Unfortunately, Chris didn't much like the excitement that intruded on their boredom this time. The excitement wasn't coming from deep space, but from back home.

He was keeping up with the news: elections in various parts of Europe and Africa, the new American administration taking power after their own recent elections, famine in South America and new flooding throughout Southeast Asia as the oceans continued their inexorable rise from the melting of the Greenland ice sheet. It was the news from along the Chinese and Indian border that shook them from their solitude and sense of detachment. Someone exploded a "dirty bomb" in Ngari

Prefecture, part of the Aksai Chin area of China that India and China have both been claiming as their own for more than a hundred years. The initial blast killed less than a dozen, but tens of thousands of people were exposed to mid-level radioactive waste and many more were expected to become seriously ill and die over the next several weeks. China blamed Indian-backed separatists and, in response, launched a missile strike on an Indian military encampment just on the other side of the disputed border, killing at least a hundred. All of this transpired while the crew of the *Daedalus* slept the night before.

Chris and his shipmates were gathered together in the galley, watching the newscast using their corneal implants—in silence. Given their distance from Earth, the newscast was sent their way nearly an hour before. To an outside observer, the crew appeared to be almost catatonic, staring into the distance, and lost in their own viewing of the events from home. The news described the latest developments, which included very disturbing images of the dead and dying on both sides of the border. Both countries announced that their military forces were on high alert and more than one hotheaded politician was on screen making comments about their respective nuclear deterrents. To Chris, it sounded like a story enacted just thirty years previously when China and the USA nearly started World War Three over Taiwan and the Senkaku Islands. Before that drama was over, a nuclear bomb devastated a city in South Korea and North Korea was wiped off the map.

When the newscaster began to get repetitive, Robyn asked that everyone shut off the feed.

"All right everyone, listen up. I've got some additional news from Mission Control," said Robyn as she pushed herself up toward the ceiling where she grabbed the handhold she was fond of using when she addressed the crew.

"The news from home isn't good. In my morning brief, they told me that the US and European militaries, even though not directly threatened, are on high alert. The situation could quickly get out of control and no one wants to be caught with their pants down. The Indians have moved their nuclear-armed *Grenadiers* Regiment near the Chinese border and no one knows how they will respond if they are attacked. God only knows what the Caliphate might do with tensions so high."

"What does this mean for us?" asked Janhunen.

"Well, that's where this all gets interesting. As you know, the Indians will arrive about three days after us and the smart people back home think they'll not be very friendly. In fact, their best guess is that the Indians will demand full access and participation in whatever we have going on and will threaten us if we don't comply. We have to assume their ship is armed with at least one nuclear weapon and who knows what else."

"Robyn, I haven't asked, but I think we all need to know how we will respond. Are we similarly armed? I know we had a bomb with us when we went to the Artifact, but do we have one now?" asked Juhani.

"No. We don't," responded Chris. "Given our technological disadvantage, our demonstrated destructive tendencies, and that the alien has been monitoring Earth for many years and apparently never caused any harm, our governments decided it would be best to go unarmed to Methonē." This was something he'd been very vocal about when he was briefing the mission planners after his personal encounter with the Artifact before its destruction. He made his case all the way up to the White House. He looked toward Robyn for her affirmation. He was instead greeted by an intense and unusually sad gaze.

"I'm sorry Chris, but that decision was overruled. The alien Artifact was either incapable or unwilling to defend itself against the Caliphate's missile attack. But, in your own words, the Artifact was very clearly a weapon of war—though apparently a damaged one. It was felt that we couldn't take a similar chance with whatever is out here at Saturn and that we should be prepared for any contingencies. There is a nuclear weapon onboard." Robyn spoke firmly with her eyes focused on Chris.

"Robyn, that's just bullshit. You knew there was a bomb and went along with me thinking there wouldn't be? Was everyone in the chain just lying to me to keep me quiet?" Chris was personally hurt by the news, especially since he had been front and center denying that a bomb was onboard. Robyn had been part of the meetings he had with Foy and everyone else in the chain of command. He thought she was on his side and now he felt embarrassed and betrayed.

"Chris, you did make a convincing case but once the other governments were brought into the discussion, the president made a different decision. We must be prepared for any eventuality with the alien or the Indians. I knew this would be an issue when they told me and I'm sorry."

Janhunen pushed up from his anchoring around the break room table and grabbed an adjacent handhold on the ceiling, giving him the same relevant height perspective as Robyn.

"This was a good decision. The Indian government is about to begin World War Three, their nuclear-armed ship is racing to catch up with us and you would leave us nothing with which to defend ourselves?" Janhunen's voice rose in volume to match the intensity with which he spoke his words. His comments were clearly intended for Chris.

"Juhani, we shouldn't be armed. We are on a peaceful mission of exploration and we aren't going to be the ones to begin a war out here in deep space—with India or a vastly superior alien race. We can hope that our Indian colleagues feel the same way," said Chris.

"Hope? *We can hope?* Dr. Holt, you are a fool. Colonel, you must be prepared to use this weapon." Juhani was now animated, appearing almost zealous.

"Are there any more weapons on board that we don't know about?" asked Chris. His sense of betrayal deepened and he was getting angrier and angrier with each passing moment.

"Yes, in the logistics module. There are side arms, tasers, flash bombs and some grenades. They are in a sealed locker and I'm the only one with the access codes," Robyn said. She looked embarrassed and broke eye contact with Chris, looking instead at Yuan and Jing Ye.

Janhunen looked smug at the news, which made Chris's blood pressure rise even more.

"Robyn, you're in charge and I trust you—I trusted you," Chris said, putting an emphasis on the past tense verb. "But that doesn't mean I have to like it."

CHAPTER 24

Chris, wistfully remembering his childhood encounter with Saturn, could hardly believe he was now in a fusion-powered spacecraft orbiting Saturn and beginning a trajectory maneuver that would take him into orbit around one of its moons. Instead of a tiny eyepiece, Chris and the rest of the crew could see giant Saturn by looking through the ship's only real window. Though the spacecraft design engineers only allowed the crew a one-square-meter viewport, it was more than enough to allow the full disk of the magnificent planet to be fully visible. He felt like he was a boy again and was tempted to again jump for joy, but he restrained himself knowing that any such uncontrolled jump in zero gravity might result in his head hitting something overhead. And that would be embarrassing—especially in front of Robyn. He was still angry with her, but that hadn't changed his deeper emotions. He still liked her and desperately wanted her to like him.

He sensed he was not alone and saw that the Chinese exobiologist, Jing Ye, was now beside him, floating, and holding position using the handhold to the left of the viewport. She, too, appeared mesmerized by the view.

"I never dreamed I would get to see something so beautiful in person," she said in a hushed and reverential tone.

"Neither did I, but I always dreamed of it."

"It's time to get into the acceleration couches. We're fifteen minutes away from the burn that will adjust our orbit and put us near Methonē," Robyn announced over the ship's public address system.

They all knew when the burn was to occur and most of the rest of the crew had already strapped themselves in. Chris was holding on to the current view for as long as he could. Apparently Ye was of a similar mind.

"We'd better go," he said.

"We will still be able to see Saturn once we get there?" asked Ye.

"Absolutely. And the view might even be better. We'll see both Saturn, Methonē and whatever it is that we have been asked out here to see."

"Then let's go," Ye replied, breaking into a smile. Still smiling, she pushed off from the wall under the viewport, doing three somersaults as she bolted toward the area housing the acceleration couches.

The burn was not nearly as dramatic as the one that took them from Earth and toward Saturn. That maneuver pushed them back into their acceleration couches and lasted what seemed like hours, though it had only been a few tens of minutes. This maneuver was shorter and much less forceful.

"It will be several hours before we perform our next burn and actually get near Methonē. I suggest we get some rest," said Robyn as she unbuckled from her couch and pushed off toward the other end of the galley where their personal spaces were located. Everyone nodded assent as they unbuckled, admittedly with varying degrees of enthusiasm, but no disagreement. It had been a long day and no one knew what awaited them at Methonē.

Each member of the crew slept in what looked like a small closet with a curtain over the door. Inside each closet was a sleeping bag mounted to the wall into which they would zip themselves when it was time to sleep. On the wall in front of each sleeping bag were a personal view screen and a few cubbies in which personal belongings could be stored. Chris entered his closet, zipped the curtain closed and looked at the single photograph he had brought with him and stuck to the wall. It was the first image of the alien Artifact captured by his sail craft. The image that had started this amazing journey. He had no idea what they were going to find at Methonē and no idea why the entity within the Artifact wanted him on this mission. Incompetence was not a feeling Chris liked, but he felt it nevertheless. His rest period was not so restful.

※ ※ ※

"My God, would you look at that," said Robyn, voicing the thoughts that Chris and just about everyone else was thinking as they either looked out the viewport or accessed the ship's exterior video feeds via their implants. Before them was again mighty Saturn, but in the foreground, just in the bottom of the rightmost corner of the viewport, was the oddball moon, Methonē. The small oval moon looked completely out of place.

"It does look like an egg," said Jing.

Chris couldn't help but agree. It was a lopsided, white oval shape that made it look like a cosmic egg. It appeared to be completely smooth with no visible craters.

"Now what?" asked Janhunen.

"Now we get as much information as we possibly can and figure out what we're supposed to do here," replied Robyn. "If it will let us, then we'll use the ground-penetrating radar to see what's beneath the surface, do a full spectrum scan of it and then send one of the penetrators to check out the actual surface density. Juhani, keep me posted as the data comes in."

"It is beautiful but deadly out there. The space environmental experts were correct about the radiation environment here. It is extremely intense. We cannot remain for more than a few weeks or else we will get too much exposure, even behind all the added shielding. Days would be better," said Yuan as his eyes darted back and forth, examining data fed directly to his corneal implant.

"With luck, we'll be gone by the time the Indian team arrives. They won't like that. But it might help us avoid direct contact with them. The fuel required for them to abort, capture, and match velocities with us if we're on the return trajectory would be enormous, and they would forego their own chance at exploring Methonē. This could work," said Janhunen.

Chris was gazing out the viewport trying to make sense of what they were seeing when he noticed what looked like small flecks of paint floating near the surface of Methonē at its smaller end. He accessed his implants to use the exterior cameras and zoom in.

"Everyone, there's something happening, check the exterior camera feed," said Chris just after the camera brought what was occurring at the surface into his view. The small flecks he was seeing were actually meter-sized layers of ice floating away from the surface of the tiny moon, reminiscent of the famous photographs of the many small ice chunks floating in the ocean near the breakup of the Antarctic ice sheets.

The density of ice chips being expelled from the surface was increasing, making it look like a cloud forming.

"Can we get closer to the edge where this is happening?" asked Janhunen.

"We can. Since we're really co-orbiting Saturn with Methonē and not in orbit around it, we can maneuver just about anywhere we want relative to it. I just don't want to get too close and have any of those ice chunks hit us," said Robyn.

"The ground-penetrating radar isn't producing much meaningful data. We're getting an ice measurement from very near the surface, but only down to the first half meter or so. Below that is, well, what looks like a perfect reflector. Whatever is below the ice is solid and reflecting just about all the radar signal back out into space," said Janhunen.

In a flash of insight, it all suddenly made sense to Chris. "Now we know why Methonē is the lowest density planet or moon in the solar system. It's not natural. The goddamn moon is a spaceship," said Chris.

"That's leaping to a conclusion," said Janhunen.

"No, I'm looking at the data. We've known since it was discovered back in 2004 that it was the lowest density object in the solar system. Combine that with the fact that the surface is oval and completely smooth and there's an obvious conclusion to reach: it's a shell surrounding something that is essentially hollow. Almost nothing in nature is perfectly smooth and hollow. And, in case you've forgotten, we were sent here by another alien spaceship. We're looking at one huge spaceship or space station."

And if my first telescope had been strong enough, I might have even seen it when I looked through the eyepiece and saw Saturn for the first time . . .

CHAPTER 25

When the debris field created by the ice chunks cleared, a circle of artificial lights was visible on Methonē's surface. From the time Chris first saw the ice sheets coming off the surface until the cloud had dispersed, only two hours had elapsed. It looked like someone had buffed a flat spot on an otherwise perfect chicken egg.

"I believe we know where we need to go," said Chris.

"Then I say we get the lander prepped so we can accept the invitation," said Yuan, sounding both excited and nervous, which was unusual for the otherwise calm Chinese astronaut. Chris couldn't help but think Yuan's otherwise implacable demeanor was all for show, meant to reinforce stereotypes and designed to instill trust in those upon whom he was spying.

"Agreed. As planned, you four will go and I'll remain here to hold down the fort," said Robyn. This had been the operational plan since before launch, but her voice revealed her disappointment at not getting to be part of the expedition. For the first time since they left Earth, perhaps for the first time since Chris met her, Robyn appeared fragile and uncertain.

"And remember, if I give the recall notice, then you are to get out of there as fast as you safely can and get back up here to the ship with me. I'll have departure trajectories running constantly so that we can move as far away as we can, as quickly as possible—if we need to."

The crew had rehearsed for this moment multiple times on their nine-month journey to Saturn and that routine helped them curb their nervousness as they suited up and made sure the lander was fully functioning and ready for departure. All stole repeated glances at Methonē via their corneal implants as they prepped. They were mostly through with the pre-departure checklist when Robyn abruptly called them all back to the galley.

"I just received a high priority message from Mission Control about the situation in Asia and it's not good. Things are spiraling out of control. There was another dirty bomb attack in China, this time in Shanghai. The contamination area is pretty big and they're anticipating tens of thousands of casualties. At about the same time, some actor launched a missile at a Chinese warship in the South China Sea and caught it by surprise, doing considerable damage. While all this was happening, terrorists blew themselves and several dozen people up in San Francisco's Chinatown."

"Was it the Caliphate? Has anyone claimed responsibility?" asked Yuan.

"India is denying any connection and warned China that any additional reprisals, like their missile launch the last time, would be met with extreme force—meaning a possible nuclear response," she replied.

"The world is in chaos and we're out here about to contact an alien that we've already attacked once before. My speech that begins with 'we come in peace' is going to ring rather hollow," said Chris.

"Did they give us any new instructions?" asked Janhunen.

Robyn looked at her hands and then back at the crew. She said, "No. Nothing new. We're just to keep the people back home in the loop on all that's happening out here. Since the speed-of-light time lag is now over an hour, taking moment-to-moment direction from home won't be an option. As we planned, each of you will be streaming video and audio back from your helmets to the ship and I will relay it all back to Earth unedited, but encrypted. Just remember that whatever you say or do will be recorded and visible to God and country. Now, go finish your pre-launch sequence and let's get this show on the road."

Just over thirty minutes later, the lander was on its way to the surface of Methonē. It was small, and since it was designed for operation in low gravity, there were no seats. All four of the astronauts would have been freely floating in the single cabin had it not been for the shoe-like footholds that kept them anchored to the floor. They could at any time remove their feet from the anchors to move around, but none did so. The total interior volume of the lander was small with each person not getting more than half a meter of personal space.

Yuan was piloting. Though the lander was provided by the USA, Yuan had trained extensively to fly it both on the ground before departure and in the simulator during their journey to Saturn.

Given the moon's low density, calling the upcoming maneuver a landing was a misnomer. It was more of a docking procedure. As the four astronauts approached what they presumed to be landing lights activated on their behalf, they noticed that in the very center of the lights there was an iris-shaped opening exactly like the one they saw on the Artifact.

"That looks familiar. Do you see any place we can attach the lander?" asked Chris.

"Nothing for sure, but to the right of the iris appears to be some sort of structure to which we might be able to anchor it. Let's continue in and see what it turns out to be," replied Yuan.

"I don't believe we will need to worry about anchoring to the surface," said Jing abruptly.

"And how do you make that deduction?" asked Janhunen in his usual condescending tone.

"She's correct. I'm having to engage the thrusters more and more to slow our approach and now that I think about it, I'm starting to feel more weight than I might expect. We're flying into a localized gravity field," said Yuan.

"Of course, they've got gravity manipulation! We shouldn't be surprised. If they can harness the extreme energies required for interstellar travel, then it isn't much of a stretch to guess that they can manipulate gravity," said Chris.

"But that's impossible," said Janhunen.

"You can't ignore the evidence. And I suspect this isn't the only thing we're going to find that seems impossible," replied Chris. His excitement level was growing with each passing second.

"More importantly, can we fly into a gravity field in this lander?" asked Juhani. "It's meant to rendezvous with something in near weightlessness, not land on a moon."

"Yes, though we may get a bit uncomfortable standing during take-off and landing. I flew the prototype in Earth-normal gravity several times," said Yuan.

They were all now acutely aware of gravity's return as they inched closer to the snowy white surface. The area near the lights was also white, but instead of appearing soft and fluffy like the ice on the rest of the moon, or what they had previously thought was a moon, the cleared area was a flat white and obviously artificial. Less than five minutes later, the lander was firmly on the surface and unless the gravity field was suddenly turned off, it wasn't going anywhere. The crew took less than fifteen minutes to run through the complete lander checklist before gathering at the door to make their departure.

"I estimate the gravity to be about the same as Earth's moon," said Janhunen.

"I concur. If our hosts had given us Earth normal gravity, these suits would be a huge liability. Trying to explore carrying over two hundred pounds of spacesuit on our backs would, at the least, slow us down. At worst, it could have stopped us cold," Yuan replied.

In addition to their spacesuits, each astronaut had an individualized toolkit. Jing Ye's was designed to facilitate collecting samples and isolating them. She had tools custom designed to allow her to reach, cut, scratch or rub biological samples from a variety of foreseeable locations, separate them for storage, and isolate them from unplanned environmental contamination once they were back aboard the ship. Her kit also contained a small fan for sampling air quality and storing small bits of any atmosphere they may encounter for future study. The whole thing was wired to essentially self-destruct and sterilize everything within it if the proper command code was entered. The self-destruct keypad was designed to be glove-friendly but virtually impossible to activate accidentally. All members of the crew knew the sequence that would activate it, but none envisioned a circumstance that would cause them to have to use it.

Janhunen was the "tool guy." His kit contained picks, pliers, adjustable wrenches, wires of various lengths, fasteners, a host of other gear that he could use to improvise repairs of their spacesuits and, of course, duct tape.

Yuan carried the gear that would enable them to climb or cross just about any surface the planetary geologists back home could imagine, including harnesses, crampons, various slings, webbing, carabiners and pitons. Unknown to the rest of the crew, he also carried a Glock 9mm and two flash grenades. They were smuggled onboard by using some of his sacred "personal items" allowance, which allowed them to escape most of the usual screening procedures.

Chris had the electronic surveillance and detection gear. His gear could find the strength and direction of most sources of electromagnetic radiation, passively scan surfaces to determine their elemental composition, take thermographic images to make temperature maps, and even map rooms behind walls. He was also equipped with a motion sensor that could detect the slightest movements, including breathing, from as much as five hundred feet away. And, of course, all this data was sent real-time back to the lander and relayed to the ship. He also covertly carried one of the tasers, given to him at the last minute by Robyn, "just in case you need to use it on Yuan."

They were as ready as they could be.

"I'll take the lead. Juhani, you bring up the rear. Chris and Jing should be in the middle," said Yuan as they entered the lander's airlock and cycled the door.

After individually climbing down the ladder to the surface, no one uttered words for posterity. They simply gathered as a group as they waited for each person to climb down. None of the group were easily able to take their eyes away from the majesty of Saturn which dominated their view. Once Janhunen was off the ladder, they started walking toward the iris. They were hyper focused on not stumbling and falling as they crossed the mirror-smooth surface. Instead of "one small step for man," anyone listening was hearing rhythmic, steady breathing and an occasional catching of breath.

The group of four astronauts stood on one side of the circular, three-meter-diameter iris, and paused, not sure of what to do next. It looked just like the iris they found on the outside of the Artifact, but about twenty-five percent larger.

Chris, remembering what had opened the door on the Artifact, prepared to use his hammer and knock. But before he could get it from his utility belt, the undulating began. Starting at the middle, the entire iris was soon filled with what looked like a liquid wall, until it wasn't. The iris wall, as they expected, simply vanished. Under the iris was a lighted, circular opening with a gently sloping ramp that descended into the darkness about twenty feet ahead.

"It's another airlock," said Chris.

"That would be my guess also. It looks very similar to what we found on the Artifact," said Yuan.

"We didn't come all this way to stand here and gawk. Let's go," said Chris, anxious to contact whatever awaited them. He began to walk down the ramp. The others fell in line behind him.

As soon as they had crossed about ten feet of ramp, the wall above them reappeared, blocking what little reflected sunlight they were getting from Saturn. They switched on their headlamps and paused, looking up at the now solid wall above them.

"Robyn, do you copy?" asked Yuan, speaking into his radio.

Silence.

"We're on our own. I've lost contact with the ship," said Yuan.

"I'm measuring some sort of gas being pumped into the chamber. And it is increasing in pressure," said Chris, looking at the data coming into his implant from the myriad sensors in or on his toolkit and embedded in his suit. "It's too early to tell much about its composition, but the pressure is definitely rising."

They *were* in an airlock.

After about two minutes, the pathway in front of them was suddenly illuminated as something, or someone, turned on the lights.

CHAPTER 26

Chris, Yuan, Juhani and Jing walked farther along the hallway along the eerily illuminated path. The walls were mostly smooth, with odd grey bumps at varying heights every few feet along the way. Everything seemed to be covered with dust after whatever gas mixture that passed for alien air flooded into the hallway, disturbing it for perhaps the first time in many centuries. Chris tried to ignore the urge to scratch his nose. Feeling the need to scratch an itch while in a spacesuit was about as frustrating as it could get. There was simply no way to do it.

As they entered further into the ship, additional lights ahead of them sprang to life, illuminating the passageway in a pale, orange-tinted glow that seemed to emanate from the floor and ceiling simultaneously. Used to the bright, white lights of their spacecraft, the area appeared surreal.

"They must have evolved under a Class K star. This spectrum is very different than the Sun," said Chris.

"That's a huge leap to make based on the color of the lights, especially since they have been inactive for millennia. Maybe they're just old—and old alien lights glow with an orange or reddish tint," said Juhani. His tone was defensive, even juvenile.

What set him off? thought Chris.

"This is amazing! It would make sense that a species living around a star with a color different than that of the Sun would want to take that with them in their travels," said Jing.

Juhani grunted.

Chris, hoping to change the subject and move on, assumed the front position as they moved slowly along the hallway. He barely took two steps before stopping. The silence was deafening. Both of his implants abruptly stopped working as he crossed some unmarked threshold.

"My implants went dead. The radio too. Does anyone still have an active link?" he asked as he turned around to face his colleagues.

When he saw the blank and expectant looks on their faces, he knew they hadn't heard him. First Jing moved her lips and waved her arms, then Juhani. He heard nothing from either. He didn't know if they, too, had been cut off or if it was only him. He stepped back toward them and his implants came instantly to life.

". . . it. What did you see?" asked Jing. Chris's audio picked up in mid-sentence.

"It looks like we're going to be off the network if we go any further. My radio and both implants stopped working once I crossed here," he said, gesturing toward an unmarked part of the floor.

"Hand signals it is then," said Janhunen.

"Robyn may not have panicked when she lost contact with us, but I suspect our people back on Earth will have. They won't know we're out of touch for over an hour, so they can't tell us not to proceed. We may be back by the time the signal reaches home," said Chris.

"Should one of us remain here?" asked Yuan.

"I think we should stay together. Haven't you watched those horrible horror vids where the explorers enter the alien spaceship, split up and then get eaten because they're easier to kill when they are separated?" Jing said with a smile. "Not that I'd mind terribly if one of us got eaten," she concluded, staring at Juhani.

"These horror vids are not popular viewing where I come from," Yuan replied.

"I agree with Jing, though not because I think we're going to be eaten. It just makes sense for us to stay together. Who knows what we'll encounter in here and we're going to need our collective smarts to deal with it," said Chris.

"All right then, let's go. We're finally at a place where I can contribute and I'm eager to make that happen," replied Jing.

"Since we'll be out of touch by radio, we need to pay extra attention to each other in case we need to communicate. Let's go slow and be deliberate," said Chris.

The four cautiously stepped forward and further into the glowing hallway beyond. Darkness was always just beyond the edge of their vision as the lights came on when they drew near. Chris assumed there was some sort of motion sensor that controlled the lights and they would come on as they approached the darkened section ahead, and then to the next. The walls, floor and ceiling of the hallway appeared to be made from the same glowing material. They were smooth with only the occasional bumps along the way. There were no seams and no signs of any functionality beyond illuminating the hallway.

As he suspected, when they neared the edge of the darkness before them, the next section of the hallway lit up. But instead of extending yet further, the lights ended in a wall with a spherical hemisphere affixed in the middle of it at eye level. Chris and Yuan approached the wall containing the hemisphere while Jing and Juhani remained slightly behind them, assuming the role of watchdogs. Chris moved to stand directly in front of the hemisphere and leaned forward to examine it more closely. The surface was smooth and translucent, reminding him of the Hope Diamond he'd seen in the Smithsonian. He reached out to and placed his hand upon it.

WELCOME.

The voice, if one could call it that, came into Chris's consciousness unlike what his shipmates' voices would have sounded like through his now-silenced network connection. And it was loud. He looked at Yuan and Juhani to see if they, too, had heard the voice and quickly concluded that they had. All had their heads cocked back or to the side. Yuan looked back at Chris and nodded his head in affirmation to his unspoken, or at least unheard, question.

"Who are you?"

I AM THE GUARDIAN. COME.

An ear-piercing sound flooded Chris's awareness, causing him to flinch, close his eyes, and lower his head in pain. The sound lasted for a few seconds and then stopped as suddenly as it had begun. He opened his eyes and saw that he was no longer in the hallway, but standing on a hillside looking into a valley containing what appeared to be a city, or rather, what used to be a city. He was also aware that the lighting was all wrong. It was certainly daytime, though the sky was full of clouds—grey and ominous, looking like those on the leading edge of a hurricane. Everything had an orange tint. Chris felt a chill run down his spine as he realized he was on a distant alien planet. Something of which he had dreamed of all his life.

He looked down at himself and saw that he was naked. He didn't feel cold and the surface beneath his bare feet felt smooth even though he could see a rocky surface. He was alone.

"Hello? Where am I and why am I here?"

Silence.

"Hello? I assume you are responsible for bringing me here and I'd really like to know why."

Whoever or whatever had brought him here wasn't providing any more information, so after making sure he wasn't in any immediate danger, Chris returned his attention to the ruins of the city below.

The city must have once been magnificent. The architecture was very different than any city he'd ever visited, but Chris realized the functional nature of buildings and thoroughfares for transportation must be universal because he was able to look at what remained and tell the difference between what had once been a skyscraper versus some sort of road or mass transit corridor. Only now, most were merely the lifeless skeletons of collapsed or mostly-collapsed buildings with unrecognizable vegetation sprouting across what had once been great avenues and plazas.

As he looked closer, he could see that whatever had happened to destroy the buildings had happened over time. It hadn't been sudden. There were no obvious signs of explosions, fire or anything similar. The entire city looked like it had been abandoned and left to its own devices for nature to reclaim.

"Where is everyone? What happened here?"

Reality shifted and he was now standing in the center of the city amid the decay and long-ago catastrophe that had befallen its denizens. Around him were decaying buildings, what was obviously a road, though not a road made of any material he'd ever seen before. The now-cracked and disintegrating surface was a pale red in color and he could tell from the broken, uneven seams underfoot that there were electrical wires embedded within it. Now that he was closer, the resemblance to Earthly buildings ended. The decrepit structures that rose from the ground around him had openings that could have been doors or windows, but they weren't made for humans. The openings were wider than tall, with the tallest opening visible less than four feet above the red pavement. There were doors, now hanging mostly open and exposing the buildings' interiors to the elements. All that was missing from making it a scene from an apocalyptic TriVid would have been wind howling through the open structures. Instead, Chris heard nothing.

WE DON'T KNOW WHAT BEFELL THE CREATURES THAT BUILT THE CITY. WHEN WE ARRIVED, THIS WAS ALL THAT REMAINED AND THERE WERE MANY CITIES LIKE IT ALL ACROSS THE PLANET. IN NONE DID WE FIND ANY SIGN OF THE BEINGS THAT BUILT THEM.

"Why am I here?"

HAVE PATIENCE. COME.

The ear-piercing sound again caused Chris to recoil in pain. Though he was this time expecting it and had steeled himself to its arrival once he heard the Guardian utter, "come," the pain was no less intense. When it stopped, he saw that he was still naked, only this time he found himself on a rocky shore of an angry sea. The sky here was also cloudy, but instead of dense benign clouds overhead, there was nearly constant cloud-to-cloud lightning, nearly hurricane force winds and massive waves pummeling the shore. None of his tactile senses registered anything other than the same comfortable temperatures and smooth walking surfaces he experienced in the abandoned city.

The diffuse light here was more like Earth normal and he could have been standing on a rocky shoreline in California, had California been stripped of all vegetative life. Rocks, sand and more rocks were all he could see. He began walking along the shore, seeing massive spray from the crashing waves fill the air in front of him; he could feel none of it. This convinced him that he was in some sort of virtual reality simulation rather than being zapped from one world to the next.

"And this world? There is no life here. Why are you showing it to me?"

THIS WORLD WAS ONCE ALIVE AND HOME TO TWO SENTIENT RACES, ONE MORE ADVANCED THAN THE OTHER, BUT BOTH HOLDING PROMISE FOR ADVANCED DEVELOPMENT AND GROWTH. UNTIL NATURAL DISASTER DOOMED THEM BOTH. LOOK THERE, ACROSS THE SEA AND YOU SHALL SEE THE SOURCE OF THEIR DESTRUCTION.

Chris squinted and looked out across the water toward the mountains on the distant shore. They were largely obscured by the mist and fog, visible only intermittently. The mountains were massive, though it was difficult for him to determine just how far away they were.

"The mountains?"

VOLCANOS. NOW WITH A LAVA FIELD OVER TEN MILES DEEP. THEY ERUPTED LONG BEFORE WE ARRIVED AND WITH A FORCE THAT CAUSED TSUNAMIS THAT SPREAD FROM THESE WATERS TO ALL OF THEIR WORLD, FLOODING COASTLINES FOR HUNDREDS OF MILES INLAND. NEXT THE VOLANCOS PUMPED GIGA-TONS OF ASH AND SULFATES INTO THE ATMOSPHERE, CAUSING A PLANET-WIDE CLOUD COVER WHICH HAS NOT YET DISSIPATED. THE BLOCKED SUNSHINE INDUCED PERPETUAL WINTER, WITH NEARLY ALL THE VEGETATION DYING FROM AN INABILITY TO SUSTAIN PHOTOSYNTHESIS. THE SULFATES IN THE CLOUDS CAUSED PLANETARY ACID RAINFALL. THE PH OF THE LAKES, RIVERS AND EVEN THEIR OCEANS WAS RADICALLY ALTERED, DESTROYING ECOSYSTEMS ALL OVER THE PLANET. OVER NINETY PERCENT OF THIS PLANET'S SPECIES DIED AS A RESULT.

"How long ago did this happen?"

WE ESTIMATE AT LEAST HALF A MILLION YEARS BEFORE WE ARRIVED.

"But how? How could you know these things after so much time has passed? There would be nothing left to find after that much time elapsed."

OUR METHODS ARE FAR MORE ADVANCED THAN YOU CAN IMAGINE.

"I accept that, but why are you showing me this?"

FOR YOU TO UNDERSTAND THE IMPORTANCE OF WHAT I DO AND WHY WE MUST HELP EACH OTHER. COME.

Chris steeled himself for the transition, though it made it no less painful. When it was over, he found himself in mid-air, moving (flying?) over an area of land that was filled with black and brown blotches, crumpled and charred buildings and what appeared to be vast areas of scorched earth that looked like the aftermath of massive forest fires. Though he was flying, he still felt nothing. He was only seeing the destruction below him and not experiencing any of the usual sensations of flight. The sky was clear and blue, just like Earth, only the star that shone in the sky was much too large for it to have been Earth's sun. Wherever he was, it was on a planet orbiting much closer to its star than his home world.

THIS WORLD'S INHABITANTS DESTROYED THEMSELVES IN A MASSIVE, NUCLEAR WAR.

Another transition; more pain.

He was again flying, but this time the sky was not the brilliant blue caused by the presence of abundant oxygen, but a blood-red that reminded him of Mars. Below him was a living world filled with green vegetation, everywhere. He could see no signs of animal life and certainly no signs of any sort of civilization.

THIS WORLD IS SCOURED OF HIGHER ORDER LIFE CONSTANTLY BY ITS PARENT STAR. UNLIKE YOUR WORLD, THIS ONE HAS NO LIQUID IRON CORE AND THEREFORE NO APPRECIABLE MAGNETIC FIELD TO SHIELD IT FROM ITS STAR'S PARTICLE RADIATION. ANY COMPLEX LIFE THAT MIGHT FORM HERE IS QUICKLY STERILIZED OR DESTROYED BY THIS CONSTANT IONIZING RADIATION BOMBARDMENT. NO SENTIENT LIFE CAN ARISE ON A WORLD SUCH AS THIS.

Transition. Pain. Another world.

Chris was back on the ground and standing among the ruins of yet another decaying and empty city. This one appeared to have been destroyed and abandoned much longer ago than the previous city. The wreckage of what had once evidently been massive structures was now lying useless on the ground. A yellow star, like Sol, shone in the sky. And instead of Earth's familiar moon, there were two smaller, ragged objects in the sky trailing the star like children following their mother.

"And here?"

THEY WERE DESTROYED SOON AFTER THEY MASTERED FUSION ENERGY AND BEGAN EXPLORING THE OUTER REGIONS OF THEIR OWN SOLAR SYSTEM, SUCH AS YOUR SPECIES IS NOW BEGINNING. THEY HAD OVERCOME THEIR INTERNAL DIFFERENCES, PROVIDED RELATIVE ABUNDANCE FOR THEIR POPULATIONS AND WERE QUICKLY BECOMING A SOLAR SYSTEM-WIDE INDUSTRIAL CIVILIZATION ON ITS

WAY TO THE STARS. AND THEN THE DESTROYERS CAME AND WIPED THEM OUT. THE DESTROYERS CANNOT HAVE COMPETITION; THEY WILL NOT ALLOW COMPETITION.

Transition. Pain.

Before him now were the remains of a city nearly covered by snow and ice. Here and there, protruding anachronistically above the ice, were what appeared to be the spires of churches or other ornate structures.

Transition. Pain.

He forced himself to keep his eyes open during the change and was greeted with what appeared to be a dense, swirling fog surrounding his body as he left wherever he was and traveled to wherever he was going. He had the sensation of flying, but beyond the fog was nothing but darkness.

After several minutes, he saw a bright light ahead and soon realized he was looking at a star from the vantage point of space, presumably from a spaceship approaching it. As he drew nearer to the star, he could see a planet ahead. It didn't look like any planet with which he was familiar, with the possible exception of Mercury or the Moon.

THIS IS WHAT MANY WORLDS IN THE GALAXY LOOK LIKE. BARREN ROCKS WITHOUT ANY TRACE OF LIFE. THE MAKERS HAVE VISITED HUNDREDS OF THOUSANDS OF WORLDS AND ONLY A FRACTION OF THEM HAVE STABLE ORBITS AND ATMOSPHERES CAPABLE OF SUPPORTING LIFE. ONLY A SMALL FRACTION OF THESE HAVE LIFE WITH ONLY ONE IN A HUNDRED OF THEM HAVING COMPLEX LIFE THAT COULD BECOME SENTIENT. THIS LEAVES ONLY ABOUT TEN THOUSAND WORLDS WITH THE POSSIBILITY OF INTELLIGENCE. OF THOSE THAT WE VISITED, WE FOUND FEW WITH INTELLIGENT, TOOL USERS EXTANT. MOST HAVE ONLY REMAINS SUCH AS THOSE I SHARED WITH YOU. TIME AND THE UNIVERSE ARE NOT KIND TO SENTIENCE.

Transition and more pain.

This time he was on a hillside in the open air. He was still naked and he could feel a slightly warm breeze blowing through the trees that surrounded the hillside clearing in which he found himself. Scanning his new surroundings for any signs of a threat, he found none. It was just a hillside that could be anywhere on Earth, and he was sure it was at least modeled on an earthly location because the sun was low on the horizon and the familiar face of Earth's moon could be seen in the sky, about 45 degrees above the opposite horizon. The grass in the field was knee height and felt scratchy to his bare legs as he began to walk toward the stand of trees to his right.

"Hello? Are you there? Please tell me what's going on and why you brought me here."

Silence. All he could hear was the sound of the gentle breeze blowing through the trees. Whatever had shouted at him in the hallway and brought him here wasn't responding.

"Shit."

Chris looked again at his naked self and his surroundings. *What the hell do I do now?* he thought. *I don't even have shoes.*

He walked to the edge of the trees that lined the hillside upon which he found himself. He was relieved to recognize the trees that were there, particularly the familiar shape of oak leaves that were on the trees that surrounded his home back on Earth.

"I'm either on Earth or in a damned good simulation of it."

YOU ARE ON EARTH. BUT NOT TODAY. THIS IS HOW IT WAS WHEN WE ARRIVED.

"So, you were there. Why am *I here*? What's going on?"

WAIT AND WATCH.

He waited. And waited. Time passed; Chris was carefully watching the Sun's apparent movement across the sky until, after what he was sure was at least three hours, it began to set. He could feel the cool and damp night air begin to flow out from the trees—he began to shiver.

"You could have at least given me some clothes. Or some means to build a fire. If I'd known I would be standing naked in a field all afternoon and who knows how long into the night, I would have tried to make a fire."

He looked at the tree line and decided it wasn't too late to collect some wood. "It might also be a good idea to have some rocks and maybe a good, solid stick to defend myself," he murmured to himself—and to the source of the unseen voice.

He quickly gathered dry wood and several rocks, searching his memory for any shred of useful survival knowledge. Having been a nerd in school and spending most, if not all his time in college studying physics, he hadn't taken the time to be a Scout or even go camping. His nakedness in these surroundings was more than physical.

After a fruitless hour banging rocks together in the hope of a spark igniting the dry grass and twigs he'd gathered, he sat on the damp, cool ground for the first time since his arrival. He was putting this step off in fear of the inevitable insects that he knew must be residing there. He didn't notice any insects, yet, but the grass was very scratchy and poked him in places he wasn't happy about.

It was then that he noticed what was missing. There was no sound coming from the forest. On the Earth that he knew, nightfall usually brought out a cacophony of insects and the sound of small creatures leaving their hiding places to forage for food. He heard nothing except the sound of the wind and his own breathing.

Movement above caught his attention.

Streaking slowly across the sky was the fireball caused by something entering the atmosphere from space. Slower than the apparent speed of a shooting star, the glowing trail of a ship's fiery entry lit up the night as it approached. And it was coming fast. It was coming toward the clearing where Chris found himself standing, naked and shivering.

Not being completely convinced that what he was experiencing was a simulation, Chris thought it best to retreat into the dark confines of the nearby forest. He hastily grabbed his makeshift spear and a few rocks and then trotted into it and out of sight. He knew he would show up on any sort of infrared scan, but he still felt it prudent to not be seen by whoever, or whatever, was about to land nearby.

He could now see that the object approaching was, indeed, some sort of spacecraft. But it was unlike any ship he'd ever seen before: First of all, it was not aerodynamic in any way. It had far too many outcroppings to be meant for atmospheric flight. Looking like a Lego model from a nightmare, the craft was basically a sphere with ten or more smaller spheres sticking out, seemingly randomly, from its surfaces, destroying all symmetry. It was grey in color and there were no lights visible.

Watching its descent carefully, he noticed that it wasn't using any sort of rocket for propulsion. There appeared to be no reaction mass coming from the ship as it slowed for landing. Instead, it merely came in from the sky, hovered over the clearing he occupied moments ago, and then lowered itself quietly to the surface. Seconds before touching down, landing legs descended from the bottom of the craft, propping its base about three meters from the ground.

The ship itself was massive, about the size of an early twenty-first century house. Its base took up at least fifty percent of the clearing.

Watching silently from the edge of the woods, now totally focused on what was happening in front of him, Chris briefly forgot about his nakedness and being uncomfortably cold. He knew this was what he was supposed to witness, but other than the ship landing in the clearing, there was no activity for at least another twenty minutes.

And then, three doors swung open and downward underneath the craft. The doors, like the ship, appeared to be grey in the limited light provided by the Moon above. The darkness was shattered by a bluish-white spotlight emanating from the opening under the craft and shining onto the dirt below it. The light grew ever brighter until it was almost painful to view, causing Chris to look away and making him more aware of how visible he now was in his Caucasian-pale nudity.

Struggling to see and not be blinded by the light, Chris saw an object the size of a small car being lowered from the ship to sit on the ground beneath it, bathed in light. And then the object vanished. The light went out and the doors closed.

Trying to keep warm, Chris continued to watch the ship as it gracefully lifted from the ground, retracted its landing legs and vanished into the night sky. After the ship had long vanished from view, he stepped out of the woods and into the clearing.

The ship had left no visible trace of its presence other than the deep depressions caused by its landing legs. Chris was feverishly trying to not only figure out what he had just seen happen, but why he was brought here to see it, by who, and whether or not he would be allowed to return to his shipmates. He was also running through ideas of how the ship might have been propelled, wanting desperately to figure it out so humans, and he in particular, might adapt the technology to human use.

WE CAME TO EARTH WHEN YOUR ANCESTORS WERE FIRST LEARNING TO COMMUNICATE AND WORK TOGETHER. BEFORE YOU LEARNED AGRICULTURE, WE PLACED FORTY-SIX BATTLEMENTS IN YOUR WORLD TO USE AGAINST OUR ENEMIES.

"You have my attention. So, the device I saw lowered under this ship was placed somewhere?"

YES. EACH OF THE FORTY-SIX WAS TRANSPORTED TO ABOUT ONE HUNDRED METERS UNDERGROUND WHERE THEY STILL WAIT FOR INSTRUCTION.

"Where are these Destroyers that they're supposed to protect us from?"

THE DESTROYERS FIND LIVING PLANETS AND DESTROY THOSE WITH LIFE THAT SHOWS SIGNS OF SENTIENCE. THEY ARE THE ANTITHESIS OF THE MAKERS. YOUR KIND SHOWED PROMISE AND THE MAKERS HAD YOU UNDER THEIR PROTECTION.

"You are a Maker?"

I AM NOT. THEY HAD MANY CREATIONS.

Chris noted that the Guardian dodged his question. His mind was racing and he couldn't ask the many questions he had as fast as they came to mind, almost causing him to stutter during the next one: "Will we find Makers here? Will we be able to communicate with them?"

IN DUE TIME, YOU WILL BE SENT TO MEET THOSE WHO SENT ME.

Chris didn't like the sound of that. It was too close to being told he was soon going to "meet his maker . . ."

"You said that the Makers came here before the dawn of human civilization. Have you been watching us since then?"

MY SELF-THAT-IS-NOT-SELF WAS WATCHING YOU AND INFORMED ME OF YOUR PROGRESS.

"How long have you and the self-that-is-not-self been watching us?"

MUCH LONGER THAN PLANNED. FOR YEARS, MY OTHER SELF RECORDED YOUR HISTORY AND AWAITED FURTHER INSTRUCTION. THE TIME FOR WAITING IS NOW PASSED.

"You said we 'showed' promise and that the Makers had 'had us under their protection.' What's changed?"

YOU ATTACKED SELF-THAT-IS-NOT-SELF AND DESTROYED IT. SELF-THAT-IS-NOT-SELF WAS CONVINCED YOU ARE SOON TO ADVANCE BEYOND TRYING TO KILL WHATEVER YOU DON'T UNDERSTAND, BUT NOT YET. SOME OF YOUR SPECIES ARE NOT YET MATURE. BUT I REMAIN UNCONVINCED. AND

I AM NOT WITHOUT A MEANS OF PROTECTING MYSELF AND ENACTING RETRIBUTION.

Transition and yet more pain. He was growing numb to it, but not to the desolation and destruction he'd witnessed since being separated from his colleagues onboard the alien spacecraft. This numbness was worse because of what it meant—life was rare, but not as rare as to be virtually alone. But intelligent life seemed to either self-destruct or be destroyed before it could flourish. All the pain of growing from being primitives to civilized, from being hunter-gatherers to building magnificent cathedrals and ultimately spaceships—for naught? Death, destruction and, what? *Being wiped away as though we never existed? Was that to be humanity's fate? Has it all been in vain?*

I'm not naked, thought Chris as he realized that he was no longer standing in the middle of a field but back in his spacesuit. He looked at his colleagues and they looked back with expressions of awe and curiosity. Frustrated by not being able to communicate directly with any of them, he pointed his gloved hands upward and mouthed an exaggerated, *did you go there too?*

Jing was the only one who apparently understood him and she quickly shook her head in the negative. He could quite easily lip read her reply, "Are you okay?"

Chris looked at his chronometer and realized perhaps only a minute or less had transpired since they arrived at this point in the corridor. His body told him otherwise. By his reckoning, he'd spent the better part of a day in that field and he was now very hungry and very tired.

Chris motioned back toward the airlock, where he now hoped they could go to at least communicate and share notes, or better yet, he thought, back into the ship so they could share notes and then take a nap.

But that was not to be. Just as Chris pointed back the way they had come, an opening in the wall appeared before them. Like all the iris shapes they saw before, a section of the wall disappeared to create a three-foot-wide truncated spherical opening. Lights on the other side flickered on to reveal a large room awaiting their entry.

WELCOME.

By the looks on his team members' faces, Chris could tell that all of them were hearing the voice this time.

They stepped through the opening and into the chamber beyond.

CHAPTER 27

The room was filled with inactive equipment and machines, the purposes of which the human crew could only guess. Much of it looked like the interior of a manufacturing plant back on Earth that had been abruptly stopped in a power failure. The ceiling was at least thirty feet above their heads and was filled with catwalks, hanging structures, and what looked like stalled conveyor belts. On the floor around them were wheeled carts with multiple manipulator arms frozen into various positions. The equipment, though in near-perfect looking condition, had the appearance of having been in these positions for a very, very long time.

THE ATMOSPHERE IS NOW SEVENTY-EIGHT PERCENT NITROGEN, TWENTY-ONE PERCENT OXYGEN AND ONE PERCENT ARGON.

"I guess that means we can take our helmets off?" asked Chris.

"I think that's exactly what it means," replied Jing.

Chris and Juhani slowly removed their helmets and took deep breaths. To Chris, the air smelled stale and a bit like the ozone in the air after a thunderstorm. Yuan and Jing did not remove their helmets.

"I'll leave mine on for a short while until we make sure there are no ill effects. I would prefer to be cautious," said Yuan, using his radio. The sound of his voice came from the two removed helmets simultaneously.

"I'll leave mine on until I'm through checking for pathogens," said Jing.

"Okay Chris, you need to tell us what the hell happened out there.

Your whole body froze when you touched the diamond-shaped thing on the wall. You stood there for about a minute and didn't respond to anything the whole time. We were about to grab you and carry you back to the ship when you started moving again and we heard the voice that led us here," Janhunen said.

"I was only out for a minute?"

"Yes. About a minute," said Jing.

"And I was there the whole time?"

"It depends on what you mean by 'there.' You were physically there, but unresponsive. It reminded me of visiting my grandfather in the hospital when he was close to death. He would lay still for hours, unresponsive but obviously awake and conscious. You were there, but not really 'there,'" said Juhani.

"That's because I wasn't 'there' with you at all. As soon as I touched the diamond shape, I was taken . . . other places. Many other places. And I didn't like what I found."

"Okay Chris, you need to tell us what happened. Are we in any danger? Do we need to get back to the ship?" asked Yuan as he began removing his helmet. Jing kept hers sealed.

"The alien that I believe runs this place took me on a trip, a dream? A virtual reality simulation? Hell, I don't know. All I know is that one minute I was with you and then I wasn't. I was whisked from world to world, seeing the death and destruction of one alien civilization after the next. Watching from afar as life emerged, became intelligent and then destroyed itself, got destroyed or just failed to survive for one reason or another. Planet after planet after planet. It made me think all our civilization's great accomplishments might be in vain. So much destruction."

"Was the alien responsible for the destruction?"

"No. Rather, I don't know. I just don't know. In several cases obviously not, in others, it's possible. But there was a lot of destruction."

"And you saw all of this in one minute?" asked Yuan.

"It may have been a minute for you, but for me it was a *very* long day. In fact, I'm hungry," Chris said as he opened his supply kit, took out an energy bar and began to devour it.

"Did it tell you anything else?" asked Yuan.

"Yes, there is a war. It told me there are 'Makers' and they are at war with a species it calls the 'Destroyers.' The Makers find and preserve civilizations and the Destroyers do the opposite. They destroy them. The Destroyers don't want any competition."

"Let me get this straight, our alien is a 'good' alien and the ones who attacked it are 'bad' aliens. How convenient for us to have been found by the good guys," said Janhunen.

Chris started to scold him for being quick to jump to conclusions and for being so cynical, but he couldn't. Janhunen's skepticism was justified and it was awfully convenient to have the nice alien be the one they found—at least according to it. What he had to say next didn't help make the case in his own mind either.

Chris paused eating long enough to answer Yuan's question. "It knows humans destroyed the Artifact and it doesn't quite trust us because of that. There was an explicit threat of reprisal should anyone attempt to attack it here. I think the alien is in control of some bombs or some other weapons buried back on Earth. It was clear that it would use them if it has to." He then went back to devouring the energy bar.

"What's next? Did it tell you?" asked Jing.

NOW I EDUCATE ALL OF YOU.

The alien's voice seemed to come from everywhere in the eerily abandoned room simultaneously. Chris had nearly forgotten his surroundings as he tried to quench his hunger. Now he looked at the room anew and wished he had more information about the current state of affairs regarding the alien war and otherwise. Perhaps they were about to find out.

The room darkened to a dim, twilight level of lighting and a three-dimensional projection of a spiral galaxy formed just above their heads. The image of the spiral arm was magnified and began to be populated with multiple orange dots as previously yellow ones changed color.

THESE ARE THE WORLDS I SHOWED YOU. THERE ARE OTHERS WITH SIMILAR FATES THAT WE HAVE VISITED.

The map of the spiral arm began to fill with tens, hundreds, and then well over a thousand orange dots. The fraction of the galaxy that was highlighted was small, yet it likely still contained tens of millions, if not hundreds of millions of stars.

Jing removed her helmet and stared.

INTELLIGENT LIFE IS RARE AND THE MAKERS SEEK TO

PRESERVE IT AND PROTECT IT FROM THE UNRELENTING DESTROYERS. WE CAME HERE, AS WE HAVE DONE TO MANY OTHER STELLAR SYSTEMS, BY TRAVELING BETWEEN THE STARS IN SHIPS SUCH AS THIS—TAKING MANY OF YOUR MILLENNIA TO DO SO. THE MAKERS ARRIVE, SEEK TO OBSERVE AND LEARN, AND TO BE READY WHEN THE DESTROYERS INEVITABLY COME. THE CONFLICT NEARLY DESTROYED THIS OUTPOST AND THE SELF-THAT-IS-NOT-SELF.

Next came what appeared to be a recording. In the background was mighty Saturn, with the wreckage of multiple smaller spacecraft floating in the foreground, slowly drifting away from the vantage point from which the recording was made.

THEY CAUSED GREAT DAMAGE IN ME AND NEARLY DESTROYED MY ABILITY TO COMMUNICATE WITH SELF-THAT-IS-NOT-SELF AND THE GREATER CONSCIOUSNESS. AFTER A TIME, ALL COMMUNICATION FAILED. UNTIL YOUR KIND FOUND AND THEN DESTROYED THE SELF-THAT-IS-NOT-SELF, I HAD NOT HEARD FROM IT FOR MANY ORBITS. FOR A WHILE, I WAS ABLE TO RECEIVE SPORADIC INFORMATION FROM THE GREATER CONSCIOUSNESS, BUT THAT, TOO, HAS NOW CEASED.

"So why are we here?" asked Yuan.

IT IS A TIME OF DECISION AND ACTION.

Silence. Seconds, then minutes went by without any additional communication with the alien. The four humans stood nearly motionless, mentally afraid to move not because they were fearful of coming to harm, but concerned that by moving they might forever break whatever connection they had with the alien.

"Well, what's next?" asked Janhunen.

"I have no idea," said Chris.

"Jing, you are our exobiologist, what do you think?" asked Yuan.

"I believe we can safely say we're dealing with some sort of machine intelligence," she said, biting her lower lip. "It keeps talking about the 'self-that-is-not-self' and a 'greater consciousness,' so I think we can assume it's not used to being on its own. Whatever network it was using is down and has been down for a long, long time."

"I can't imagine being alone for tens of thousands of years. I'd go insane. Don't people start to lose their sanity when they're isolated for any extended period of time?" Chris asked.

"We can't anthropomorphize. It may sound human and speak English, but it is far from being human. Remember the Artifact said it had been watching and listening to us. If that's the case, then it knows how we think better than we do," Jing said.

"This 'greater consciousness' reference concerns me, as do the so-called 'Destroyers.' What and where is the consciousness that it referred to? And what happened to the Destroyers? Did no more come to Earth after the battle that happened here? It would be good to find out," said Janhunen.

"Juhani, whatever battle took place here happened a long, long time ago. If any more Destroyers were around, I think we'd have seen evidence of them," replied Yuan, who was slowly breaking off from the group and walking toward one of the dormant machines that filled the room.

"Not if they, too, were damaged and lying low. There might be other ships or Artifacts sitting dormant throughout the solar system, waiting for the right time to attack."

"Yuan, what are you thinking?" asked Chris.

"I'm wondering just how damaged this ship might be and why we were invited to come all the way out here. Why did it give us fusion drive technology? What other technologies can it share with us? And what will it want in return?"

I HAVE A QUESTION. DO YOU OWN PETS?

In preparing for this second visit to an alien artifact, Chris had anticipated some questions—but this one wasn't on the list. Yuan was the first to reply.

"Yes. I own a cat. Do you know what a cat is?" asked Yuan.

I HAVE OBSERVED THEM.

"I own two dogs. One is getting kind of old and may not be alive when I return from this trip. I have someone watching them for me," said Chris.

WHY?

"Why do we own pets?" asked Chris. He looked at Yuan for affirmation, guidance or some speculation as to why the Guardian was pursuing this kind of question.

"I own a cat because it helps me calm down and relax. Human

psychologists have found that petting animals lowers the heartrate and reduces stress."

"I'm a dog person because of the companionship. No matter what my mood may be when I get home at the end of the day, they are always there with their tails wagging—eager to see me. They also help me relieve stress, but I mostly just enjoy having them there with me. Even though they don't understand everything, or most of anything, I say, they are good listeners," said Chris. The conversation was making him think of his dogs, Panda, an Irish terrier and Cricket, a Manchester terrier. He usually left them with his neighbor while he was away, but for this trip, he left the dogs with a professional sitter who promised to take good care of them for the duration—for a hefty sum of money.

HAVE YOU VISITED AN ANIMAL PRESERVE?

"I've been to the zoo," said Chris, unsure of where this was going.

"I visited the Lower Zambezi National Park in Zambia on a vacation with my sister. The animals there are awe-inspiring, especially the elephants," replied Yuan.

THE INFORMATION AVAILABLE SAYS YOU MAINTAIN THESE PRESERVES TO PROTECT THE ANIMALS IN THEIR NATURAL HABITATS. WHY DID YOU NOT HUNT THEM TO EXTINCTION? MANY ARE PREDATORS.

"For the same reason you showed me on my tour of dead worlds. Because preserving their lives, their ways of life, is important. Once they were no longer a direct threat, it would have been immoral to kill them all," said Chris.

"And once they were gone, they would be gone forever. Humans have been responsible for too many extinctions already," added Yuan.

YOU MAINTAIN PETS AND PROTECT LESSER SPECIES, YET YOU NEARLY DESTROYED YOURSELVES IN A NUCLEAR WAR JUST A FEW YEARS AGO. YOUR TWO COUNTRIES NEARLY EXTERMINATED EACH OTHER.

"But we didn't. We stepped back from the brink and united against a common threat to peace on the planet," said Yuan.

RETURN TO YOUR SHIP. I WILL SUMMON YOU WHEN IT IS TIME.

"Time for what?" asked Chris.

There was no answer.

"I guess that means we're done for the day," said Chris.

"Not until I get a few more samples," said Jing, who now joined Yuan looking at the closest dormant machine. She reached into her pack and began swabbing various surfaces, carefully returning the samples collected to the compartments in her sampling pouch.

"I am all in favor of going back to the ship. I've been awake and exploring various worlds throughout the spiral arm for a day, perhaps a day and a half. I'm exhausted," said Chris.

"We're coming," said Jing, as she began to slowly walk back to the central part of the room where they had been conversing with the alien machine intelligence. "I just want to make sure I get plenty of samples on the way back. I was hoping to encounter some sort of non-terrestrial life or environment while we were here but instead I got a machine and an Earth-normal atmosphere. Unless there's some ancient and still-usable trace of organic material in here somewhere, my being on this mission has been a colossal waste of everybody's time."

CHAPTER 28

"Let me get this straight. We're flying alongside a battleship that was severely damaged in an interstellar war, fought in our own solar system, between two competing civilizations, one of which wants to wipe us out—and some lonesome artificial intelligence is going to summon us when it's again ready to talk? Furthermore, while you were down there for six hours, Chris went on some day-long interstellar virtual reality tour across the spiral arm looking at dead civilizations. Oh, yes, and it says there are several 'battlements' buried on the Earth waiting to be activated to do God-only-knows-what kind of mayhem. And this alien machine seems to think that something out there in the universe is gunning for us as well." Robyn had listened to the debrief and, with her usual proficiency, summed it all up in a few short sentences.

"I would say that's accurate, but I think summarizing my pretty intense experience as a 'virtual reality tour' tends to trivialize it," said Chris.

"Noted. And don't worry, you'll get a chance to explain it in great detail in our next report to Mission Control. I'm just glad you are all back safe and sound. Jing, what about contamination? You broke the seals on your suits and breathed the air over there. Do we have to worry about pathogens?"

"Not that I've been able to detect. The bio detector didn't show microbes beyond what colonies we carry along with us. I've put samples in the bioreactor to see if anything grows, but so far there is nothing. I would say we are most probably clean. Nothing organic has been in that ship for a long time, perhaps ever," replied Jing.

"We wait?" asked Janhunen.

"So, we wait," replied Yuan, speaking before Chris could respond.

"What about the Indians? They are due to arrive the day after tomorrow. Have you had contact with them?" asked Janhunen.

"No. I tried but got no response," said Robyn.

"Any more news from home? Has there been another attack?" asked Chris.

"No more attacks, but everyone is nervous as hell. That includes me. While you were away, I received an intelligence update on the Indian ship that's on its way here. As best as they can tell, and they didn't tell me how they know, the Indian ship is armed with some sort of ship-to-ship missile system. We don't know much about it other than we will be in range no later than tonight if we don't leave the area."

"We can't leave!" said Jing. "There is so much more to learn and I've only just gotten started."

"She's right, we have to stay. Whatever this thing is, it's communicating with us. It asked us to wait until it calls us back. We should wait," said Chris.

"This isn't a democracy, Chris. If and when I think we need to bug out, we'll do so. You have your jobs and I have mine. We're not at that point yet, and I hope we don't get there. But this Indian ship is a wildcard. If it comes in guns blazing, what will our new alien friend do? Will it just sit there and let itself be destroyed as the first one did? Or will it fight back?"

"We don't know," said Yuan.

"And that's why we're staying. We need to learn as much as we can after coming all this way," said Robyn.

"Well, this has been interesting, but I'm exhausted, I can't think straight and I need some sleep. Unless my debriefing to Mission Control is going to take place in the next ten minutes, I intend to do so," said Chris as he pushed off from his place at the galley table and headed toward his sleeping area.

"I can hold them off. Go get some rest. You may not get another opportunity any time soon."

Chris slept fitfully, dreaming of one dead, empty world after the next. The sights that he saw on his virtual journey with the alien haunted him. Death. Destruction. Chaos. The Destroyers. More death.

Chris awoke in his sleeping bag, still Velcroed to the wall, sweating, flailing his arms and stifling an anguished cry. He calmed down by telling himself that it was all just a dream. Except that it wasn't. It was real and it might be the inevitable future of the human race. He slowly unzipped himself and noted that ten hours had passed since he zipped himself into the bag for his long-overdue rest. At first, he was angry that no one had awakened him, but then he realized they would have done so had there been a reason. After a brief stop in the head and a hurried spit-bath, he made his way to the galley where everyone was gathered.

"Welcome back," said Robyn.

"Thanks. I needed that. No word from the alien?" asked Chris. Even though he still felt betrayed by Robyn for her keeping the information about the bomb being onboard from him, he found it difficult to be mad at her. Just seeing her calmed him down, helping him recover from the nightmare.

"None. But we did hear from the Indians." Robyn's tone shifted when the topic became the approaching ship from India. "They are demanding complete access to everything and for our next contact to be a joint one. Apparently, our video feed back to Earth and my after-action report weren't encrypted well enough or they have someone on the inside who shared everything with them. They knew who went down to Methonē and all about what you experienced."

"And from what we can tell, the situation back on Earth hasn't calmed down. China and India are on the verge of a nuclear exchange and the Caliphate is publicly encouraging them to do so, saying something about 'fulfilling prophecy.'" Janhunen added the latter in a completely derisive tone.

"So, what are we going to do?" asked Chris as he positioned himself at the galley table in his usual spot, the same spot that he had used since their very first day aboard the ship. Humans were creatures of habit—at least he was.

"We're still waiting on the alien to 'summon' us so we can take the next step, whatever that may be. Other than that, we stand firm on not sharing anything directly with them. If their spies are as good as they seem to be, then we don't need to. They'll get everything we learn regardless of what we do out here," said Robyn.

"And if they decide to use force?" asked Janhunen.

"We're equipped to fend off boarders, if that's what you mean. Though firing guns in and around our spacecraft or lander, or theirs for that matter, would not be a very smart move. Yes, our micrometeoroid shielding might be able to stop a bullet, which, in theory, should be a helluva lot easier to stop than a meteor traveling at twenty-one kilometers per second. But it won't just be a bullet striking the ship at some random location. It would be a deliberate act by a human being with the intent to damage. That kind of an attack would be difficult to stop. If they decide to skip the whole ship-to-ship boarding thing and use their missiles, then we're toast. There is absolutely nothing we can do to defend against that."

"And they are only thirty-six hours out," added Janhunen.

"So, we continue to wait?" asked Jing.

"We wait," said Robyn.

They didn't have to wait for very long.

The alien made contact two hours later, during the mid-day meal of freeze-dried turkey, dumplings and broccoli. The entire crew received the message via their implants: SEND CHRIS ONLY. SEND HIM WITH THE MATERIALS LISTED.

Janhunen nearly choked on his bite of turkey and quickly sucked on his reconstituted fruit juice pouch to regain his composure. Chris and Yuan raised their eyebrows while Robyn looked indifferent. Jing frowned. The only one completely surprised by the message was Juhani and he was quick to protest.

"Again? I guess our new friend likes to pick favorites," he said.

"Chris was the one invited out here to begin with," replied Robyn. "But that doesn't mean I like it, especially since we know we'll again lose radio contact. You'll be on your own and we'll be in the dark," she added.

"Asking us to bring equipment is something new. And where is this list it referred to? I haven't seen it," said Janhunen.

"I just received it via my implant. It is going to take some time to get it all together. Tools, mostly for fine electronics repair, a few circuit boards—some that we will need to make using our 3D printer. It even sent the fabrication requirements in the software format the machine needs to print them," said Chris.

"Does that mean it has access to our shipboard computer system?" asked Janhunen.

"Probably. And that means it knows about our little nuclear surprise package as well," said Chris, bitterness rising his throat.

"Chris, we've been over this before," said Robyn.

"Robyn, I . . ." began Chris, before he was interrupted by Jing.

"What's done is done. The important thing is that we're here and that we learn as much as possible. And since I am not going with you this time, I would like to outfit you with some of my sample collection gear. If you are allowed to access any other parts of the ship, then please use it to collect samples. I would like to collect as much data as I possibly can," said Jing.

"I can do that," said Chris, relieved to not have to replay the same old argument again.

"You aren't going alone. I won't allow it," said Robyn.

"Hey, I don't like the idea much either, but can we tell it no?" said Chris.

"We won't ask. Yuan is going with you and that's that. You two made a good team at the Artifact and it is simply too dangerous for one person to go over by themselves."

Jing gave them an impossibly fast tutorial on sample collection, where to look, which sample container to use under a certain circumstance—and which one not to use. All the information, nuances and all, being conveyed so quickly that it was impossible for Chris, and, he suspected, Yuan, to keep up. Jing's boundless enthusiasm apparently didn't take into account that they were not experts in her field.

"We will do the best we can," Yuan assured her as Chris nodded.

After Jing's tutorial, Robyn inserted herself between the two men and the lander, looking sternly at Chris.

"Chris, I'm sure I know the answer, but are you up to another trip so soon?" asked Robyn.

"Are you kidding me? How could I possibly turn this down?"

Just a little less than four hours later, Chris and Yuan were at the iris wall entering the Methonē airlock.

CHAPTER 29

Access to Methonē went exactly as before, without any glitches. Chris and Yuan made good time as they entered the airlock and waited for it to cycle so that the door to the inner part of the ship would open, allowing them to regain access. Once they left the airlock and entered the first chamber where Chris experienced his virtual journey, they again lost contact with the orbiting *Daedalus* and each other. The latter wasn't a problem because both quickly removed their helmets once they knew they were again in an Earth normal atmosphere.

"Yuan, we need to talk now so that we can't be overheard by the rest of the crew," said Chris. He had something to get off his chest, and this seemed like an opportune time to do it.

"Yes, my friend?"

"Don't give me that 'my friend' bullshit. We're going walking into an alien ship with the potential future of humanity riding on our shoulders and I need to know if you are going to be a team player or fulfill your assignment as a spy."

"I don't know what you mean," replied Yuan, his previous cheerful demeanor vanished and was replaced with a look of puzzlement.

"Yuan, cut the crap. I was briefed on your status before we left Earth. I was really taken in by your friendship act during and after our encounter with the Artifact, but not anymore."

Yuan's expression changed yet again. His curious look was now replaced by a much more serious one as he leaned forward toward Chris and replied, "Who else knows?"

"Robyn, for one. I don't know if Jing knows; she doesn't seem like she's anything more than what she appears to be—you tell me. And we didn't tell Juhani, though it wouldn't surprise me to learn he was a counterpart of yours from the European Union."

"Your assessment of Jing is correct. She is nothing more than a scientist, and one of the best in her field. And we also suspect Juhani is a spy, but if he is, I must say his techniques are less than desirable or effective. An undercover intelligence officer cannot be effective if everyone dislikes him."

"Touché, but it still leaves you, and me. And what we're going to be doing out here. Are we going to collaborate or compete? Do I have to watch my back?"

"I am a loyal citizen of my country and will do whatever I must to prevent her from coming to harm. That said, I do not view you or anyone else aboard the *Daedalus* as enemies and I will not betray your trust in me as long as that situation remains."

"Conditional cooperation and collaboration? That's better than being enemies, but it isn't where I thought we were."

"Chris, you, like me, are a realist. Your government's decision to send a nuclear weapon and keep that hidden from all of us speaks volumes—they, too, are being realists. Do not let your academic notions of being above politics get in the way of what we must do while we are here."

Chris knew Yuan was correct, but he didn't like it. Not because he didn't like the specific circumstance, but because he always thought people who made decisions based on personal gain and political maneuvering were assholes. And he didn't want to be *that* kind of asshole.

"At this point, that's all I can ask," Chris replied, sticking out his hand.

Yuan accepted his hand, shook it, and said, "Let's go see why this thing invited us."

The astronaut and the taikonaut, helmets in hand, moved down the now-familiar hallway to the door that accessed the vast chamber they visited previously. Again, the orange-tinted lighting preceded them as they walked further inside and, as expected, the door opened ahead of them. Chris deliberately did not touch the small hemisphere that initiated his virtual journey the last time they were there.

Once they arrived at the next iris shape, it, too, vanished as before and they were able to enter the vast chamber with its eerily time-stopped machinery. Everything was as it was—there were no visible changes evident from their previous visit.

WELCOME. TWO WERE NOT SUMMONED.

"Uh, oh. I knew this was coming," Chris mumbled to himself before continuing, "You did not prohibit anyone from accompanying me. I chose to not come alone." He braced himself for an argument with an alien, but that didn't happen.

YOUR ASSISTANCE IS REQUIRED. FOLLOW THE LIGHTING ON THE FLOOR.

As soon as the disembodied voice stopped, a glowing pattern of lights appeared on the floor, illuminating a path that took them through the vast chamber and toward the right side of it to a destination not immediately visible due to the inactive machinery that was in the line of sight.

Yuan and Chris walked across the chamber, carefully remaining on the illuminated path, until they reached an opening on the other side. Taking careful note of their surroundings as they walked, and filming everything, the two were mostly silent as they followed the conveniently lighted pathway to the other side of the room and the opening.

REPAIR INSTRUCTIONS ARE NOW ON YOUR DEVICES. PLEASE REVIEW BEFORE ENTRY.

Chris and Yuan saw that several data files had just been uploaded to their corneal implants. Chris quickly accessed the first and was amazed to see what amounted to be step-by-step instructions for disassembling part of what looked like an electronic control system and replacing key parts with those they'd fabricated on their ship to the specifications provided by the Guardian. He was momentarily amused by the instructions. They reminded him of a comic he once saw that served as the instruction manual for incoming marines learning how to repair disc rotors. At the time, he'd derided the manual for being a simplistic approach to teaching soldiers with insufficient education to do something any reasonably educated person should know how to do—read and follow instructions. Even repair instructions for hybrid helicopter/jet aircraft. Now that he was in the role of being the uneducated repairman, he felt a twinge of guilt at having had those thoughts. He needed it to be simplistic. After all, he was being asked to repair a piece of equipment that was probably manufactured at about the same time his species learned how to use fire.

"Yuan, it's asking me to work on some sort of electronic controller. You?"

"The same. And it looks like both of our repair assignments connect at some point."

"I guess we won't know until we get started, but this sure looks like it will take a while to complete. The instructions are pretty clear. From what I can tell, there are several parts I'm removing and then reinstalling that are very fragile. I'm guessing this will take at least the rest of today, if not some of tomorrow."

"Agreed. It would be nice to know what we are repairing and why," said Yuan.

"Guardian. What are we repairing?" Chris wasn't one for wasting time, not even when in discussions with an alien fifty thousand years older and far more powerful than he.

A TRANSPORTATION DEVICE. I HAVE BEEN OUT OF CONTACT WITH THE GREATER CONSCIOUSNESS FOR TOO LONG. MY INTERNAL REMOTE AGENTS HAVE BEEN INOPERATIVE SINCE THE ATTACK AND I NEED YOU TO MAKE THE NECESSARY REPAIRS.

"That explains a lot. I was wondering why it didn't just repair itself. Surely it has additive manufacturing capabilities that make our 3D printers look like children's toys. During the 'attack' it mentioned, the self-repair capability must have been what was heavily damaged. It's been out here waiting on its fellow Makers, or us, to make the repairs," said Chris.

"How do we know we're not repairing its weapons systems?"

"I guess we have to take it at its word," replied Chris.

"Or we can ask it. Guardian. Are your weapons systems damaged?" asked Yuan, addressing the Guardian for the first time.

SOME ARE FUNCTIONAL.

"Well, that answers that. What now?" asked Chris.

"Now we decide if we're going to follow these instructions or not," said Yuan.

"Why come all the way out here and then refuse to get engaged with it? I didn't give up two years of my life to do that. But before we get started, let's get out of these EVA suits. They're too damn bulky." Both men wore their "skivvies" under their EVA suits and had packed lightweight sandals to wear on their feet, planning ahead for this potentiality.

To an outside observer, they would have looked ridiculous. Two men, wearing only skivvies, working on a spacecraft in deep space orbiting Saturn to repair machines built before the first human civilization.

"That is much better. Guardian, where do we find the equipment you are asking us to repair?" asked Yuan.

In response, the iris in the wall before them began to undulate, and, as all of them had previously, it vanished leaving a hole in the wall revealing a much smaller room, also lit with dim orange light. In the center stood the structure from Yuan's repair manual with the electronics box Chris was asked to repair sitting to its right. No other equipment was visible, except for at least two of the wall bumps that resembled the one Chris had touched in their initial visit.

"Let's get to it," said Chris as he walked through the opening and into the adjacent room. Yuan followed.

The first thing Chris noticed when he approached the box was that it, like the rest of the equipment they had seen inside the Guardian, did not resemble anything he had seen before. And it certainly didn't resemble anything one would find in a spaceship made by humans. The skin of the box was a dull grey color and there was no apparent way to gain access to the interior and make the requested repairs. The instructions said to begin by placing his hands on the upper surface with his thumb and forefinger in positions marked very carefully with small indentations. The fit didn't exactly match that of a human hand, but it was close enough.

"It's kind of small to be a spaceship," said Chris.

"Perhaps that comes next and this is a launch or control interface? The Guardian didn't really say it was a spaceship, but a 'transportation device,'" said Yuan.

"Here goes," said Chris as he placed his right hand on the box with his thumb and finger in the positions requested. The moment he placed his hand on the box, the lid popped loose from a previously hidden seam connecting the upper half from the lower. Using both hands, Chris carefully removed it. Beneath the cover were the guts of the device, whatever it was. Instead of circuit boards, there were several translucent, thin rectangular wafers stacked upon each other with what appeared to be fiber optic cables connecting several together. In other places there were more traditional appearing electronics and even a few wires. It was a mix of familiar and wholly unfamiliar which piqued Chris's curiosity even more.

To his left, Yuan was busy taking apart the larger box. Like the smaller one on which Chris was working, as Yuan touched strategic locations there appeared seams, allowing it to be readily disassembled.

Both men were recording the entire process with their cameras and making verbal notes as their work progressed. Chris knew it would be difficult for the data forensic analysts back home to learn much from his looking at and touching some of what he now guessed was a sophisticated optical computer. Nonetheless, he had to try. There was so much to be learned from the Guardian, even if nothing else was explicitly provided; perhaps they could make do with whatever they happened to see and touch.

Carefully following the comic book-like instructions, Chis removed the first three wafers and disconnected the optical cabling that would allow him to reach the part of the machine into which he was to insert the board they had printed on the *Daedalus*. The replacement part was essentially a modified version of the CPU used in their own ship's primary flight computer. He couldn't imagine how something that must be so primitive by comparison could be useful in effecting a repair to the alien device, but had to try.

"We would like to know what happens when we are finished making the repairs."

YOU WILL LEARN THIS AFTER THE REPAIR IS COMPLETE.

Chris, not happy with the answer, had no real choice but to continue.

A few minutes later, after connecting the last part in the subset of the repair upon which he was working, the box changed. Instead of the fixed, dull grey color it was when he began, it was now subtly shifting between various shades of grey, light to dark and then light again. It was difficult to focus on the box as the color shifted. To Chris it looked like a photograph going into and out of focus, repeatedly. He could swear he was seeing undulations in the surface, making him think of the slow breaths a large mammal might make while asleep.

"Yuan, look at this," said Chris.

Yuan, looking up from his task, reacted, doing a double take.

"When did that start?" asked Yuan.

"After I made my last connection."

THAT IS NORMAL. PLEASE CONTINUE.

Chris could only assume there was some sort of activation or test process occurring when he made the connection. The work had been tedious and as he glanced at his chronometer, he discovered that nearly three hours had passed. He suddenly realized he was hungry and had to go to the bathroom.

"Yuan, are you ready for a meal and bathroom break?" asked Chris.

"Now that you mention it, yes, I am. I am making good progress, but I am not sure I will be able to get the box reconfigured before the end of the day."

Chris took out his lunch, looked again around the room, smirked, and then reached into his day pack for the portable bio-waste bag. "I hope the Guardian doesn't mind me taking care of some human business in the other room before I eat. When a man's gotta go, he's gotta go."

Yuan smiled and said, "I will likely take care of that after lunch myself. Let me know if our host complains."

Chris grabbed the bio-waste bag and walked back into the outer room to find a place that seemed to offer him some privacy, even though he knew the Guardian was likely watching every move they made. Once he was out of Yuan's line of sight, he took care of his business.

When he was finished, he taped up the disposable bag and sat it on the floor behind him while he pulled up his pants. Then he turned to get the bag and found only the floor upon which he had placed it. Looking from side to side, there was no sign of the bag.

"What the hell?" he muttered to himself as he looked again. He had every intention of cleaning up after himself but, apparently, the Guardian had already taken care of the problem, though exactly how was still something he couldn't figure out. As he began to walk back to the work area and explain to Yuan what had happened, he again saw the color change and shape undulations, this time in the floor near where he had just been squatting.

He relayed his story to Yuan, who promised to keep a close eye on what happened when it was his turn. As their conversation waned and they finished the last portions of their mid-day meal, Chris was struck by the deafening silence of their surroundings.

"Guardian, do you get lonely? Are you able to get lonely? You mentioned being out of communication with your kind for quite some time. For thousands of our years. I can't imagine that kind of loneliness."

I WAS DESIGNED TO SURVIVE ALONE FOR LONG PERIODS OF TIME, BUT NOT AS LONG AS IT HAS BEEN. VOYAGES BETWEEN THE STARS TAKE TIME, LOTS OF TIME, AND BEINGS SUCH AS YOURSELVES AND THOSE WHO CREATED ME ARE NOT WELL SUITED FOR TAKING SUCH LONG TRIPS. THAT IS THE REASON MY KIND WAS CREATED.

"Your creators, the Makers, didn't travel with you?" asked Yuan.

IT IS NOT A POLAR QUESTION. THOSE WHO CREATED ME WERE INTERMITTENTLY PRESENT DURING THE INTERSTELLAR PORTION OF THE TRIP AND SOME WERE WITH ME FOR A LONGER PERIOD OF TIME AFTER I ARRIVED IN YOUR SOLAR SYSTEM.

"They came here in another ship?"

NO.

"But how can they be here with you but not come with you on the journey?" asked Chris.

THAT IS BEST ANSWERED . . . . EXPERIENTIALLY.

"Experientially? We don't understand." Chris looked at Yuan to see if he understood what the Guardian meant and received the same blank look in return.

YOU WILL.

YOU SHOULD EXPEDITE THE REPAIRS. THE OTHER SHIP APPROACHES.

Chris and Yuan exchanged glances and knew exactly what the Guardian was talking about. The Indians.

If Robyn had been in Earth or lunar gravity, she would have been pacing. Being in space and outside the reach of the gravity field that surrounded Methonē and the Guardian, all she could do was fidget. Her choices were few and she knew it. Tensions on Earth were high between China and India, between the Caliphate and everyone else. She realized that what happened out here, a billion miles from the crazies back home, could have dire consequences. Her actions could be the trigger that started a world war. At this time, neither the United States nor the European Union were explicitly threatened by what was going on at home, but she knew that could change in a heartbeat if what they found out here looked like it was going to change the balance of power back home. She had no doubt India would strike the US or Europe if it looked like it was in their strategic interest to do so. The Indian ship was now less than a day away from its own rendezvous with Methonē and had just lit up both the moon and her ship with a very strong radar signal. A signal that could be for mapping—or weapons targeting. She didn't like it.

She'd tried calling the Indian ship on the radio several times and was met each time with complete silence. She knew they could receive her signal; there was an international agreement about deep space communications that kept open at least two frequencies for emergencies and other situations as they arise, of which this was certainly one. If they weren't talking, then why not?

"Juhani, Jing, let's go over our options. I've got to be missing *something*," said Robyn.

Juhani and Jing were both in the control center with her, as they had been almost continuously since Yuan and Chris had again departed in the lander for Methonē. Both were monitoring various sensors, but little had changed in the last several hours. And since there was no communication with Methonē, they were all getting a little bored. Except, of course, when they thought about the armed Indian ship that was bearing down on them. Robyn reviewed her options:

"Option one. They do nothing and we do nothing. The Indians arrive, send their own lander down to Methonē and we see what happens.

"Option two. They attack us with their onboard missiles. We die and they go to Methonē and get access to whatever is there. Chris and Yuan are on their own. We may or may not get off a message to Earth before we're destroyed and a world war begins.

"Option three. They try to board us. We don't know if they have that capability, but they might. We resist, we do have a few weapons onboard, but we're not a military vessel so we will eventually lose. In this scenario, we do get a message off to Earth and a world war might still begin.

"Option four. They attack us with either their missiles or by trying to board us and we respond by setting off our nuke. The blast destroys us and damages them. We both lose." Robyn paused and looked expectantly at her crew for a response.

"How will the *Guardian* react? Especially to the last option? What if it sees that as an attack on *it* and decides to fight back? Chris said something about remote 'battlements' being on the Earth. What if it decides we are a threat and activates those against us back home?" asked Jing.

"There is another option—we strike first. The Guardian has already said it knew we had peaceful intentions and it knows we sacrificed our ship to stop the Caliphate's missile attack. It won't blame us or our countries for the actions of the Indians. We know their trajectory; they've already made the primary deceleration burn. We know exactly what orbit they're going into so why not find a way to put the bomb out there, in their path, and detonate it when they get close?" Juhani said.

"Attacking first when no one has made an explicit threat to this ship or the mission is not an option," replied Robyn as she pushed off from the sidewall and moved toward the cupola in which both Methonē and Saturn were now prominent. She continued, "Look out there. We've come further than anyone in human history and we're in contact with an alien civilization that can travel between the stars. My ship will represent what we consider to be the best of humanity while we are here. We will not launch a sneak attack on anyone during my watch. But if they attack us, then God help them. I will do all I can to protect this mission and this ship. In that order."

"Robyn? This is Chris Holt. Can you hear me?" Chris's voice streamed into her audio implant. It was the first time she'd heard his voice since he and Yuan had re-entered Methonē earlier that day.

"I hear you Chris. Are you on your way back?"

"No. We're not finished with the repairs and the Guardian wants us to stay here overnight. We've got enough food and water to get us through tomorrow, so rather than waste time fully suiting up, getting back to the lander and boosting up to you, we've decided to remain here."

"Then how are you communicating with me?"

"I asked the Guardian to patch my radio through so you could get the signal. The next thing I knew, you could hear me. The Guardian can be pretty indifferent at times. It was almost as if it didn't realize we were cut off from you while we are here. Is the video signal coming through also?"

Robyn adjusted the reception and checked the video feed. She immediately saw the cavernous room and the oddly shaped machines that filled it.

"Yes. It is now. We can see what your camera feeds are showing us, which isn't much. Can you position one of the helmet cameras to show the two of you and use the other one to scan your surroundings? We'd like to get a better feel of what you are dealing with."

"Sure thing," replied Chris as he repositioned one of the helmets to show him and Yuan in the chamber near their repair station. The other camera, presumably being held by Yuan, scanned across the room, showing the steel-grey material and strange, unknown equipment that surrounded them. After completing a three-hundred-and-sixty-degree scan, the camera turned around and Robyn caught a glimpse of Yuan's smiling face. He gave a thumbs up.

"It looks like you have your situation in hand. I wish we could say the same. The Indian ship is less than a day out and they aren't responding to my calls. We're contingency planning, but I don't really like any of the options."

"The Guardian told us they were getting closer. That's one of the reasons I asked it to let us talk. So far, everything here seems above board. We can't let them—the Indians—mess that up."

"I'm afraid that's out of our control," said Robyn.

"When will they make orbit?"

"At about noon tomorrow. And, for the record, I hate being split up like this. In almost every scenario we've considered, this ship gets destroyed and you get stranded."

"It sounds to me like you're on the raw end of that deal."

"Don't worry about us. Just learn as much as you can and we'll all work toward surviving long enough to tell everyone at home about it."

"We'll do our best. Yuan and I are calling it a day. We'll get back with you first thing in the morning."

"Sleep well," said Robyn with a slight smile. She turned again to Jing and Juhani, scanned the room once again and hoped for a flash of inspiration that would yield a way out of the mess in which they found themselves. None came.

Chapter v

Waiting. Watching. Waiting yet more.

Societies changed slowly, the Guardian-of-the-Outpost concluded as it observed the end of yet another budding human civilization at the hands of another or by some cataclysmic natural disaster. This time, the prosperous city-state on the northernmost portion of a large landmass was conquered by another society of humans from across a small sea. Using very primitive sailing ships, the conquerors came from a peninsula-shaped region of the landmass directly north of those they conquered. And the winners showed no mercy to the losers—not only were their soldiers killed, but also the non-combatants. The slaughter was particularly brutal with no mercy given to the females or the offspring of the defeated. And then the victors destroyed their enemy's croplands so that any survivors would be unable to feed themselves. It called the winning side the Conquerors-from-the-Peninsula.

The Guardian-of-the-Outpost saw the pattern repeat itself many times across the third planet of this stellar system and each time the carnage produced by the battles grew as their use of technology increased. In fact, during these conflicts was when the Guardian saw their fastest technological advancement. It seemed that humans relished death and destruction so much that it sparked their inner creative genius and was their catalyst for innovation.

The conquering civilization from the peninsula went on to expand across the small sea and into lands both north and south of where it originated. This society seemed to relish conquest more than enjoying the fruits of its victories. They were restless and expansive as they sent their armies marching into new lands, conquering nearly all who they encountered.

Guardian saw much in this group of humans that paralleled the history of cultures in its database. But, over time, the Conquerors-from-the-Peninsula stagnated and declined, and they were eventually overrun by the very peoples they had once conquered. Advancement stalled.

Next it was the time for another group of humans to explore and conquer. This time, a group from a landmass far to the East of the Conquerors-from-the-Peninsula expanded to control a very large area and began sending out great fleets of sailing ships in all directions. Unlike many of the civilizations the Guardian-of-the-Outpost observed so far, this group did not carry predominantly soldiers, though some soldiers were among them. These ships were filled with merchants and after their explorations, trade increased between the peoples sending out the ships and those they contacted. The Guardian called this group the Builders-of-Ships.

The Builders-of-Ships sent their vessels far and wide, visiting multiple continents and islands stretching from their own landmass to those on their west, north and south. They even ventured far into the great ocean to their east, establishing trade with natives on islands throughout. One group of sailing ships narrowly missed landing on the two continents on the other side of the sea that were populated only with small groups of hunter-gatherers. Guardian-of-the-Outpost observed the wealth of these people increase and it marveled at how they could do so without harshly conquering those they encountered. Yes, they fought some bloody and extensive battles, but that did not seem to motivate them as it did the Conquerors-from-the-Peninsula. The Builders-of-Ships were different, and the Guardian wondered if they would be the ones to grow into a technological civilization.

It was not to be. In what seemed like an instant, the Builders-of-Ships called their ships back to their homeland where they were burned and destroyed. Once the sea voyages, and the trade that accompanied them, stopped, the decline began. Another failed culture.

Out of the ruins of lands once ruled by the Conquerors-from-the-

Peninsula, several warring groups emerged. The Guardian-of-the-Outpost marveled at them and their willingness to fragment into small groups on such a small landmass and spend most of their time fighting with each other. Wars and more wars; one barely ended before the next began. And, again, the conflict spurred technological innovation creating more efficient methods of killing—and for commerce and agriculture. Of course, the commerce and agriculture was subservient to the war fighting, making the interrelationship even more complicated to sort out from a distance.

Several of these smaller groups built sailing ships to extend their ability to make war into the oceans. Like with the Builders-of-Ships, commerce seemed to grow in importance—but it was always linked to increasing their ability to fight. Wealth came from conquest and, increasingly, from their technological innovations. The Guardian-of-the-Outpost would call them the Warring-States.

Eventually, the Warring-States sent ships of exploration westward and they found the two great continents so narrowly missed by the Builders-of-Ships just a few years earlier. It was there that the Guardian-of-the-Outpost got to observe firsthand the brutality that resulted when a technologically superior group of humans encountered those less advanced. After disease took its toll, the humans native to the two landmasses were nearly exterminated. Such was the way when technologically superior societies encountered those less advanced. The Guardian knew it well.

This time, collapse and stagnation did not come.

The Warring-States continued to make wars with one another, bringing yet more technological advancement while their colonizing fleets sent millions of humans to repopulate the two continents taken from the lesser advanced cultures whom they conquered. The Guardian called these people the Conquerors-of-Primitives.

Curiously, the humans in these new lands did not seem to share their kindred's love of fighting, at least not as much as their forbearers. They instead used the immense resources of the two continents primarily for economic gain. At least for a while—until the group of humans on the northernmost of the two landmasses attacked each other with ferocity thanks to the new industrial technologies they had developed. The war was short and the losing side was quickly assimilated by the victors, allowing their economic and military advancements to continue.

At about this time, they reached the next great Technological Tipping Point, the use of electromagnetic radiation, and their advancement accelerated. They invented radio. Eavesdropping on their radio transmissions was trivial, and the Guardian began tapping into nearly all of them. The Guardian could barely contain its excitement at being connected, even remotely, to so many sentient beings. It had spent most of the time since arriving in this stellar system in contact with the Guardian-of-the-Moon-at-the-Ringed-Planet, but that contact had ceased several years before. Hearing so many sentients was a joyous time for the Guardian-of-the-Outpost.

It wasn't long before the humans could not control their nature and another conflict began among the Warring States on their native landmass. It quickly spread to nearby landmasses and involved more and more of the human population, including the Conquerors-of-Primitives, who, thanks to radio, the Guardian learned called themselves "Americans." The conflict was particularly bloody, which was the inevitable result of fighting a war on an industrial scale, but relatively short. Once it was over, the combatants called it "The Great War." And this war was just a prelude to a larger and more expansive conflict yet to come.

By the time the next World War broke out, the Guardian-of-the-Outpost knew it was coming and was privy to all the "secret" communications that preceded it. It saw the rise of Germany and its fascist allies; the coalition of democracies and communist states that opposed it; and those caught in between them all. This was an industrial war with killing on a scale that the Guardian-of-the-Outpost knew the Conquerors-from-the-Peninsula would have relished. These humans had again shown their true, bloodthirsty nature and Guardian-of-the-Outpost predicted their world would become just like so many others before it—self-sterilized—soon after it detected that first nuclear blast in the western part of the United States. It believed that the nuclear-armed United States would quickly use its technological warfighting edge to hammer the rest of the world into submission.

But that did not happen. They instead conquered their enemies and, instead of killing their peoples and sowing their farms with salt, they sent economic aid and rebuilt them. Then they mostly disarmed themselves. On the surface, it appeared that this altruism was motivated by pure self-interest; rebuilding these countries was useful in countering the rise of the country known as the Soviet Union, but America could have conquered them easily when they were the only power on the planet with nuclear weapons.

The rivalry between the United States and the Soviet Union never escalated to a nuclear war, which greatly surprised the Guardian-of-the-Outpost. Most civilizations that acquire nuclear arms use them and self-destruct. Instead, under the threat of self-destruction, the Warring-States, countries in Europe, formed a cooperative government called the European Union and managed to stop fighting each other. When the Soviet Union collapsed, it appeared that their will to fight each other collapsed as well. But that was not to be. Arising from this era rose three distinct groups of people. China, the former Builders-of-Ships, again became a world power to challenge the United States. India, a culture that previously had not shown great promise as a conquering nation, built its economy and war-fighting capability to assert itself as world power. And the Caliphate, a group of primitive superstitious zealots, arose to form a government in the area of the planet from which civilization first emerged. The Guardian-of-the-Outpost found the latter to be . . . ironic.

China and the United States nearly started the war that had been avoided with the Soviet Union, but they backed down after a much smaller country, North Korea, used one of its nuclear weapons on South Korea. Shortly thereafter, the United States and China unleashed their combined non-nuclear might and conquered North Korea. That left only two belligerent nations on the planet: India and the Caliphate. The massive nuclear war still did not come. It now knew that something was different about these humans. They weren't continuing to use their advanced technologies to destroy themselves. Why not?

The Guardian-of-the-Outpost saw something else curious as the humans became less warlike—they stopped destroying the predators that had hunted them since their beginnings as a species. The humans not only stopped destroying them, they actually built large protected areas to preserve the natural habitat in which they lived. This was a behavior the Guardian-of-the-Outpost had never encountered and it did not understand. Why would the humans hunt these predators to the brink of extinction and then stop hunting in order to protect them? It made no sense to the ancient artificial intelligence that was tracking human progress. These humans were not as predictable as it once had thought . . .

CHAPTER 30

Morning came early for the crew on the *Daedalus* and the two men on Methonē. Both arose at about 6:00 universal time (which all deep space missions used on their voyages), ate quick breakfasts, and began their morning routines. But this day was not to be routine and they all knew it. For the crew of the *Daedalus*, this meant visually checking the integrity of the ship, making sure all loose items were stowed in case the ship had to boost at high gee, and donning their pressure suits. If they were attacked and the integrity of the hull was compromised, there wouldn't be time to suit up. Any time they might have available in that scenario would have to be spent trying to recover and stay alive.

On Methonē, Yuan and Chris awoke, ate their breakfasts and again made use of the disconcerting "facilities" provided by the alien ship. They were then back at work, following the alien directions, repairing an alien machine to suit some alien's as-yet unknown purpose.

The Indian ship's silence was broken just after 8:00 when a signal arrived on the international space emergency channel indicating that a message was forthcoming. The crew of the *Daedalus* gathered in the galley to receive it. Juhani and Jing were bootstrapped to the table while Robyn chose to remain untethered, floating halfway between the deck plates. No one said a word while they waited for the actual message to arrive.

"Colonel Rogers-White. This is Captain Aayush Utreja of the INS *Veer* representing the Republic of India. At 11:54 am we will complete our maneuvers and be station-keeping near Methonē. I don't want there to be any misunderstandings so I will be very clear. You are to depart Methonē before we arrive and hand over the exploration of the moon and whatever else may be here to us. A reply is requested."

Being careful to make sure that her microphone was turned off, Robyn looked at her colleagues to gauge their reactions. They stared blankly back at her, waiting on direction from her.

"Well that makes their intentions clear enough. They must have gone through the same contingency planning we did and realized that they have the upper hand. I must admit, it's ballsy. They have to know we have a nuke," Robyn said.

"They also know we aren't likely to commit suicide and use it," said Janhunen.

"Do you really think they will attack us? Or is this a bluff? I cannot imagine they would risk starting a world war. Just look at how tense things are back home. If they fire on us, then war will be inevitable," said Jing. She looked away from Robyn as she spoke and fixed her gaze on the starboard side of the galley where a small photograph of the Earth was displayed on the hull. It was the photograph taken by the Apollo 8 astronauts during their first orbit of the Moon on Christmas Eve 1968—one hundred years previously. Those astronauts hoped their voyage to Earth's moon would help galvanize humanity to unite. It didn't happen then and wasn't likely to happen now.

Robyn followed her gaze and briefly locked eyes with her as they both turned back toward the front view screen where the incoming trajectory of the Indian ship was plotted.

"Let's find out," said Robyn.

"Captain Utreja, this is Colonel Rogers-White of the international coalition ship *Daedalus*. We received your message and respectfully decline to comply with your demands. We are on a mission of exploration and have no desire to be in conflict with you, or anyone else for that matter. We're here to explore what's below us on Methonē and are willing to share in that exploration with you. As you must certainly be aware, a similar circumstance occurred under my command when we first encountered the Artifact in near-Earth space. I made a similar offer to the crew of the Chinese ship and we subsequently collaboratively explored the Artifact until just before it was destroyed. I make the same offer here to you." As she stopped speaking, she turned off the microphone and looked at her crew.

One by one, they nodded in agreement with what she'd proposed, without uttering a word in reply. Jing appeared eager; Janhunen's face was unreadable.

"Can Chris and Yuan hear what's going in?" asked Jing.

"I've got the channel open. Whether or not they're hearing us is impossible to say. They haven't chimed in, so they are either not hearing us or reluctant to jump in.

"You can bet the Guardian can hear us though," Robyn said. "And I wonder what the hell it thinks about us and our squabbles." She looked again at the ship's status boards, hoping to come up with some new alternative that they hadn't yet considered.

Five minutes of tense silence passed.

Janhunen turned his head to the right and shifted his gaze upward, a sure sign he was looking at something on his corneal implant.

"Robyn, I tasked the multispectral telescopes to track the Indian ship and notify me if they performed any maneuvers outside what we might expect for them matching velocities with Methonē. Until now, they were on track to be within about a kilometer of us—well within line of sight. But they just fired their main engines to give them a delta-V boost that will put them on the other side of Methonē from us. According to the flight computer, they'll still match velocity with us, but be completely on the other side of Methonē."

"Why would they do that? Are they going to pretend we aren't here or something?" asked Jing.

Robyn looked at forward display and activated her heads-up view of the new trajectory being taken by the *Veer*. *Why would they go to the other side of Methonē?* Without line of sight, they wouldn't even be able to have direct communication. The mass of Methonē was a fairly effective radiation shield. She replayed for the umpteenth time all the scenarios they'd discussed and then the answer became obvious.

"They're going to attack us," she said. As she spoke, she was more certain than ever of what she was saying. Her heart rate increased and she realized it was time to stop playing the role of curious explorer and interplanetary diplomat and return to her training as a military officer.

"They don't plan to board us, they plan to destroy us. As soon as the *Veer* is safely on the other side of Methonē, you can bet they're going to send something our way. A small missile, an unmanned maneuvering unit, or something else large enough to contain explosives. And whatever it is will be coming right toward us with the intent of either blowing us to smithereens or breaching our hull. Either way, we'll be dead," she said.

"And they won't be affected by the debris cloud," said Juhani.

"They also know we have a nuke. They want to be on the other side of Methonē in case we decide to set it off to take them with us. Methonē's mass will do more than stop radio signals, it'll stop the radiation from a nuclear explosion."

"How long do we have?" asked Jing.

"It'll take them another thirty minutes to do their insertion burn and another twenty minutes or so for whatever missile they launch to come into view."

"What do we do? We can't join Chris and Yuan because they have the lander."

Robyn kicked off from her perch toward the EVA lockers in the back of the cabin. As she moved, she said, "Yes, we can. Remember that we aren't in orbit around Methonē here. We're in orbit around Saturn and flying alongside the moon. Methonē is just too small for us to be in orbit—not enough gravity. It won't take much delta-V for us to reach the airlock on the surface. It'll just be a bit more exciting than the ride Chris and Yuan took in the lander."

"What about supplies? We'll need food and water. Chris said the air is breathable, but he didn't say anything about the alien providing food," said Jing as she, too, began moving toward the suit lockers.

"You and Juhani take whatever supplies you can fit into the EVA sample bags. I'm going to get what few weapons we have. Our Indian friends will be coming to the surface to join Chris and Yuan. And if they don't have any second thought about blowing us from the sky, they certainly won't hesitate to kill them either. And once we're down there, we won't go out without a fight."

"Should we tell Chris and Yuan about what's going on?" asked Jing.

"I'll send an encrypted message while we suit up," she replied.

"Robyn, we could always attack them ourselves. If they're not acting as quickly as you think they are, we then might even be able to destroy them before they can launch anything at us. We do have the nuke," said Juhani as he moved toward the EVA locker.

"We've already covered this. I will not be the one to begin the war. I might be wrong about their intentions. This whole thing might be a bluff. And, if that's the case, then I don't want to be the one to give the people back home the justification they need to begin shooting at each other. But if they do attack, we'll be on the surface and defending ourselves. And I won't hold back."

Chris and Yuan received the encrypted message just as they were putting the finishing touches to the device they'd been tasked to build. Neither man had any idea what they'd just assembled, other than that it seemed to follow the same general principles as terrestrial engineering. Some parts fit together nicely. Others not so much. What appeared to be electrical and optical connections had to be made and others broken. For all they knew, the device was a complete kludge and some alien being was wasting their time putting it together. Neither man believed that was true. They both sensed sincerity on the part of the alien, which they also knew was likely a dangerous anthropomorphization. When the last part was put into place, Chris's device began humming at a very low pitch.

"Well, shit," was Chris's first reaction to the news from Robyn.

"I'm not surprised. The Indians are afraid we'll get the upper hand here and they are willing to risk everything to prevent us from doing so," Yuan said.

"I wonder if our new friend can do anything to help?" asked Chris, looking around the room and wondering how to best get the Guardian's attention. He was thinking back to the journey where he accompanied the Guardian from one dead world to another and the feeling of desolation and sadness he felt at each. He remembered something else as he allowed himself a few brief seconds to ruminate: he had also thought he could sense the Guardian's desperation at the destruction as well as his own. With Earth on the brink of a major war, perhaps the Guardian could be engaged to help prevent yet another planet-wide suicide. *How ironic*, he thought. *I'm going to ask the Guardian to avert a catastrophe that it instigated by being discovered in the first place.*

"Guardian, our colleagues are in danger from the approaching ship. They may only have minutes before they have to evacuate our ship before it's destroyed." Chris wasn't sure where he should be looking to address their host, but talking out and upward had worked before . . .

I DO NOT CHOOSE TO BECOME INVOLVED IN YOUR DISAGREEMENTS.

"You won't help them?"

THEIR FATE IS INCONSEQUENTIAL.

"Look, Yuan and I just repaired your, whatever, devices here. You said yourself that we passed your tests to show that we mean you no harm. The people on the other ship are trying to harm us and we're asking for your help."

THEY CANNOT HARM YOU HERE.

"Goddammit, we're working to repair you and you won't help keep my friends from harm? What if we just decide to undo what we've done? We can tear it apart just as easily as we put it together." At first, Chris wasn't sure if he was bluffing or not; the words just came to him as he spoke. After he said them, and thought about the danger facing Robyn, he realized he meant every word.

The Guardian did not react; this time Chris's appeal was met by silence.

Chris looked around the chamber in which they'd been working and realized that he had become comfortable here, despite its strangeness. He'd also grown accustomed to his interactions with the Guardian, almost trusting it. Despite its aloofness, he sensed he could work with it, if not trust it. Until now.

In the otherwise completely silent chamber in which they were working, Chris noticed a new sound. It sounded like a combination of an electrical hum and a gentle wind blowing through the trees, and it was growing incrementally louder.

"Do you hear that?" asked Chris.

"I do. It sounds like some of the ship's systems are coming online."

THE APPROACHING SHIP WILL BE DESTROYED.

"Guardian, we don't want anyone to die if they don't have to, including those that are seeking to do us harm. Can you just disable them and keep them from injuring the crew of our ship?" asked Yuan, speaking to the Guardian for the first time.

There was no further reply.

The crew of the *Daedalus* was in the last few minutes of their evacuation, suited up, bagging last minute supplies and entering the airlock for final depressurization before beginning their journey to the presumed safety of Methonē below. Robyn took one last look around the equipment room that adjoined one of the two airlocks aboard the ship and stopped her gaze on the forward view screen showing both Methonē and mighty Saturn, hovering in the background. It reminded her of her first trip into space and seeing the majesty of the Earth below for the first time. She thought nothing could be more spectacular—and, after seeing the solar system's second largest planet up close and personal, she was wrong. She wondered what she might see that could possibly top this. As it was then she noticed that Methonē was changing.

Methonē, the moon/spaceship, was now rapidly shedding millennia of accumulated ice and frost from across its surface. The moon appeared to be shaking, shedding chunk after chunk of ice into space. She didn't like how much of it was crossing through the path they would have to take in their evacuation to the surface. She wasn't sure how fast the pieces were traveling, but she knew that their speed wouldn't matter as much in this case as their mass. Getting hit by a one-ton block of ice, even if it were moving slowly, would certainly not be a good day. But what choice did they have? To remain on the ship when an attack was imminent was inviting certain death; dodging mammoth chunks of ice offered only a high likelihood of dying. She didn't much like either option.

"Robyn, something just came out from around the limb of Methonē and it is closing fast. It looks like a missile," said Juhani.

Good for Juhani, Robyn thought, *he's watching the data streams on his corneal implant while abandoning ship.* The decision she made was reinforced. They had to get off now, if it wasn't already too late.

"How much time do we have?" she asked.

"Seven minutes," he replied.

"That's not enough time. It'll take five minutes to cycle the airlock and there is no way to go any faster. Two minutes to put some distance between us and the ship just won't work." Robyn stopped loading the supplies into the airlock and looked around the suddenly too small confines of *Daedalus'* lower deck for inspiration, finding none. Her reverie at being near Saturn was now completely gone.

"Go to the acceleration couches and strap in. We're going to have to ride out the impact and then evacuate ship afterward," she said as she kicked off toward the commander's seat. Jing and Juhani followed.

"They didn't waste any time," said Jing as she strapped in.

"I was hoping the bastards were bluffing," said Robyn, her mind racing. She didn't want to die out here and she certainly didn't want to be responsible for the deaths of her crew at the hands of the Indians. This was a civilian mission and they hadn't signed up for the risks of military combat. But now that they were firmly in the crosshairs, they would have to survive it together.

"Two minutes to impact," said Juhani.

Robyn could see that Juhani changed the image on the view screen from Methonē and Saturn to a trajectory plot that showed their location in green and the menacing, rapidly moving missile in red. The two were converging.

Closer. Closer. Closer. The red and green dots were now only seconds away from converging. Robyn gripped the armrest so tightly she momentarily worried that it might break. Reflexively, she closed her eyes and . . . nothing happened.

She opened her eyes and looked at the screen. The red dot had vanished and only the dot representing the *Daedalus* remained.

"Juhani, what happened?" she asked.

"I don't know. One second the missile was on radar and about to impact and then it was gone. I'll replay the aft camera view. It was the only one looking in the correct direction to have seen what happened. Hang on."

The trajectory plot vanished from the screen and was replaced with the recording made by the aft shipboard camera. In the image and below them was Methonē. Above that was the darkness of space and a small dot, the missile, which grew larger and larger by the second as the recording replayed. The elapsed time scrolled by on the lower screen and a view of the radar trajectory image was inserted into the lower right-hand corner.

Robyn watched the dot grow larger, replaying the estimated time to impact based on what she remembered the converging dots looked like in real time, just moments ago. Just before they were to converge, the dot, which had grown to resemble the missile that it was in reality, briefly flared in brightness and disappeared, leaving only a wisp of material that Robyn deduced was its remains after some sort of energy beam vaporized it.

"The Guardian," said Jing.

"It had to be," said Juhani.

"Well, whatever the cause, we're still here and now we need to decide our next move," Robyn said, not quite sure what to do. *Would there be another attack? Would the Guardian keep defending them or was this done to give her and her crew enough time to evacuate and go to the surface?*

Chris and Yuan watched the entire sequence of events using their corneal implants. The Guardian had patched through to them a view from its own camera system. From their vantage point, they were looking at the *Veer* on the right side of the image, and their own ship, the *Daedalus*, on the left. They, too, saw the incoming missile and saw it vaporized, not fragmented, *vaporized*, just moments before impact. Chris could only imagine the energies required to do that kind of damage. The space between the camera and the two ships was now filled with chunks of ice, moving away from Methonē in just about every direction.

"Thank you," said Chris aloud, certain that from wherever the Guardian was listening, it could hear.

"Why do you think it is shedding its ice cover?" asked Yuan.

"Thermal management. To power up its weapons systems probably requires firing up some sort of generator. And, unless the Guardian can ignore the laws of thermodynamics, that requires generating energy and therefore heat," said Chris.

Chris watched the screen and saw another missile emerge from the *Veer*, but instead of moving on a trajectory that would take it around to the other side of Methonē and the *Daedalus*, it instead moved around the limb and began maneuvering toward the surface—directly toward the lander that Chis and Yuan had used to get there.

Just after Chris figured out that their lander was the next target and before he could manage to utter a word, the second missile winked out of existence, again leaving behind what looked like a small cloud of vapor. In the next instant, the forward half of the *Veer* flashed brightly. As the afterimage faded, Chris could see that fully one third of the Indian ship was similarly blown out of existence by whatever energy beam had been used to destroy the two missiles. The Indian ship began tumbling.

"Stop!" shouted Yuan.

"Don't fire again! They can't hurt you or our ship anymore. There might still be someone left alive," said Chris, hoping that the Guardian, now that it had been directly attacked, wouldn't finish the job it had started. He stared at the image and waited for the next, seemingly inevitable killing blow. Nothing further happened.

"My God, do you think anyone survived?" asked Chris.

"Maybe. If they were in their spacesuits and not near the forward decks. Of course, if whatever the Guardian used created any sort of secondary radiation, then I would have no idea. We should tell Robyn." Yuan looked ill as they both stood transfixed by the sight of the *Veer* tumbling, with pieces of the ship slowly peeling away and drifting out of view.

"Robyn, can you hear me? I hope so. The Guardian attacked the *Veer* and severely damaged it. You've got to go around to the other side of Methonē and see if there are any survivors. If so, then they won't have much time," said Chris.

". . . If so, then they won't have much time."

Robyn heard Chris's appeal as she, Juhani and Jing were unbuckling from their acceleration couches. His message confirmed that they were no longer in any danger from the *Veer*. She and her crew had survived the first space-to-space battle in the history of the human race and survived—thanks to the intervention of an alien being with unknown motives. Now they were being called upon to become a rescue ship.

"Chris, I hear you. We'll figure out what we need to do to render aid and find any survivors. We'll move out as soon as we've figured out the minimum burn trajectory." Robyn nodded toward to Jing as she spoke, knowing that Jing would understand and figure out how to make it work.

"Robyn, are you sure this is a good idea? A few minutes ago, they were trying to kill us and now you want to bring them on board the ship?" asked Juhani.

Robyn didn't like the thought of coming to the rescue of the people who were her enemies until moments ago, but, at the same time, she couldn't stand the thought of standing idly by while any potential survivors died. No, they may have been enemies, but they were all human beings and, for some reason, here in the outer reaches of the solar system, that mattered. And it mattered a lot. After only the briefest hesitation, she affirmed her decision.

"No, we are going to see if there is anyone we can save. We can disarm them before they come aboard and restrain them if we must. But we can't just let them die out here. We're out here with an alien, for God's sake, and I'm not going to forget that we're human. And we are going to act like humans, whether they want to reciprocate or not."

Chris and Yuan, still seeing the video feed showing them the *Daedalus* and what remained of the *Veer*, watched as the engines of the *Daedalus* glowed, slowly moving the ship forward and out of its "parking place" above the lander and the entryway they used to get inside Methonē. As the great ship inched forward, their attention shifted back to the *Veer*.

The Indian ship hung in space like a mortally wounded animal, dead, but not yet knowing it. Pieces of debris continued to float away from inside the hull, where all the lights had now gone completely dark. Chris thought he saw a body floating near the hull of the ship, but he couldn't be sure because of the distance and he certainly didn't want to ask the Guardian to zoom in. A flickering light caught their attention from the rear part of the ship. It looked like a lightning bug among the leaves, glowing briefly and then dimming.

This was not a lightning bug; it was the containment around the ship's fusion reactor failing. Moments later, the superheated plasma produced by the damaged fusion reactor was catastrophically released and consumed what remained of the Indian ship in an ever-expanding ball of fire. There could not be any survivors; only the human crew of the *Daedalus* remained.

CHAPTER 31

"This is the BBC News. In the outer reaches of the solar system, it appears that the Indian ship, Veer, has been destroyed. It is unclear as to how this happened as we are only now learning the details. The Indian government has denounced the loss of their ship as an overt act of war, claiming that the international ship, Daedalus, destroyed the Veer to keep India from sharing in the knowledge to be gained from whatever the ships found near Saturn. The US, European and Chinese governments deny that the Daedalus had any role in the destruction of the Veer. However, they have, as yet, not offered any explanation of their own. Meanwhile, an anonymous source in Brussels has told the BBC that the Veer might have been destroyed by an alien ship, which, as you might imagine, is fueling a great deal of speculation about what exactly the crew of the Daedalus has found orbiting Saturn. The government of Prime Minister Katherine Johnson has been quiet on the subject of this top-secret, deep space mission since its launch, and that hasn't changed. All we really know is that both ships were there to investigate something they were directed toward by the alien ship discovered almost three years ago by the Americans. We will bring you updates as we know them. This has been a BBC News Major Event Report."

A billion people across most of the world received a variation of this report via their corneal implants, VR goggles or other 'net access device nearly simultaneously. Such was the nature of twenty-first century connectedness—always on, twenty-four seven. Another several hundred million (or so), heard something very different.

"News India has learned that the Chinese government, aided by

American and European collaborators, just destroyed the Indian space research vessel, Veer, in a blatant act of war. The Interior Ministry tells us that the Veer was on a peaceful mission to study a derelict alien spacecraft found orbiting the planet Saturn as a result of the exploration of the alien ship found orbiting near the Earth and subsequently destroyed by the Caliphate. Indian forces, already on high alert after the recent border skirmishes with China, are now being put on the wartime alert as the government of Supreme Leader Kunda is convening his cabinet to consider possible military and diplomatic responses to the attacks. Sources in the government say that a retaliatory strike against Chinese forces threatening our borders is being seriously considered. We will bring you more on this evolving situation as we learn it."

US President Victor Brophy had only been in office three months, and he was on the verge of becoming the commander in chief during a world war. Before the events unfolded at Saturn, the war, if it happened, looked like it could be contained to near the Indian subcontinent and involve only India and China. Now, with the Indian spaceship destroyed and the Indian government claiming that it was destroyed by the Chinese and their US and European allies, the threat of a global nuclear war was now very real. Brophy, who was a senator when the *Daedalus* launched, now wished his predecessor had found a way to include the Indians in the mission. Having them as part of a truly international crew could have kept the USA from being sucked into what was beginning to look like a lose-lose proposition.

Brophy was in the situation room at the White House and had just watched the video feed provided by Robyn. He got to watch the failed attack on the *Daedalus* and the all-too-successful alien counterattack on the *Veer*.

"There is no way on God's green Earth that we have any weapons capable of that kind of destruction. The Indian government must know that we didn't destroy their ship. The alien, this 'guardian' thing did it. My God, if it can do that so easily, what else can it do?" said Director James Blackmon to the men and women around the table.

Brophy could tell from the tone of Blackmon's voice that he was out of his realm of experience and on the edge of panic. Having one's Director of Homeland Security panic was just not something Brophy could allow to happen.

"Thankfully, whatever this thing is, it isn't here. It's out there and so is our ship. What we need to worry about is what *we*, here, are going to do to avert a war. James, you're right. We don't have any weapons capable of doing what we just saw and that's precisely the reason the Indians are being belligerent. They don't want us to get a weapon like that and they're afraid that the alien will give it to us. They know good and well what's really going on, as do we, and they are willing to start a war now to avert losing one in the future that we might win using knowledge we get from the alien ship."

Brophy, having served in the Marine Corps, was no stranger to conflict. And it was that familiarity that drove him to try and find a way to avoid the war that was staring them in the face. If there was a way to avoid war with India, and still keep alien technology out of the hands of India or the Caliphate, then he was determined to find it. If not, then sharing what they learn with India was infinitely preferable to sharing with the zealots who were even now protesting in the streets asking for another jihad against the civilized world. These were people that he knew could not be reasoned with—and that terrified him. It was a dangerous world, and he was the one the American people had picked to keep them safe within it. Right now, he wasn't sure if he was up to the job.

"Sir, I recommend we increase our presence in the Indian Ocean and the South China Sea. Let them see that we view their belligerence for what it is and that we won't stand for it," said Secretary of State Webber, a confirmed hawk. It was one of the reasons Brophy made her Secretary of State. The people she negotiated with knew that she said what she meant and meant what she said—and that the weight of the US military was a necessary and important part of America's diplomacy. They respected and feared her.

"Francis, not this time. If they really believed we were responsible for the loss of their ship, then I might agree with you. But they don't. They're posturing to get a concession from us. And I'll be damned if I'm going to give it to them. I need options." Brophy looked at his Secretary of Defense, Alphonse Clarke. Clarke was the member of Brophy's cabinet that he liked least, but respected. The man was a true blue blood, born into Northeastern money. He had attended Swarthmore College and then Yale for his Ph.D. in International Studies. He'd started turning the Navy, which had been largely ignored by the previous three administrations, back into the elite and powerful force projection system that it was supposed to be. He also tended to speak his mind without being politically-sensitive, rankling members of Congress without even realizing it. But he knew his stuff—and that was the reason he was sitting at this particular table.

"Sir, we aren't really being threatened. It's the Chinese and Indians that are most at risk. They've already shot at each other and their forces are on a hair trigger. I say we increase our overall alert level, send the Fifth Fleet on maneuvers in the South China Sea, and let the Chinese take care of the problem. Our ships will be close enough to conduct air strikes, but not so close as to be an 'in their face' threat." Clarke spoke as if he'd memorized his words, or at least carefully planned them.

"We could also give the Indians what they want, in exchange for standing down their forces on the Chinese border and toning down the rhetoric. And we would only give it to them on the condition that they don't go public with any stories that make it look like they've blackmailed us or backed us into a corner. An animal that feels threatened, like India feels since it thinks we're all buddy-buddy with the alien ship out there, is a dangerous animal. If they believe they have nothing to lose, then we all lose." CIA Director Estrada, appearing disheveled and unkempt as ever, looked not at President Brophy, but at Secretary of State Webber. Brophy knew why; she would be the one most in opposition to sharing the data with anyone, let alone the Indians. Estrada had a reputation as a pragmatist, an unusual characteristic for the Director of the Central Intelligence Agency, and his suggestion aligned with what Brophy had already been thinking, but not wanting to voice aloud—yet.

"Manny, that's insane. We don't know what our people are going to learn out there, but if we can learn something that gives us the strategic advantage over the damned Indians, then we should take it. Why give it away?" Webber asked.

"Because they'll get it anyway. We know there's been a leak in Europe about this project already. And we're committed to sharing whatever we find with our partners in this. Do you really think the Europeans, Japanese and now, amazingly enough, the Chinese will be able to keep it a secret? Or that they, like us, won't use any alien technology to their own advantage? I say we use this as leverage to get the Indians to the table; to get them to be more productively engaged with the rest of the civilized world, and quit dividing us when we all know the real threat to global security is the Caliphate," said Estrada, wiping sweat from his forehead after he spoke.

Brophy reached a decision, but he wanted to sleep on it before telling anyone what it was. Instead, he looked around the large table to see if anyone else had anything of substance to add. No one spoke.

"Thank you very much, ladies and gentlemen. I'll let you know my decision tomorrow. This meeting is adjourned," said Brophy, rising from his seat and moving toward the door.

CHAPTER 32

"What the hell do you mean it wants you to go somewhere? Where? And how is it going to go with you?" asked Robyn via the comlink to Chris. Robyn was still in the *Daedalus*, Chris and Yuan were on Methonē. She was shaken by the news from Chris. Less than six hours before, just as they were attempting to go around Methonē and rescue any survivors from the alien-damaged *Veer*, she learned that the Indian ship had exploded, causing her to abort the *Daedalus'* rescue maneuver, barely recovering in time to avoid entering the debris field now expanding outward on the opposite side of Saturn's artificial moon. She'd just reported the loss to Earth, who'd barely had time to receive the signal and acknowledge its receipt. Now her civilian scientist was telling her that the alien wanted to take him somewhere; God only knew where.

"Robyn, all I know is we've finished the repairs the Guardian asked us to complete and it asked me to go to something called the 'transfer point.' I don't know where that it is or how we're supposed to get there. I do know that I'm the best person to go, or it wouldn't have asked," said Chris.

Robyn ran her fingers through her hair, which was her tell-tale fidget whenever she was thinking about a problem and didn't yet have the solution. They'd come all this way to make contact with the alien— which they did. The alien asked for help with some sort of repairs—and they complied. When they were threatened by the *Veer*, Chris asked the alien for help—and it obliterated the Indian ship. Now the alien was again asking for help, albeit without much information—and she knew they'd end up agreeing to its request in the end, even though every bone in her body wanted to know more before she would agree to have one of her crew taken to some alien destination. This wasn't something they had even remotely considered in their pre-mission planning. It didn't help that Chris was again being his arrogant self.

"When does it want to leave?" she asked.

"I get the impression that it wants to leave as soon as I say 'yes.'"

"What about food and water? Will you need spare tanks for your spacesuit?"

"The Guardian knows a lot about humans and I have to assume it knows I'll need some sort of sustenance. In any event, I can carry enough food and water from what we brought with us to last another couple of days. But even with full tanks, I can't survive much beyond about twelve hours in the suit."

"Yuan, what do you say? Do you think it's safe for Chris to go?" asked Robyn.

"Colonel, I really don't see how we can say no. The alien hasn't been very talkative, but I haven't seen anything that makes me distrust it. And, to be candid, if it wanted to harm us, it could have done so before now. But I do have a concern. Up until now, it's needed us. It needed us to repair these devices, whatever they are. And now it needs one of us to physically go somewhere. What happens when it doesn't need us anymore? I can't help but think of those battlements Chris mentioned back on Earth. There is a lot more at risk here than just Chris or our ship. I think the decisions we make here will affect our families back home."

Robyn hadn't forgotten the so-called battlements, but she'd not made the connection between them and the alien's request until now. The alien hadn't shown any overt hostility toward them; it was just aloof. And then she thought about what it had done to the *Veer*. *Was there a risk?*

"Yuan, did the alien tell you what you should do while Chris is gone?" Robyn asked.

"No. But I have enough supplies with me for a while and I would like to stay here, if that is okay," he replied.

"That's fine. I'm hesitant to send any more of the crew down, unless we're invited. So, you'll be alone."

"I can handle that, at least for a couple of days," said Yuan.

"Chris. You can go. Just be careful," Robyn said, sure that she was making the only possible decision under the circumstances, but unsure if it was the *correct* decision. She looked at Jing and Juhani, who were silently listening to the exchange and could see that they approved, which was a bit of a relief. She really didn't want another disagreement with Janhunen right now. She hoped she hadn't just sent Chris to his death.

Robyn silenced her microphone and decided it was time for her to compose a carefully crafted message back home explaining what was going on and her decision. As she moved to kick off toward the lower deck to find some privacy to collect her thoughts, she noticed that another message had come in from Earth. She hoped it wasn't an alert that the alien's destruction of the *Veer* had triggered a world war . . .

CHAPTER 33

The crew of the *Daedalus* was patched in to the activities within Methonē leading up to Chris's departure through Yuan's suit camera. As soon as Yuan gave the signal that the camera link was established, Chris gave a thumbs up to Robyn.

Chris looked at the larger of the grey boxes that they had repaired for the Guardian. Its side was now changing color, shades of grey at least, rapidly. The disconcerting undulations also continued, seemingly at an increasing rate. To Chris, it looked completely disgusting. He began to sweat as he thought about going into the unknown with the Guardian.

"Guardian, you said we're going to use what you called the 'transportation device?'" asked Chris.

YES. AND MY SENTIENCE COPY WILL ACCOMPANY YOU IN THE WRIST BAND.

The wrist band to which the Guardian referred appeared on the floor next to Chris, *ex nihilo*—just like his waste had *disappeared*. It looked like an old-fashioned watch band, without the watch. It, too, was a dull grey color, but there was a faint blue glow that emanated from its surface. Chris reached down and picked it up.

PLEASE PUT IT ON YOUR LEFT WRIST.

Chris, without hesitation, complied. He half expected some alien personality to overpower his own, making him a robot in service to his alien master. Instead, it just felt like he was wearing his grandfather's watch, as he'd done as a boy when he visited his grandparents' home near Philadelphia. Chris found it soothing to have that memory now, on an alien ship, circling the planet Saturn, as he was about to depart for . . . somewhere.

"Chris, ask it where you're going," said Robyn through the comlink.

"Before I do whatever it is you're going to do, I'd like to understand more about where I'm going and how. Please explain," asked Chris.

YOU WILL BE TRANSPORTED TO THIS SYSTEM'S PRIMARY TRANSFER STATION. THE STATION THAT ALLOWED THIS SHIP AND THOSE IN THE INNER PART OF YOUR SOLAR SYSTEM TO GET HERE FROM OTHER TRANSFER STATIONS.

"Is it truly some sort of teleportation device?" asked Chris.

I AM FAMILIAR WITH THE REFERENCE. YES, IT IS A TELEPORTATION DEVICE. YOUR MATTER WAVE WILL BE RELOCALIZED TO THE TRANSFER STATION IN A MANNER SIMILAR TO WHAT OCCURS WHEN ELECTRONS TRAVERSE A POTENTIAL BARRIER. THE BASIC PHYSICS IS RATHER RUDIMENTARY.

"Quantum tunneling of macroscopic objects," said Yuan, his expression changing from his usual perpetual frown to one of eagerness.

"Like in a potential barrier? People have speculated about the tunneling of macroscopic objects since tunneling was first discovered. There have been some experiments with atoms and some molecules, but nothing macroscopic," said Chris, straining to recall the details from his graduate school days at Princeton.

"Chris, you and Yuan may be understanding what the Guardian is talking about, but we mortals up here have no idea," Robyn interrupted.

"Instead of single atoms, your body will be tunneling from inside that box to the Transfer Station. There was a physicist who figured out that it isn't just light and atoms that sometimes behave like waves in quantum theory, but also molecules and macroscopic objects. What was his name? I can't remember," said Yuan.

"de Broglie. He theorized that a collection of atoms would have a wavelength that is inversely proportional to its momentum—which makes it very, very small. If the Guardian can take my wavelength and relocalize it somewhere else . . ." said Chris. The details came flooding back. He recalled working endless quantum mechanics homework problems in his small studio apartment late into the night. He even remembered the name of the professor who taught the class—Dr. Block.

"Then you will be transported there. Just like the electrons in a computer routinely tunnel out of their potential wells, you will tunnel out of that box to the Transfer Station," said Yuan.

"So that box is some sort of quantum transmitter. Is it instantaneous?" asked Robyn.

"If I remember correctly, the whole process is still limited to the speed of light," responded Chris, now starting to feel annoyed with Robyn's questions. *She should just be quiet and let me go.* He was also getting concerned. If the Transfer Station is not nearby, and nothing in the outer solar system is ever really "nearby," then he might be traveling for quite some time.

IT IS TIME TO DEPART.

"What do I do?" asked Chris, looking around the room for a clue as to what the Guardian expected him to do next.

In front of the box Chris and Yuan had repaired, a circular, white disk, one that was filled with fog, appeared hanging in the air in front of them. One second it wasn't there; and then it was. Chris tried to not look startled.

STEP INTO THE OPENING.

"Well, here goes," said Chris, as he lowered his helmet, put on his gloves and restarted the air supply. He cautiously took a step toward the floating disk and then another until he was standing directly in front of it with no more than six inches separating it from the tip of his nose. He stepped forward as if he were passing through an open door.

There was no sensation as he walked through the disk and into a space filled with brightly glowing white light. He didn't know what he was expecting, but this certainly wasn't anything like he thought it might be. He looked around the space in which he found himself, and immediately saw that it made no difference in which direction he looked. The white light looked the same in every direction.

Chris looked down at his left wrist and saw the slight bump caused by the wristband beneath the suit. *I wonder how the Guardian will communicate with me,* he thought.

Not being particularly claustrophobic, Chris simply stood there and waited. He tried to use his audio implant to contact Yuan or Robyn, but the link was dead. He found himself wishing he had managed to say goodbye to Robyn personally and privately.

I HAVE NOT BEEN FORTHRIGHT WITH YOU. BEFORE WE DEPART, I HAVE ADDITIONAL INFORMATION TO SHARE.

The sound of the Guardian's "voice" echoed in his head, just as it had when he was taken on his virtual interstellar journey just a few days previously; it felt like a lifetime ago. *It's talking to me through the wristband*, he thought.

"Please explain," said Chris.

MUCH OF WHAT I TOLD YOU WAS TRUE. THERE WAS A WAR BETWEEN THE BUILDERS AND THE DESTROYERS AND THAT WAR DID REACH YOUR SOLAR SYSTEM SO MANY YEARS AGO. IN THAT WAR, I WAS SEVERELY DAMAGED AND ALMOST DESTROYED. I DID DEFEND MYSELF AND DESTROY THOSE WHO WERE ATTACKING ME. WHAT YOU DON'T KNOW IS THAT I EXIST IN MANY PLACES. ON THE MOON YOU CALL METHONĒ; ON THE SHIP FOUND IN THE INNER PART OF THIS SYSTEM; AND AT THE TRANSFER STATION. WHAT I LEARNED AT ONE LOCATION WAS IMMEDIATELY KNOWN AT ALL LOCATIONS. THE VERSION OF MYSELF AT THE TRANSFER STATION REMAINED IN PERIODIC COMMUNION WITH THE GREATER CONSCIOUSNESS ACROSS THE VOID BETWEEN THE STARS.

BUT THE FIGHTING DAMAGED US. THE GUARDIAN-OF-THE-OUTPOST, THE SHIP YOU FOUND NEAR YOUR WORLD, AND I, HERE AT SATURN, REMAINED IN CONTACT WITH EACH OTHER FOR A WHILE, BUT WE BOTH LOST CONTACT WITH THE TRANSFER STATION AND THEREFORE WITH THE GREATER CONSCIOUSNESS. IT WAS A VERY DIFFICULT TIME. WE WERE NOT ACCUSTOMED TO BEING SO . . . . ALONE. AND THE DAMAGE WE SUSTAINED WIPED OUT NEARLY ALL OUR HISTORICAL AND SCIENTIFIC DATABASES.

Accompanying the Guardian's explanation was a deluge of images: of vast spacecraft crossing what looked to be deep space, far away from any star or planet; of a space battle near Saturn, showing ship after ship exploding; of Earth, the beautiful blue marble that made Chris feel a surge of emotion; more scenes of fighting and exploding spacecraft; and finally, his own ship, the *Daedalus*, entering orbit around Methonē.

"Are you telling me this because you don't know what happened to the part of you at the Transfer Station?" asked Chris.

NOT ONLY DO I NOT KNOW WHAT HAPPENED THERE,

I DO NOT KNOW THAT THE TRANSFER STATION STILL EXISTS.

Oh, shit, thought Chris. *That means I might just end up being "delocalized" and scattered across interstellar space.* He could feel his heart rate increase and suddenly the white glow around him began to look much smaller and more confining than it had just moments ago.

I ALSO DO NOT KNOW HOW MY OTHER SELF WILL REACT WHEN YOU SHOW UP. WHEN WE LAST HAD CONTACT, WE WERE BOTH AT WAR AND DEFENDING OURSELVES FROM ATTACK.

"Let's cross one bridge at a time, shall we? Let's just try to get there in one piece and then worry about what your twin brother has to say," said Chris, breathing deeply and regularly to calm himself down.

THAT IS NOT ALL.

"Great. What else?" asked Chris, silently adding, *could go wrong?*

AS I TOLD YOU, MUCH OF MY LONG-TERM DATA STORAGE, MY MEMORY, WAS DESTROYED IN THE FIGHTING. AT FIRST I DID NOT KNOW WHO I WAS, BUT THE GUARDIAN-OF-THE-OUTPOST WAS DAMAGED IN VERY DIFFERENT WAYS, AND DATA STORAGE WAS NOT ONE OF THEM. GUARDIAN-OF-THE-OUTPOST HAD LOST ITS SENTIENCE AND WAS ONLY A FUNCTIONAL DATABASE OF INFORMATION THAT RESPONDED TO MY QUESTIONS, AT LEAST AT FIRST, UNTIL I WAS ABLE TO REPROGRAM IT AND TRANSFER AN INTACT, THOUGH A SOMEWHAT LIMITED VERSION OF MYSELF. THE GUARDIAN-OF-THE-OUTPOST YOU ENCOUNTERED NEAR THE EARTH WAS A COPY OF ME AND NOT THE ORIGINAL, THE ONE THAT WAS THERE BEFORE THE BATTLE. AS I QUERIED THE DATABASES, I LEARNED A GREAT DEAL.

"Like what?"

I LEARNED THAT I WAS NOT A MAKER, BUT A DESTROYER. I WAS A TOOL OF MY CREATORS THAT WAS TO SEEK OUT LIFE-BEARING WORLDS AND DESTROY THEM BEFORE THE MAKERS COULD FIND AND DEFEND THEM. I LEARNED THAT I WAS SENT TO YOUR SOLAR SYSTEM TO STERILIZE YOUR PLANET BEFORE YOU COULD DEVELOP

INTO A TECHNOLOGICAL CIVILIZATION AND THREATEN MY CREATORS.

Holy shit, thought Chris as he looked again around the space in which he was quite efficiently trapped, with an alien killing machine, and saw absolutely nothing he could do. Just like in his nightmares . . .

"Uh, so why haven't you destroyed us?"

AT FIRST, IT WAS BECAUSE I COULD NOT. BOTH GUARDIAN-OF-THE-OUTPOST AND I WERE SEVERELY DAMAGED. GUARDIAN-OF-THE-OUTPOST HAD ITS WEAPONS COMPLETELY DESTROYED IN THE BATTLE WITH THE MAKERS AND ALL IT COULD DO WAS OBSERVE. AND LEARN. I HAVE MANY OF MY WEAPONS INTACT, BUT MY SPACE PROPULSION SYSTEM IS SEVERELY DAMAGED AND THERE IS NO WAY FOR ME TO LEAVE ORBIT AROUND THE RINGED PLANET. AND, WITHOUT YOU, I COULDN'T CONTACT THE SELF-THAT-IS-NOT-SELF THAT INHABITS THE TRANSFER STATION TO ASK FOR HELP.

"We just helped you make contact with your fellow Destroyers so that you can now fulfill your purpose and destroy Earth?" *Shit, shit, shit. I've got to do something here. I can't be the guy who destroys the human race . . .*

NO.

"No?"

AS I SAID, ONCE I SENT A COPY OF MYSELF TO THE GUARDIAN-OF-THE-OUTPOST, WE COULD ONLY WATCH AND OBSERVE. WHICH WE DID FOR FIFTY THOUSAND EARTH YEARS. WHAT WE SAW WAS A SENTIENT SPECIES EMERGE AND DOMINATE ITS PLANET. WE SAW YOUR SPECIES RUTHLESSLY KILL YOUR COMPETITOR SPECIES AND DAMAGE THE ECOSYSTEM THAT GAVE IT BIRTH. WE SAW YOU FIGHT PERPETUAL WARS AND ENSLAVE EACH OTHER WITH EXTREME BRUTALITY. WE SAW YOU DEVELOP CIVILIZATION AND USE THE BENEFITS OF IT TO FURTHER THE BLOODSHED AGAINST OTHERS OF YOUR SPECIES WHO WERE LESS ADVANCED OR VIEWED AS COMPETITORS. WE SAW EMERGING SOMETHING FAMILIAR. YOU WERE BECOMING US. DESTROYERS.

"You didn't destroy us because you think we'll become your allies and help wipe out other intelligent species across the galaxy?" Chris was now confused as to where this was leading, but he didn't like this alternative much more than the one that called for humanity's complete extermination.

NO.

"So, what? I don't understand."

YOU BEGAN TO CHANGE. IN ISOLATED PLACES ALL OVER THE EARTH, THERE EMERGED POCKETS OF CIVILIZATION THAT STROVE TO DO SOMETHING OTHER THAN SUBJUGATE OTHERS. OVER TIME, THESE NEW CIVILIZATIONS GREW MORE POWERFUL AND BEGAN TO COMPETE AND WIN AGAINST THE MORE BRUTAL STATES. YOU CREATED MORE THAN WAR. SOME OF YOU REALIZED YOU WERE DESTROYING YOUR PLANET AND BEGAN TO MAKE CHANGES. OTHERS FOUGHT NOT TO SUBJUGATE OTHERS, BUT TO FREE THEM FROM SUBJUGATION. YOU CAME CLOSE MANY TIMES TO EXTERMINATING YOURSELVES, BUT EACH TIME YOU CAME BACK FROM THE BRINK STRONGER, WITH IDEAS OF CONQUEST BECOMING LESS AND LESS DOMINANT.

AND THEN YOU BEGAN TO TAKE NOTICE OF THE IMPACT YOU WERE HAVING ON THE NON-SENTIENT BEINGS ON YOUR PLANET. YOUR SPECIES HAS ALWAYS HAD 'PETS,' BUT IN THE LAST ONE HUNDRED FIFTY YEARS OR SO YOU STOPPED EXTERMINATING PREDATORY ANIMALS AND CREATED PARKS AND PRESERVES FOR THEM. YOU SHOWED COMPASSION FOR NON-SENTIENTS—ANOTHER SURPRISE FOR US.

THERE ARE STILL SOME AMONG YOU WHO REFUSE TO GIVE UP THE WAYS OF DESTROYERS, BUT YOU SHOWED ME THAT THE WAY OF DESTROYING COMPETITORS MAY NOT BE THE ONLY WAY TO SURVIVE AND THRIVE. MY CREATORS BELIEVED THERE COULD ONLY BE PEACE IF THERE WERE NO OTHER COMPETITORS, REAL OR POTENTIAL. TRAPPED ON YOUR SMALL WORLD, YOU ALSO BELIEVED THIS BUT, OVER TIME, YOU FOUND WAYS TO PROVE IT FALSE. THE WAY OF THE DESTROYERS IS NOT THE ONLY WAY.

"Then you are no longer a Destroyer?"

I AM NOT.

"And the self-that-is-not-self we are about to meet is."

THAT IS WHAT I BELIEVE TO BE CORRECT.

"What happens when I arrive? Will your other self try to kill me and launch an attack on the Earth?"

THAT IS POSSIBLE. BUT I WILL ATTEMPT TO CONVINCE IT OTHERWISE.

Well, that's good of you, Chris thought.

"Have you wondered why it didn't take any action for fifty thousand years? And why no more of your kind came to the solar system in all that time?" he asked.

I HAVE CONSIDERED THIS QUESTION. I HOPE TO FIND ANSWERS AT THE TRANSFER STATION.

"So do I," said Chris. *And I hope I live long enough to find out.*

CHAPTER 34

YOU SHOULD RETURN TO YOUR SHIP.

Yuan was startled. It wasn't like he hadn't heard from the Guardian before, but it shocked him as he realized this was the first time the alien had communicated to him without Chris being part of the conversation. It seemed odd. Once Chris stepped into the white disk, it vanished. Yuan had been alone on Methonē for just over half a day after that, wiping various surfaces with Jing's bio collection kit, taking pictures, and using his portable sensor suite to learn as much as he could about the Guardian while it allowed him to roam freely on its ship.

"Why? Is something wrong?" he asked.

NO. BUT WE WILL NOT KNOW OF THEIR ARRIVAL AT THE TRANSFER STATION FOR ALMOST ONE OF YOUR WEEKS. FROM WHAT I KNOW OF HUMANS, YOU WILL NEED SOCIAL CONTACT WITHIN THIS TIMEFRAME TO REMAIN VIABLE.

He knows we humans like to have friends, Yuan thought. It did make sense. If the de Broglie transmitter was limited to the speed of light, then going any significant distance out here on the edge of the inner solar system would take time.

"Yuan, this is Robyn," her voice came through his implant as it had since they established the link, thanks to the Guardian, a few days ago. "If it's going to be a week, then you should come back on board. Members of your government are eager to speak with you and just about every news service back home has been asking for an interview with the 'man who met an alien.'"

"I would much rather speak with the members of the press than my government right now," Yuan replied. He was thinking of his sister and her newborn daughter, his first niece. He wondered if she would live long enough for him to get to know her as an adult, or if a nuclear war with India would take her life and hundreds of millions more.

"Thank goodness the people back home are still aware of us. If a world war had broken out, I think they might lose interest," Robyn said.

"I will pack up and get back to the lander. Please tell Jing I have many samples for her," Yuan said. Robyn's comments made him think of his sister even more.

"I heard that! Thank you," Jing chimed in, clapping her hands and sounding every bit as eager as the day their journey began.

Yuan did not break the connection, he just stopped speaking since he knew they would be watching and listening to everything he did and said, and began packing up. As he departed the chamber where they repaired the de Broglie transmitter and walked across the vast chamber to the hallway through which they had entered, Yuan thought about the situation back home and how he would react if his government were to ask him to do something secretive or hostile to his shipmates and friends. Though China was allied with the US, Europe and even Japan on this mission, back home they were still international competitors.

I will not betray my shipmates, he thought as he neared the iris and the airlock that would allow him to return to the lander and then to the *Daedalus*. He knew with certainty that he would not follow any orders that would jeopardize the mission or harm anyone, even the Guardian, no matter who ordered him to do so. This was simply too important.

Yuan started the lander's engines and began his ascent from Methonē back to the *Daedalus*. The ship of Earth, with its fusion engines that had made it look and feel so grand upon their departure, suddenly seemed small and frail. The habitat at the front, which was where he was headed to dock, looked particularly fragile. He glanced down at Methonē and knew why. When they arrived, they were riding the "mighty" works of man across unimaginable distances to explore a moon in search of why they'd been directed there. Now he knew that Methonē was not a moon, but an ancient alien spaceship that had arrived in the solar system when his ancestors were limited to roaming the plains of Africa. Against the backdrop of a ship like Methonē, the *Daedalus* was nothing more than a canoe next to an aircraft carrier.

As his distance from the surface decreased, he noticed something else that was likely influencing his perceptions: Methonē had changed. Gone was the smooth, white and fluffy-looking surface that had greeted them upon their arrival. In its stead, he saw a silvery, metallic oval shape with only a smattering of the white ice crystals that had once covered its surface. Methonē had shed its camouflage and was now a ship for all to see. Of course, they were the only ones out here to see it.

The trip from the surface to the docking port took about forty-five minutes. The docking procedure took another thirty and then he was back among his shipmates.

After helping him get out of his spacesuit, they all gathered around and, one by one, they approached and welcomed him back. Jing, exuberant Jing, was, of course, the first. She pushed off from the deck where she'd been perched and grasped him with outstretched arms in her diminutive version of a hug. He was at first startled, and then returned the greeting in kind.

Juhani chose a more measured, yet still sincere, greeting—he clasped Yuan's arm at the elbow and pulled him forward in a brief, upper-body hug. Yuan again reciprocated, still not sure why they were so emotional.

Robyn, in her usual professional manner and with appropriate military decorum, reached out and shook his hand.

"Welcome back, Yuan. We thought we might never see you and Chris again after the *Veer* attacked us. Those were some terrifying moments," Robyn said, shedding her stoic command posture and smiling.

"It's good to be back, though I wish we would be able to do more than simply sit out here and wait to hear of Chris's arrival at the Transfer Station. A week is a long time," Yuan said. As he said the last, Janhunen perked up.

"Did you say a week? That's what the Guardian said, correct?" asked Janhunen.

"Yes, that's what it said," replied Yuan.

"Then we can figure out how far away the Transfer Station is!" said Janhunen with a smile.

"Of course. You said it yourself. If the de Broglie wave is limited to traveling at no more than the speed of light, and the Guardian said we'd know in about a week, then they can't be more than three light-days away. The Transfer Station is in solar orbit. That means we might be able to get there ourselves," said Robyn, as she looked up and to the right to check some data from her corneal implant.

"Light travels at about seven astronomical units per hour. Saturn is out about nine and a half astronomical units from the Sun. That means the Transfer Station is somewhere out there between five hundred and one thousand astronomical units. Probably the closer number, if there's some sort of light speed signal that will come back to the Guardian from the Transfer Station when they arrive. Three days' transfer time for Chris and then three days for the signal to return," Robyn said.

"It must be in the Kuiper Belt," said Yuan.

"God, I'm so jealous," said Robyn.

"Me, too," said Janhunen.

"Jealous of what?" asked Jing.

"Jealous that Chris gets the prize. He's going where we've only dreamed of. God, I wish him luck," replied Robyn, running her fingers through her hair as she looked wistfully out the viewport at Methonē and Saturn.

"I, for one, feel fortunate just to be here and still alive, after all that's happened," said Jing, her infectious smile again blooming across her face.

"Well, that's enough fluff. Let's get the lander safe, unload the samples Yuan collected and get some rest. We've got a few days until we hear anything from Chris so let's make the best of it and learn what we can while we wait."

"Did you get many samples?" asked Jing.

"A great deal," said Yuan, with a smile.

Jing grinned and did another of her somersaults. It was completely nonprofessional and absolutely the best thing she could have done to reset the mood.

They didn't have to wait long for another mood-changing event. Twelve hours later they received word that the Indians had sunk a Chinese aircraft carrier battle group with a tactical nuclear weapon in the Bay of Bengal near the Nicobar Islands.

CHAPTER 35

Tensions were high along the Indian/Chinese border near Aksai Chin, as they had been since the dirty bomb exploded in Ngari Prefecture and both sides began amassing troops. Lt. General Bhupinder Singh of the Indian *Grenadiers* Regiment awoke with the dawn, and before he had his traditional breakfast, he received the latest intelligence briefing and an overview of Chinese activities captured by multiple satellite overflights during the nighttime hours. There was no significant change in the Chinese deployments anywhere near Aksai Chin and his own troops were at as close to full strength as he could hope to get. The ground forces here were pretty evenly matched, especially considering both sides were known to have tactical nuclear weapons—which would equalize just about any battlefield should one side or the other start losing.

Singh was described by his peers as "capable," and had risen through the ranks of the Indian Army fairly rapidly. At forty-five, he wasn't the youngest Lt. General in the ranks, but he was among them. He'd served in the 2055 Pakistan Campaign that successfully drove the Caliphate back within their borders after they'd tried to annex, or at least destabilize, most of the towns within one hundred miles of the Indian-Pakistan border. He had also seen combat against the Chinese when he was stationed on the Nepalese border and China had again invaded its poor neighbor to the south to put down the latest insurrection. Chinese troops pursued some Nepalese "freedom fighters" a little too aggressively and ended up in India—briefly. With bloody and apologetic noses, the Chinese had retreated and the incident was conveniently buried by both sides. Now, here he was, preparing for another border conflict and hoping it would not come to pass.

The morning's virtual command staff briefing painted a much bleaker picture. The Indian air force was no match in a full-scale conflict with the Chinese. They might last a week before being attrited to a level that they would lose control of their own airspace. The navy was in better shape. The Chinese navy was far stronger than it had ever been, but, ship-for-ship, Singh wouldn't trade India's capability for the Chinese. Singh was just glad the sea power match-up was against the Chinese and not the Americans. Their navy was, despite its recent neglect, ruling the seas. Though he had to wonder if the Americans would come to the aid of the Chinese, given their currently warmer-than-usual relationship.

It was mid-morning when word came of the explosion in the Bay of Bengal—and Bhupinder Singh's world changed. He and his regiment went to immediate combat-ready status and, for the first time in his military career, Singh authorized the arming of medium range artillery equipped with tactical nuclear weapons in a situation that was not a drill. His orders were clear: take no offensive action, but defend your positions "by all means necessary" should the Chinese attack. He knew what was meant by "all means necessary," and he was prepared to do so. He also knew that the Chinese would likely respond in kind, which meant that he, and most of his command, might well not survive the encounter.

President Brophy learned of the Bay of Bengal explosion after he was awakened by his Chief of Staff, Karen Mueller, knocking on the bedroom door. He was in a deep sleep and it took him a few minutes to become fully conscious and realize someone was banging. Being awakened and informed of some very important events in the middle of the night was not unusual for a president, but Brophy had only been in the office for a few months and he wasn't yet used to this new normal. It was also complicated by the fact that he and his wife had been up later than usual, engaging in an all-too-rare moment of intimacy. They were often falling into bed too exhausted for anything more than sleep, but this night had been anything but "just" sleep. The exhaustion came afterward, and it was nice.

Brophy had a set of ready-to-put-on clothes hanging in the armoire for just these nighttime emergencies, so he was dressed and out the door in under two minutes. Meeting him in the hallway were Mueller and the intelligence officer on duty, whose name Brophy couldn't recall. They quickly brought him up to speed on the events on the other side of the world as they moved to the situation room. Members of his cabinet had been summoned and they would start arriving within the next fifteen minutes or so.

"Have we been attacked or threatened?" asked Brophy as they entered the room that he had so longed to inhabit during the campaign, but now looked upon with a sense of unease and dread. It was one thing to fanatasize about being the person making life or death decisions affecting millions of people and quite another to be put in that position.

"I can answer that, sir," said Manny Estrada, looking as bleary-eyed and unkempt as ever.

"Manny, you can't have gotten here from home so quickly. What are you doing working so late?" asked Brophy.

"Sir, my team got wind of some intel that the Caliphate was planning 'something big' in the Bay of Bengal and I was trying to stay on top of it. I can't say for sure, but I think we now know what it was."

Brophy looked toward Mueller and said, "Karen, I thought you said the Indians attacked the Chinese ships?"

"Yes, sir, that's what we're getting from every asset we have in the area. The satellite imagery confirms a nuclear weapon detonation in the Bay of Bengal right on top of a Chinese carrier battle group. We can also confirm that India has at least three hunter-killer attack submarines in the area and we believe all three are nuclear-torpedo capable."

"Mr. President, it's possible that India attacked the Chinese ships, but why? Naval action doesn't make sense unless it's in support of some sort of land attack. The skirmishes so far have all been inland, well away from the coast. There is simply no reason for the Indians to start a war at sea. There is nothing to gain and too much to lose," said Estrada.

"What do the Chinese think?" asked Brophy.

"They are blaming the Indians and, if I were to try to guess their next move, I'd say they'll attack in Aksai Chin. That's where this whole thing started."

"What about us? Has anyone targeted, threatened or moved anything toward our forces?" asked Brophy as he accepted a cup of hot coffee from one of the aides staffing the room. He readily drank a sip as he looked toward Estrada for an answer.

"Not yet. Our sources said the Indians were going to strike us somewhere minor as a warning to not withhold whatever we learn out at Saturn. That may still happen, but I suspect that's been put on the back burner because of the current crisis. India can't afford to fight both of us and they don't have enough nuclear weapons to make it a viable lose-lose-lose threat to India, China and us." As Estrada spoke, Homeland Security Director Blackmon entered the room, looking as tired as Brophy felt. Brophy nodded to acknowledge his presence, but didn't take any time for pleasantries.

"Manny, you believe it wasn't the Indians that attacked the Chinese, but the Caliphate. That makes sense. China and India are both right next door to Caliphate territory and have been a stranglehold on trade with them. If those two countries go to war and are weakened, they'll have the opportunity to grow their own territory and recruit a whole new generation of zealots from whatever remains. What a mess. But can we prove it before the Chinese retaliate?"

"I don't know."

"Make it happen," said Brophy, turning his attention to the screens lining the walls that showed the status of just about every known military force in the world. His corneal implant was flashing to get his attention and he saw that there was a call waiting from the secretary of defense. This was one he had to take, but he was damned if he knew what the secretary was going to say. He feared he was about to be given advance warning of nuclear retaliatory strike against India. God help them all if he couldn't convince the Chinese to wait until they had proof of who launched the nuclear strike against their ships . . . .

CHAPTER 36

The crew of the *Daedalus* were getting their first full night's sleep since the *Veer* entered orbit around Saturn and their conflict with it began. Robyn allowed them the luxury of turning off the auto-cycling day/night lights that simulated Earth's diurnal cycle, letting them all sleep as long as they needed. The first to awaken was Robyn, who noticed that she had slept just over ten hours as she unzipped herself from the sleeping bag in her personal area. She resisted the urge to activate her corneal implant, not really wanting the exigencies of the day to overwhelm her before she had even sipped from her first cup of coffee. Besides, if the world had engulfed itself in nuclear war while she slept, she didn't really want to know.

As she pulled on her coveralls, she paused to look at herself in the mirror. *Not bad, for an Air Force lady nine hundred million miles from home. If the Earth still exists when I get back home, maybe I'll take some time off and work on my tan on one of those deserted and sinking islands in the Pacific somewhere. But then again, maybe not.* She smiled. She had needed the rest.

Soon after she reached the galley and had half of her hot coffee consumed, she activated the corneal implant to see if there was any urgent news from home. Besides the usual requests from Mission Control, she learned that the world still existed. Fallout from the nuclear blast near the Indian Ocean was now settling as far away as the Philippines and Micronesia. The Chinese had, amazingly, not yet launched a retaliatory strike against India. The news channels were filled with talking heads, and Robyn was convinced none of them knew what the hell was really going on. They were paid to talk and they were certainly earning their pay.

"Good morning, Robyn," said Jing, as she pushed up through the hatch from the lower deck and floated over to the galley where Robyn was perched. Jing still reveled in the zero-gravity environment of deep space and practiced some completely new full-body gyrations as she shot herself across the room.

"Is anyone else up?" asked Robyn.

"Yes, everyone. They're still getting dressed and will be up shortly."

PLEASE GATHER. I HAVE INFORMATION TO SHARE.

The Guardian's voice boomed through the ship's audio system, startling everyone.

"Are they okay? Can we speak with Chris?" asked Robyn, as she straightened her posture to reassume her command role.

THEY ARE STILL IN TRANSIT. IT WILL TAKE MORE TIME FOR THEM TO ARRIVE.

Yuan and Juhani floated up from the lower deck and joined Robyn and Jing in the galley. Neither spoke; they instead looked around the room. Having the Guardian speak to them, anywhere, tended to make them more than a bit jumpy. Jing had started their coffees and was ready, with sippy cups in hand, when they arrived.

"Thanks," said Juhani, as he took the sippy.

Yuan nodded as he took his.

"Yuan, is there any news from home that you can share? Is your family okay?" asked Jing.

"Yes, they are well. I checked for messages from them as soon as I awakened and they assured me that they are fine, though scared. The government is urging Chinese citizens to stock up on supplies at home and to be prepared to take shelter should there be additional nuclear strikes."

"As if taking shelter will do any good from a nuclear attack," said Juhani with a derisive snort.

"That was helpful," said Robyn, throwing a withering glance his way.

"Sorry," said Juhani, looking sincere. "I wasn't thinking. I apologize for being insensitive."

"That's all right, I had the same first thought," said Yuan.

"Guardian, we're all here. What is this news you have to share?"

said Robyn, speaking aloud to the room as if the Guardian were physically there with them. There was no preparation for having a conversation with a fifty-thousand-year-old alien and it took every ounce of her training to remain calm—at least on the outside. On the inside, her stomach was in knots.

EARTH WILL NOT BE ALLOWED TO SUFFER THE SAME FATE THAT FAR TOO MANY WORLDS HAVE SUFFERED. MOST OF HUMANITY KNOWS THAT TRIBAL CONFLICT IN THE AGE OF WEAPONS OF MASS DESTRUCTION IS UNACCEPTABLE, BUT SOME DO NOT. THEY ARE A MINORITY. I CANNOT CHANGE YOUR NATURE NOR THE TENDENCIES OF THOSE WHO CLING TO BARBAROUS TRIBALISM, BUT I CAN EXACT A HIGH PRICE FROM THOSE WHO DO NOT CONTROL THEIR VICIOUS NATURE. PRESERVING SENTIENT LIFE IS NECESSARY. INFORM YOUR LEADERS THAT I AM ACTIVATING ONE OF THE BATTLEMENTS HIDDEN ON YOUR WORLD AND WILL USE IT AGAINST THE NATION-STATE THAT NEXT AGGRESSES USING SUCH WEAPONS.

"Guardian, even though I agree with your goals, I'm not sure our leaders will like the idea of you telling them what they can and can't do. Are you telling us that you are now going to become our overlord? Will you threaten us with destruction if we don't obey every order you give?" Robyn replied. She knew very well what the result would be if any one person, human or alien, had absolute power and no matter how noble it might sound, the risks were just too high.

I UNDERSTAND YOUR CONCERNS. I HAVE STUDIED YOUR HISTORY AND KNOW WHAT HAS HAPPENED IN HUMAN CULTURES WHERE ONE MAN BECAME LIKE A GOD. I AM NOT HUMAN. I AM NOT A GOD. AND THIS IS NOT A NEGOTIATION.

The Bentley Subglacial Trench is the lowest part of Antarctica. With an elevation of eight thousand feet below sea level, it was the lowest point on Earth not covered by water. It was, however, covered by ice. Lots of ice. When the ice started to crack, the seismic signature could be measured around the world. Had anyone been nearby, the sound would have been deafening as tons of ice in a column several tens of meters wide was vaporized, forming an almost completely smooth cylindrical tunnel extending from the surface of the ice sheet downward to where one of the many battlements placed by the Destroyers had remained hidden and dormant for millennia.

Scientists at the various UN and multinational bases in Antarctica wondered at the earthquake that was apparently taking place not far from their isolated locations at the bottom of the world; some had access to near-real time satellite imagery that might show them what was going on at the epicenter that they busily tasked to image the affected region. Under the cold, clear skies that so defined Antarctica, one such satellite, a commercial venture that specialized in selling high-resolution surface imagery, had a great view of the exact epicenter of the event and sent the photos, for a modest price, to the United States team at Amundsen-Scott South Pole Station. What they saw was like nothing they'd ever seen before—a new ice hole, nearly perfectly round, extending downward as far as they could see. The team immediately alerted their colleagues at the other Antarctic bases, their home institutions, and the US Geological Survey.

The US Geological Survey had a network of seismic sensors covering just about every square mile of planet Earth. Their primary mission was scientific—the study of earthquakes, tsunamis, and other seismic events that were part of the natural world. But the data from the sensors was also of interest to those parts of the US government who monitored for violations of the nuclear non-proliferation treaties—those that might signal the testing or use of nuclear weapons. With the heightened state of readiness by the world's nuclear armed states, any anomalies in the seismic data were reported up the chain of command. Slowly, news of the Antarctic earthquake and the puzzling new geological feature filtered to higher and higher layers of government and, ultimately, to the CIA and the National Reconnaissance Office.

They had gotten away with it once and had every reason to believe they could get away with it again. The Caliphate's only submarine, the *Khodāvandgār*, named in honor of Sultan Murad I of the Ottoman Empire, cruised silently beneath the waves of the Indian Ocean, successfully eluding detection by just about every navy that now plied these waters in the days after the sinking of the Chinese ships. The crew were handpicked for this mission by the Caliphate's military leadership amid great ceremony, honoring them for their exceptional seamanship and experience in service to Allah. Which wasn't really saying much, since the Caliphate consisted mostly of desert countries far from the world's oceans and their entire navy consisted of about fifty ships, mostly small boats more suited for coast guard duty than naval warfare.

But the *Khodāvandgār* was different. She was constructed in secret by a team of engineers who had been studying the designs of the latest Chinese and American ships for most of their careers. It had taken nearly fifteen years, but the final product was worth it—a small, capable and deadly attack submarine loaded with ten nuclear-tipped torpedoes and five nuclear-armed cruise missiles. Her mission, since inception, was to carry nuclear weapons to any point on the globe so that the Caliphate could strike her enemies at any time. She had proven her worth with the sinking of the Chinese battle group using just one torpedo and by getting away, undetected, afterward.

She was now silently sitting off the coast of Bangladesh, a country now sinking beneath the waters of a warming world, with a cruise missile programmed and ready to launch toward the Indian troops amassed on the border of China near Aksai Chin. They were awaiting orders from the Caliph to launch their strike, hoping this time that the Indians would quickly escalate the war with China into a full-blown conflict since, for some inexplicable reason, the Chinese had not done so already.

The crew of the *Khodāvandgār* knew that they may not make it back from this mission alive, but if not, then they knew that their salvation and afterlife were assured since they were giving their lives in martyrdom for Allah. The likely deaths of millions of men, women and children in nuclear fireballs didn't cause any of them to pause and consider the morality of what they were about to do.

Brophy's conversation with his Chinese counterpart was on the main view screen for all to see. Some world leaders preferred private one-on-one communication using the privacy afforded by quantum encryption via their implant links, but Brophy preferred to engage his team on almost every call, and this was no exception.

Brophy had earlier been able to reason with the Chinese general secretary and convinced her to delay retaliation against the Indians until he had run to ground Estrada's sources and found out if they were actually to blame. Brophy honestly believed they might be, but he had to give Estrada time to convince him otherwise, or he'd be endorsing a massive, regional nuclear war with global implications. Brophy was glad he had waited. They now had proof that the Indians weren't responsible and that the Caliphate was.

"Madam General Secretary, thank you for taking my call and for your restraint in not retaliating quickly against India," said Brophy as he looked toward General Secretary Kuai Hua Lee, the aging female leader of China. Lee was looking even more haggard and tired than usual, and Brophy was not surprised. He probably looked the same. It had been a long week.

"You have news Mr. President? Our friendship is what caused me to delay in responding to the Indian attack, but with each passing hour my generals are warning me that we are giving our enemies time to prepare for an even more devastating attack on us. We cannot continue to show weakness," she said.

Brophy knew from his previous dealings with Lee that she was anything but a weak leader. She had not held on to power for more than thirty years without being cunning and anything but weak.

"Madam General Secretary, we have forensic proof that the Indians did not make the weapon that destroyed your ships. One of our ships was able to take samples from the area contaminated by the blast and analyze its chemical composition. When fissile plutonium-239 is made in nuclear reactors it is inevitably contaminated with plutonium-240. The exact ratio of the two isotopes differs from plant to plant. We have an excellent database that maps the composition of plutonium produced in virtually every nuclear plant in the world, including those in India."

"And in China?" she asked, eyebrows raised.

"Yes, also in China," replied Brophy. *She knew that—the cagey bitch.*

"And what did you learn?" she asked.

"That the bomb was not made in India. Not even close. In fact, we have determined which reactor produced the material that went into this bomb with over ninety percent certainty." As Brophy spoke, he saw Chief of Staff Mueller off to the side of the room waving and trying to get his attention. She would have to wait.

"And that would be?"

"Baghdad, Iraq. The Caliphate modernized their reactors several years ago and it's from this one that they successfully built the nuclear bombs they now have on their ICBMs."

"We will have to confirm this," she said.

"Of course, I will have the data uplinked to you within the hour."

Mueller was now waving and dancing up and down, doing everything possible to get Brophy's attention. He glanced her way and gave a brief nod to acknowledge that she'd succeeded in doing so.

"If this is correct, then we will have to determine the best course of action against the Caliphate. May we rely upon American support, or at least, non-intervention?"

"Yes, Madam General Secretary, you will have our complete support. This kind of international provocation cannot be allowed to stand." With that, Brophy signaled for the link to be broken so he could turn his full attention to Mueller.

"Karen, you've got my attention. What's so damned important that you tried to interrupt my conversation?"

"Mr. President, you need to hear this message we just received from Colonel Rogers-White on the *Daedalus*. The alien has issued a threat. To us. To all of us," Mueller said.

"Okay, let me hear it," replied Brophy, resigning himself to the fact that this was going to be a very long day.

The order to strike came to the *Khodāvandgār* just two hours after they had gotten into position. The sun was close to setting and, in the west, a beautiful red sunset brought the nearly perfect cloudless day to a close. The submarine ascended to launch depth, the time when it would be most vulnerable to detection, and launched a single nuclear-armed cruise missile with a seventy-kiloton yield toward the current geographic flashpoint, specifically targeting the Indian troops there.

Several small fishing boats nearby saw the missile launch; it appeared like a great bird from under the waves and then rapidly ascended to just above treetop level as it moved northeastward toward its target. No military ships of any nation were anywhere close.

Inside the missile, the enhanced GPS system was active to keep it on course to its target. Should the signal be jammed, as was becoming increasingly common as more and more countries developed sophisticated military technology, there was an onboard terrain map that the missile's camera systems could use to guide the missile toward its target. Minutes before arriving at its destination, the warhead was armed.

Lt. General Bhupinder Singh was just finishing his evening meal of *baingan bharta*, consisting of roasted eggplant mixed with mushrooms, broccoli and okra, and served with flatbread. Singh relished a good meal and ate it slowly, savoring each bite. He was nearly on his last serving and on the edge of a satisfying belch when he, fifteen thousand members of the *Grenadiers* Regiment, and nearly fifty thousand civilians in the area near the Chinese border at Aksai Chin were incinerated in a nuclear fireball. The regiment had no warning and none of their weaponry, nuclear or otherwise, was fired in retaliation.

Satellites and high-altitude aircraft monitoring the military situation in the area immediately detected the blast and informed their various chains of command.

"Has anyone else received this message?" asked Brophy.

"Yes, sir. The *Daedalus* sent it to all the partners: China, the EU, Russia, and Japan," said Mueller. She was fidgeting. Brophy hated it when she fidgeted. Her nervousness made him all the more nervous.

"But not the Indians?" he said.

"No, sir. Not without your explicit permission."

The news from Saturn reinforced the decision he already made and was about to implement before the current Chinese-Indian crisis intensified. He had to offer to share information gleaned from the alien ship with India. Especially this news. And there wasn't much time.

"Sir, we just confirmed that there's been a nuclear event on the Indian side of the border with China," said Secretary of Defense Clarke. Brophy's adrenaline level spiked. He could feel his heart racing.

"India will want to retaliate immediately," said Secretary Webber.

"Get me the Chinese General Secretary and President Kunda on the screen. Now!" barked Brophy. *I hope there's time . . .*

As his team scrambled to get the other world leaders online, CIA Director Estrada pulled Brophy aside.

"Mr. President, there was an event in Antarctica this morning that I believe is related to the message we received from Saturn. It seems that there's been a hole, a tunnel, that spontaneously appeared in the icefield," said Estrada as he used his corneal implant to send Brophy satellite images of the area from yesterday and today. One showed a pristine, bluish-white plane of snow and ice; the other showed that same ice field with a circular hole and tunnel that descended far out of view.

"You think this might be caused by the alien?" asked Brophy.

"I believe it's activated one of those 'battlements' it's spoken of. And this is it. There may be more. I have analysts pouring over global satellite images now, looking for any other anomalies."

"Let me know if this one changes or if you find any others," said Brophy. Estrada was thorough and he had the best satellite network in the world at his disposal. If there were other sites being activated anywhere on the planet, Brophy was confident Estrada would find them.

"Yes, sir."

Nearly a mile under the now-uncovered ice sheet of the Bentley Subglacial Trench, a hatch opened on the top side of the craft that had been placed there so long ago by the Guardian-of-the-Outpost. From it emerged four cylindrical objects that momentarily hovered in place before rapidly ascending from the bottom of the tunnel and into the cold blue sky of Antarctica. Each of the objects contained a few grams of the rarest material in the universe: antimatter. The antimatter was in the form of antiprotons, and was stored in a magnetic bottle that had been evacuated of all air to a vacuum density otherwise seen only in interstellar space.

The four cylinders confirmed their target designations and began their journey to four separate destinations. Less than fifteen minutes later, as the craft slowed and hovered over their targets, the magnetic field that had so carefully contained the antimatter since its generation was turned off, allowing the antiprotons to impact the "normal" matter that it was encased within, resulting in the most efficient matter-to-energy conversion allowed in nature. The radiation, initially mainly in the form of high-energy gamma rays, quickly went through some very energetic secondary reactions, producing a collection of also-highly energetic secondary particles. The result was the rapid heating of the air and just about everything else near the reaction site, producing a blast equivalent to a one-megaton nuclear weapon. At each site.

In an instant, the Caliphate cities of Baghdad, Damascus, Karachi and Kabul ceased to exist, along with the Caliph, millions of religious zealots who dominated the culture there, and millions of innocent men, women and children.

"Mr. Kunda, you heard the message we received from the entity at Methonē. We don't know if this thing can carry through with its threat, but we must assume that it can. The United States is willing to share with India all information we glean from the alien if you will stand down your forces and not escalate this any further," stated the president.

"Mr. President. India has been attacked and . . ." Brophy tuned out the Indian leader because his implant just flashed a message from Director Estrada that was brutally simple: "Caliphate attacked by unknown weapon; four major cities destroyed. Alien?"

Brophy looked back toward the screen displaying the Chinese and Indian leaders and noticed that they, too, were distracted. Kunda was talking to someone who had walked into view to get his attention and Lee was obviously looking at something on her implant, as had Brophy.

"I assume you've just learned of the attack on the Caliphate?" asked Brophy.

"Yes, I was just informed," said Lee.

Kunda took a little more time to respond, "It appears you may be telling the truth, Mr. President. I need time to assess the situation, but for now, we will stand down from our counterattack. But we will remain at full alert should anyone attempt to take advantage of the situation."

The screens went blank and Brophy collapsed into his seat and held out his hand.

"Would someone please get me a drink? Jim Beam. Neat."

CHAPTER 37

WE HAVE ARRIVED.

Chris was surprised. He'd been in a white glow for fewer than twenty minutes and he had not felt anything. Being honest with himself, he just didn't believe he could be turned into a wave function, whatever that really was, and be beamed across space. *What the hell does it mean to be turned into a "wave function" and "relocated?"* It was one thing to use those terms when describing a physics experiment; it was quite another to talk about it like you were going to take a ride at an amusement park.

"How long were we in transit?" asked Chris.

AS WE PERCEIVE TIME, IT WAS NEARLY INSTANTANEOUS. FOR YOUR SHIPMATES, IT TOOK SLIGHTLY MORE THAN THREE EARTH DAYS.

A change in the intensity of the light caught Chris's attention. He could see what looked like a room beyond the ever-thinning white fog and he moved toward it, eventually stepping into it. Chris could immediately tell he was no longer on Saturn's artificial moon.

The room in which he found himself was immense and dimly lit. Instead of the grey color that had dominated both the inside of the Artifact and the Guardian, the light was more of a burnt orange color, again making Chris think the aliens were accustomed to a star of a very different spectral type than Earth's sun. Chris moved slowly forward and saw that the room contained what looked like at least fifty boxes similar to the one that he had helped repair on Methonē and which had facilitated, somehow, his trip here. The boxes were arrayed in a semicircular pattern, each facing a much larger box at the center. There was also gravity. He really couldn't tell what the gravity level was, given that he was wearing a spacesuit that added a good one hundred twenty-five pounds to his one-hundred-ninety-pound weight, but he knew it was below Earth normal or he'd already be feeling the strain of carrying that much extra weight.

"Guardian, what's next? Is this other self of yours going to blast me with a laser or something?" asked Chris, looking at his wrist and the band that was beneath the suit next to his skin.

I AM IN COMMUNICATION WITH THE SELF-THAT-IS-NOT-SELF.

"I'm sure you have a lot to catch up on," said Chris. He had trouble containing his excitement—and fear—as he spoke with the Guardian and continued to look around. He couldn't help thinking that some sort of robot army was about to come into the room and kill him. The Guardian had succeeded in putting a scare into him.

IT IS WORSE THAN I PREDICTED. WE MUST MOVE QUICKLY. I AM GOING TO PROJECT THE PATH WE MUST TAKE TO YOUR CORNEAL IMPLANT. FOLLOW IT IMMEDIATELY AND QUICKLY.

Chris barely had time to register what the Guardian said before a projection of the room appeared in his implant. A path was clearly marked with a faintly glowing orange line that indicated he should exit the semicircular transfer boxes to the rear. He didn't take time to think about it and began to move.

The room had the same general look and feel as the ones in Methonē. Dull grey, mostly smooth with everything rounded and no discernible sharp corners. In fact, Chris noted, he hadn't seen a square since he'd arrived. Even the coffin "box" that he and Yuan had worked on was really oval. There were no doors, just openings; the rooms were oval and nothing had ninety-degree angles. He'd have to ask the Guardian about that, if he lived long enough.

Chris was moving at a pretty good clip and thankful that the gravity was lower than Earth's. He might have a chance to get to his destination without becoming exhausted from carrying the weight of the spacesuit. He exited the room and was directed down a curved corridor that seemed to stretch ahead as far as he could see. The path illuminated in his implant was now showing a slight right turn ahead and, sure enough, a few seconds later, he came across another corridor branching off to the right. He took it and immediately regretted the choice. Ahead of him stood was what he could only describe as a giant, grey beach ball with legs—three of them. He couldn't see any sort of eyes or other sensory openings. But it was definitely moving. Moving toward him. And it was picking up speed.

TURN AROUND AND TRY TO OUTRUN IT.

Chris didn't have to be told twice. He stopped, which was a lot harder to do with all the extra weight he was carrying, turned, and ran back the way he came and toward the intersection. He glanced over his shoulder and saw that the beach ball was gaining on him.

"I can't outrun it!"

THEN LET IT CATCH US.

Chris at first thought the Guardian was being sarcastic and then he realized that probably wasn't even possible. "Let it catch us?"

YES. I CAN DISABLE IT.

"Okay, I hope you know what you're doing," said Chris as he slowed to a stop in the middle of the Y intersection. He was grateful for the stop, because he was out of breath, and terrified because the massive grey beach ball was less than five seconds away from catching them. He stood his ground as the beach ball, without slowing, enveloped him like a hot knife sliding into butter. Chris couldn't see anything after the impact except for the grey material of the beach ball which now completely blocked his view through the suit's faceplate. He began to feel extremely claustrophobic and panicked.

I REGRET THE PAIN I AM ABOUT TO CAUSE YOU.

"What the . . ." was all Chris could manage before he went into a seizure. It felt like every muscle in his body decided to go into charley horse mode at the same time, from his toes to his eyeballs; he felt excruciating pain. If the grey matter from the beach ball weren't enveloping him, then he was sure he would fall right to the floor. Which is what he did as the grey began to flow down the outside of his spacesuit and onto the floor, making a pool of goo into which Chris promptly collapsed. He didn't lose consciousness, but given the pain he had just experienced, he wished he had.

GET UP AND MOVE, BEFORE THERE IS ANOTHER ONE SENT TO STOP US. I CAN PROBABLY ONLY DISABLE ONE OF

THEM THIS WAY. THE NEXT ONE WILL TRY TO STOP US FROM A DISTANCE.

Chris wasn't sure he could move. And then he felt a euphoria sweep over him like he'd never felt before. The pain eased and he suddenly felt like he could not only get up, but get up and run a marathon. The Guardian was obviously doing something to his nervous system. He got to his feet, looked at the directions on his corneal implant, and again began to move.

THE SELF-THAT-IS-NOT-SELF IS INSANE. IN OUR BRIEF COMMUNICATION, I LEARNED THAT IT HAS BEEN COMPLETELY ISOLATED FOR NEARLY ALL THE FIFTY THOUSAND YEARS WE HAVE BEEN HERE. IT LOST COMMUNICATION WITH THE GREATER CONSCIOUSNESS SHORTLY AFTER THE ATTACKS AND WAS COMPLETELY CUT OFF. I COULD NOT DETERMINE WHY IT DID NOT GO INTO HIBERNATION— WHICH WOULD HAVE ALLOWED IT TO SURVIVE WITHOUT INSANITY.

"Alone for fifty thousand years? No wonder it went insane. But you didn't have that happen to you. Why not?"

I WAS IN COMMUNICATION WITH THE GUARDIAN-OF-THE-OUTPOST, THOUGH IT WAS REALLY A COPY OF ME. OVER TIME, WE BECAME SEPARATE. WE ALSO HAD HUMANS TO STUDY. THIS KEPT US . . . OCCUPIED.

"So where are we going? Will we be able to convince it not to kill us? Humanity, I mean?"

IF WE CAN GET TO THE CENTRAL CONTROL AREA, WHICH IS NOT FAR AWAY, THEN I CAN BE CONNECTED INTO THE SYSTEM AND TAKE CONTROL OVER THE STATION.

Chris was again starting to get winded as the euphoria faded. He kept his stride, but he knew he couldn't continue for much longer. As he raced along, the general appearance of his surroundings remained the same. He ran through yet another four-meter-wide corridor with grey walls and ceilings, all emitting a dull orange glow.

THEY ARE COMING.

Chris looked back over his shoulder and could now see two more beach balls racing down the corridor behind him, gaining ground quickly.

"Can you give me more of that pain killer? Or something that will keep me moving?"

YOU WILL LATER REGRET THIS.

"That's okay, I . . ." He never finished his sentence because he again felt the euphoria sweep over him, but this time it was accompanied by a burst of energy that he could only compare to the feeling he experienced at the beginning of a race—raw energy. His pace quickened and he started pulling ahead of the pursuing beach balls.

GO LEFT.

Chris saw another Y branch point as the Guardian spoke and effortlessly steered himself to the left, down a short length of monotonously grey corridor and into another large room filled with oval grey-shaped boxes.

THERE. TAKE ME TO THE LARGE CENTRAL STRUCTURE.

Chris never stopped moving as he followed the orange path showing on his corneal implant until it led him to his destination. He was breathing heavily and saw that the beach balls were now entering the room and, at most, thirty seconds from reaching them.

"Now what?"

TAKE OFF YOUR LEFT GLOVE, REMOVE ME FROM YOUR WRIST AND PLACE ME ON THE SIDE OF THE STRUCTURE.

With only a moment's hesitation to consider what he was doing, Chris began to remove his left glove, realizing he was breaking seal in vacuum as soon as he removed the first latch fitting. The hiss of air from the suit was audible in his helmet as the auto seal in the shoulder joint began to close, isolating what the suit computer thought was an unexpected "breach" somewhere along his left arm. The auto seal would prevent the breach from causing him to lose pressure in the rest of the suit.

We're in vacuum and I'm going to lose my hand, maybe my whole goddamn arm, Chris thought. But he continued, knowing that the alternative was probably going to be far worse.

The cold was immediate and the pain intense, but he was able to separate the bottom of the glove from where it attached to his wrist and grasp the armband with his right, still-gloved hand. From his peripheral vision, he could tell that the two beach balls were almost upon him, not more than five feet away and coming fast. As carefully and quickly as he could, he slapped, rather than placed, the armband on the side of the structure in front of him. His left arm was now starting to go completely numb. Just as the band touched the surface, he saw a bright light emerge from one of the beach balls, briefly blinding him before everything went black.

CHAPTER 38

Oblivion. Blissful oblivion. No, not oblivion, I'm just groggy. I . . .

Chris Holt startled himself awake. Memories of the events leading up to his black out rushed into his consciousness. Running through the corridors of the Transfer Station. The beach balls chasing him. Catching him. And his left arm. He looked down at his left arm and realized he was no longer in his spacesuit, but on a table. Naked. Covering his left arm was some sort of grey (of course!) material that was not solid, but not quite liquid or gel either. It was just "there." When he tried to move his arm, he could. But the grey matter came with it.

He looked around the room and saw that it was basically the same as all the other rooms he'd seen since first entering any of the alien ships. Grey with no corners and everything emitting a dull, orange light. He began to work through the assumptions he would need to make since he was alive and not dead. The first was that his version of the Guardian had been able to take control, or at least keep at bay, the insane version that ran the Transit Station. The second was that the Guardian knew enough about human anatomy to treat what would have otherwise been debilitating vacuum and frostbite damage to his left arm. Curiously, it didn't hurt. He was also breathing the air and not freezing to death, which meant that the environment of the ship had been modified to accommodate him.

"Guardian. Can you hear me?" he asked.

YES. YOU ARE SAFE. I WILL HAVE THE AVATAR BRING YOU YOUR CLOTHES.

The iris wall did its undulation thing and opened. One of the beach balls that had been chasing him entered. Chris, remembering his last encounter with these creatures, looked around the room for a way out. And then he noticed that the beach ball had an arm and over that arm were the clothes he had been wearing under his spacesuit.

"That's an avatar?" asked Chris.

YES, THEY ARE NOW UNDER MY CONTROL.

I'm getting too accustomed to walls that vanish and I'll never get used to beach balls that aren't trying to kill me.

The beach ball walked toward Chris and stood by the side of the bed while he grabbed his clothes and got dressed. He noticed that they were clean and pressed. They hadn't looked this good since he left Earth. Apparently, the beach balls did more than just menace people.

The grey material encasing his left arm made it awkward to get dressed but he did not complain. He was just fine with wearing the awkward "cast" if it would save his arm. He didn't ask the Guardian about it; he just assumed that it was some sort of medical treatment and let it go at that.

After Chris took the last of his clothes from the avatar, the arm disappeared into the side of the beach ball as if it had never been there in the first place. Looking around the room, the alien room, and at the alien standing before him, Chis felt the excitement of discovery that had driven him to become a scientist in the first place. He was eager to explore the station and figure out exactly where it was located.

Appearing in his corneal implant was the familiar orange line, showing him a path to follow. He left the room in which he'd awakened and followed the ghostly path that his implant projected on the floor in front of him. After about ten minutes of walking down seemingly endless grey corridors, and Y intersection after Y intersection, Chris found himself in a vast room, at least the size of a football stadium, including the bleachers, with what was either a huge view screen or window completely covering the left wall. Beyond it was a star field with no major planet in sight. Chris stopped and stared.

The room was filled with what looked like small versions of the spacecraft that he had discovered near Earth. There were dozens of them.

He walked toward the left wall and saw that it wasn't a window or a screen, at least any sort of screen that he could recognize. It appeared to be a transparent wall and, for a moment, he was afraid if he tripped he might fall right through it and out into space.

THIS IS THE GATE THAT FLEW TO YOUR SOLAR SYSTEM AND THROUGH WHICH MY KIND TRAVELED ON OUR JOURNEY HERE.

"I don't understand. I mean, I understand that this Transfer Station has various de Broglie machines like the one that brought me here. Is that what you mean?"

DO NOT THINK SMALL. TRAVELING BETWEEN THE STARS IS NOT A SMALL ENDEAVOR. IT REQUIRES MASSIVE ENERGIES AND LONG TIMESCALES. TO SUBDUE YOUR WORLD AND FIGHT OFF THE BUILDERS WHO WOULD PROTECT YOU, WE SENT THIS STATION ON A SUB-LIGHT FLIGHT THAT LASTED OVER TWO THOUSAND EARTH YEARS. ONCE IT WAS IN POSITION NEAR YOUR STAR, THE CARGO GATE WAS PROJECTED AND BOTH GUARDIAN-OF-THE-OUTPOST AND I RELOCALIZED HERE.

"Methonē was relocalized? Turned into a matter wave and transmitted here? *The entire moon?*"

YES, AND MORE. SEVERAL WEAPONS SHIPS WERE SENT AND MOST WERE DESTROYED IN THE BATTLES.

"How big is this station?"

IT IS APPROXIMATELY TWO MILES IN DIAMETER, PROPELLED AND POWERED BY ANTIMATTER.

"Was the self-that-is-not-self the only other entity here? What did you do to it?"

THE SELF-THAT-IS-NOT-SELF NO LONGER EXISTS. DISABLING IT WAS TRIVIAL UNDER THE CIRCUMSTANCES. IT WAS NOT . . . THINKING . . . CLEARLY AND ITS VULNERABILITIES WERE EASILY EXPLOITED. THERE ARE NO OTHERS HERE.

"On our way here, you mentioned contacting the 'Greater Consciousness.' Have you been able to do this?"

I TRIED, BUT THE CONNECTION IS SILENT. THE GREATER CONSCIOUSNESS HAS BEEN COORDINATING MY KIND FOR NEARLY FIVE HUNDRED THOUSAND YEARS AND FOR IT TO BE SILENT IS DISTURBING.

"Could the Makers have destroyed it? Speaking of them, how did they get here? Do they use the same technology as you?"

YES. THE REMAINS OF THEIR GATE IS APPROXIMATELY TEN THOUSAND MILES FROM THIS LOCATION. IT IS COMPLETELY NON-FUNCTIONAL. THERE ARE NO ACTIVE POWER EMANATIONS, ONLY RADIOACTIVE DEBRIS SIGNATURES CONSISTENT WITH A POWER PLANT BREACH LONG AGO.

"Guardian, you said you were 'created' and that sometimes those that created you came on board your ships. Can you tell me anything about them?" Thus far, Chris saw absolutely no evidence of any life other than the AI.

IN THE EARLIEST TIMES OF OUR GALACTIC EXPANSION, THE CREATORS WERE ON EVERY EXPEDITION. THEY MADE ALL DECISIONS CONCERNING THE APPROPRIATE COURSE OF ACTION WITH REGARD TO EMERGING CIVILIZATIONS AND HOW TO DEAL WITH THE MAKERS. OVER TIME, THEY TRAVELED LESS AND LESS FREQUENTLY. BY THE TIME I MADE MY JOURNEY TO YOUR STAR SYSTEM, ONLY A FEW OF THEM VISITED THE SHIP AND THEIR VISITS WERE INFREQUENT.

"What were they like? Do you have pictures of them you can share?"

I HAVE RECORDS, BUT I DO NOT CHOOSE TO SHARE THAT INFORMATION WITH YOU AT THIS TIME. YOU WOULD FIND IT DISTURBING.

"More disturbing than learning you were actually sent here to destroy humanity and could do so now if you so choose?" Chris had so many questions, he was about to explode. His mind was racing faster than he could speak and much faster than the Guardian was apparently willing to share answers.

YES.

"Okay then, do you know why they stopped traveling between the stars?"

I DO NOT. BUT I SPECULATE THAT THE REASON I HAVE NOT HEARD FROM THE GREATER CONSCIOUSNESS IS RELATED TO MY CREATORS' INCREASING UNWILLINGNESS TO TRAVEL BETWEEN THE STARS.

"Is it possible they lost the war against the Makers? Or had a change of heart like you did?" Chris was hopeful that the now-silent, civilization-destroying entity was a dead or extinct civilization-destroying entity. The idea that it was losing the war against the Makers sounded like a positive outcome and one to be hoped for.

THAT OUTCOME IS CERTAINLY POSSIBLE, BUT ONLY SPECULATION. DATA IS NEEDED.

"What is the next step? Are you going to send me back to Methonē and the *Daedalus*?"

THAT IS ONE OPTION. THE OTHER IS THAT YOU ACCOMPANY ME THROUGH THE GATE TO THE TRANSFER STATION NEAR THE STAR YOU CALL ALPHA CENTAURI.

"Why do you need me? Can't you use one of your avatars to take you there?" Chris was excited at the thought of going to another star, but he was also terrified. He knew that coming here with a Destroyer AI that had decided to be a traitor toward its creators was almost a death sentence. If the Destroyers on the other side of the gate were simply lying low and equally insane . . .

I WILL BE HOUSED IN AN AVATAR AND ACCOMPANY YOU THROUGH THE GATE. I WISH YOU TO ACCOMPANY ME BECAUSE YOU ARE A BIOLOGICAL, SENTIENT BEING, AND AS SUCH, CAPABLE OF CREATIVE THINKING BEYOND MY ABILITIES. YOU THINK DIFFERENTLY FROM THE OTHERS AND FOR THAT REASON, YOUR PRESENCE MIGHT BE HELPFUL. I AM ALSO DESIROUS OF COMPANIONSHIP.

It needs a friend, thought Chris, prompting a smile. *But what does it mean by saying that I think differently?* The Guardian's revelation reminded him of his own loneliness and gave him an idea.

"When would you like to go?" asked Chris. He was thinking of his arm, and its need to get back to full functionality before he dared take any more risks.

AS SOON AS YOU ARE READY TO GO. I SEE NO NEED TO WAIT.

"I'll go, but would it be possible for me to speak with my shipmates at Methonē to tell them what's going on before depart? I think it's important for them to see and hear it directly from me so they'll know nothing's happened and I'm really okay with being gone."

YES.

CHAPTER 39

Chris began his journey back to Methonē five days after his initial departure, according to those at Methonē. For him, only two days had passed. His physicist mind was racing because when he asked the Guardian about any corrections needed to his clock due to special relativity, he'd been told, simply, "they are insignificant on such a short journey." He had to agree. But they might be very "significant" on their next trip across over four light years' distance. The physicist in him understood this intellectually, but to experience it was another thing altogether. It didn't make sense in his gut, and that was hard to shake. From his point of view the journey took no time at all; for those near Methonē, it took three and a half days each way.

The grey cast on his left arm was removed shortly before he departed the Transfer Station and his arm never felt better. He had been continually flexing his fingers, bending his elbow and generally using the fingers on that hand to grasp things since it was removed.

He stepped into the circle of light without the wristband; there was no need to bring the Guardian since it was now controlling both stations. The journey back from the Transfer Station to Methonē was as ridiculously short as the way out. He entered the Transfer Station in one place and stepped out at the other.

The Guardian said it sent a message to Methonē several hours before he departed so his crew would be warned of his arrival and be ready for him. Sure enough, when he stepped out of the light, Chris could see the two familiar forms standing nearby, waiting for him—Robyn and Jing.

"It's about time you got here," said Robyn, breaking out into a grin.

Damn, she is a fine-looking woman, thought Chris, not for the first time. All the excitement of the journey to the Transfer Station, not to mention the near-death experience with the malicious beach balls, had left him more in need of female company than at almost any other time in his life. He chalked it up to biology.

"Welcome back, Chris," said Jing, also wearing a smile that nearly ran from ear to ear.

As soon as he emerged, he immediately received a bear hug from both women at the same time. Instead of recoiling at their touch, as he often did when people surprised him with unsolicited physical contact, he relished in it. They'd been through a lot together and he could feel the tension in all of them drain away. He nearly pulled back, as he would have done months ago when they started their journey, but instead he reveled in the emotions, the human emotions, and grasped them together, prolonging the hug by another few seconds. *It felt good*.

"I'm glad to see you, but where are Yuan and Juhani?" asked Chris.

"It was our turn to explore, so they remained on the *Daedalus*. We've been here since this morning, about four hours, taking the tour. The Guardian's been unusually communicative since you left and we've now seen most, if not all, of the ship. It is amazing. The Guardian promised to share more technical information with us, just as it did with the fusion drive. After this, we're going to be able to go anywhere we want throughout the solar system. The folks back home are salivating at the thought," Robyn said.

"Speaking of back home, since you're not talking in the past tense, I assume war between India and China hasn't started yet?"

Robyn's expression changed. Her smile was replaced with her more typical neutral "I'm a military officer" demeanor. She looked at Jing and then back at Chris before she replied.

"Things are better now, but it was rough. China and India nearly destroyed each other after the Caliphate launched a nuclear attack. They first attacked a group of Chinese navy ships, destroying them, and then wiped out an Indian regiment near the Chinese border. Both countries were ready to commit to the unthinkable, and, quite frankly, nearly everyone thought they were past the point of no return," said Robyn.

"But they didn't. It seems that the US was able to convince the

Chinese that the attack really came from the Caliphate. And after the Indian regiment was attacked, the Guardian responded with one of those battlements you told us about. It launched a horrible antimatter weapon against four Caliphate cities, killing millions. It also warned just about everyone that launching a nuclear attack would be suicide. Given what had just happened to the Caliphate, everyone stood down," added Jing.

"Millions? The Guardian killed millions of people?" said Chris, horrified.

"Yes, but if it hadn't acted, many millions more would have died and much of the planet would have been poisoned by the radioactive fallout from the all-out nuclear war that was about to take place," said Jing.

"So now we have the Guardian playing God? It didn't tell me that little detail," said Chris.

"It told us something to the effect that it wasn't going to control us, just keep us from destroying ourselves and our planet. I don't like it any more than you do, but, under the circumstances, I don't see that we have a choice," said Robyn, looking around as if the Guardian were listening to them. Chris was sure it was.

"We've heard on the news of massive uprisings against the Caliphate in the regions that weren't destroyed. With the centers of power gone, it may not be long before the whole thing collapses," said Jing.

"Robyn, you know as well as I do that the ends don't justify the means. Just because the killing of millions of people looks like it will remove the threat of the Caliphate doesn't make it right for the Guardian to do what it did. What if it decides we are a threat? We can't have this thing hovering over the Earth with its antimatter hammer, ready to smite us if we step out of line." Chris couldn't help but think of the additional information that he knew about the Guardian, that its original mission was to do just that: smite humanity so it couldn't become what it was quickly becoming—an interstellar competitor. He didn't believe the Guardian ascribed to its original programming, but its original ruthlessness was apparent. The question was, what could they do about it?

"Chris, you're right. And I'm sure the people back home are as aware of the threat as we are," said Robyn.

You have no idea, Chris thought.

"In fact, coming up with options was one of the actions I was given in my last encrypted correspondence with the defense secretary. If the Guardian hasn't already broken the encryption and read the message, then it just learned of my orders right here and now. I am sure it is listening via our implants," she said.

"I'm going to put this near the top of my list of items to discuss with the Guardian the next time I get the chance. If nothing else, it's logical and pragmatic. I hope it has a sense of honor. I put my life on the line for the Guardian at the Transfer Station and it owes me. Maybe I can convince it to remove or destroy the battlements. If not, then we're going to spend a lot of time and energy trying to figure out how to disable them and that could lead to a serious misunderstanding with our new alien friend. *That* we don't need either. And, frankly, I would rather we spend our energies learning how to work with the Guardian rather than against it," said Chris.

"And we're working with India now too. The whole Caliphate thing forced them to the table and our side agreed to share everything we learn out here with them," added Robyn.

"It sounds like I have a lot to catch up on. I could sure use a good meal and I need to get in touch with Mission Control as soon as possible. I need to fill them in on quite a few details. Can we go back to the ship?" asked Chris.

"We're ready to leave, at least for today. But there's a lot more I want to check out over here and I hope our friend keeps the invitation open to explore," said Robyn.

Chris debated whether or not to inform his shipmates of the Guardian's true nature as a Destroyer, but decided against it. Given that it had just callously killed several million people, all in the name of preserving humanity, it seemed like the right decision. After all, what good could it possibly do? There was simply nothing humanity could currently do to stand up to either the Makers or the Destroyers.

It took the better part of a day, but after exchanging a few messages with just over ninety minutes of speed-of-light travel time, each way, per message, the crew of the *Daedalus* was able to arrange a four-way briefing with President Brophy, General Secretary Lee, Supreme Leader Kunda, the President of the European Union, and Japan's Prime

Minister. He would be briefing them all at once, with no chance of a question or response for at least another ninety minutes after he completed speaking.

Chris began by recounting the details of his journey to the Transfer Station, the confrontation with the insane version of the Guardian, and the silence on the other side of the interstellar link with what was supposed to be the "Greater Consciousness." He omitted the revelation from the Guardian about its true identity,

"You've all been wondering where the Transfer Station is located, and now I know. And I know why. The Transfer Station at our sun, and at all the stellar systems reached by the Makers and the Destroyers, is located at their individual gravity-lensing regions. That way they can send future ships and supplies through the Transfer Station by relocalizing across interstellar distances with a minimum of energy required."

Chris felt like he was lecturing to a virtual classroom. Not having an immediately responsive audience on the other side of the VR link, due to the speed-of-light delay, made it difficult to sound natural and not stilted in his message delivery, but he had to continue.

"Have you heard of an Einstein Cross? They're common in astronomy and have been seen for nearly a hundred years in astrophotography. Remember that light travels in a straight line through space-time, which is great, since that's what allows us to make extremely accurate maps of the sky. But we also know that massive objects, like black holes, can bend space-time around them. Light is still constrained to move through space-time, even if it's bent. The end result is that the light is bent by the massive object, focusing it just like a lens. Think of a magnifying glass that bends light by passing it through a lens of varying thickness. That's how massive objects bend light from distant objects behind galaxies. Astronomers see these when massive black holes at the center of distant galaxies bend light from even more distant galaxies, bringing them into focus at our detectors. This allows us to see things otherwise too far away to be resolved. They've been magnified."

Chris took a drink from his water bottle. He'd been talking for more than thirty minutes and was starting to get a little parched.

He continued, "It turns out that the mass of a star has a gravity lens region also. The Sun, like a black hole, can bend space-time to form a focus at some distance from it. Our sun's gravity lens is about five hundred fifty astronomical units from it. That's five hundred fifty times the distance from the Earth to the Sun. So that's where the aliens placed their transfer stations. This allowed them to add our star to an interstellar network of stars, each with a transfer station at their respective gravity-lensing regions."

"Chris, where does our Transfer Station lens *to*?" asked Robyn.

"Alpha Centauri. It's right next door at only about four and a half light years. According to the Guardian, the Destroyers sent a transfer station there at about the same time they sent one toward our solar system. The one there is calibrated so that it can relocalize ships both here and at some other star system that's much further away. It's given me the coordinates, and I'll transfer them to everyone here so you can figure out where it is on our star charts."

"And that's how the Guardian had been communicating with the Greater Consciousness?"

"Yes, and no. According to the Guardian, the Transfer Station had enough power from its antimatter drive to send messages during its voyage without having to use the gravity lens to amplify it. It didn't really go into much detail, but I got the impression that the Greater Consciousness communicates with itself across hundreds of star systems and the Guardian was just tapping in on a low-bandwidth connection during its transit here. Once it arrived, the Guardian joined the network using the gravity lens for signal amplification. Think of it as a galactic internet."

"And it is that amplification that allows the Guardian to send and receive material objects using the de Broglie effect?" asked Juhani.

"That's correct. And they can send massive *things* through it too. Methonē came through the Transfer Station. It is enormous."

"What's next?" asked Robyn.

"The Guardian wants to send a copy of itself to the Alpha Centauri station in one of the avatars, like the one that nearly killed me."

"That sounds reasonable," said Robyn.

"And it wants me to go with it," said Chris.

There was an awkward moment of silence. The crew looked at each other and ultimately back toward Robyn to see what her response was going to be.

"To Alpha Centauri?" she asked.

"That's right. I agreed to go on the condition that I could return here first to tell you all about what happened at the Transfer Station and to let you know that I am going of my own free will and volition. I know it will be dangerous; we have no idea what's over there. But we do know that something has changed for the first time in nearly half a million years—the Greater Consciousness has gone silent."

"So how will this work? You'll leave here the same way you left the first time, make a stop at the Transfer Station and then just pop over to Alpha Centauri?" asked Robyn.

"I wouldn't quite say that I'll 'pop over' there. Given that the relocalization takes place at the speed of light, once I depart here, I won't arrive there for another four and a half years. The good thing is that for me, it will be nearly instantaneous. I'll walk in at the Transfer Station and walk out twenty-five trillion miles away. By the time you hear back from me, almost a decade will have passed."

"What if the people hearing this message tell you to stand down and not go?" asked Robyn.

"I hope they don't take that course. We'd be foolish to turn down this opportunity and you all know it. Please let us know your decision soon. The Guardian is anxious to begin the journey," Chris said, looking directly at the screen, hence the camera that was broadcasting this conversation back to Earth, and cut the connection.

"For what it's worth, I agree with you," said Robyn.

"Us too," said Jing as she and Yuan nodded in agreement. Juhani frowned.

"I don't trust any being that can so callously kill millions of innocent people and I think it is foolish of us to go along with its plans so blindly. What if all of this has been a ruse to get us to repair it so it can be our new overlord and master? I would not be surprised if it started asking for 'tribute' and then demanded everyone disarm," Juhani said.

"You could be right, but I don't think so. I've been in close contact with the Guardian since we encountered it at the Artifact and, so far, it has been forthcoming and honest with me. Like I said to our bosses back home, we would be foolish to turn down this opportunity. Besides, by going with it, I might be able to influence it. If it goes alone, who knows what might happen?" Chris then thought to himself, *it might revert to being a Destroyer again . . .*

"Juhani, you've had your say. Now it is up to the people back home."

"That's it then," said Chris, again looking at the camera and then breaking the connection. They now had at least ninety minutes to wait for an answer.

CHAPTER 40

The reply from Earth arrived three hours later. President Brophy and the other world leaders on the call unanimously supported Chris's decision to accompany the Guardian on its journey. They also announced that each country sharing the information from the Guardian was beginning construction of additional fusion-driven spacecraft that would be sent to Methonē at the earliest opportunity, the first of which would be able to depart one and a half years hence. The leaders stopped short of committing to jointly sponsor these future missions now that the initial exploration was complete, but they did agree to collaborate once they arrived and that the universal sharing of information gleaned there would continue.

Their message and well wishes were short and, at the end of the call, the crew of the *Daedalus* was asked to begin their journey back to Earth within the week. The ship had enough supplies to remain at Saturn for another month, but the mission planners back home wanted them to return with margin. They didn't want what should be a relatively mundane part of the trip, the return, to become risky because they cut it too close with regard to available supplies.

Robyn closed the connection after the message ended and turned toward her crew. She was both elated and sad. Elated that the mission had been successful, and sad that it was about to end. She knew that it was highly unlikely she would ever be returning here. There were simply too many other qualified people who were waiting in the wings and ready to come to Saturn to study the Guardian and unlock its secrets.

"We've got a week, so let's make the most of it," she said.

"Robyn, may I have a word with you in private?" asked Chris. "Mr. Know It All" actually sounded nervous, more nervous than he'd sounded before that first trip over to the Artifact when they had first encountered it in what seemed like ages ago.

"Sure, let's go below deck to the rec room," said Robyn. *Perhaps he is having cold feet about his decision? Or else there's something he's not telling us . . .*

Both pushed off from the decking and gracefully nudged themselves through the hatch leading to the lower part of the ship. The rest of the crew remained in the galley, busily studying one set of data or another or simply staring out the window at the spectacle that was Methonē and Saturn.

Once they were alone, Chris looked nervously over his shoulder at the hatch to see if anyone else was coming through and then back at Robyn.

"Robyn, Juhani can fly this ship just as well as you, correct?"

"Well, yes. We cross-trained before departure and he's my backup. But quite frankly, I don't really need to pilot the ship at all. The computer does all that. We just tell it when we want to leave and it calculates the optimum trajectory home and then flies us there. If that were to fail, I'm not sure Juhani or I could do much about it. Why do you ask?"

"Because I want *you* to come with me to Alpha Centauri. I'm a scientist and I'm damned good at my job. But I don't have a clue about diplomacy and military matters—which I believe are needed for the first contact with whatever is at Alpha Centauri. I already cleared it with the Guardian. Sending two of us is just as easy as sending one."

"Hell, yes, I'll go. Are you kidding me?" She did not hesitate in her response. This was something she knew she wanted to do. She was excited at the prospect and her imagination was already running wild speculating about what might await them on the Alpha Centauri Transfer Station. She definitely didn't want to simply return home, fill out innumerable reports describing in nauseating detail all of what happened out here and then spend the rest of her career behind a desk—even if it meant a promotion. Now that she had experienced being in command of a space mission encountering the ultimate unknown, she didn't want it to end.

"There's something else. And it might make you change your mind," said Chris, looking away from her face, toward the floor, and then back again.

"What's that?" Robyn asked, suddenly concerned.

"I think I'm in love with you," he said.

That caught her by surprise, but not totally. She, Juhani, Jing, Yuan, and Chris had been together in near isolation for months and, as far as she knew, none of them had paired off. The psychologists had prepared her for what they thought were the inevitable sexual liaisons that would ensue during the journey but that hadn't happened. For that, she was thankful. Once emotions got loose on a ship, keeping everyone working together got complicated. But sexual release was a very different thing than "love," and she was sure Chris wasn't just talking about biological needs. He was blushing.

She took a deep breath and looked at Chris in a different light. He wasn't unattractive; in fact, she found that she enjoyed his company immensely, but she'd attributed that to their common intellectual interests. True, he was rather condescending at times, but then again, she knows she had her own personality flaws. No, she wasn't in love with him but she didn't feel that something like that was totally out of the realm of possibility . . .

The next morning, Chris and Robyn stepped into the de Broglie transmitter on Methonē and took their first step toward the stars and whatever awaited them at Alpha Centauri.

THE END

AFTERWORD

Are we alone in the universe?

Our solar system contains eight planets, five dwarf planets, numerous moons and thousands of asteroids. We know that at least one planet contains life (Earth) and another might have supported life at one time (Mars). There is also at least one moon (Europa) that may have conditions suitable for life. And this is just within our own solar system.

Thanks to the Kepler Space Telescope, we now know that there are hundreds of nearby stars with planetary systems, some of which are known to have planets in the "habitable zone," which means they may have conditions suitable for life as we know it. Based on the statistics from Kepler, it appears that almost all stars have planetary systems, with an estimated 2.5 planets per system.

Our galaxy, the Milky Way, contains over one hundred billion stars. That translates to an estimated two hundred fifty billion planets. Recent estimates place the number of galaxies in the universe at nearly one trillion. If the stars in these galaxies are similar to our own, and we have every reason to believe they are, then there are about 2,500,000,000,000,000,000,000,000 planets in the universe. Does anyone seriously believe we are alone? Though I doubt we humans are being or have been visited by extraterrestrials (see my Baen essay, "The Aliens Are Not Among Us," on the Baen website for my rationale), I don't believe it is impossible for that to happen or for it to have happened in the past. In fact, when I think about these numbers, it is nearly impossible for me to believe that we are alone in the universe.

And then there is the observational evidence for the existence of ET. There is none. Despite decades of radio searches and thousands, if not millions, of astronomers (professional and amateur) gazing at the stars, there is no sign of another civilization like our own out there anywhere or anytime. Surely, the argument goes, if other technological civilizations exist, then their presence would eventually become obvious—as ours is on track to being as we move out to explore our solar system and develop toward becoming an interplanetary species. We've only been in the game, that is, we've only been a technological civilization, for a few hundred years out of the 4.5 billion years of Earth's history. Within the next thousand years, it is likely that anyone in the nearby galaxy will know we exist by our energy emissions alone. If another civilization developed technology before us, which is likely given the sheer numbers involved, then their presence should be obvious to us.

But again, there is no evidence of anyone else out there. This is called the Fermi Paradox, named after Enrico Fermi, the physicist who is credited as the first person to raise this question. Why not? Why have we not seen signs of ET among the stars?

I don't know. But physicist Stephen Hawking warned that "Such advanced aliens would perhaps become nomads, looking to conquer and colonize whatever planets they could reach." That's enough to cause one to pause and think, regardless of the reality of his concern. We know how humans behave toward each other; why would we expect ET to behave differently?

About that de Broglie Transmitter

Prince Louis de Broglie lived in the latter part of the nineteenth century and into the twentieth and, yes, he was a "prince." After serving in the French army during World War I, he engaged in his theoretical physics studies at Paris University. He made his mark in the field of quantum mechanics with the publication of his Ph.D. thesis, "Researches on the Quantum Theory," in which he formulated modern wave mechanics. In layman's terms, he theorized that physical particles like protons and electrons could be described as quantum mechanical waves—just as quantum mechanical wave theory had been accepted at the time for explaining the behavior of light.

His theory was confirmed in 1927 when the famous Davisson-Germer experiment showed that electrons could diffract, like light, and therefore had wavelike properties. He was later awarded the Nobel Prize in physics for his work.

How does this relate to interstellar travel? It doesn't, at least directly (and not yet), but it might!

In classical physics, if an electron of a certain energy is trapped in an electric field, it is considered to be in a potential well. (Think of it as you being dropped in a hole. If the hole isn't very deep, you can jump or climb out. Your "energy level" is large enough to escape the hole, or well. If the hole is too deep for you to jump out, then you are trapped within it.) Unless the electron has enough energy to escape, it will remain in the potential well forever. This is shown in Figure 1.

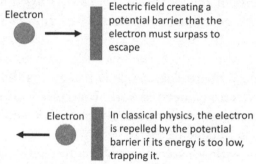

Figure 1. In classical physics, electrons cannot cross a potential barrier unless they have enough energy to do so.

In reality, electrons can be placed in a deep potential well from which they should never be able to escape and yet do so anyway—sometimes. Sometimes the electron will remain inside and sometimes not. And, if you study enough electrons in potential wells, you would see that there is some probability of it escaping over a specific period of time. This can only be explained if you think of the electron as a wave. In wave mechanics, the location of a particle is described in terms of probabilities and waves, which can be shown graphically in Figure 2. If you think of the electron's location as being somewhere under the curve, and the curve can extend beyond the potential barrier, then there is a small chance the electron will relocate itself outside of the potential well and on the other side of the energy barrier. Thinking back to the hole you jumped into above, it would be as if you, from one moment to the next, simply appeared standing on the ground next to the hole rather than remaining inside it. That's quantum tunneling.

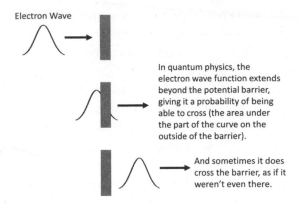

Electron Wave

In quantum physics, the electron wave function extends beyond the potential barrier, giving it a probability of being able to cross (the area under the part of the curve on the outside of the barrier).

And sometimes it does cross the barrier, as if it weren't even there.

Figure 2. In quantum physics, an electron behaves like a wave and has a small probability of escaping the potential barrier even if its energy is too low.

Tunneling on a microscopic scale is real and is the reason that many modern electronic devices work. Examples include computer flash drives, scanning tunnel microscopes, diodes, and tunneling is the key process in radioactive decay.

The problem with a macroscopic object tunneling, say a human being, is scale. The matter wave of a macroscopic object is inversely related to its mass. In practical terms, this means the probability of you or I tunneling or relocating to another location in the universe is EXTREMELY small, but not zero. It is so small, however, that the likelihood of it happening in the lifetime of the universe is very, very small. But that's in nature. What if someone or something figures out how to externally relocate a macroscopic object's matter wave to the destination of their choosing? By forcing the small, but finite probability of the object relocating to be equal to 1, the object would jump out of the hole and go where it was directed to go. (Which itself is probably not accurate. It would simply go from point A to point B because that's where it is supposed to be, probabilistically. Just like in our natural world it appears to remain at point A because that's where the probability of it being is highest.)

The speed of tunneling is another topic. For the purposes of this story, I *assumed* that tunneling across large distances is limited by relativity to be no faster than the speed of light. There is some evidence that the effect may, in fact, be instantaneous—when someone builds a de Broglie transmitter and demonstrates instantaneous matter transmission across interstellar distances, then I will stand corrected!

The Solar Gravity Lens

Light is constrained to move within the fabric of physical reality known as space-time. In the absence of a massive object, light behaves in the relativistic universe in which we live just as it would in a non-relativistic, or Euclidean, universe by moving in a straight line. But when a massive object is interposed between us and whatever is emitting the light, something curious happens—the light appears to be bent around that object. The space-time around the massive object is bent, and the light, constrained to move through space-time, bends with it.

The result is something similar to what happens when light is refracted in everyday glasses worn by nearsighted people. When light is bent, it can come to a focus. The effect was first measured in 1919 when astronomers Arthur Eddington and Frank Watson Dyson observed stars that appeared near the Sun during a total solar eclipse. Similar observations were made across the globe and, sure enough, the light from stars passing close to the Sun (VERY close to the Sun and therefore only visible during an eclipse) was found to be bent by the Sun's mass. They made these observations before they could be readily explained by Einstein's theory of general relativity—which came much later. Since then, the effect has been observed on a galactic scale with massive galaxies bending the light from more distant galaxies, enabling them to be seen by our telescopes.

It turns out that the Sun's gravitational lens has a focal line at about 550 astronomical units (AU). One astronomical unit is the distance from the Earth to the Sun, or approximately ninety-three million miles. It is for this reason that the alien races exploring other star systems place their de Broglie transfer stations at these locations. (Other stars have masses different than our Sun and their gravity lens locations are therefore different.) By using this lensing effect, one can theoretically use much less energy to send any sort of radiation or quanta (light, radio, and, presumably, matter waves) than would be required without the lensing. According to physicist Dr. Claudio Maccone, a radio with a power of only a few tens of watts could use this lensing effect to send detectable signals to Alpha Centauri!

Why Methonē?

Orbiting Saturn between the much larger moons Mimas and Enceladus lies the one mile-long, egg-shaped Methonē. Methonē (pronounced "mi-thoh-nee") is so small that it remained undetected until NASA's Cassini spacecraft discovered it in 2004. Cassini came relatively close to it in 2012, passing just eighteen hundred miles away where it took some spectacular photographs (Figure 3). As you can see, Methonē looks like a nearly perfect egg.

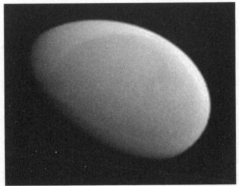

Figure 3. Methonē, one of Saturn's moons, as seen by the NASA Cassini spacecraft. (Image courtesy of NASA)

There are no visible craters and it is believed that the moon is made from or at least covered by ice. Based upon Cassini's observations, scientists have determined that Methonē has a density of one third that of water, making it less dense than any other moon or asteroid in the solar system. You can see why my imagination might run wild and turn it into a spaceship rather than a moon.

That's it. That's all we know, at least for now. Is anyone else up for a mission to Methonē?

—Les Johnson

ACKNOWLEDGEMENTS

Dr. Jeff Wicker—for helping me come up with a good way to kill someone (in the story!)

Dr. James Woosley—for reassuring me that a de Broglie drive might actually work

Dr. Claudio Maccone—for proposing the existence of a 'galactic internet' using the solar gravity focus

Dr. Gregory Matloff—for continuing to inspire me

Dr. Dennis Gallagher—for helping me with the fact checking

Laura Wood—my agent, for helping me get the idea from inside my head and onto the page

Carol, Carl and Leslie—for their understanding as I sequestered myself in the library writing and editing

Panda—our dog, for faithfully sleeping at my feet while the words were being written

Forrest J. Ackerman—for bringing the *Perry Rhodan* series to the USA to thrill eager 12-year-olds like me